STARS AND BONES BOOK 1

Thief in the Castle

BEATRICE B. MORGAN

Authors 4 Authors Publishing
Marysville, WA, USA

Published by Authors 4 Authors Publishing
1214 6th St St
Marysville, WA 98270
www.authors4authorspublishing.com

Library of Congress Control Number: 2019947195

E-book ISBN: 978-1-64477-126-6
Paperback ISBN: 978-1-64477-127-3
Audiobook ISBN: 978-1-64477-128-0

Edited by Rebecca Milkkelson
Copyedited by Brandi Spencer

Cover design ©2021 Brandi Spencer. All rights reserved.
Interior layout and artwork by Brandi Spencer.

Authors 4 Authors Content Rating and copyright are set in Poppins. Book title is set in Allura and Bilbo Swash Caps. Series title and other headers are set in Cinzel. All other text is set in Garamond.

STARS AND BONES BOOK 1

Thief
in the
Castle

BEATRICE B. MORGAN

Authors 4 Authors Content Rating

This title has been rated 17+, appropriate for older teens and adults, and contains:

- Intense implied sex
- Intense violence
- Moderate language
- Mild alcohol use
- Child slavery

Please, keep the following in mind when using our rating system:

1. A content rating is not a measure of quality.

Great stories can be found for every audience. One book with many content warnings and another with none at all may be of equal depth and sophistication. Our ratings can work both ways: to avoid content or to find it.

2. Ratings are merely a tool.

For our young adult (YA) and children's titles, age ratings are generalized suggestions. For parents, our descriptive ratings can help you make informed decisions, but at the end of the day, only you know what kinds of content are appropriate for your individual child. This is why we provide details in addition to the general age rating.

For more information on our rating system, please, visit our Content Guide at:
www.authors4authorspublishing.com/books/ratings

DEDICATION

To my good friend, Ryan, whom I know I can bounce any
fantasy idea off of.

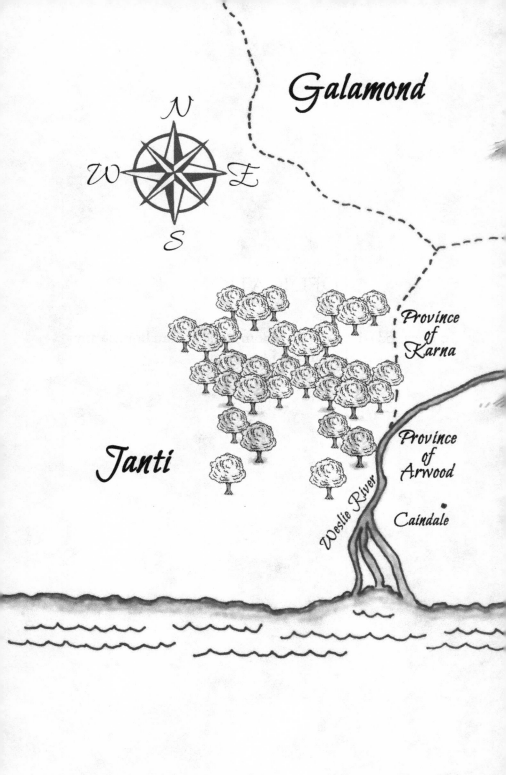

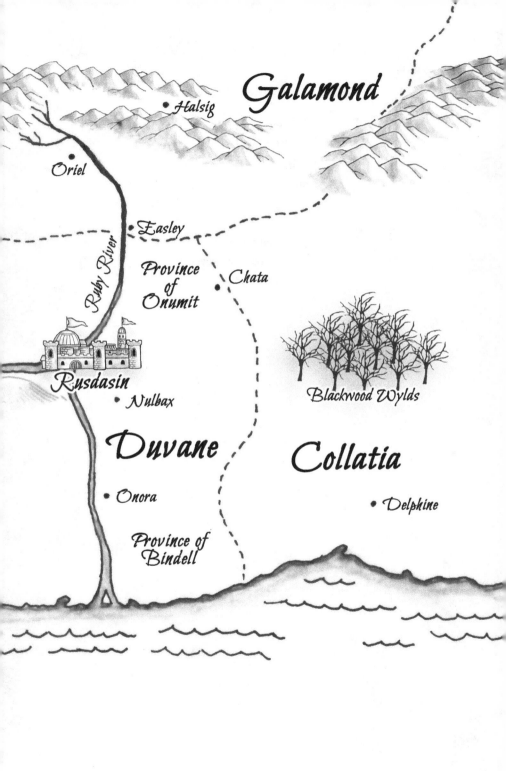

WORKS BY BEATRICE B. MORGAN

Stars and Bones:
Thief in the Castle
Mage in the Undercity
Dreams in the Snow (Spring 2021)

Hard as Stone:
Hard as Stone
Thick as Blood
Strong as Steel (Summer 2022)

TABLE OF CONTENTS

TABLE OF CONTENTS

CHAPTER ONE

Not just any thief could sneak into Bradburn Castle, but Juniper Thimble wasn't *just any thief*. She crouched on the ugly weathered head of a stone gargoyle, one of hundreds that lined the parapets and towers. The gargoyles were an ancient tradition meant to keep assassins and thieves just like her from slipping into the castle undetected. In her experience, gargoyles did little more than provide handholds for climbing an otherwise lackluster stone wall.

Down below, the Royal Guard made rounds in the front garden, patrolling from the grand stairs to the front gates, faces unyielding and blank. The flickering torchlight lit the curved double-headed ax on each bronze breastplate: the symbol of Bradburn and, for the past one thousand years, of the Kingdom of Duvane.

One set of guards reached the steps of the castle and turned. They started back toward the castle gates as the second pair of guards made their way toward the stairs.

Juniper smiled to herself. Neither of them had even glanced up to where she crouched. Of course, in her dark thieving clothes, there wouldn't be anything to see. Her midnight blue scarf covered her mouth, nose, and hair, leaving only her eyes visible. Juniper glanced sideways at Amery, her partner for the night, who perched on an equally ugly and useless gargoyle a few feet away. Her onyx eyes glittered. For all the talk of how well trained the Royal Guard was, the two of them had gotten surprisingly far without trouble.

Tonight, they would become the best thieves in Duvane's capital city of Rusdasin. They weren't stealing just any old jewels. No, they were going to steal the king's crown. Tomorrow, every thief in the Undercity would be raging with jealousy.

Moving in mirrored silence, Juniper and Amery scaled the castle. The rough, weathered gray stone provided plenty of handholds. Juniper avoided looking down; she'd never been afraid of heights, but the thought of falling often left her with an uneasy stomach.

Juniper and Amery had taken turns memorizing guard rotations, doors and windows, the routine of the servants, and the layout of the castle.

1

They had spent weeks planning the heist, secretly, as per the advice of Maddox Hawk, their guild master. He'd chosen this night because according to a source he wouldn't disclose, the wards surrounding the castle would be down. For a skilled thief, the impregnable stronghold would be briefly vulnerable. He knew Juniper and Amery would get the job done, which was why he entrusted the secret heist to them. It would throw their names into history; it would solidify Maddox's name in the Undercity.

Sneaking through the castle itself would be impossible with the Royal Guard and an army of servants and staff. However, Bradburn Castle had a number of rooftop courtyards; the courtyard to which Juniper and Amery climbed led straight into the Royal Chambers.

By the time Juniper and Amery neared the top of the tower, Juniper's arms and thighs burned from the climb. She bit down on a swear when Amery reached the tower's edge a fingertip before she did.

The two thieves hung at the edge of the courtyard, bodies pressed against the stone, listening.

"...says something else is happening tonight," said a rough-voiced guard. "But I don't know. I half think the man's gone senile."

"I overheard the captain talking about something like that, but as soon as I came around the corner, he hushed up."

"What do you think they're doing at this hour?"

"Gods only know, and it's not our business. I'd rather stand out here than have to worry about the prattling of the rich."

The other guard grumbled in agreement.

Juniper met Amery's stare. Her onyx eyes returned Juniper's confusion. What was happening tonight?

With her hands starting to cramp, Juniper risked a peek over the edge. Both guards had their backs to her. Cigar smoke puffed out in time with slow breaths, easing toward the sky on the gentle night breeze. Unlike the patrolling guards, they did not wear bronze armor; instead, they wore the black and gold doublet of the Royal Guard.

Juniper hoisted herself over the stone railing and into the courtyard. The mossy ground softened her silent landing. Amery landed swiftly beside her, barely a shadow in the shade of the trellises choked with morning glory, towering lavender, and thorny aloe. Unlike the front gardens, this courtyard had been dimmed of light, save for a single lantern on the ground beside the guards.

The doors at the far end of the courtyard were dark. Unwatched.

Juniper and Amery moved like twin hands; in less than a few seconds and a few unison jabs to the neck, both guards fell backward into their waiting arms, unconscious.

Unconscious, as Maddox had requested, although *why*, Juniper didn't understand. He'd never had a problem with casualties before.

They laid the guards softly on their backs. They had a couple hours before they would wake, and five hours until the next rotation, to slip into the Royal Chambers, find and steal the crown, and get out before anyone noticed.

Amery made it to the darkened doors first and tested the handle. Unlocked. The courtyard doors opened silently into a dark lounge; the pitiful light from the lantern didn't stretch far over the threshold. The cold hearth gave the lounge a haunted feel. It smelled vaguely of butterscotch. A book lay open on the coffee table. A golden bookmark had been set on the open page. Someone had been in this room. Recently enough for their scent to linger.

On the far side of the lounge was a set of grand wooden doors with elaborate brass handles. Those doors would take them into the Royal Chambers. According to Maddox, the Royal Chambers took up as much space as a city block, despite there being only three Bradburns currently inhabiting them. Once, each of the fifteen bedrooms had been in use, when the king took more than one wife. Luckily, the current King Bradburn had taken only one.

Amery pressed her ear to the seam of the doors, listening. A beat passed. Amery turned the handle and gently pushed one door open—she kept her knees bent, ready to jump at the sound of creaky hinges. The doors made no sound, and she slithered into the corridor. Juniper crept after her. Where the lounge had been cozy, the corridor felt cold with all gray stone.

Torches burned in iron brackets, illuminating the portraits that lined the walls, the suits of polished armor, and the decorative side tables and hutches. Before her, a gold, crimson, and black tapestry hung. The golden thread wove in and out of the red and black, creating an elaborate curved double-sided ax.

The corridor was empty. No guards stood watch. On either end.

Strange. Not unheard of, but strange.

That tiny voice that dwelled somewhere in the back of her mind whispered: *What's happening tonight?*

3

Juniper pushed the thought down and focused on the goal. The crown. No time to be paranoid. She started one way down the corridor and Amery, the other; they parted ways without a glance. There were two ways into the royal jewel room where the crown slept.

Two ways.

Two thieves.

Twice the luck.

Twice the risk of failure, but Juniper pushed that thought down too.

Juniper eased through the shadows of the corridor, wary of where the thicker shadows gathered, of the circles of light cast by each torch. The light glinted off the portrait frames and the suits of armor—the armor dated from different periods of Duvane's history, redesigned by each king. When the light hit the armor just right, it flickered like an incoming blade, and Juniper jumped more than once. She cursed herself silently each time.

Despite that, she found herself in awe. Bradburn Castle had the charm of the ancient world with its curved stone arches, coiled iron brackets, and white marble pillars, of when dragons flew free in the skies and the southern forests were full of singing trees and fairies. A thousand years had passed since the Great War that had taken with it the old magic, and the magical creatures that had once thrived had dwindled into nonexistence. Juniper had never seen a dragon or heard a singing tree, but this castle made her want to believe such things might still exist out there in the far corners of the world, untouched by man's war.

She kept her ears and eyes open for any footsteps, sighs, or any other such humanly sounds, but only silence pressed in against her, making each of her footfalls sound like thunder. Where were the bustling servants attending to all the hearths, the gathering dust, the polishing of the armor? Where were the guards? Where were the *mice*? She did not believe for a moment that a castle this large hadn't a swarm of mice.

It's nighttime, she told herself as she crept past a grand set of mahogany doors. She paused and listened. No sound. Not even the calm breathing of sleep. Not even the scurry of mice. She continued toward her goal. The crown.

She crept toward the intersection of two corridors. Then, the silence shattered with the opening of a door. Juniper froze where she crouched. Footsteps sounded—armored footsteps.

She slunk underneath a dainty wooden table. Across the corridor, a sour-mouthed woman with silver hair stared at her from a rosewood frame. Her eyes seemed oddly downcast as if the portrait indeed *looked* at Juniper.

Nonsense. A trick of the paint.

Still, she stole her glance away from the woman's dark eyes.

The footsteps came closer, closer, closer, but no one appeared from the corridor. They halted. Juniper forced her breath in and out in even, calm beats. Then, the footsteps retreated, each footfall sounding farther away. Juniper dared not move until those footsteps faded completely with the opening and closing of another door. She slid out from the shadow, and without looking up at the sour old woman's portrait, she continued down the corridor.

According to the plans Maddox had acquired, a left turn at the end of this corridor, then through a set of doors, and then she would be standing in the queen's dressing room, which would then lead her into the royal jewel room. To the crown. Amery would be making her entrance through the king's dressing room on the other side.

Juniper crept to the end of the corridor and to the mahogany doors of the dressing room. No guards. She pressed her ear to the seam. Nothing.

Again, that voice in the back of her mind whispered, *No guards?*

Focus. The crown.

Juniper slid her gloved fingers around the elaborate brass handle and pulled. The door eased open, the mechanism sighed, and she slipped into the queen's dressing room, into near-total darkness. She eased the door closed behind her, shutting out what little light she had from the corridor.

It didn't matter. Juniper had always had good night eyes. She blinked a few times, and the dark hues of the room lightened. The pure black became shades of deep purple, midnight blue, and charcoal. She could see the outline of the room and the shadowy furniture inside it. Most of it centered around a large flat stepping stool. A pedestal. With plenty of cushiony seating for the ladies in waiting while the queen marveled over her clothes.

Instead of portraits, the walls held shelves. Shoes. Jewelry. Hanging or folded shirts, tunics, and underthings. Dresses. Dresses. And more dresses. In every color and style. With belts, sashes, scarves, and all manner of useless accessories. The movable racks of clothes hugged the sides of the room and gave the eeriest impression that she tiptoed through a room lined with people.

Why did the castle have to be so creepy?

Juniper slid through the shadow of two circular racks of shoes in all shapes and colors and styles. How could one woman possibly wear so many shoes? Juniper had two pairs of shoes, both plain all-purpose boots. One pair in black, the other in brown. What purpose did pointed toes and sharp heels serve other than to mar the human foot? Juniper eyed the sharp heel of a sleek snake-like boot. It looked more like the tooth of a long-dead beast than footwear.

Maybe that's why women wore them. One of those heels would go through an eyeball like a knife.

She tiptoed through the dark dressing room and to the doors that would take her into the jewel room. Juniper felt a jolt through her spine, a prick of success. She listened at the seam, heard nothing, not even Amery's cat-like footsteps, and let herself into the jewel room.

Shelves covered each wall, lined with ancient precious stones, tiaras, bracelets, scepters, and all manner of royal jewelry and ceremonial dress. In the dark, they did not glitter or gleam; they appeared nothing more than common river stones. Her prize slept along the far wall, set upon a white marble pillar, resting atop a velvet cushion.

The king's crown.

Worn by every Bradburn king since the founding of Duvane nearly one thousand years ago, when King Lenden Bradburn had it forged from the gold he had plundered from the empire before. The crown was a masterwork of gold, encrusted with flawless rubies, diamonds, and pearls.

Juniper crept up the small dais, fingers itching to feel the cool metal, to see the look on Maddox's face when she strolled into his office with the king's crown on her head. She could almost feel the weight of it.

Her fingers hovered over the crown.

A shadow slithered—something hard knocked into her chest, sending her sprawling to the floor. She struggled to stand, but something cold and putrid-smelling pressed against her nose and mouth. Hands grabbed her shoulders, her legs—pinning her; she had no choice but to breathe in the horrible odor.

Movement slowed. The room darkened. She barely saw her attackers, shadows among shadows.

Then, darkness swallowed her whole.

CHAPTER TWO

Juniper had a vague sense of movement that stretched through her entire body like thorns in her bloodstream. She felt pain, felt the stiffness in her bones, but her groggy state refused to let her worry about it. When she finally came to, she found herself lying on a hard bedroll in a small dark room with four walls of cold gray stone and a matching ceiling. To her dismay, a single door of tight iron bars was the only break in the stone.

Prison—no, a dungeon. Bradburn's dungeon.

Caught. How had she gotten caught?

She couldn't move. Each breath took effort. Her head throbbed. Her fingers felt like limp river weeds. The rest of her body hadn't fared any better. Whatever knock-out drug they'd given her had done a marvelous job.

She lifted her limp fingers and wobbly arms to her sides, to her daggers. Gone. All of them. They had disarmed her. And by the cold, dank air touching her neck, ears, and cheeks, they had taken her scarf too. She wiggled on the bedroll to make sure they hadn't completely stripped her. She kept the basics of her clothes: tight dark pants, close-fitted tunic, dark jacket, and...bare feet? They'd taken her boots. She liked those boots.

Luckily, she had been out of it during their search of her. She shivered at the thought of hands wandering freely, searching.

Armor clanked outside the cell. A tough male voice said, "This one's awake."

She strained her neck and shoulders to see the speaker. A royal guard stood at her door. The torchlight flickering behind him cast his face into shadow. He wore a doublet, not armor.

A second pair of footsteps sounded in the stone hall, then several more behind it. Two royal guards appeared beside the first. A man appeared in the doorway, his skin bronze and his dark hair streaked gray at the temples. The other guards gazed at him with silent respect, and he looked down at her like something rotten that had washed up on a riverbank.

Captain Sandpiper of the Royal Guard.

Lucky her.

"Open this door," barked the captain. One of the guards stepped forward and unlocked the gate with a heavy metal *clack*. The captain stepped into the cell and rested his gloved hand on the pommel of his blade. "One move, thief, and your head rolls. Now get up."

Juniper struggled to move on her limp bones. *One move...* She could barely move at all! She grunted and gasped, her muscles stretching too far and not enough, and managed to push herself onto her elbows. Gods...everything hurt. *What* had they given her?

The captain huffed. A few short footsteps, and then a guard appeared at her side. Strong gloved hands gripped her upper arm and yanked her to her feet so fast that the cell twisted sideways. She went limp. The guard dropped her. She hit the bedroll on her knees, doubled over, and emptied the pitiful contents of her stomach on the stone floor.

The captain grunted in disgust. A hand fastened around her arm again, but this time, the guard lifted her slower. He tugged her toward the cell door. Her feet barely listened, and she wobbled with each step. The hay-strewn floor bit into her freezing feet.

The captain barked into the corridor, "Get someone in here to clean this up."

Juniper wanted to retort that the vomit wasn't entirely her fault, but she hadn't the strength to speak. The taste of bile made her feel like vomiting again. She clamped her mouth shut and wiped her mouth on the sleeve of her dark tunic. The stone between her pale feet swayed; she shut her eyes tight.

A pair of cold manacles clamped onto her wrists.

Juniper's eyes shot open at the sudden weight. The captain turned the key, yanked it out, and it vanished into the inside breast pocket of his black and gold jacket. Another guard held the chain attached to her manacles and gave it a sharp tug. She fell forward and careened toward the opposite wall. She twisted; her shoulder took the brunt of the impact instead of her face. Pain flared from her shoulder.

The captain drawled, "Don't hurt her too much."

Juniper seethed at the captain, who looked nothing but amused. When she got out, she'd kill him first. She didn't need her daggers to snap a neck. His amusement faded, and a scowl twisted his lips downward. Daring her to try.

They started a slow procession through the dank dungeons. The guard holding her chain took the lead, two walked on either side of her, and the captain walked a step behind.

She could have easily taken out four guards with her weapons. She

8

might have been able to without her weapons, but with her head pounding and her stomach feeling queasy, she didn't stand a chance. Any sudden movement on her part would likely earn her a sword to the throat or through the heart.

The narrow halls of the dungeon had barely enough torchlight to see by. They must have been far below the castle. She didn't hear any other prisoners, and she doubted Bradburn's dungeons to be so empty. No, they'd taken her somewhere special, somewhere away from the common street scum and riffraff. She supposed she should feel honored, but the spike of pride didn't ease the tremor of panic.

Walking gave her back some balance—a small consolation. The cold of the floor penetrated her feet, sinking into her bones. The numbing started at her toes and moved slowly toward her ankles. Not that it mattered. They surely walked her to her execution, either a blade through the heart, a beheading, or the gallows. That knowledge pulled her heart into her groin while simultaneously pushing it into her throat.

Their procession continued down empty halls, up narrow stairs, then down a hall slightly better lit than the others. At the end of the hall was a simple wooden door. The guard leading their procession paused before it and stepped aside.

The captain knocked once, waited a beat, then knocked again. He said to the door, "We've retrieved the prisoner."

"Enter." The deep male voice that spoke came out clear and heavy, a command given by a man used to being obeyed.

A lock slid back on the other side of the door.

The captain entered first. The guard holding her chain entered next and yanked her after. The room was not very big and had no windows. It looked more like a large cell than anything: dank, dreary, and forbidding. On the other side of the room sat three men at a rough wooden table. Another stood to the side.

Juniper recognized the man sitting in the middle at once. King Bentley Bradburn.

She swallowed, throat suddenly tight.

The king stood. Even without his royal regalia, the king had a commanding presence. He wore a gray tunic, dark pants, and a thick leather sword belt. He carried a real sword, one whose pommel had been well-used, not some cheap decoration like the nobles wore. From his past as a general, he knew how to use that sword. His dark blond hair was streaked with gray; he wore his crown.

9

To the king's left sat a silver-haired old man in dark purple robes—the color of a master mage as declared by the Marca, the Order's school for mages. Mason Hobbs, the court magician of Duvane. His gaunt, severe face and piercing eyes made Juniper feel as though he could see right through her.

To the king's right sat Adrian Bradburn, the Crown Prince of Duvane. He shared his father's dark blond hair. Unlike his father, Adrian did not command the room. He sat back in his chair, almost bored. Even with his bored expression, Adrian was easily one of the most handsome men Juniper had ever seen.

Adrian's gaze met hers. He looked at her with a strange curiosity that sent a shiver down her back. A cat eyeing a mouse.

She shifted her attention to the fourth man, a tan young man standing near the wall. He wore silver armor, like the knights, but no seal of the Order adorned the breastplate. Not a knight—a squire. A knight-in-training. His dark eyes met hers briefly. The hand on his sword twitched.

"What happened to the other one?" King Bradburn gestured toward Juniper. "You mentioned two thieves."

"The second narrowly escaped," answered the captain. He gave the king a slight bow of his head.

King Bradburn's gaze bore into Juniper's. "I see."

The other one. It took Juniper a moment to realize they spoke about Amery. The other thief. She'd escaped, according to the captain. Without the crown.

King Bradburn studied Juniper a long moment, his hazel eyes—like his son's—weighing thoughts in his head. Calculating. No one spoke. The only sounds came from their breathing, shifting clothing and armor, the flicker of the torches, and the infinite dripping of water somewhere in the dungeons.

The king maneuvered around the wooden table, his footsteps sure, his hands folded behind his back. He stopped halfway between the table and Juniper.

Finally, the king said, "This one will do."

The court magician stood and stepped around the table with grace that defied his old age. He reached into his flowing purple robes and pulled out a parchment scroll.

Her panic flared at the sight of the scroll. Her shoulders tensed, and the guard holding her arm squeezed.

She managed to ask, "Do for what?"

No one answered her. The king watched with indifference—another trait his son inherited—as the court magician glided toward her, his purple robes flowing like they had been stitched together with magic thread. Of course, given his position and notoriety, they might have been. The court magician came to a halt in front of her, along with a subtle metallic scent. Magic. Her heart skipped a beat. Juniper leaned away from the old man, but the guard behind her held her firmly.

What sort of botched execution was this? Why not display her death at the public gallows? The City Watch would drink for a week, knowing that Juniper Thimble had finally been put down.

The king settled his icy indifference on Juniper. He stood at least a head taller than her, still built from his warrior's prime, and with him looking down his nose at her, she found it hard not to feel insignificant.

The king took a step closer. Every guard had a hand on a blade. Waiting.

"I have need of someone with your particular skill set," said the king, his words carefully chosen. "Juniper Thimble."

Addressed by the king himself. She steeled her shoulders, trying not to let the trembling in her bones show. But her voice betrayed her, shaking as she said, "The king knows my name."

"All of Rusdasin knows your name, thief," the king said sternly. His voice bore the ferocity and calmness of a commander. "Larceny, murder, forgery. The list of your crimes is longer than most in my dungeons. For all you've done, you deserve no less than an execution. Rusdasin deserves your execution." A twinkle appeared in his eye, and Juniper felt a chill run down her spine. "However, this need not turn into one, Thimble."

The way he said her name, like a question, irked her.

"You have two choices before you." King Bradburn stepped closer.

The captain tensed. The hand around his sword adjusted for an easy killing blow. The guard clenched her arm tighter. The squire on the far side of the room took a stance beside Prince Adrian, who watched the scene unfold before him with mild interest.

The king continued, "You can return to the dungeons as a prisoner slated for execution, or..." The king paused to let that choice sink in.

"Or?" Juniper croaked. What did he want from a criminal? To hunt down some other criminal? To be a rat for the Undercity? To feed him information?

"Or," King Bradburn said, a grim smile tugging on his lips. "You can spend your sentence as a servant to the crown."

She chuckled halfheartedly. *Saw that one coming.* "Doing what? Hunting down your enemies for you? Or would it be something less extensive like polishing silver and warming beds? I'll warn you, Majesty, I'd be better at the first option," she said shakily.

For a brief moment, the king's lips twisted upward, then his face resumed his grim-as-death frown, and he said, "Something much more dire, I'm afraid."

Though her gut twisted, she forced a smile onto her chapped lips. "And what shall I be doing that is more important than bed warming?"

Prince Adrian chuckled. His beautiful face stretched into a smile, and his hazel eyes glittered at Juniper. He cast a sideways glance at the squire, who scowled.

The king's gaze slid to the scroll in the court magician's hands.

Juniper took a better look at that scroll. The old, thick paper had veins of pale gold running throughout the fibers. She'd seen that type of scroll in the Undercity's markets, in the stalls in front of the Marca and in the homes of the wealthy and distrusting. A magical contract.

King Bradburn frowned. "If I tell you, and you refuse, then you will not leave this room alive. It is a matter of utmost secrecy."

That explained why so few people had accompanied the king into the pits of the dungeons.

She swallowed, but it felt as though her throat had closed. Though she tried to stand tall, a tremor weakened her knees. If she didn't agree, she'd be killed. If she refused, she'd be killed. It didn't matter what she chose—the king had forced her to choose between the magical contract and her death.

The king's dark brows came together. Not confusion. Worry.

She nodded. In a small voice, she said, "Okay."

King Bradburn considered her, and at last, he said, "Someone is threatening the life of my son."

Juniper's gaze drifted to Adrian. He made no move to confirm or deny. "Is that not what the Royal Guard is for?" she asked.

The captain huffed.

"Adrian is the only heir to the Bradburn line. Should he die, the entire lineage will end with him. I am too old to sire another heir." The king's frown deepened. "I need someone to protect my son in ways that the guard cannot. In ways that no one will be able to detect. In exchange for your life, I am offering you the role as his royal protector."

CHAPTER THREE

Juniper blinked. Once. Twice. She imagined herself strutting a step behind the prince in the black and gold of the Royal Guard, armed to the teeth.

"What could I do that the guards can't?" Juniper glanced at the captain. He didn't look happy about this arrangement at all. The court magician looked even more dire. The silence in the room thickened. Her thoughts returned to the magical contract in the court magician's hands. "Unless all of this secrecy... You think the threat is coming from within your own castle."

King Bradburn stiffened. He glared down at her with a mixture of relief and distaste. "Smarter than she looks."

"Indeed," drawled the captain.

"I received an education." Juniper held her shoulders straighter. Dumb thieves never lived long.

King Bradburn and the captain exchanged a skeptical look.

"Your Majesty?" The court magician held up the scroll. "We need to be finished here before dawn, or our absences will be noticed."

The king nodded. "Yes. Proceed."

The court magician released the scroll, but it did not fall. With his hand instructing it, the scroll magically unraveled. She eyed the contract; the words were punctuated with archaic dots, slashes, and strange symbols. It radiated magic. Powerful magic. She could feel it prickle against her skin. A faint scent of metal, like freshly polished silver, tickled her nose.

The court magician clamped a bony hand around her fingers and lifted her hand. She panicked and pulled against him.

"You will be magically bound to the prince," explained the court magician. "To prevent any unsavory ideas on your part."

Her hand shook without her consent, but she did not release it to the court magician. His hands didn't tug on her, although she suspected he could if he wanted to.

They wouldn't force her hand, she realized. They were giving her the option.

"I will not ask you more than once, Juniper Thimble," said the king. The captain unsheathed his sword. "Sign the contract, or die in this room."

The captain stepped into her immediate view, sword at the ready.

She swallowed; she heard the *thwack* of the chopping block, the wet crunch, the thud. She shivered. She could do this. She could survive being a royal protector for a while, then steal the crown. She might have to steal ten thousand gold worth of jewels to make it up to Maddox, but she'd have time to think about it.

She loosened her tense arm, and the court magician lifted her hand. Her other hand hung limp in the manacle beside it. He held her index finger between his, gave it a slight squeeze, and a magical poke made her jump and hiss. He pressed her finger to the bottom of the contract, which floated on its own accord.

Something cold zapped through her body, through her bloodstream, like an icy wind.

The court magician pulled her finger away from the parchment. The red splotch of her blood soaked into the fibers; it burned a bright blue before drying.

Signed. A blood signature. There'd be no easy way to break it.

The court magician repeated the process of finger-poking on Adrian, who did not jump or hiss at the pricking. He'd been prepared. Adrian's blood signature became the twin of hers. With both signatures, she felt a tingle that started in her fingertips and wormed its way down every vein, every bone, every hair. It prickled on her scalp and spider-walked down her skin. Adrian wore discomfort; he felt the strange sensation too. A mirror of her own.

"The binding ritual is complete." The court magician waved his hands around the scroll, and it rolled itself tightly. He tucked the scroll into his purple robes. "I will personally see to its sealing and safe-keeping."

King Bradburn nodded toward the court magician. "Thank you, Mason."

The court magician bowed his head lower. "My honor, Your Majesty."

The guards holding Juniper hauled her to the side so that the court magician could pass. She saw the looks they gave the old man. Suspicious. Wary. They didn't trust him.

Regular humans distrusting mages? Shocker.

The king spoke to Juniper, exasperation on his tone: "While you are here, you will be under the supervision of Squire Sandpiper." The young squire stepped forward. The torchlight glinted off his silver armor. "If you step out of line, endanger anyone within my castle, or give him any reason, he has my permission to end your life."

Juniper met the squire's indifferent stare. More of a scowl, really. His name, Sandpiper—he must have been related to the captain.

"Squire," said King Bradburn. "She is all yours."

"Majesty," said Sandpiper in a clear, articulate voice.

King Bradburn left. Adrian followed him, hands in his pockets, as calm as if he had taken a stroll through one of the many courtyards of the castle. Once the door shut, the captain grabbed Juniper's manacles and shoved the key into the lock. The heavy lock clinked, and the guard beside her yanked the manacles from her wrists.

"No need to be so rough about it," Juniper whined, rubbing her cold, achy wrists.

The captain turned toward the squire. "Do you require a guard escort?"

"I've got it from here," said Sandpiper. "But thank you."

The captain left, followed by his guards. Just like that, only Juniper and Sandpiper remained in the room; however, one of the guards held the door open. Watching.

Sandpiper stood with one hand on his sword. Did he know she could just twist his neck and be done with it? Of course, with the guard watching, she would have to be lightning quick to avoid a commotion. No, best not to start something this early.

Up close, the squire's brown eyes looked more like dark honey. He kept his chestnut brown hair cut close. He was not exceedingly handsome, though she wouldn't call him unattractive.

She took one step toward the door but slipped on her freezing feet. She caught herself on the doorway and breathed a colorful curse.

Sandpiper growled. "We're running out of time," he barked. He grabbed her by the arm and half-pushed and half-pulled her into the corridor beyond.

He hauled her down the corridor and through a simple wooden door, behind which a spiral staircase rose. He pushed for her to go first. Good on his part. She might otherwise find something to stick through his neck. She started up at a leisurely pace, mostly to avoid falling. She had to look at her feet to make sure they landed properly on the stairs.

"Where are we going?" she asked.

"Your chambers."

"I get chambers?" She smiled over her shoulder at him and nearly fell

15

because of it. After that, she kept her eyes on the stairs. "Do I get a uniform and a plethora of weapons with which I can better protect our dear prince?"

"Be quiet and keep going."

The spiral stairs led into a dim room of barrels, brooms, and buckets. A few old paintings in need of new frames were stacked against the far wall. Sandpiper led her through a wooden door on the other side and into another, slightly less dank corridor. They were still in the dungeons.

This time, she could hear prisoners. Cries and moans echoed off the stone. Pain. Misery. Boredom. Hunger. The crack of a whip made her jump.

They walked through the populated dungeons, but Sandpiper didn't take her past any of the cells. She didn't ask why; she didn't want him to change his mind about it. They might pass someone she knew. They walked down several more corridors, up a staircase, and through another corridor of the dungeon. She heard less punishment and less pain. A lesser level, she supposed.

"I didn't realize the castle dungeons were this extensive," she said, if only to break the silence.

"There are plenty of scum who need a cell." He didn't look at her when he said it, but she felt it in his words. He meant her too.

"Is that why you put me in the lowest corner you could find? The one reserved for the worst?"

"Don't be so proud of that."

She smirked. She knew it had been for the purpose of secrecy, but how many others had witnessed the lowest level of Bradburn's dungeons and walked out? She would have yet another tale to boast about.

They climbed another staircase, wider than the others, which brought them to a brightly lit room. At a wooden desk sat a guard, one who had been in the room with them.

The guard nodded to Sandpiper. No words passed between them.

Sandpiper led her through a set of doors, dark like those in the Royal Chambers, that led into a bright corridor, lit with dozens of torches in elaborate iron brackets, and *windows*. Through the windows, she saw the nighttime landscape of Rusdasin. Lights speckled the dark. Dawn had not yet broken.

The lingering winter chill seethed through the windows worse than it had in the dungeons. Juniper shivered as a draft swarmed her neck like gripping hands. They kept walking up, around, and through corridors that all looked strikingly similar to one another. Sandpiper dragged her through narrow passageways between floors—servants' passages, she realized. He pushed her into curtained-off alcoves at the sound of voices or footsteps, only to pull her out once the speaker or walker had passed.

"I'm starting to think you don't want anyone to see me," she mused, wishing dearly for a fire to warm up by.

He didn't answer, only glared and urged her to move faster.

They went up, up, and up, and finally, to a set of grand mahogany doors. Two guards whom she recognized from the room in the dungeons stood on either side. They gave no hint that they recognized or even noticed them as Sandpiper pushed her through the doors and into—she gasped—the Royal Chambers.

He didn't give her time to gawk. He dragged her down a corridor that didn't look familiar—or at least the grim portraits didn't—and stopped in front of a set of mahogany doors. Torches gleamed on either side, glinting off the brass handles.

He nodded toward the doors. She folded her cold hand around the handle. When he didn't object, she pushed the doors open.

Her mouth fell open.

She walked into a spacious sitting room worthy of a duchess, with luxurious red seating angled around a roaring hearth fire. A beautiful red, gold, and cream rug circled the seating area. On the other side were a fine wooden table with a bench on either side and a small candelabra in the center. Bookcases lined one wall, and although the books were sparse, she could imagine them overflowing with colorful spines.

She went to the hearth and moaned as the warmth soaked into her freezing hands and feet. She hadn't even realized how cold the rest of her had become. She held her hands dangerously close to the fire but felt only the warmth.

The fireplace had been carved from white and gray marble. Delicate vines with leaves and blooms twined up the sides of the fireplace and onto the mantel where the vines burst into star-shaped flowers. Above the mantle, the Bradburn crest was carved into the marble.

Once her hands and feet thawed, she moved through a door on the other side of the sitting room. It led into a spacious bedroom with a canopied bed large enough for five people and enough pillows for twice that many. Red and cream curtains hung on the thick wooden bedposts, tied with golden cords. Matching drapes hung on the windows. Through those windows, gray and misty blue dawn glowed in the east.

Two doors led from the bedroom. One led into a spacious dressing room. The other led into a grand bathing room of white and gray marble with a bath large enough for two, at least.

She ran her fingers along the brass faucets. Running water too. Only the wealthiest in the city could afford such a luxury. The finely crafted oak cabinets held basic but expensive toiletries: scented soaps, oils, hair tonics, perfumes. She closed the cabinets and found the squire standing in the doorway to the bedroom.

"It's like they were expecting someone to be staying here," Juniper said. She walked back into the bedroom and absently fingered the golden castings on the writing desk, which had been stocked with paper, ink, and a wax seal.

"They were."

"Oh?" Juniper crossed her arms as a pang of bitterness shot through her. "The king was so sure that I would agree to his bargain?"

"If not you, then someone else."

She huffed. No doubt the king would have worked his way through a list of criminals until someone took his bait. How many had he gone through before Juniper?

Sandpiper said, "You were the first he asked."

She raised a brow at him. "How did you know I was going to ask that?"

"Because you had that look on your face."

"Oh? You know my face so well already?"

He scowled. "Knights are trained to notice such things."

She looked him up and down. His silver armor fit him well. Strong jaw. Broad shoulders. Muscular arms and legs. Warrior-built and knight-trained.

A hearth fire had been built in the bedroom as well, and she knelt beside it. The last of the chill began to melt from her bones. She asked, "How am I supposed to protect the prince if I'm not allowed any weapons?"

Not that she needed them. But she would like them.

"Nothing so obvious." Sandpiper meandered to the window, each step with a warrior's controlled grace. "Prince Adrian is expecting a visit from Lady Roslyn Derean of Galamond."

Juniper had heard of her; most people had. The prince's supposed lover, who lived so far in the north that few had seen her. Some thought Roslyn Derean a myth.

She glared at Sandpiper over her shoulder, hoping he didn't mean what she thought he meant. "I'm sharing a room? With a lady? *That* doesn't sound very wise, squire. Ladies always travel with precious jewels and other such easily pilfered things."

She would know. She had robbed countless nobles along the White Road.

A wicked glint flashed in his honey-colored eyes. "No. You're not sharing a room."

Juniper carefully stood on legs that had become weak and tired. She stiffened. Sandpiper was grinning at her. He was much more attractive when he smiled.

She asked, "Where *is* Lady Roslyn Derean?"

"*You* are Lady Roslyn Derean."

CHAPTER FOUR

Juniper blinked, sure that she'd misheard. She, Lady Roslyn Derean? No. She didn't believe him. Sandpiper regarded her with an arrogant smirk, which only twisted her disbelief into anger.

"And the king has graciously left me to explain it." The squire sauntered closer with slow, confident steps. "Few outside that meeting know anything about your capture or the plan to protect the prince. The story everyone else will hear is of how Lady Derean arrived late last night on a surprise visit to her beloved. They will expect you to be a lady, and you will act the part. No one is to know who you really are. Understand?"

She shook her head. "I don't understand," Juniper said, glaring at him. "How am I supposed to protect him while I'm pretending to be some ninny? Won't they be a little suspicious if I have to fight off some assassin?"

"You won't be the one to fight," Sandpiper said quickly. He gripped the pommel of his blade.

She frowned. "And how am I to protect him without fighting?"

"That is what the binding spell is for."

Rolling her eyes, she said, "Which no one has told me about beyond that it exists." A convenient point to leave out. She waited for Sandpiper to elaborate. He didn't, so she continued, "How am I supposed to pretend to be someone I don't know?"

"That is what I am for, as well as the prince himself. He will be able to tell you about Lady Derean more than anyone else."

She blinked. "Wait, is there a *real* Lady Derean?" He nodded, but before he could speak, she said, "*What*? How am I supposed to pretend to be someone who actually exists?"

"Because few have seen her, and fewer have met her," Sandpiper said, his voice coated with agitation. "She lives in the northern reaches of Galamond, and most believe her to be a mythical woman who the prince claims to have met on a visit to our northern neighbor."

"Does the real Lady Derean know she's being impersonated?"

"I don't know." Sandpiper started to say something else, then closed his mouth. He shook his head. "I was not informed of the specifics, only that you are to be identified as Roslyn Derean."

Juniper half laughed. "How absurd. They want me to pretend to be the prince's lover to draw out the person wishing to do him harm."

Sandpiper raised a brow.

"Isn't that obvious?" She crossed her arms. "This way, you've given his assassins another target by which to harm him." And that fact gave her a horrible pitting feeling in her stomach. "As the royal protector, I expected to be defending the target, not wearing it."

Sandpiper regarded her with indifference. "The king has appointed me your personal guard during your stay. To everyone else, that is what I will be. To you, I am the one keeping you from the gallows." A warning. "If all goes well, few people will actually see you up close to notice the difference between you and the real Roslyn."

She turned to the fire. She covered her unease with a dramatic sigh and said, "At least he's pretty."

"You arrived a few hours before dawn. You've had a long ride and wish to rest this day," he said as though she hadn't spoken at all.

"Oh, I do?" It came out bitterly.

"Yes," Sandpiper said sharply. He walked into her view but out of her reach. He patted the pommel of his blade. "Part of my job is to ensure you don't do anything stupid or reveal yourself—"

"Or you'll kill me," she said dismissively.

"As well as to ensure your general wellbeing," Sandpiper said through gritted teeth. Not a man used to being interrupted. "I suggest you wash up before breakfast arrives. The Royal Seamstress will be here this afternoon to fit you to the part. Best to be well rested and—" he sniffed; his nose crinkled "—clean. You smell like a slum." She clicked her tongue at him, retort at the ready, but he spoke over her as he started toward the bedroom door. "I'll be in the sitting room."

Guarding the exit, is what he didn't say.

The squire left her in the bedroom and closed the door behind him. His armor clinked on the other side. Juniper stood by the hearth, unable to formulate words. Bastards. Every one of them.

She stormed to the window and yanked it open; she'd used windows plenty in her escapes and heists. The window itself was narrow, but she could squeeze. The drop on the other side, however, would surely kill her. People moved about on the grounds far, far below. She'd forgotten how high the Royal Chambers were. Few ledges to hold onto and none wide enough for her fingers.

Someone had chosen the least thief-friendly side of the Royal Chambers to put her on. Clever bastards, then.

She pulled herself back into the bedroom and shut the window. Fine. She could play their game. Until she found her way out. Until she slipped out of their grasp, crown in hand.

✦

She lit several candles in the bathing room and shut herself in. Perfumed candles, she soon realized as a fruity scent filled the air. She took a deep breath—gods, was that her? She lifted her shirt to her nose. Urgh—she did smell like a slum. Like unwashed bedroll and vomit. Oh, she *had* vomited. The crusted remains lingered on her sleeve.

She turned the knobs on the bathtub for hot water, and while it filled, she stripped her nasty clothing away. She searched the cabinets and took advantage of the finery offered, adding a sweet honeysuckle oil to the water and a handful of pink bath salts. By the time she turned off the water, the bathing room smelled like a floral shop in spring.

She let out a moan as she submerged herself into the hot scented water. The heat of the water soothed the ache in her muscles and leeched the worry from her mind. Maybe pretending to be Lady Derean wouldn't be so horrible, not if she could live in this sort of luxury while doing so.

Her, Juniper Thimble, an Undercity rat, disguised as a lady! She laughed at herself, the sound echoing off the marble walls.

Sandpiper shifted in the other room; his armor clinked.

At least he couldn't sneak up on her.

Amery would have returned to Maddox by now. She would have told him what happened last night. Was it last night? Juniper hadn't thought to ask how long it had been. Would Maddox send someone for her? Or would he accept the loss and find someone else to take her place?

Juniper let the water soak out her worries about Maddox. Later. First, her bath. She scrubbed the scented soap into her skin to rid herself of the stench of dungeon and vomit. She couldn't identify the scent of the soap, but between the oils in the water, the salts, and the candles, the smells ran together.

Once the water started to cool, she dried herself with soft towels and rubbed a gentle-scented oil into her skin. Juniper used a comb made from bone with small rubies encrusted on either end. The tonic she used on her hair left it silky smooth. She'd never been able to afford tonics as nice, and her auburn hair had always been left in a wild mess. The tonic brought out a copper hue to her hair she'd never seen before.

Wrapped in a towel, she meandered back into her bedroom in much better spirits. That mood didn't plummet even when she spotted Sandpiper standing in front of her open dressing room door.

At the sight of her, he stiffened. His honey-colored eyes quickly darted along her towel-draped body and snapped back to the closet.

She laughed and started toward the dressing room with an exaggerated swagger. "What? You think I would put my dirty clothes back on? Nonsense." Especially ones that she'd puked on. "A *lady* never wears the same thing two days in a row."

Sandpiper held his tongue and forced his gaze to the window. She didn't take her eyes off him. She found too much delight in his obvious discomfort. She paused in the dressing room doorway.

Was that a tint of blush on his cheeks? In the natural sunlight that had come streaming in since she went to bathe, his skin appeared more bronze than before. A complexion too rich to simply be due to the sun. She would bet coin he had some southern blood in him. His eyes darted to her, then to the dressing room over her shoulder. He cleared his throat.

Juniper turned. A servant, a young woman no older than eighteen, stood in the dressing room. Her light brown hair was tied back into a no-nonsense bun, but she wore innocent amusement on her freckled face. Her golden yellow eyes were bright.

The servant bowed deeply. "Good morning, my lady. My name is Clara, and I will be attending to you during your stay here at Bradburn Castle. No need to pretend in front of me. I don't know who you are, but I know who you are not."

Behind her, Sandpiper released a low sigh of relief.

"What would you prefer to wear this day?" Clara asked. She gestured to the closet, which held considerably more than it had before. She must have been stocking it. The previously empty shelves now held linens, blankets, and towels, as well as a stock of simple dresses.

Juniper held her shoulders straighter, her chin a bit higher. Clara didn't know who she was, only that she wasn't Roslyn Derean. "Something comfortable," Juniper said. She waved her hand toward the dresses. "I need my rest today."

Clara nodded and reached for a dress of pale blue.

Juniper quickly added, "No pastels. They wash me out."

"Of course, my lady." Clara reached for the next dress, a dark gold.

Juniper glanced at Sandpiper with a satisfied grin. *See how well I can play along?* She then loosened the towel. His honey eyes widened, and he quickly stepped out of her immediate view. She didn't wait for him to leave the room—she dropped the towel. He made the smallest of disgruntled sounds.

She tried not to smile, but then she caught the small, knowing grin on Clara's face.

Juniper whispered, "If I have to be stuck with a grumpy squire, then I'm going to at least get some enjoyment out of making him uncomfortable."

"I might have done the same, my lady."

CHAPTER FIVE

Clara helped Juniper into a soft underdress and the dark gold dress. Without the corset or a tight-fitting bodice, it fit more like a glorified dressing robe. Clara set a pair of warm fur-lined house boots at her feet and offered her a thick shrug. With Juniper's permission, Clara braided her damp hair into an elegant rope that draped over her shoulder.

She reentered the bedroom and found Sandpiper standing by the far window, his back to her. She strolled over to him, her gait that of a simpering, long-legged lady.

The risen sun bathed the grounds in a gilded blue haze. On the far side of the grounds, she spotted the barely-there Royal Greenhouses.

She turned to the squire, but whatever thought she'd had vanished as a wonderful aroma filled her nose. She sniffed; her mouth watered. "What is that?"

Sandpiper answered, "A late breakfast."

She pushed past him and followed the smells into the sitting room. Her stomach growled; the wooden table was laden with a spread fit for a king: bread, butter, eggs, ham, sausages, porridge. Juniper rushed to the table. She grabbed a roll, warm to the touch, and sank her teeth into the soft flesh. The buttery bread melted in her mouth.

On her second bite, she sank onto the bench. Sandpiper sat down across from her, eyeing her warily.

"What?" she asked, mouth full.

He cleared his throat. "Use a lady's manners."

She glared at him as she chewed. His gaze darted over her shoulder, and soft footsteps traveled from her bedroom door to the main door in the sitting room. Without a word, Clara left her chambers.

Juniper swallowed. She understood. Servants talked. Even though Clara knew a fraction of the truth, if she overheard anything strange, she might convey that information to the other servants. Juniper had bought plenty of information about her targets from servants. The more disgruntled the help, the cheaper the information.

Sandpiper selected a roll and tore a piece off; the feathery bread steamed. "Consider this your first lesson. How to eat like a lady." He plopped the piece into his mouth.

"I eat like a lady."

"You tore into that roll like a starving dog."

Indeed, the bite from her roll had not been dainty or sophisticated. She'd thought of her stomach first. She took another hearty bite and said, "I *am* starving."

"Two, don't talk with your mouth full."

She chewed and swallowed, then stuck out her tongue.

"Three, take small, delicate bites."

She shoved the rest of the roll into her mouth, chewed, and swallowed. She reached for another, but he slapped the back of her hand with his spoon. She yanked her hand back, rubbing the back of it.

"See that plate in front of you? It's called a place setting. That's where your food goes."

"I know that," she snapped. "I've eaten meals at a table before."

"Then act like it." Sandpiper grabbed the dainty serving spoon in the eggs and brought a portion to his plate. He set the spoon back into the eggs and gestured for her to do the same.

She took hold of the spoon. She fought the urge to throw eggs at him. Reluctantly, she brought a large spoon of eggs to her plate. Oh, they smelled delicious. She repeated the action with the other dishes, and finally, when she thought she could at last eat, the lesson on silverware began.

Her stomach did not have the patience to learn how to properly use a fork, knife, and spoon.

"You're gripping your fork too tightly," he said.

She let it hang loosely between her fingers and stabbed at her eggs.

Sandpiper stood, and for a moment, she feared she'd pushed him too far. He walked around the table and grabbed hold of her hand. She sucked in her next breath; a chill ran down her spine, and her heart skipped a beat. His fingers, larger than hers by several sizes, folded over hers. Callouses lined his hand from where he'd held a sword.

He adjusted her grip on the fork. "That is how you properly hold a fork."

He released her hand and returned to his side of the table. Her panic subsided.

While she ate, Sandpiper instructed her on posture, manners, and etiquette. By the time she'd been able to eat her fill, she wanted to throw the remaining food at him. She set her silverware on either side of her plate and refilled her crystal goblet with tea. It was not the plain black tea she'd grown used to, but a rich, bold tea bursting with fruit flavors. She couldn't drink enough of it. She tilted her glass up, draining the tea into her mouth. She set it down to find Sandpiper glaring.

"Yes, yes, I'm such a heathen." She stuck her tongue out and refilled her glass.

A knock landed on the door, a calm three-knock.

"That must be the seamstress." Sandpiper stood and crossed the room to the door. "She's early."

"Why do I need a seamstress?" The dress Juniper wore fit fine. She didn't need it altered.

"You can't be expected to wear that." He gestured to her simple dress. "You'll need to look like a proper lady. You'll need more appropriate attire, a noble's attire."

Not off-the-rack attire like the dress she wore.

"Oh, I am looking forward to that," she said flatly, sipping the fruit tea. Puffy gowns, useless shoes, and squeezing corsets. She hated them all. She preferred the freedom of a tunic and pants. She'd seen some of the noble's gowns during her pilfering, those giant puffs of fabric, held together with ties, clasps, and buttons. It took a team to properly put one on. A *team*. Juniper could dress herself.

Sandpiper opened the door. Juniper twisted around on the bench to see; his face changed ever so slightly into a scowl. "Good morning, Your Highness."

Prince Adrian strolled into the room. He'd changed since that morning and looked like a dream in an exquisite sage tunic. His hazel eyes, alight with good humor, slid from Sandpiper to Juniper.

"Oh, stop with all the formalities, Reid. It's just us," said Adrian in a lighthearted tone.

Adrian sauntered inside and sat down beside Juniper. She dared not move; she had never sat so close to royalty before. Sandpiper quickly took up his place on the other side of the table, surveying the distance between Juniper and Adrian as if she might attack.

Adrian grabbed one of the rolls and sank his teeth into it. Not minding *his* manners at all, he said, "And what motivating conversation have you two been having this fine morning?"

"We've just been discussing the proper strength with which to hold a fork," she said as sweetly as she could. Should she address him properly? She glanced at Sandpiper, but he didn't correct her.

Adrian laughed. "Honestly, Reid?"

Sandpiper bristled. "She'll need to act the part. And if she can't eat like a lady, people will notice."

Adrian shrugged, dismissing the issue. "Roslyn comes from Galamond and from a very sturdy-minded family." The way he said it, Juniper didn't know if he meant *sturdy* as a compliment or not. "When she was sixteen, her father blindfolded her, took her out into the woods, and left her there with nothing but a knife. Told her to find her own way back home. His birthday present to her."

"In Galamond?" asked Juniper. Galamond was a horrible place to be left outside. In the winter, the snow piled high enough to bury smaller houses and drift higher still. The warmer months brought hail large enough to puncture anything not made of thick wood or stone or reinforced with iron.

"Oh, don't worry, she made it home well within the time limit," Adrian said proudly. "Roslyn is a bit eccentric and hard-headed, especially when someone suggests she can't do something because she is a *lady*. Which is why no one will question why she arrived in the middle of the night." Adrian nodded to Juniper. "Or why her table manners are lacking." He chuckled. "Duke Derean, her father, raised her to be a survivor. I'm sure that even if she knows how to use a fork properly; she chooses not to."

Adrian laughed, and the way he looked sideways at her made it feel as though a warm raindrop were sliding down her spine.

A voice in her head chimed, *The prince's lover.*

Adrian took a helping of eggs. "Are you adjusting well? The accommodations up to your liking, dearest?"

Dearest. He said it so easily, so sweetly.

"Yes, very well, my dear prince." Her voice did not roll as sweetly off her tongue. "If at any time I find it not to be so, I will inform you."

"I would have it no other way." He smiled; it stretched over every inch of his face.

A heavy hand knocked on the chamber door, snapping Juniper's attention away from Adrian. Sandpiper moved to answer it. This time, a hurried, plump woman of about fifty rushed inside with a servant quick on her heels. She wore a measuring tape around her neck and large colorful pins in her hair.

The plump woman's over-plucked eyebrows rose at Juniper.

Adrian cleared his throat. "I should take my leave."

"Your Highness." The seamstress bowed deeply. The measuring tape around her neck draped to the floor. "I know you must desire time alone with your beloved, but no doubt, you will also want her in better attire."

"Of course," Adrian said to the seamstress. He glanced at Juniper and winked. "I do love a woman in fine clothes, but between you and me, the simpler dresses are much easier to remove."

Juniper crinkled her nose. She hated when people talked about her like she wasn't there.

Adrian left, and several sets of footsteps began to walk with him. His personal guard.

Sandpiper cleared his throat. "Lady Roslyn, this is Miss Flox Jenson, the Royal Seamstress."

"Greetings, Miss Jenson." Juniper gave a dramatic curtsy.

"Oh, you've got a lot to learn about a lady's manners," Miss Jenson said, hand over her heart. "Now, up. We're wasting time." She sighed. "And we'll have to do something with your hair." She reached and fingered Juniper's hair.

Juniper knocked her hand away. "And what is wrong with my hair?"

"It's the wrong color." Miss Jenson reached into the leather bag the servant carried and pulled out a bottle of what looked like ink. "Roslyn has black hair."

Juniper reached up for her auburn hair. "Dye it?"

"Or someone might be concerned why Roslyn Derean, the raven-haired beauty of the north, is suddenly a redhead."

Juniper sighed but didn't argue.

The dye needed to set, and Miss Jenson didn't waste any time. She pulled Juniper into the bathing room and smothered her hair with the black dye, magically imbued to not fade, she said. Her hair would grow black too. Then she wrapped it in a thick turban, which began to heat, pressing against her hair and scalp. A shiver ran down her spine in response.

"Now, let's talk clothes."

Miss Jenson proceeded to measure every possible length of her body while talking nonstop of fabrics, styles, trends, and colors. Juniper listened and agreed when necessary. Although the idea of her own personalized wardrobe was alluring, she couldn't let it distract her. Binding spell or no, she wouldn't give up that easily.

Once she had a better layout of the Royal Chambers, she would steal the crown. She'd have to get away from the squire first. Sandpiper kept a hand on the pommel of his sword constantly, like he couldn't wait for the chance to depart her head from the rest of her body. She could handle a squire. All she had to do was wait.

CHAPTER SIX

Not in the mood to listen to women prattle about clothes, Reid Sandpiper left the thief in the hands of the seamstress and took up a post outside her chambers, where he couldn't hear them.

Juniper Thimble. She'd done more than enough to buy a ticket to the gallows. If the council caught wind of her presence in the castle, they would demand it. Immediately. He did not like having her in the castle, and he really did not like having her in the Royal Chambers.

Reid had dealt with enough fast-talking criminals to know not to trust a single word Juniper said. That silver tongue of hers had been trained for lies and deceit, and it would only get her, and him, into trouble if he didn't play it safe. It would also help her fool the rest of the castle if she played along.

She would. If not, he'd end her.

Still, the way she had tensed when he'd grabbed her hand and adjusted her grip on the fork bothered him. Like she had expected the worst of him. Like she had expected him to shatter her hand for the offense. Did she have such an outrageous view of the law?

The king had asked him before he'd offered him the position of her guardian: *If it comes to it, could you kill a girl?* The question had taken Reid by surprise, but he had nodded. If it meant protecting the royal family, protecting the people he had grown up so close to, yes.

A part of him wished the king had asked someone else to guard her, but at the same time, he felt proud to have been chosen. The king had recognized him. With such a secret and important task as guarding the prince's protector, the king must trust him. If he could prove himself with handling the thief, surely, he would be called upon soon for a king-given quest and finally become a knight.

Patience. A knight had unlimited patience. Or so they were supposed to. The truth of his task had to remain secret, even to his fellow squires. They, like the rest of the castle, believed he had been appointed the personal guard of Lady Derean.

Reid kept his ears on the doors behind him. If he listened close enough, he could hear the faint chatter between Juniper and Miss Jenson.

He wished he could lock the thief in, but the doors locked only from the inside. Switching it would have been suspicious. Of course, if the rumors about Juniper Thimble were true, a simple lock wouldn't have mattered.

A single pair of footsteps sounded in the corridor. Instinctively, Reid put a hand on his sword.

However, the lone pair of feet belonged to Adrian. He strolled down the corridor toward Reid, hands in his pockets, no guard in sight.

Reid released his sword.

"Someone looks angry." Adrian chuckled. He nodded toward the closed doors. "Has the lady insulted you already? Gods, what will happen when you have to be in there longer than a few hours? I could give you a few pointers on how to keep them quiet."

Reid frowned.

"Don't worry; none of them involve ropes."

Reid's frown deepened. "You wouldn't be thrilled either if you were stuck on watch duty. Where is your guard?"

"With you on duty, I'm sure she'll become the epitome of a lady in no time," Adrian said, ignoring the question. "I never knew you to be so knowledgeable about table etiquette."

Reid glanced down the corridor. No guards or servants in sight. That didn't mean no one listened, and he kept his voice low. "You'd rather her embarrass herself should she eat in front of someone?"

Adrian chuckled. "Father's made it clear that she should be kept away from as many people as possible. People only need to see her from a distance. At which, I'll add, she looks as much like a lady as anyone else."

Footsteps sounded from within Juniper's chambers. Soft steps of indoor shoes. The main door opened a fraction, and Juniper leaned out, brows furrowed. The stringent odor of the hair dye came with her.

Her midnight blue eyes settled on Adrian, and at once, her brows smoothed. "I thought I heard voices. Whatever could you two gentlemen be talking about?" she asked.

"Making you the epitome of a lady." Adrian smirked. "With Reid's help, of course."

"Ah, that's what I thought." She leaned against the closed door, her posture more bully than lady. She rolled her eyes over Reid and crinkled her nose. "Man talk. Can't stand it. If you'll excuse me, dearest, I've an appointment to finish."

Adrian bowed his head toward her, his smile devilish.

She slipped back into the room.

Adrian nudged Reid with his elbow. "I think she likes you."

Juniper whispered something foul on the other side of the door.

Adrian grinned wider. "What did she say?"

"I'd rather not repeat it," said Reid.

Juniper's voice murmured from the seam in the doors, "I called you a—"

Reid thumped his heel against the door. "Keep your mouth shut, and be respectful."

She harrumphed, and her soft footsteps stormed back toward the bedroom.

Adrian laughed and took several leisurely steps down the corridor. "Walk with me, Reid. It's been too long since we've spoken. You're becoming too serious for your own good."

Reid considered it. He hadn't spent much time in the past few months with his friend. The seamstress would be a while, and she could keep Juniper preoccupied with talk of clothes. Her hair would take time too. There were guards scattered about the Royal Chambers; Juniper wouldn't get anywhere without someone seeing her.

Reid followed Adrian down the corridor.

Adrian said, "She can't be all that bad. She's got spirit, and she's pretty."

"No," Reid warned. He had seen that wild look in Adrian's eyes plenty to know what it meant. He saw the thief as a challenge, an obstacle to be tackled. "She's not to be trusted."

Adrian laughed, shrugging. Adrian could pull out his best charms when he wanted to, reserved for courtiers, parties in the city, and attractive strangers in taverns. But when no one watched, when he had no one to impress, Adrian relaxed into a natural, friendly charm. Into the young man who currently walked beside Reid. That charm made the idea of someone wanting to kill him hard to believe, but Reid had seen the threats himself.

They turned a corner into another corridor. A group of young servants scurried at the other end, carrying a heavy basket of clean linens between them.

"Where did your guard go?" Reid asked.

"I lost them through the old hidden door trick. I went into the Lavender Lounge through one door and out another."

Reid frowned. "Your father won't be amused."

Adrian's grin never faltered. "My father is rarely amused, even when there's no one trying to kill me."

"You should be more careful. You're not even armed."

"And I came straight to you." Adrian clapped him on the shoulder. "No assassin will stand a chance when Squire Sandpiper is with me."

Reid tried to look proud at the statement, but it left him feeling the weight of responsibility. If they were to be attacked, and something happened to Adrian, it would be his fault. Of course, Reid would die before he let anyone at Adrian.

If the binding spell worked as the court magician alleged, it wouldn't come to that.

Adrian and Reid walked into one of the rooftop courtyards. This one did not have a stunning view, or any view at all. It connected four corridors, all closed with mahogany doors. A veranda lined the courtyard, a simple stone awning supported by marble pillars. Blue hydrangea bushes grew within the center of the courtyard. They grew tall and wide enough to block the view from the other side of the veranda and from the clearing between the bushes. In the center of that clearing, a fountain sprayed from a mermaid's mouth into a shimmering pool of painted fish. The small square of sky was a clear clue.

As Reid and Adrian walked down one side of the veranda, a door opened, and two servants appeared, each carrying a tray laden with a finished meal. One charmed smile from Adrian sent both young women blushing bright pink. They giggled as they hauled the trays down the veranda, toward the corridor that would take them to the kitchens.

"Perhaps..." Reid paused, in case more servants appeared. "Perhaps you should keep the flirting to a minimum now that you are...otherwise engaged."

Adrian flashed him a wicked smile. "Being on a leash doesn't mean I can't look."

Reid wanted to reprimand him for the logic, but he held his mouth shut.

Adrian laughed. "I see that look. I know what you were going to say."

"And what was that?"

"To mind my leash."

"Something like that," Reid said, although he wouldn't have called a relationship a leash.

"Speaking of that leash," Adrian said, "my servants tell me that the news of Roslyn's midnight arrival has spread out of the castle already. She's become a legend overnight."

"I beg you not to tell her that," Reid said. "She'll be beaming with pride."

Adrian nodded. A breeze whisked through the hydrangea bushes. Adrian paused and leaned against a marble pillar. "Do you think she will adjust? Roslyn, I mean. This must be a drastic change from her home in Galamond."

From the Undercity to Bradburn Castle? Reid wanted to laugh. "From a professional opinion? I would say no." He glanced for any listening ears. With the bushes, anyone could be listening and remain unseen. "She was raised to survive in Galamond. That's her home. It's in her blood. It's hard for one to adjust their habits to new surroundings."

Once a thief, always a thief.

"But you will keep an eye on her for us all." Adrian nudged him. "You'll report any discomfort she might have."

"Of course."

Adrian's eyes narrowed at the tone.

Reid couldn't help the disappointment he felt. He should be out hunting apostates or burning bandit hideouts, not playing babysitter for a thief. He hadn't told Adrian any of that, but he suspected the prince knew. He was always observant.

Adrian clapped Reid on his armored shoulder. "Don't worry. My father trusts you with this task because he knows I trust you with it. He knows what an asset you are. It's a shame you hadn't stayed in the Royal Guard. I'm certain you would have made captain once your uncle retired."

"That might be twenty years from now," Reid said. His uncle wasn't that old. Forty-five wasn't old for Captain of the Royal Guard. His predecessor had served as captain until sixty-seven.

"And you've got his attitude." Adrian drew his arms closer to his body as a chill wind blew over the courtyard. "Professional to a point. No sense of humor when it comes to work. All business."

"It's a continuous duty to be the captain." An unrelenting, demanding duty. The entire castle's safety rested on the captain's shoulders.

"Yes, yes. No time for fun," said Adrian.

"Not everyone can frolic all day."

Adrian frowned. "I do not frolic."

Reid chuckled. "And what is it that you do?"

"I...*saunter*."

They laughed. They turned onto the last side of the veranda and

35

started back toward the Royal Chambers. A group of servants came from one corridor, carrying tins of silver polish and reeking of the scent. They bowed respectfully to Adrian, who smiled warmly back at them, and continued on their way.

"They are either working on the suits of armor or the silverware," Adrian said absently as they approached the open door.

Both men nearly jumped out of their skins as three young women burst from the corridor, each dressed for an afternoon at court, with pinned hair, heavy jewels gracing their slender necks, and thick skirts swishing about their legs like petals.

"Oh! Your Highness," chimed a young woman in pale green. She curtsied nearly to the floor. Her tightly pinned dark hair didn't move. "I didn't expect to run into you today! My sincerest apologies."

The giggling of the other young women suggested otherwise. How long had they been lying in wait for Adrian to pass?

"Lady Dudley," Adrian said with forced pleasantry. He held out his hand for hers, and she eagerly placed her manicured fingers into his. Adrian lifted her hand to his lips. "Pleasure."

Lady Dudley's flanking friends received similar kisses on their hands. Their eyes shifted to Reid, as though they expected similar treatment, but he would give them none. He had no wish to be a part of the court's clawing drama.

The two ladies eyed him suspiciously and then looked at each other. They spoke without moving their lips.

Reid forced his face into neutrality. No doubt, they spoke silently about Nanette, the young woman he'd courted the summer before, and they would likely speak aloud once Reid could no longer hear them. As her name fluttered through his mind, he felt the similar grip of grief, heartbreak, and rage that had consumed him for the better part of the autumn.

"I hear that Lady Roslyn Derean has come to visit," said Lady Dudley. By the way her eyes shone with the words, Reid would have bet gold her entire meeting here had been planned around that question. "Is she well after such a long trip?"

"Yes," Adrian said, placing a hand over his heart. "She set a grueling pace to get here. She will need a few days to rest up and adjust to the warmer weather."

"When will she be at court?" A cleverly disguised threat.

"When she is ready," Adrian said.

Even though Reid would rather keep the thief away from the court as long as possible, he knew she'd have to make something of an appearance. She would have to learn manners before then, or meeting hawks like Lady Dudley would surely end in disaster. Though, it would be interesting to see her and Lady Dudley match wits.

"Although"—Adrian lowered his voice—"the northern parts of the country are a bit different. She might come across as a bit brash to the ladies here."

Lady Dudley's eyes flashed. "Oh, I wouldn't hold a thing against her!"

After a few long minutes of simple, unimportant chit chat and flimsy promises of future talks with Lady Dudley and her friends, Adrian and Reid continued along the veranda and toward the Royal Chambers. Reid held in his panic as best he could; he had already been gone far longer than he would have liked. He should have stationed someone...but whom? He couldn't tell anyone who was behind those doors. He should have made something up to the nearest guard—that Roslyn hadn't been feeling well.

Adrian groaned softly. He murmured, "They're following."

Reid listened to the corridor behind them. Sure enough, several pairs of heels clicked against the stone a short distance back. "They're not very sneaky," Reid muttered.

Adrian grinned and nudged Reid's arm. "Maybe we should introduce them to Roslyn."

"That would be an unwise decision," Reid said, keeping his voice low. "At least, until she learns manners. I dare say your lady friends want to learn where Roslyn is staying as to pay her a visit themselves."

"And that is why there are guards at every entrance to the Royal Chambers," Adrian said, motioning to the two guards standing alert on either side of the mahogany doors. As they walked through, Adrian greeted the guards by name. The guards nodded their respect. "And, no one will get a toe through her door with you standing watch."

Which only reminded Reid that he was currently *not* standing watch.

As Adrian predicted, the ladies did not follow them into the Royal Chambers. Reid knew they wouldn't. He had been in the guard. He knew his uncle trained his men well; those guards would sooner run Lady Dudley through than grant her access to the Royal Chambers.

Reid walked a bit faster. Adrian kept up with him but said nothing.

They made it to the thief's chambers, and to Reid's great relief, he heard her humming on the other side.

Adrian put a hand on his shoulder. "See? Epitome of a lady. She's already abiding by the rules." He chuckled. "I'm glad we could find time to talk again. I miss having you around. I must go before my guard tears down the castle, looking for me. Father has meetings planned this afternoon, and he wants me to attend. All of them. Dreadfully boring, these politics. I could go my entire life without hearing any more of bandits or apostates or market regulations."

"Might as well get used to them." Reid recognized the tune she hummed but couldn't recall a single word of it.

Adrian sighed dramatically and waved as he departed. Reid was relieved that he didn't have to go to those ridiculous meetings. Had he followed his uncle and remained in the Royal Guard, he would have. Dozens of meetings each week to discuss castle procedures, possible dangers, prison management, guard positioning, training, discipline reports, expenditures, and salaries... Dreadfully boring.

Not that the Order's meetings were any more exciting, but at least they traveled and did something other than guard doorways and windows while trying not to look bored out of their wits.

The humming hit a high note, which she missed.

Reid let himself into her chambers, mind on encouraging her to get some sleep, but he stopped on the threshold. His heart skipped.

Clara, the servant, was dusting the bookshelves. Humming. She nodded a quick greeting to him. "Squire Sandpiper."

He rushed past her and into the bedroom. The bedroom was empty. The dressing room was empty. The bathing room, to his dismay, was empty.

No Juniper.

Heart thudding against his breastplate, Reid dashed back into the sitting room. Clara stood by the bookshelves, eyes wide. She clutched the feather duster to her chest, spotting her dress with dust.

"Where is she?" he demanded.

Clara paled. Her throat bobbed. "I—I don't know, Squire. I thought she'd gone for a nap. I've only been here a few minutes."

Reid dashed back into the corridor. Empty. Not even a guard to question.

Which way would she have gone? The guards wouldn't have let her out of the Royal Chambers. They had been told, however discreetly, to keep Roslyn inside unless she had an escort. With him and Adrian both occupied, only the king or the queen would have taken her beyond the Royal Chambers. Either option made his heart drop into his groin.

Assuming she hadn't left the Royal Chambers, that still left him with a sizable area to search for a thief trained to be unseen.

Reid started down the corridor, toward where he and Adrian had come from. Once he reached the end, he turned the opposite way. If she had gone the way they had, they would have run into her.

He dashed down another corridor, pausing at the end of it, looking down both adjoining corridors, feeling about as hopeless as he could, when he heard the distinct swish of steel through air. He followed it. He turned around a corner, hand on his blade, and there she was.

Black hair done up in a braided crown, she leaned against the stone wall, gazing out the window, midnight eyes focused.

She lazily tossed a dagger into the air.

CHAPTER SEVEN

Juniper sensed Sandpiper's rage. It rippled like heat in the peak of summer. She didn't look at him; she held her gaze on the distant green blur of the Royal Greenhouses. The dagger came back down, and she caught it by the hilt.

"Where did you get that?" Sandpiper snapped. He stormed to her with all the contained rage of an insulted man and lifted his sword a few inches out of the sheath.

"You were gone, and I was bored." She glanced at him; his eyes burned. Oh, she had *infuriated* him. "So, I went exploring on my own. So many nice things in the castle."

She had also gotten a better idea of the layout of the Royal Chambers. The corridors connected in a rectangular fashion. Not so chaotic.

Sandpiper's tan face reddened with anger. He gritted his teeth. His fingers tightened on the hilt of his sword. Aware of how angry she'd made him, she tossed the dagger up. It flipped gracefully in the air and landed hilt-first in her palm.

Sandpiper's knuckles had gone white. His pursed lips paled.

"Is there a problem, Squire?" she said sweetly. She tossed the dagger up.

"You know what the problem is." He sheathed his sword and grabbed her arm; his other hand caught the dagger out of the air and held it out of her reach. "My problem is *you*. You are not to go anywhere in this castle without me."

The sun coming in through the window turned his honey-brown eyes to gold. Juniper tried to twist her hand out of his grip, but he held her tighter.

"Does that mean you missed me, Squire?"

He released her arm but stepped closer; he grabbed her roughly by the shoulders, one hand still holding onto the dagger, its blade now angled dangerously toward her throat. He pushed her back into the stone wall between windows, shadowing them both. In a deadly whisper, he said, "Do you understand what could happen if you wander off? You are *bound* to the prince. Do you understand what that binding spell did?"

She dared not move for fear of the dagger, whose blade she could almost feel. "I am bound to the darling Prince Adrian," she said. "I didn't get a good look at the scroll itself, but I've never been good with poetry."

He growled, a rather unsettling sound from the back of his throat. The dagger wiggled. "It means, if he gets sick, you take that sickness. If he is wounded, you take that wound from him. If he dies, Juniper," he hissed her name like a curse, "then you die for him."

"If he dies, I also die?"

"You will die *for* him. You take that death so that he will live."

Oh. Her heart tumbled into her stomach. "And you intend to kill me to save someone else the trouble?"

He glanced again at the dagger. He leaned back, releasing her shoulders and removing the dagger from her throat. He flipped it into the air and caught it by the hilt, now angled at her ribs. "No. Because the spell binds you to him until it is lifted or until you fulfill your duty with your death. If someone sneaks into his room in the middle of the night and slices his throat, yours will open, and his will heal. You will bleed out for him. Any wound he receives is magically transferred to you so that he will live."

She could just wake up in the middle of the night with a lethal wound? She felt herself blanch. "It doesn't work in reverse?"

"No, thank the gods it doesn't." Sandpiper glanced down at the dagger with disinterest. "I suggest you start taking this job seriously. Your life literally depends on it."

His gaze on the dagger narrowed. He studied the elaborate metalwork along the hilt, a masterwork of scrolling steel and crusted lapis lazuli with a bit of witherite. The dark blade shimmered as if sapphires and diamonds had been crushed into powder and folded into the steel during its ancient forging. In the sunlight, the blade glittered.

"Where did you get this?" he demanded, his fury mixed with astonishment. He knew exactly where she'd gotten it.

"I borrowed it," she said simply.

"Lying sneak thief!" he hissed. "You stole this from Lendon's Lounge. This isn't a toy, this is Gem Cutter! A Bradburn heirloom, a priceless artifact. The king would gut you himself if he knew you'd laid your sinful hands on it."

That would explain the glass box and the cushion and the oversized portrait of the long-dead King Lendon Bradburn. She said, "Now, now, Squire, calling me names will not make me like you."

He growled. "Who said I wanted to be friends with you? We are not friends. You are a thief worthy only of the gallows. I am a squire, a future knight. It is my duty to end people like you."

Worthy only of the gallows.

She would have been lying if she said those words hadn't hurt, even a little, but they were not words she hadn't said to herself. Regardless, she didn't let it show. "I thought knights were supposed to end only apostate's lives?"

Reid radiated anger, and a part of her loved it.

Apostates were mages who refused to go to the Marca, thus ignoring the Order and breaking the law. According to the Order, apostates were lawless, sinful, terrible human beings—users of black and forbidden magic.

"We are, but that doesn't mean I can't run you through and blame it on your wandering hand," he said, each word dripping with dislike. "The king wouldn't question my judgment, and we would find another thief to take your place." A servant came around the other end of the corridor. Sandpiper seized her arm and yanked her after him, back toward her chambers. "With you dead, there would be no one to doubt me."

Her humor deflated. "You don't have to be so nasty about it."

He didn't say another word as he dragged her back through the corridors. They passed a few servants, all of whom seemed too busy to pay them any mind. He finally came to a halt in front of her chambers, threw open the doors, stormed inside, and hurled her into one of the armchairs. He slammed the doors closed.

Juniper gathered herself and stood, her fury rising at being manhandled, a retort forming on her tongue, along with a colorful name for him, but as he spun to face her, she nearly careened into his breastplate. Fury twisted his features into a mask of hatred. He seethed, but she did not back away. She stood her ground.

They stood close enough to share breath; she smelled the sweat on him, the leather, the steel. This close, she spotted lighter golden streaks in his brown eyes.

He grabbed her arm in a vicious grip.

"You are here only because His Majesty allows it," Sandpiper said so quietly that no one but she could hear him, even if they pressed their ear to the door. "If it were up to me, you would have gone straight to gallows, if the guards hadn't run you through. That's still an option." He patted his sword. "Should His Majesty change his mind or decide against you, you can be fitted for a noose, not a dress. I suggest you mind your manners, mind that tongue, and keep your hands to yourself."

He released her and left the chambers, slamming the door hard enough to rattle the few books on her bookshelves. By the lack of armored footsteps stomping down the corridor, he had taken up a post outside.

She placed a hand on her arm where he'd grabbed her. She felt the beginning of a bruise.

He'd meant to hurt her, hadn't he?

"You don't have to be so nasty about it," she said, quieter than before. Oh, she would make sure to pay him back in full before she left.

CHAPTER EIGHT

Juniper collapsed onto the cushy bed and snuggled underneath the mound of silken blankets, one of them a luxurious down, and barely thought anything more before a heavy sleep took her. The exhaustion-driven dreamless sleep flashed past, and Juniper woke up in a groggy daze, unable to move within her cloud of silk.

Sandpiper stood at the bedside, scowling.

The sunlight had faded from glorious midmorning yellow-white to a gilded evening gold.

"Hmm?" she murmured to Sandpiper.

"Dinner has arrived," he barked.

She peeled herself from the bed. His nose crinkled at her wrinkled dress. She ignored him; dinner smelled as marvelous as breakfast had. The table in the sitting room was laden with dishes. This time, she had a bit more self-control, and she reached first for the decanter of wine. She poured a healthy amount into her crystal goblet and sipped.

Sweet. Flavorful. Expensive.

Sandpiper sat across from her, scowling. Not wanting to engage him in direct conversation so soon after waking up, she delicately piled a little bit of everything on her plate. Rolls, cheesy casseroles, smoked meats, fresh fruits, and buttery vegetables. By the time she had finished filling her plate, her mouth was watering. She started eating without a glance in his direction, although she did use her fork properly.

Gods, the food was delicious!

Sandpiper cleared his throat.

She raised her brows innocently. *What?*

He carefully positioned his fork and knife and sliced cleanly through a chunk of smoked pork. "Manners, Lady Roslyn."

He delicately placed an artfully cut piece of pork into his mouth. He chewed, swallowed. They ate for a while in silence. Juniper took bites of everything on her plate, systematically trying to figure out which she liked best while ignoring the looks Sandpiper gave her. She felt his eyes watching her, studying her manners, analyzing her every move.

With that sort of indifferent attentiveness, he certainly would make a good knight.

After devouring her entire plate, she set her utensils to the sides.

"You did fine," he said, tilting his wine to his lips. "A bit overly dramatic, but I'm sure the court will fawn over it. They crave dramatics."

"You're not a fan of court?"

He hesitated to answer. He didn't seem like the type to enjoy the dancing, chatting, and mindless spite and subtle passive-aggressiveness. He took a long drink of his wine, then said, "It is not my favorite way to spend an afternoon."

She had the strangest urge to say something. She took a drink from her wine and let the crisp taste linger on her tongue. Sandpiper was staring into the bottom of his goblet. She thought about laying her arm on the table and pulling up her sleeve so he could see the tinted skin of the bruise he'd left her with, but decided against it. It would make her look weak to whine about her injuries.

She reached for another roll. He didn't object. He was still gazing into the glass, into the dregs of the wine.

Leaning onto the table, she asked, "How long have you been a squire?"

He didn't look up. "A year."

"How long is one usually a squire?"

"It varies." He took his eyes from the wine dregs to her, his gaze calculating, debating whether to tell her or not. "A year is not a long time. The shortest time spent in squirehood belongs to Sir Gomedia, who spent two months training before he accepted the doomed quest of slaying Hunimtor, Dragon of the South. It had killed five squires before him, and two knights."

"Your eyes got bright."

He blinked. "What?"

"Your eyes." She motioned to those golden discs, which had gone bright at the tale of Sir Gomedia and the impossible dragon. "They got bright. They nearly glittered."

He cleared his throat and looked away, although he couldn't hide the red that flushed his cheeks.

She prodded the roll in her hands and tore off a corner. "Why a knight? You would make a decent royal guard."

"I joined the Royal Guard at fourteen at the behest of my uncle," Reid said, eyes on his wine. "I gained acceptance into the Order as a Pledge at sixteen. Became a squire at eighteen."

Which would make him nineteen. Only two years her senior.

She had unknowingly squeezed her roll; she'd left finger marks in the soft crust. Setting it down on her empty plate, she said, "What changed your mind about being in the Royal Guard?"

"I never wanted to be in the Royal Guard." His jaw twitched. His lips parted, but he closed them quickly. He said instead, "I've wanted to be a knight since I was a boy."

"Then why start in the guard?"

"My uncle is the captain," he said irritably, like the answer should have been obvious. "He raised me. I joined the guard because he wanted me to. For all that he did for me, I couldn't refuse the offer. The guard is an elite family, hard to get into, and I felt honored to wear the uniform."

His uncle, Captain Sandpiper. If his uncle had raised him, then his parents were not capable. Not alive. Sandpiper turned his scowl away from her and onto the hearth fire.

"I see you and he inherited your kindness and pleasant demeanor from the same side of the family," she crooned.

His frown deepened.

"And that lovely smile of yours! Oh, it must set all the ladies aflutter."

He huffed, his tanned cheeks turning a shade of red. "Did you always want to become a thief?"

She pretended to think about it, then said, "No, I can't say that I did."

"What made you choose that path?" He asked it casually, but she heard the inflection in his tone, the intrigue.

She tore at her abandoned roll. "It was mostly a series of unlucky circumstances on my part. I was kidnapped by bandits at an early age, and they sold me in the Undercity like a cut of meat."

Sandpiper frowned. His brows came together in such a way that he looked ready to run someone through. Not unlike the always-angry City Watch. No doubt he had heard of the child market in the Undercity. Most ignored it like a myth; others rallied against it to little avail. Too many hands had earned too much gold selling lost children and orphans to underground guilds and slavers.

"You were sold?" he whispered, his voice crisp.

She nodded, poking at the remains of the roll. "Maddox Hawk bought me. I've been in his keep ever since."

Sandpiper fixed her with a gaze full of a guard's concern and an outsider's pity.

She shrugged, then said in a lighter tone, "But being a thief is much better than being a courtesan. I'd rather kill men for a living than sleep with them. Lucky for me, Maddox thought I'd make a better assassin than whore."

Sandpiper didn't chuckle at her attempted humor. His mouth didn't even twitch. After a heartbeat, the red returned to his cheeks, and he looked her up and down. Red came to her cheeks then.

Something flickered in Sandpiper's face before it became a stoic mask once again. He cleared his throat. "Before I forget, you are to dine tomorrow morning with Adrian. His request."

"I look forward to it," she said as dreamily as she could.

Sandpiper scrunched his brow, then shook his head. "No, I don't believe you'd have made a very good courtesan."

She frowned as her cheeks burned. "You have experience to back that up, Squire? I thought knights were supposed to take vows of celibacy?"

He coughed. "No. To both."

A knock on the door interrupted any further discussion. Sandpiper stood quickly to answer it. Juniper twisted to see her visitor, and to her delight, the seamstress scurried through the doorway with a half a dozen dresses thrown over her chubby arm. Her servant carried another six in hers, nearly drowning the poor girl.

Juniper jumped to her feet, squeal on her lips.

"Now, these are hurried, mind you, mostly dresses I've had in the shop. Did a few quick adjustments for your shape," warned the seamstress as she walked them into the bedroom. The servant followed on her heels.

Juniper rushed after her, not minding the glare from Sandpiper. She'd been looking forward to her noble wardrobe, but she didn't think it would arrive so soon!

Juniper sat in the chair in the dressing room, admiring each dress as the seamstress showed them to her. Each looked marvelous and expensive, if not a bit plain, but the finer material and luxurious colors made up for the lack of elaborate sashes or ribbons or beading or detailed threading. Juniper quickly found her favorite: a silky purple gown with golden accents on the skirt and lace on the bodice, although the cream and cobalt gown looked exquisite.

"Oh, these are beautiful!" Juniper ran her fingers down the silken sleeve of the purple gown. "Just wait until His Highness sees me in these."

Miss Jenson beamed. "I am glad you approve. I'll have something better tailored to your shape by the end of the week."

Juniper could only imagine how lovely *that* gown would be. Miss Jenson gave a short bow and left, her silent servant on her heels.

Juniper stood in the dressing room for a while, admiring her new gowns in turn. She had brought a few well-made tunics too.

Sandpiper came to stand in the doorway.

"Should I have thanked her?" Juniper asked him.

"You did."

"But I didn't say—"

"You implied it," Sandpiper said. "Which means more to someone like Miss Jenson. You haven't taken your eyes off those gowns, and your eyes went a bit misty when you looked at that one." He pointed to the purple gown. "No words could have said what your eyes did."

"Am I that easy to read?"

"Sometimes." He smirked. "When you're not trying." He took a step out of the dressing room. "Wear the purple one tomorrow."

That tone— "Are you leaving?"

He nodded. "There is a guard posted in the hall for the night. Don't worry."

She scoffed. "I am not afraid of the dark, Squire."

"They are there should you need something or should you try something." He took a step closer to the dressing room, and his eyes hardened. "You are not to leave this room, understand?"

"Fine."

Sandpiper headed for the bedroom door. His footsteps clanked across the sitting room, then out into the corridor. Juniper stayed in the dressing room a while longer until she had sufficiently studied her new assortment of gowns. She had seen dresses like them in shop windows in the high-end markets, always out of her price range. Not that she had ever had an occasion to wear something so nice.

Despite her afternoon nap, she washed and readied for bed. Maybe, she thought as she climbed back into the bed, being Lady Roslyn Derean wouldn't be so bad.

Chapter Nine

Reid was halfway to his chambers when he met his uncle in the corridor. Captain Sandpiper had hastily pulled his black and gold jacket over his shirt, leaving it unbuttoned. His brow furrowed at Reid, but his surprise quickly vanished.

"Reid," said Captain Sandpiper, not bothering to halt. His green eyes, the same eyes that Reid's father had had, bore into his—something had stirred him.

"Is something the matter, Uncle?"

The captain motioned for Reid to follow. He spoke in a low, calm tone of urgency. "Another servant has been reported missing. A cook this time."

"Another?"

His uncle nodded. "The word has just come to me. I want to inspect the site before anyone else catches wind of it. Come, assist me."

Reid walked quickly to match his uncle's pace. He had missed the time spent with his uncle. His squire studies and duties had kept him busy over the last year.

His uncle took a servant's passage that wound down into the kitchens. The kitchens were the oldest part of the castle; according to historians, they had belonged to the castle King Lendon Bradburn destroyed in his conquest. From massive brick ovens to stone countertops to narrow ventilation shafts vanishing into the ceiling, everything looked ancient. The floors were flat bricks set in a curving pattern not used in at least a thousand years.

Reid held in his awe at the implied age, the number of feet that had crossed those bricks, the meals prepared.

Even without the boiling pots, simmering stews, rising bread, and resting pies, the kitchens smelled wonderful, like every spice and spout of flavorful steam had soaked into the stones and mortar. A thousand years of soaking. A thousand years of gossip too—servants saw everything. What would the servants of kings past have to say to them?

Reid shook the feeling of being watched by generations of servants and followed his uncle into the far corner of the kitchen, behind a row of wide brick ovens. A boy of maybe fifteen was holding onto the pudgy arm of a middle-aged woman who had her face buried in the folds of her stained apron.

The servant boy's gaze flashed between the captain and Reid. He gave them both a quick respectable bow of his head.

"Captain Sandpiper," said the servant boy, his voice cracking. "Squire Sandpiper."

The woman's head snapped up, eyes swollen and soggy, cheeks red from tears that had stopped not that long ago. A few clung to her bottom lashes. Her soft brown hair had been tied up into a bun, but the recent events had shaken it loose. She looked at Captain Sandpiper with a mournful hope.

"It's taken him, hasn't it, Captain?" she whispered, her voice hoarse.

The way she said *it's* sent a chill down his spine, like *it* truly existed. Whatever the servants believed *it* to be.

Reid schooled his face into a neutral expression, like his uncle had taught him, like he'd taught all of his guards. Reid had heard the servants gossip about the thing they believed lurked between the stones in the walls, down forgotten corridors and secret passageways, stealing unsuspecting servants. From what they said, it could have been a dozen different monsters, each as ancient as the ruins on which Bradburn Castle had been built. Each as unlikely.

"You are?" Captain Sandpiper asked calmly. He suspected, but he didn't want to assume; he'd taught Reid never to fully assume.

"His wife, sir, since we were seventeen," she murmured, eyes straining to keep the tears back. She pointed to the oven closest to them. Scorch marks from hundreds of years of roaring fires marred the inside pitch black. "He came in here to clean the ovens, and he did by the look of them, but this one here. Look, sir, it's only partially clean."

Reid followed her stare to the oven, the last oven in the row. Where the racks of the other ovens were indeed clean, the cleaning of the last rack had stopped halfway through. The crud of several meals and soot from the fire below caked half of the iron bars, whereas the other half had been scrubbed free of it. The rack had fallen into the ash below, not yet scraped out as it had been in the other ovens, as if the person holding the rack to clean it had suddenly stopped holding it.

"It appears as though he was interrupted," said Captain Sandpiper.

Reid stepped away from the oven and glanced down. A small splotch of ash had landed on the floor. It had been smeared. The smear did not give away a footprint, but it pointed at the wooden door that led into the larder.

Both men stepped toward the door in unison. His uncle reached the door first. Reid expected to see the missing middle-aged man slouched near the wine barrels, drunk and out cold. It wouldn't be the first time.

The larder was empty.

Reid stepped inside. Towering wooden shelves lined the room, thick with supplies: cooking dishes, serving dishes, utensils, cleaning soaps, bags of dried ingredients, jars of spices, barrels of rice, flour, and potatoes. Reid went one way, and his uncle went the other. Reid scoured every detail of the shelves, but nothing looked to have been disturbed. No broken bottles or moved barrels. No signs of ash. No bodies. No blood. No struggle. Nothing seemed even remotely out of place.

Reid met his uncle on the far side of the larder, the farthest point from the open door where the wife of the missing man waited. She'd refused to step inside.

"Anything?" asked the captain.

Reid shook his head. "No."

The servants would be listening, and neither man said anything more. Reid started to walk back to the door but paused. The back wall of the larder, unlike the rest of it, held no shelves. Barrels were stacked on either side, but one barrel stood cockeyed. The dust on the floor suggested it had once been in front of the wall, but someone had recently moved it. Why move it away from the wall?

His uncle noticed his stare and stepped closer to the wall. He whispered, "A passage to the old castle. One that a long-dead king sealed. See this seam here?" He ran his forefinger along the old stone. "It's been filled."

Reid saw it. A barely visible seam ran along the stones in the shape of a narrow door. It had been filled with something that had long dried into stone. Reid had a horrible feeling in the bottom of his stomach. Suspicion, maybe. Or dread. A hidden and forgotten door in the same place where a servant vanished? He did not like coincidences.

Reid pressed his hand against the old door, but it didn't budge. Solid as stone.

"Nothing could get in or out this way without leaving a sizeable mess behind," his uncle said. He grinned at Reid and whispered, "Unless there's a ghost in here who can drag people through solid stone."

Reid didn't laugh. He offered his uncle a smile in return. He would bet gold the servants would be terrified of ghosts next.

Captain Sandpiper promised the missing man's wife that the guard would be looking for him and that he would inform the City Watch as well. He did not promise, nor even suggest, they would find him. He knew better.

The two men left the wife to mourn and blubber to the younger servant. They did not speak again until they were nearly to the corridor where they had met.

Reid asked, "What do you make of it?"

His uncle ran a hand through his chestnut hair. The gray at his temples seemed more pronounced, as did the lines around his eyes. "I will speak to Glenda. She knows her servants better than anyone else. It could be something as simple as the man was a drunk. Maybe he hated his wife enough to leave. Who knows. But..." He heaved a powerful, quick sigh. "It's too many servants. Too many have gone missing in the past six months. This man, if I remember correctly, will push our number of missing servants into the sixties."

Reid gaped. "*Sixty*?"

He knew a number of them had been reported missing, but he had no idea it had been so many. As a squire, he didn't hear about the Royal Guard's troubles.

His uncle nodded grimly. "The other servants have noticed. Some have willingly turned in resignations. Fewer people are coming to the castle looking for work. Rumors are spreading into the city. Everyone from the king to the tax collectors has been blamed. But the truth is, no one knows where they've gone. They're just gone."

"Do you think..." Reid paused and looked about the corridor; finding no one to easily eavesdrop on them, he continued lowly, "...it has something to do with the threats against the prince?"

His uncle didn't answer immediately. He chewed his thoughts, and then said, "I can't say one way or another. Two strange things that happen at the same time are often blamed on each other, but there is no way to connect them. But I agree. It can't be mere coincidence. I refuse to believe it."

They walked to the barracks in silence. They reached the corridor where they would part ways, and the captain said, "Reid." His uncle wore a serious glimmer in his green eyes. Was that the same grimness the thief claimed Reid had inherited? His uncle closed the space between them. "Something is indeed happening within this castle, be it by human hands or otherwise. Stay alert, and be wary of whom you trust."

Reid nodded. "I will."

With that, his uncle strode toward his office, no doubt to think, brood, and stare out the window that overlooked a courtyard where the guards trained. Reid started toward his chambers with his uncle's words fresh in his mind.

Be wary of whom you trust.

On which side did the thief land?

CHAPTER TEN

Juniper slept better than she expected for having slept most of the previous afternoon. The bed felt like a thick cloud, supportive without protruding or poking. The comfort of the bed mixed with the heat of the hearth fire, and she rolled over to find another pocket of that glorious sleep.

The sleep did not last. A knocking prodded her from it.

She opened her eyes to find the squire standing at the end of the bed, knocking his knuckles against the bedpost.

"You're still in bed?" His usual frown looked deeper.

She moved her arms underneath the covers. The drowsy peace of the morning took any snippy comment she might have otherwise made. She stretched her arms and legs into the cooler reaches of the blankets. "Yes, I slept well. Thank you for asking, Squire."

He stalked to one of the windows. He wrenched the curtains open, splashing the space with blinding morning light. She snapped her eyes shut at the light, but they quickly adjusted. Moving to each window in turn, he opened them all with the same yank of his wrist. The sunlight gleamed off his silver armor.

She slowly pushed herself onto her elbows. Sleepiness made her too happy for her own good, for she said, "You look quite surreal in the sunlight, Squire. Surely you must be off to slay a dragon or sweep an unsuspecting maiden off her feet?"

"What?" He raised a brow. It might have been the dreamy light or the sleepy daze, but she thought his frown seemed to flicker ever so slightly upward. His stern tone didn't change. "Get up. You'll not want to be late for your breakfast with Prince Adrian. He is looking forward to spending time with his beloved Roslyn."

She blinked. Oh, he meant *her*.

"Yes, yes." She waved her hand at him. "Wouldn't want to keep His Precious Highness waiting."

She reluctantly pushed the blankets down her body. The cooler air leeched the warmth from her skin. Shivering, she stuffed her feet into her fur-lined house boots and pulled her dressing gown over her shoulders. She stepped into the bathing room.

Washed, freshened, and awake, Juniper found Clara in the dressing room, preparing the purple gown.

"My lady." Clara curtsied, positioning her brown slippers perfectly. "Squire Sandpiper said you preferred to wear this gown today."

"Yes." Juniper held her chin high like a lady.

Clara helped her into the soft underdress and then into the purple gown. She tied the corset with adept fingers.

"You look marvelous, my lady."

Juniper harrumphed.

Clara's calm smile straightened. "Do you not think so?"

"No, no, it's not that."

Clara's lips pursed. She looked almost motherly. "What is it, my lady?"

Juniper bit her lip. *Complain about something.* "It would look better if my breasts were larger." She placed her hand underneath her breasts.

"Nonsense, my lady." Clara gestured to Juniper with her hand. "You've got a body women would torture themselves for." She placed her hands on her hips. "I've worked with noblewomen my whole life. I know the mad things they do to themselves to look a certain way. I once served a lady who ate once a week, and barely a sandwich at that, so that her ribs would show."

"What happened to her?" Juniper asked.

"She snapped out of it when her husband died. Her brother-in-law took over the estate, and she is now fat and happy. Well-loved, I hear."

Juniper nodded her approval.

Clara smirked. "So, trust me when I say you're a sight."

"Even as apple-breasted as I am?"

Clara laughed, a warm sound that filled the dressing room. "Yes, my lady, even so. Although, they're larger than the average apple. Grapefruits, I'd say."

"Grapefruits, then."

Clara combed and braided Juniper's black hair into an elaborate updo and wrapped a thick shawl of gray and yellow wool around her shoulders. Finally ready, Clara led Juniper into the sitting room. Sandpiper ushered her into the corridor without a word.

"Don't be afraid to compliment me," Juniper said to him. She held her chin high. "I am quite aware of how good I look this morning. You were right about the purple gown, Squire."

"If you're so aware, then why do you need me to confirm it?"

"Maybe a lady enjoys hearing her own thoughts confirmed."

"That means you don't think what you say you think."

She snapped her head to him. "I know what I think. I walked past the mirror."

"Ah, you enjoy the chit chat, then?"

"I *am* a lady, Squire."

He glanced at her. A slight smirk twisted his lips. Approval.

✦

They walked through the Royal Chambers, up a narrow yet grand staircase that wound around a hanging candelabra, and into a corridor. It didn't take long to find which door held the prince. Two royal guards stood on either side of mahogany doors. They stood still as statues, yet their eyes followed Sandpiper and Juniper as they approached.

Sandpiper opened the door. The first things she saw were windows. It was a lounge; the far wall was a stock of floor-to-ceiling windows. A set of doors in the windows let out onto a small balcony. Juniper blinked. Dainty white and gold seating had been angled around the burning hearth. A wicker basket and a tray of steaming tea set on a table between the white sofa and the hearth.

Prince Adrian was sitting on the sofa, his long legs stretched out in front of him. At the sight of her and Sandpiper, a charming smile spread over his lips. He unwound his ankles and rose to his feet with royal grace. "There you two are. I thought we'd have a picnic in one of the courtyards, but Blugo is tossing a cold snap on us."

Blugo, the God of Winter, was notorious for delaying spring.

Adrian held out his hand for hers. No guard stood inside the lounge; the three of them were alone.

"It's cozy in here," she said, placing her hand into his.

He pulled her closer, nearly chest to chest, and then he tugged the wrap from her shoulders. His breath hit her brow. Could he hear how loudly her heart beat? He hesitated, then leaned away from her to place her wrap over the back of the sofa. He sat, and she sat beside him. Sandpiper stood by the door.

Adrian reached for the teapot and poured the reddish-amber drink into two delicate china cups with a spiraling leaf pattern. Adrian picked up one of the cups; the liquid inside barely jostled within his touch. He handed it to her. As she took it into both of her hands, her fingertips grazed his.

She brought the cup to her lips.

Adrian sipped his tea. "Mmm. Tell me, how has your stay been?"

He spoke sensually, as if he truly spoke to a lover. Juniper wasn't sure how she felt about his ease with it.

"Amazing," she told him without hesitation.

Despite the circumstances, staying at Bradburn Castle had so far equated to staying at the nicest hotel in the city. She'd never been inside as a guest, but she had snuck inside enough times to see the luxury in which guests were swathed.

She detected movement—Sandpiper. He stood by the door, his arms at his sides like a royal guard, his eyes on her. Ever the patient watchdog.

Adrian leaned toward her. Close enough for her to catch the butterscotch tones of oils or soaps or maybe even an aftershave. He whispered softly so that only she could hear, "He's harmless."

She whispered back, her breath bouncing off his lips, "And a bit cranky."

Adrian chuckled. "He's always been the serious sort. To a fault. He has a lighter side, but he's too honorable and loyal to show it."

She fought the urge to see if Sandpiper had heard him. "Have you known him long?" she asked.

"Since we were boys," Adrian said. He sipped his tea. It didn't even appear to touch his lips. She thought he would say more about it, but he leaned away. He pulled the wicker basket closer and unpacked their picnic himself.

"The prince doesn't call his servants?"

He smirked at her. "By not asking them to come in, they are left to wonder what's really happening in here."

The breakfast, while not as expansive as her other meals, smelled no less grand with boiled eggs, sliced ham, warm rolls, and cinnamon tarts.

"Your favorite." Adrian motioned to the cinnamon tarts. "Every year since we met, I've sent you a jar of cinnamon for your birthday."

"How sweet of you." She liked cinnamon tarts, but she wouldn't claim them as her favorite. But as per the game, she could play.

The breakfast picnic turned out to be a lesson on the real Roslyn Derean.

Born during the autumn, Roslyn claimed Boxel—God of the Harvest—as her patron. House Derean was proud and believed strongly in the survival of the fittest. According to Adrian, she had been raised to hunt like a mosscat, curtsy like a lady, and rule like a queen.

By the end of breakfast, Roslyn sounded like someone Juniper would like to meet. She sounded useful, unlike most ladies she'd encountered, who wouldn't know a bow from an ax.

"I think that covers the basics," Adrian said, running a hand through his dark blond hair. It flounced back into place. "It's at least enough to keep the ruse to outside eyes."

"What if someone comes to the castle who knows her and knows that I'm not her?" she asked. The thought had crossed her mind several times.

Adrian's eyes went to her black hair. "Galamond is a vast kingdom," he said. "The Derean Estate is to the northern extreme of it, tucked into the base of the Dolomin Mountains. Few people go that far north. Those who live there rarely leave. Even if someone knew what Roslyn looked like, you look enough like her that no one would openly say otherwise."

She sipped her tea. It would be her luck that someone would recognize her to be an impostor, and she would be either thrown back into the dungeon or killed.

Adrian draped an arm across the back of the sofa. Behind her. His fingertips grazed her shoulders.

"Tell me," she purred, trying to mimic his lover's tone, "why do I need to be in a ruse with you at all?"

He considered her, his hazel eyes working through intelligent calculations and judgments. He brushed her hair from her temple, and her heart thudded. Touched by a prince.

"My father has enemies." His smile turned into a grim line. "He made more than a few when he sided with southern Collatia, and more for waiting so long to do so. And with the rise of bandit gangs in the south, slavers in the west, and mages in the east..." He heaved a breath. "There are some who think Duvane would be better off under different leadership, that the Bradburn line has run its course."

"But the war ended twelve years ago." Juniper didn't remember it at all. She'd been five years old.

Collatia, their mountainous neighbor to the east, had long had struggles between its prominent provinces. The king's older brother wanted to be king and led a military coup against the royal family. The north and south came together in a devastating clash; Duvane entered the war with the south and, when the kingdom collapsed, took control of the prosperous silver mines on the border, which were later annexed. It made Duvane the wealthiest kingdom on the continent and left Collatia in near ruins. Some semblance of order remained in the south, where the last bit of the royal family resided.

"Yes," said Adrian. "But some of the Collatian rebels in the north think Duvane stole their victory from them. Some in the south think Duvane stole their mines, leaving them without a major source of revenue."

Adrian adjusted himself on the sofa so that their thighs touched. She tried her best not to think about it.

"You think those rebels are the ones threatening you?"

Adrian shrugged. "We don't know. Rebels are causing problems in their kingdom, and rumor has it, they've started to flood over Duvane's borders."

Sandpiper coughed. A warning. *Don't tell the thief too much.*

Adrian finished his tea. It clinked as he set it down on the saucer. "I don't envy my father or his advisors. We don't know who is behind the threats, where they are coming from, or what the end goal is. If we did, we might be able to stop them."

"That is a lot of unknowns," she said.

He nodded. A sprig of his worry wormed through his external charm.

Real assassins—the professional ones—didn't threaten. They simply assassinated their target. No show, no talk, just action. But why threaten the prince at all? Why not threaten the king himself?

"What kind of threats are they?" she asked.

Sandpiper let out a low sigh, but Adrian wasn't paying attention to him. The prince's shoulders slumped, and he said, "It started out with unsigned letters threatening my life. They grew more detailed, listing what they would do. Torture. Specific torture." He gave a shudder. "We ignored them. I...stopped reading them entirely. My father gets threats on a daily basis. We added to my personal guard, kept my outings to a minimum and to respected establishments only. Nothing happened. I thought the threats had stopped, but...then, about a month ago, it changed."

He glanced toward the windows. The sun had steadily risen, and the dawn haze had vanished. The clear blue sky promised of incoming spring.

"Birds would fly straight into the windows of whatever room I occupied," Adrian said darkly. "Spiders would follow me around. Dead animals would somehow find their way into my room, rodents and cats mostly, even though the guards in the hall reported no one entering or exiting. A week ago, I was headed into the city, but I didn't make it past the front steps." Adrian's eyes drifted over her shoulder, to something unseen. His smile waned. A somber horror replaced his humor. "An arrow pierced the throat of the guard in front of me. Right through him. The bloodied arrow stopped an inch in front of me."

"Sounds more like an elaborate plot to scare someone witless," Juniper said. Fear flickered in Adrian's eyes, and she had the urge to calm that fear. "But I understand. Watching someone die so suddenly, so close to you, it rattles nerves. A lot of them. But normal assassins don't bother with such theatrics or drawn-out nonsense like that."

"That is what we decided too. We were not dealing with an ordinary assassin," he said. He twisted his fingers together. "My father and the court magician decided to use a binding spell, just in case. And not a week later, you were...hired."

She harrumphed. Better than *caught.*

Convenient, said the little voice in her head, *that you arrived so soon.*

"My father told me of some of your crimes," Adrian said, straight-mouthed, but his gaze held a charmed glint, curious and cautious. "You've played the assassin before."

She swallowed. "I mostly play the thief."

"But you have killed before," he said.

She nodded.

Maddox often had his guild members learn a secondary skill. While Amery had learned the skills of the courtesan, Juniper had learned the skills of the assassin.

"I have many skills and talents you don't know about," she said, though her face warmed. She sipped her tea.

His grin turned wolfish. "Except in the bedroom."

The red in her cheeks, which had almost faded, returned brighter and hotter. She coughed but laughed it off. "Of course, you'd remember that."

"How could I not? A lady mentions bed-warming, and a man isn't supposed to pay attention?" His shining hazel eyes scanned her body. She felt that gaze slide down her chest, her torso, her hips, and back up again.

The blush felt like fire.

She'd heard about Prince Adrian Bradburn. Everyone had. He knew exactly how women worked underneath their fluffy gowns, and he didn't bother to be shy about it.

He leaned closer and set a hand on her waist. The warmth from his hand seeped through the material of her dress. His gaze flickered to her lips, just once.

He did not kiss her.

He leaned away, and she released a slow sigh of relief. At the same time, she felt a twinge of regret that he hadn't come closer.

Juniper and Adrian talked for a while longer about less horrible things than assassins and threats; all the while, the sun rose higher and higher in the crisp blue sky. Adrian told her about himself, things that Roslyn would know, his favorites, his shared memories with her. By mid-morning, she had learned more about Prince Adrian than she could possibly remember.

With the food gone and the tea cold, they called their picnic finished. Adrian had duties to attend to; he seemed none enthused.

Standing, Adrian said, "Lastly, has Reid mentioned my birthday?"

"No."

"It's in three days," Adrian said, glancing over at Reid. "I plan to go to the Temple of Bala to make an offering. It would be splendid if you would accompany me."

She blinked and slowly stood. "You would be willing to take me out of the castle?" There would be countless opportunities to run.

"Unless you've made other plans?" Adrian glanced at Sandpiper again; something silent passed between them. "My father thinks it would be beneficial for people to see you, even if it is from a distance."

To further this ruse and to let the would-be assassin see her.

"If I said no, would it matter?" she asked. To be honest, she'd rather stay in her new cozy room in the castle. It had been too long since she'd had a vacation.

Adrian's grin flickered downward. He cleared his throat. "There is also the matter of Bala's Ball."

All thoughts of vacations and long soaks vanished. Juniper gasped, "Bala's Ball?"

Amusement flashed across Adrian's face. "Of course," he said. "The ball isn't for a while, but you should be prepared."

Bala's Ball celebrated Bala, the Goddess of Nature. It was the event of the year. Held at the spring equinox, they still had considerable time before the laurels were hung and wreaths of spring flowers dotted every archway and lamppost in the city.

Then her heart fell. "Do you plan on me still being here by then?"

Again, Adrian glanced over her shoulder at Sandpiper. "It is something we need to consider."

"Just in case," Sandpiper answered. "There is always the chance the problem will be solved before then."

Adrian chuckled. "I've heard rumors that it is the doing of my evil twin."

"Nonsense," said Sandpiper.

"Some would argue with you, Reid." Adrian slipped his hands into his trouser pockets. "Some of the servants are feverish about the subject."

"That you have an evil twin?" Juniper felt skeptical.

Adrian leaned toward her. "The story goes that before the civil war in Collatia had spread to our doorstep, my father had another child. The mother of that child varies with the stories: sometimes it is my mother; other times, a servant; other times, a traveling merchant. Regardless, my father, in fear that war would spread, sent that second child outside the castle for safekeeping. That child was then raised in secret. However, the worst never happened, and so that child has remained a secret."

"That sounds like something a royal family would do." Especially of a man who would enslave a criminal like her to give her life in place of his son.

"That's the logical part of the story," Adrian said. "The fun part of the story is that this bastard brother of mine discovered his heritage and has returned to Bradburn Castle, full of cold fury and the desire for revenge, and has been causing trouble ever since. He is blamed for all manner of things. In this case, trying to kill me."

"There are no records of such a child, however," Sandpiper said flatly.

"Reid has never been the superstitious sort," Adrian whispered to Juniper behind his hand, loud enough for Reid to hear.

Juniper shifted her eyes to Reid. "Yes, I can see that. It would fit the rest of him."

Adrian smiled. Reid frowned.

A bird fluttered by the window, hovering near the highest corner. Nesting, no doubt. Another bird flew after it, tweeting excitedly. Their shadows raced across the floor and out of sight.

Adrian shifted on his feet. "So, the temple?"

"I would be honored, my prince," Juniper said dramatically.

"You'll have to behave," warned Sandpiper.

"I wouldn't dream of it," Juniper said, aghast. She placed a hand over her heart. "Not with Bala's Ball dangling in front of me." She couldn't throw that opportunity aside.

Adrian flashed her that lovely smile. She felt, although she would never admit it, a small kernel of jealousy for the real Roslyn.

CHAPTER ELEVEN

Three days passed in quiet seclusion. Juniper spent the majority of her time lounging or napping. On the morning of Adrian's birthday, Clara wove Junipers's hair into an elaborate braided crown and helped her into a dress and cream and gold. Sandpiper walked her to where Adrian waited; he wore his crown, a ring of pointed gold and rubies.

"Someone looks marvelous this morning," Adrian said as he beheld her. "Almost as marvelous as me."

"Someone is full of himself this morning," she chimed, looking him over.

He laughed. "And witty!"

They walked arm in arm through the castle. An audience awaited them in the entrance hall. Staff, servants, and courtiers lined both sides of the room.

A perfect place for an assassin to hide.

Juniper tensed her grip on Adrian's arm, but nothing happened. They made it to the end of the stairs and to the grand set of doors on the other side of the hall without incident. Guardsmen opened the doors for them in perfect unison, and she and Adrian paused at the top of the wide stone steps into the front garden.

Sixty guards, at least, stood in the garden, armor shined and polished. She counted a dozen knights, their silver armor standing out from the guards' bronze. The Royal Guard and the Order made their presence known. Such security. Then she remembered Adrian's story. The last time he had left the castle, a guard had been shot through the throat. Suddenly, the prospect of leaving Bradburn Castle did not feel very appealing.

The coach that would take them to the temple was a marvel of cream, gold, and crimson. The curved double-sided ax donned the door in shining gold. The horses had been bred for beauty, each a stunning white. The driver, a slender man with a sword at his side, wore a cream-colored coat with the royal seal embroidered on the back.

Royal Guards on horseback, armed with arrows, swords, and daggers, took up positions all around the coach.

With each step toward the coach, Juniper waited for an arrow to fly. None did. The footman opened the coach's door and bowed low. Adrian held his hand out for hers.

"My lady," he said, flashing that charming smile at her.

Such a gentleman! She placed her hand into his and carefully stepped up into the coach. She knew all eyes were watching her. One slip, one broken ankle, and— She sat in the cushioned seat, and Adrian sat beside her. The door shut.

The interior was just as luxurious as the outside, with velvet seats in a rich red, buttoned velvet walls, and soft cream curtains on either window. The floor had been polished, but heels and boots had hopelessly scuffed the rosewood.

The coach began to move. Juniper let out a sigh and sank into the cushioned seat.

"Are you all right?" Adrian leaned back, stretching his legs and letting his shoulders slump. "You did well. Reid was worried you'd fall before you made it to the coach. The shoes, I take it?"

Juniper lifted the hem of her dress to show him the shoes in question. Lovely cream-colored leather with a thin wooden heel longer than her longest finger. "I'd love to see you men walk in these nightmares."

Adrian gave her a grateful smile, one that meant he would rather not walk in such shoes.

The garden passed slowly, and the hooves of their guards' horses clicked and clacked. The guards riding within her view had sharp eyes and straight-line mouths, like Sandpiper. Waiting for commotion, watching for trouble. Like her life meant something.

"It's so dreamy," she said. "I never thought, not in a hundred lifetimes, that I would get to play a princess."

Adrian looked out of her window as if to see what she found so dreamy about it. He blinked, then shrugged.

"Of course, you wouldn't see it like I do," she snapped. Adrian's hazel eyes widened in surprise. She cleared her throat; she hadn't meant for her words to come out so bitterly. "I mean, you've lived in this kind of luxury your whole life. You've never had to worry about where your next meal was coming from or getting your jobs done so you could eat or keeping a boss off your back or if you'd be jumped on your way home."

He shifted in his seat to see her better. His brow furrowed. "Did you have to worry about those things?"

She was saved from answering by a squeal of iron; the massive castle gates began to open. The coach passed through, and they started down Royal Avenue, the main street in Rusdasin. The wide sidewalks on either side were packed with people waving, shouting, and whistling; they clamored for a view of their prince.

"My, my, aren't you the popular one," Juniper mused, gazing at all the eager faces.

Adrian obliged; leaning closer to his window, he waved and smiled.

Juniper let out a bitter chuckle. "If you're so worried about an assassination, I wouldn't give them such a clear view of your head," she said plainly. She leaned forward to scan the rooftops. "It would be easy to wait for the coach to come by and shoot an arrow through the window, right through your lovely face."

Adrian paled and pulled himself back into the seat. "I hadn't thought about that."

"Which is why your father hired me," she said proudly. "He wanted someone to think like an assassin."

Adrian gave her a halfhearted chuckle. "I won't argue with that."

Silence thickened between them. Juniper had the sinking feeling that it had been her fault. Had it? She leaned back into the seat and then said, "I am sorry if my view of your life seems tilted. I've spent my life looking up at the castle, thinking how easy life is for those inside, while I fought to survive one day at a time. I've had to work for everything that I have, every meal, every gold." She paused. She could feel his eyes on her, and she dared to meet his gaze. To her surprise, she found curiosity looking back at her, not the pity she anticipated. "I find it easy to be bitter at those that have an easier life than mine."

Adrian nodded. "I can understand that. I admit that it is not the easiest thing for me to relate to what you've gone through. What many in this kingdom go through." He lifted the golden crown from his head and set it in his lap. The rubies gleamed in the sunlight. His hair had taken on a slight indentation from the crown. "I am also sorry that things happened the way they did. If it is any consolation, you are expanding my understanding of the struggles people face. But what's done is done, and there isn't anything we can do to change the past." That charming smile mixed with something else—sympathy? "All I can ask is that you be patient with me."

Adrian's charming smile faltered. She blinked at him; sincerity shone true in his hazel eyes. A prince, the Crown Prince of Duvane, had *apologized*. To her.

She didn't even have the words to respond. After a moment, Adrian chuckled. "I take your speechlessness as acceptance. This is your only chance to correct me."

She didn't.

He replaced the crown atop his head. Juniper immediately moved to adjust it; her fingers grazed the priceless crown, but Adrian never flinched. She lifted it from his head, and while holding the crown in one hand, she smoothed his hair with the other. Adrian kept still, eyes on her face. Satisfied, she replaced the crown on his hair and brought her empty hands into her lap.

"There," she said. "You don't look so haggard."

"Thank you."

A warmth flooded into her cheeks. She'd never imagined the prince so cordial. She laced her fingers together; she could still feel the cool metal against her skin. She had held the crown in her hands. Not the king's crown, but close.

Adrian held his hand palm-up to her. For hers. She set her hand into his, and he laced their fingers together.

She chuckled. "A gutter rat is sitting in a gilded coach holding hands with a prince," she said. "Who would have thought?"

Adrian winked at her.

They rode in silence for a while, each gazing out at the crowd that had gathered along Royal Avenue. The wide sidewalks were packed with people waving and shouting. Most stores along the road wore CLOSED signs in their windows. The side roads had been blocked off by the City Watch, and plenty of watchmen and watchwomen meandered through the crowds, hands on pommels, eyes darting for thieves and street rats looking to take advantage of a distracted crowd.

The thief inside of her quivered at the thought of so many unattended coin purses, keys, and loosely attached blades. In a crowd like this one, no one would think twice of a bump on the side, the shoulder, or the hip, or the confused and embarrassed face of a girl.

Would Amery be out in the crowd today?

"Wave to look important," Adrian whispered.

She did as he asked; she waved to a group of young girls who hung on the skirt of an older woman. Each of their young faces brightened.

"You're a natural," he said, smiling.

Sitting with Adrian like this, talking like friends, she understood what made girls fall so irrevocably in love with him. A game, she reminded herself. She played a game. An act. Pretend. There could be nothing between a thief like her and precious Prince Adrian. After the assassin was caught, she would be thrown out of the castle on her ass, and she would be once again gazing up at Castle Bradburn with bitterness.

CHAPTER TWELVE

The coach passed through the towering gates of stone and ivory and into the courtyard of wildflowers and berry bushes. Despite the lingering winter, Bala's Garden was in full bloom, as it was every day of the year. Purples, pinks, yellows, and greens in all shades dotted the garden. The rich floral scents fluted through the window. The buzzing of bees filled the air like a song.

The Temple of Bala was known for its delicious mead, hinted with herbs and flowers and berries, as well as its prosperous honey.

The coach came to a halt. The thundering hooves of the guard stopped alongside them, flanking every side of the coach. Adrian stepped out first and held his hand out for Juniper. She took it and gracefully, carefully, stepped down to the cobblestone.

Cobblestone. Whoever had picked out her shoes had not considered that.

They walked up the stone steps to the temple arm in arm. She avoided the temples when she could. The stone, the silence—they felt more like tombs. She knew tombs. She had plundered enough of them to know the heavy, otherworldly feeling they gave off. A warning to the weak-willed.

How would Bala, Goddess of Nature, who favored the compassionate, feel about a thief, murderer, and liar walking into her hallowed halls?

Adrian and Juniper paused in front of the simple wooden doors worn by weather and time. The doors opened in unison—two priestesses in identical yellow-white robes greeted them on the other side, warmth on their pleasant faces.

Neither spoke. No matter the god, their priests often took vows of silence, or at least vows of moderate silence—something about tongues being the main avenue for wickedness. Juniper had never paid much attention to the teachings.

The halls were dark, lit only by torches along the barren stone walls. The walls themselves seemed to whisper, hundreds of years of prayers, tears, and hopes soaked into the gray stone. Shadows thickened, swirling as if to see the two guests better.

Very tomb-like indeed.

She tightened her grip on Adrian's arm. His calm smile flickered downward. His brow furrowed.

"Roslyn?" he whispered.

"I'm fine." Her tone didn't convince her either. Her entire body shook.

Adrian reached for her hand on his arm. He folded his fingers around hers, loosening her grip on his sleeve.

The silent priests and priestesses stood along the main passage, their yellow-white robes glowing in the darkness, and kept their heads bowed as Adrian passed. The deeper they went into the temple, the more deafening the silence, until only their footsteps on the stone remained. They came to the offering chamber. Bala's statue, carved from limestone, stood waiting to receive and to bless. She stood proud, her robes carved with flowers and thorns and bees. A sparrow perched on one hand, and the other held a sprig of chicory. Her stone eyes gazed downward at the offering plate between two fires.

No priests watched the offering chamber. They didn't need to. Bala's stone eyes watched the chamber.

"Juniper?" Adrian whispered, worry deep in his eyes.

With no one looking, she confessed. "I sacked this temple this past winter."

He frowned, an expression of exasperation, not anger.

Before she could stop herself—"I took twenty gold from the offering box."

"That money is supposed to go to the poor."

"It did," she said, her voice several pitches higher. "I hadn't eaten in a week. I was starving. I was desperate."

Bala's stony eyes glared down at her, knowing what she'd done. Admitting it had only made it slightly better.

"And now you've confessed," Adrian said. His hand landed on her back. He hesitated, but she couldn't see his expression—she couldn't take her eyes off Bala's statue.

I'm sorry.

How many had starved to death so that she could eat that week? How many children had gone to bed hungry so she didn't have to?

Worthless. Only a terrible human being would take food from a hungry child.

Adrian's hand left her. "This will only be a moment."

She had half a thought to reach for him. Without him, without his earnest presence, she felt utterly alone and vulnerable under Bala's glare.

Adrian took from his pocket a slender glass bottle. He knelt and emptied the jar's contents, a pewter powder, into the silver offering bowl. He took a long matchstick from the pile below the offering bowl and lit it in the fire. He set the wooden stick burning-side first into his offering. The powdery offering began to smoke; then a rich earthy scent filled the space.

Juniper only half-listened to Adrian as he recited the prayers to Bala for his family, his kingdom, his friends, and his future.

She'd not once been to a temple to give thanks or an offering of any kind, not even her own patron's. Seeing Prince Adrian Bradburn down on his knees in offering, humbling himself, only deepened her feeling of inadequacy.

Maybe she deserved her fate. Maybe she should have just let herself starve. Save the world the trouble she caused.

After the offering had burned, he stood. He offered her his arm, and she took it in both hands.

"Silver lime stem," Juniper blurted, suddenly realizing the delicate scent. The stem of the rare and expensive silver lime. Used in healing potions. The tree only produced a few fruits a year. Only a prince would be able to afford such a thing as an offering.

He blinked at her in surprise. "Yes. I could think of no better offering than that."

They retreated from the temple, and Juniper gladly awaited the sunlight. She wouldn't step into another temple for a long while after this.

Halfway to the open doors, Adrian asked, "What god marks your birth?"

"Blugo."

"Ah, God of Winter. Favors scholars. Protector of weary and lost souls." Adrian glanced at her with a humored curiosity.

Before he asked, she said, "No, I've never been to his temple."

"Not that. I thought it curious. Given your talents and occupation, I would have pinned you for a product of Bera."

Goddess of Shadow. Favors the shy, ambitious, and clever. And, notoriously, thieves.

"I choose not to dwell on such superstitions," Juniper whispered as they passed through the main doors and into the sunlight. The sickly-sweet smell of wildflowers rushed to meet them. She did not speak again until the coach began to move. "I choose to set my own path, not some preordained one because I was born under Blugo's stars."

"I see," Adrian said, nodding. "I can respect your thinking."

"You don't think it makes me a fool? Most others say so."

"I think it makes you headstrong, but there's nothing wrong with that." He grinned. "Isn't stubbornness a trait of Blugo's?"

She rolled her eyes.

The city she knew so well rolled past, the storefronts, the sidewalks, the window displays, the taverns and clubs, and the alleys where she'd lost more than a few of the City Watch. If only her fellow thieves could see her now, dressed and treated like a princess, sitting beside the Crown Prince of Duvane, so close, their thighs touched.

"Thank you for accompanying me," Adrian said as they turned back onto Royal Avenue. "You've made this trip less odious. I'm sorry if it took a toll on you."

"Anything for you, my love," she crooned.

The coach pulled through the gates and rolled into the quiet front garden. The guards kept the people to the sides as the gates clattered to a close. Juniper fixed her gentle slouch into that of a lady's straight spine. She could practically hear Sandpiper's rant about slouching.

At least they'd arrived back at the castle, and no assassin had tried to slay either of them. Admittedly, she felt relieved.

Sandpiper was waiting for them just inside the castle doors, scowling.

"Walk me back to my chambers, Roslyn?" Adrian said to Juniper, loud enough that the servants cleaning the floor on the far side of the room heard. "I've a meeting with my father this afternoon, and I'd rather change into something more comfortable."

"Glady, my love."

Sandpiper stalked a step behind as they sauntered back to the Royal Chambers. Adrian's chambers were frighteningly close to her own. No wonder Sandpiper had been so angry when she had gone exploring. She could have been in and out without anyone knowing, pilfering whatever she wished from his chambers.

His guard arranged themselves in the corridor outside the door, and Adrian turned to her with a priceless, beloved smile. Even if he had not been born a prince, he would have had women swooning into his bed every night for that smile and those eyes. He would have been the most popular courtesan in the city. And expensive.

His fingers ran along her knuckles. He leaned toward her, eyes on her lips—a goodbye kiss. Adrian didn't give her a chance to panic. He kissed her; he moved his lips slowly against hers, allowing her to memorize his motions. She followed his lips with her own while a horde of winged insects batted around her chest.

The kiss did not last long. Adrian gave her a wolfish grin, then walked through the doors and into his chambers. She placed a cool hand on her warm cheek. She had just kissed a prince.

She turned to return to her own chambers, and her gaze fell onto Sandpiper, who looked like he had stumbled into a foul mood along the way. She opened her mouth to point it out to him when a particular stench touched her nose. Like a rotting corpse.

She shut her mouth and inhaled. Sandpiper's brow furrowed. Sandpiper's nostrils flared; his eyes widened.

That smell. She knew that foul smell.

Panic, hot and fluid, flooded her veins. She threw herself at Adrian's door and yanked it open. Sandpiper raced in behind her, unsheathing his sword as he crossed the threshold. A murmur went through the guards.

Adrian stood across the room, in the doorway to his bedroom, hand on the top button of his tunic, hazel eyes knitted in confusion.

Juniper ignored him. She scanned the room. That smell grew stronger with each breath. Beside her, she heard the squire sniffing. For once, she felt glad to have his sword so close to her.

There—within the flickering shadows cast by the hearth fire, crouched on top of the bookcase. She spotted the glinting eyes of the creature a heartbeat before it leaped through the darkness.

Chapter Thirteen

The creature leaped into the air, a mass of dark fur and patchy, leathery skin. It opened its jaw wide, exposing needle-like yellow teeth. Its curved talons raised toward Juniper, primed for ripping into flesh and bone.

She reached instinctively for her dagger—gone. Weapon...she had no weapon!

Sandpiper appeared in front of her, sword extended, and as the creature came, his sword caught it in the mouth. The steel clanked against its teeth. The creature howled and stumbled back, its spindly, bony legs thumping into the delicate furniture. The creature's foot caught one of the armchair legs, and in frustration, the creature kicked it across the room, slamming it into the wall. Wood splintered on impact.

Blood oozed from the creature's broken jaw where Sandpiper had struck it. A growl rumbled from the back of the creature's throat.

The doors to the chamber burst open; guards poured in around them, joining Sandpiper against the creature, shepherding Juniper and Adrian away from it. Adrian, his face pale, grabbed Juniper and pulled her several steps into his bedroom.

Adrian's hands trembled. Like she could talk. She balled her fists in her skirts to keep anyone from noticing how badly they shook.

She'd never seen anything like that beast. By the worried looks on the guards' faces, neither had they. But that smell...it lingered. Sandpiper stood firm, leading the offensive, his face a stoic mask. A warrior's mask.

The creature seemed to be calculating its odds; something terrifyingly like thought passed behind its brown eyes. It looked from guard to guard and to Sandpiper.

"What is it?" asked a guard.

"A rabid dire wolf?" suggested another.

"No." Sandpiper glared at the monster with all the wrath of the world. "It is a demon."

She heard Adrian's sharp intake of breath at the same moment she felt her own. His hands tightened on her shoulders. A demon. A *demon* had been waiting for Adrian in his bedroom. Waiting. *Stalking.*

The demon adjusted its haunches, the bones maneuvering underneath the taut hide. Blood dripped from the wound Sandpiper had inflicted on its jaw, which hung at a stomach-twisting angle. Worst of it all, the smell. It burned through her nose like the ash of the foulest of creatures, born of hatred and black magic, like rot and decay, like death.

She shuddered. Adrian's hands gripped her tighter.

The demon lunged at a guard who countered easily, although he did not exude the confidence that Sandpiper did. The guards attacked. Their blades cut through the beast's tough skin, leaving it crisscrossed with bleeding gashes, but the beast fought as though no wounds marred it.

Sandpiper took up a defensive position in front of the bedroom threshold. As the beast lunged for him, Juniper could have sworn the beast's eyes glanced over Sandpiper and to Adrian.

Its target.

She sucked in her breath. If that beast got past Sandpiper, there would be nothing for her to defend them with. No sword. No dagger. Just a frilly dress not made for combat. She'd be useless. She and Adrian would both die.

Sandpiper met the demon's lunge with a powerful swing of his sword, cleaving down the demon's side with a sickening wet crunch. Yet the demon pushed past him, even with its bleeding wounds leaving a bright red trail of blood behind it, even with its back leg barely attached to its body.

Demon. No other creature would have survived that attack.

The demon landed on the bedroom floor, its blood squelching underfoot. Sandpiper turned and dashed, but for a terrifying moment, nothing stood between Juniper and the demon.

She could push Adrian in front of her and escape through the window, or even through the main door. In the chaos, she could sneak out of the castle. She and Amery could be laughing about it by sunset.

The demon came at them. She shoved Adrian out of the beast's direct path, and she lunged in the other. The demon landed with a hard thump between them, sliding in its own blood, teeth clicking unevenly.

On the floor, Juniper didn't see what happened, but she heard it. Sandpiper engaged the beast; Adrian let out a terrified yelp; the beast went quiet with the crunch of steel on flesh and bone. She scrambled to her feet in time to see Sandpiper standing above the beast, his sword bloodied. The demon's head lay still, separated from the rest.

Adrian lay behind him, clutching his chest.

"Alert the king," Sandpiper commanded at once. Several pairs of feet dashed from the sitting room.

The demon exploded into black dust. The ash rained down like black snow, but she had little time to admire the dangerous beauty of it.

A searing pain started near her collarbone. She gasped; she couldn't breathe. Juniper pulled her hand away from her collarbone to find it slick and shiny with blood. It seeped from the wound, staining the cream bodice of her dress. The greedy threads leeched it from her, drinking it up as quickly as she bled.

Something exploded inward from the wound, searing, burning, ravaging through her insides; she screamed. She cried out and reached for the invisible blade but found nothing. She felt the blade in her skin, a rough, uneven blade, impossibly sharp, slightly curved. The pain slowly made its way along her chest, between her breasts, and curved to the right where it finally ended.

Adrian lay slouched near the bed, his shirt torn from neck to navel. The jagged edges were stained red, but the pale skin of his chest lay unbroken.

The binding spell. She'd taken his wounds.

Sandpiper helped the prince to his feet, examining his lack of wound.

She tried to stand, but her legs couldn't hold her weight. Then Sandpiper knelt in front of her, moving impossibly fast. He grabbed her by the shoulder and tore his dagger along the front of her dress.

"It hurts," she gasped, tears stinging her eyes.

"No one can know about the binding spell," he said with a hint of remorse. Behind him, Adrian removed his torn shirt, threw it into the hearth fire, and pulled a clean shirt over his head.

The world wobbled dangerously. Darkness played on the edge of her vision, coming ever closer.

"You'll need a healer," Sandpiper said from somewhere far away.

Distantly, she heard the clamor of swords and armed guards. They spoke, but she couldn't make out the words. Juniper shut her eyes. In the darkness behind her lids, all she knew was pain.

"Breathe," Sandpiper instructed.

She listened. In and out, in and out, even with his breaths.

And then nothing.

Chapter Fourteen

Juniper felt a strange, warm nothingness. It welcomed her. Beckoned her closer. Maybe it was the final tug on her soul that would send her into the burning blaze of her afterlife.

Bala had tried to warn her: *Repent now. It's your last chance.*

"Roslyn." He sounded an ocean away. "Look at me."

She fought to open her eyes, to find that steady voice. She found him. Sandpiper stood at the bedside.

"You need to drink this," a soft-spoken male voice said.

She shifted her gaze; it took what energy she had. A slender boy of maybe seventeen stood beside her bed. He wore robes of deep green and a purple sash, signifying him as a trained mage of the Marca. He stood shorter than Sandpiper and half as wide. He had short dark hair and steel-colored eyes that beheld Juniper with an analytical gaze. The boy held a silver tray, on which sat a glass of green liquid.

"Lady Roslyn Derean," Sandpiper said to her, "this is Ison Rolin, the court magician's apprentice and the castle's potions master. He's brought you a healing tonic."

Sandpiper regarded Ison with a cold stare. A squire looking at a mage. A squire waiting for a sign of black magic, any hint of defiance, so he could rid the world of another dangerous, rule-breaking mage. Typical.

She opened her mouth to respond, but no words found their way from her blurry mind to her tongue.

Sandpiper took the tonic from the tray and leaned over the bed. His calloused finger touched her chin, tilting it upward. He set the lip of the glass against her mouth.

She drank it slowly, one tiny gulp at a time. He never forced it down but carefully kept the glass poised. She didn't taste it. She didn't feel it move down her throat. She barely felt her muscles moving with the action.

Sandpiper pulled the glass away from her mouth. Empty.

"Thank you," he said to Ison, who nodded his leave. Sandpiper turned his attention back to her. "Sleep. You need it."

He didn't have to tell her twice.

Juniper woke in the welcoming silken folds of her bed. She couldn't move, but she had little desire to. The curtains of the windows were drawn, but the raw gray sunlight of a stormy morning seeped through. Thunder rolled, distant and lazy. The stormy light shifted as lightning followed the thunder.

The hearth had gone cold.

Breathing—someone was breathing.

She turned her head as far as she could. Sandpiper slumped in the chair beside the bed, head lolled onto his shoulder, brown hair messed. Gentle breaths issued through his mouth. His chest rose and fell. Asleep.

Should she say something? She tried, but she had not the energy or the words.

The demon.

She'd lived, so Adrian had too.

Gods, everything hurt. She inhaled slowly, gently to avoid excess movement. It felt like she had shattered every bone in her body and ripped apart a few muscles.

Sandpiper, as if spurred by her thoughts, shifted in his chair. He inhaled and blinked his eyes open; he ran a hand through his hair, leaving it more of a mess. Upon his exhale, he straightened, and his eyes fell on her. He groaned and stood. After starting a fire in the hearth, he meandered to the window. He pulled back the curtains enough for the stormy daylight to stumble in, shading himself in bright gray.

He did not wear his armor; instead, he wore a red tunic, dark pants, and a handsome leather sword belt, on which he had his sword and two daggers. Without his armor, the broad expanse of his muscular shoulders had nothing to hide under. Of course, as a squire, he would have to keep in the best of shape, of body and of mind. By the look of him, he was.

In a weak voice, she said, "You look less intimidating without your armor, Squire."

His stoic expression didn't change. "Do you see what the binding spell does?"

"Yes." She couldn't nod without stirring the pain.

"Now you know. The prince's life is in danger." Sandpiper started to pace between the bedside and the window. "Someone is trying to kill him, someone mad enough to summon demons to do it."

Bile rose in her throat. "Demon?"

Sandpiper frowned. "It could be nothing else. That beast was not of this world. The only way to bring a demon here is to thin the veil between our world and the underworld. It is black magic, forbidden magic."

"If you hadn't been there," she said, then paused at the look on his face. He knew. If it hadn't been for Sandpiper, that demon would have killed everyone in the room.

"That smell was of the underworld," said Sandpiper. He stepped toward the bed. The fire behind him shadowed his face and made his brown eyes appear black. "You smelled it before I did. You've encountered it before?"

She didn't want to talk about it. She didn't want to think about it.

She bit her lip as the memory of that smell came to her. She squeezed her eyes shut as the demon's broken jaw and hungry eyes resurfaced.

A warm, steady hand touched her forearm. "It's all right. You don't have to talk about it. I understand." He didn't ask her any more about it. Instead, he said, "Summoned demons can't go far from their source. For those demons to have gotten into the prince's room, they would have to have been summoned within the castle."

She snapped her eyes open and met his downcast gaze. She whispered, "There's an apostate hiding in the castle?"

Not just an apostate, but one who had resorted to summoning demons. Black magic. She'd heard of the deplorable, inhuman things apostates did to themselves, to others, to innocents, to gain their black magic. Sacrifices of children and virgins, dismemberment, disfiguration... She did not wish to encounter anyone of the sort.

"It is very likely that our assassin is an apostate, or one hired by the assassin to kill the prince." He grimaced. "Either way, our culprit would have to have access to the castle."

She swallowed, but her throat had gone dry. There was an apostate hiding somewhere within the castle, summoning demons. The king had suspected it or, at least, suspected the possibility that someone within his own castle could be working against him.

"Luckily," Sandpiper continued, "none of the guards saw the beast attack the prince. By the time the guards had entered, the wound had already transferred to you, making it look as though it attacked you initially." His gaze slid along the wound hidden by blankets and bandages. He had slashed through her dress too, and that he had probably seen her breasts sent a prickle along her skin. "If anyone found out about the binding spell, they would know to kill you first, then the prince."

"Or torture him until his wounds stopped transferring." She knew assassins who would do that too.

Sandpiper's eyes grew darker, even in the shadow. He meandered to the other side of the bed.

"Demons have a stout poison," he said. "The healer said it might get worse. Men twice your size have been killed by a smaller dose."

"That's why I feel so awful?"

"Yes. If the healer had been any later, you might not have woken up at all. I...stayed to make sure you didn't stop breathing between sundown and dawn."

"You've been here all night?" Her feelings of disbelief must have shown, because Sandpiper glanced away. "Thank you."

"The healer patched you up as best she could with the time she had. Ison brought a tonic soon after. It put you out for a while. You slept soundly after that."

"I remember." A glazed memory of Ison, of Sandpiper holding the tonic to her lips.

She tried to sit up, but her arms wouldn't move more than an inch. The effort stung, her crushed bones and shattered muscles whining in protest.

"Do you need anything? I can grab a servant if you require the bathing room," said Sandpiper.

She considered herself. "No, not right now."

"I will send word to the kitchens that you're awake. You need to eat something." Sandpiper stalked out of the bedroom. She heard muffled voices, but her rattled brain couldn't pick out the words. She closed her eyes and retreated into the painlessness of her exhaustion.

CHAPTER FIFTEEN

A small bowl of seasoned broth arrived, and Juniper managed to swallow a few spoons of it. She had no appetite.

Feeling slowly returned to her body, along with a strange numb sensation. She felt bandages along her middle, from her collarbone to her navel. They wrapped her breasts, granting her mild modesty. She felt nothing more than her underthings on her bottom half as the silken sheets hugged her legs.

"What will they do about the demon?" Juniper asked Sandpiper, who stood guard by her door, one hand on the pommel of his blade.

"The king has ordered the knights to scour the castle. The apostate would not have been able to summon a demon without leaving a trace of magic behind. It should still be fresh." He lowered his voice, adding, "There will be knights posted in the Royal Chambers as an extra precaution."

She swallowed. Her throat felt tight.

Knights. She could picture them, all tall, broad, and immaculate in their silver armor. The owl and chain adorning the front a gleaming reminder of what awaited rogue mages. They wore weapons forged with Mage's Bane. It made the blades darker and feathered with red.

She had never seen the Mage's Bane weapons used, but she had heard enough about them. Even a small amount would freeze the magic in one's veins, slowly, painfully draining them of it, turning the magic against its user. The mage was devoured from the inside out. Depending on how much Mage's Bane entered their system, their torturous death could last days. A death by a sword would be a mercy to a mage stricken with the bane.

She shivered at the thought, despite the fire warming the chill air.

Sandpiper stalked from his post to the foot of the bed, his expression sullen, just as a clap of thunder shook the windows. Lightning soon followed, brightening the window with blinding light. A shadow darkened the lower half of his face. It gave him a rugged look, unlike the immaculate knights. She liked it better; it made him look less serious.

"Juniper," he said but paused. He spoke her name in a tone she knew. He didn't know the right words to say what he wanted.

"Squire."

"When we..." He glanced toward the door to the sitting room. He fidgeted. "When the healer cleaned your wounds..."

What could make *him* nervous?

"Out with it," she barked, sounding like she'd swallowed sand.

He turned sharply and met her gaze. "What is that on your back?"

Oh. She hesitated with the answer. His eyes remained on hers, expecting, relentless, and fierce.

"A brand," she said.

He didn't say anything. He looked tired then, like the thought had been rolling over in his mind for hours since he'd seen it. He did not look away.

She clarified, "Maddox's brand."

She wore the brand in the center of her back: a jagged spiral. She had blocked out the worst of the memory: the searing pain as Maddox pressed the white-hot iron to her bare skin, the tears that streamed down her cheeks, the pain in her teeth as she clamped down on a block of wood to keep herself from screaming. Maddox had ordered her not to cry out. She hadn't. She had obeyed him, become a part of his keep.

Sandpiper didn't say anything or look away—like he could see through her chest to her back.

"It's a claim," she added. "It marks me as one of his. It prevents me from taking work elsewhere or joining another keep."

"Like cattle."

She broke his stare and looked instead to the ceiling, which didn't care if she wore a brand. "Branded like cattle, sold like cattle to the highest bidder...it does seem to be a recurrent theme in my life."

Sandpiper appeared in her peripheral. He sat in the chair beside her. Thunder rolled, rattling the entire castle with its mighty, vicious *crack*. Lightning flashed instantaneously. The first of the rain spat against the windows.

He leaned onto his knees. "When this is over, what will you do?"

She didn't have much choice. "Go back."

"To Maddox? Why?"

"Why?" She furrowed her brows at him. "Because I'd rather not freeze to death in some alley. I can't do anything else. If I defected, Maddox would hunt me down. His people would hunt me down to the ends of the world and either kill me on the spot or drag me back so Maddox can take his time with it."

"He doesn't own you." Sandpiper's voice came out small.

The brand said otherwise. "Try arguing with Maddox about it."

Sandpiper leaned forward and set his hand atop hers, over the blanket. "I'll make sure he doesn't come to claim you."

A fierceness in his brown eyes gleamed with determination, a certainty of his words that made her want to believe him. In that moment, he looked more like a knight than he ever had.

But... "Why?"

He didn't answer immediately. The heat from his hand traveled through the blanket and onto hers. "Because no one should be owned by another. What happened to you, being sold, it's unfair. It's not right. It's one of the reasons I want to become a knight. To stop injustice like that from happening, to stop families from getting ripped apart."

"Even to scum like me?"

He held her gaze, and something different passed behind his eyes, an emotion she hadn't yet seen on his face. Before she could catalog it, it vanished.

"Yes," he said. "Even to girls like you. I would like to think that given the chance, you would not have turned into a thief. Life has been unfair to you, and you've acted accordingly so far. And, like it or not, I care about what happens to you."

Juniper's tongue turned to stone. Even if she had words to respond with, she wouldn't have been able to utter them. No one had ever said such words so bluntly to her. The closest she had were the threats from Amery or Maddox not to die on a mission.

She'd never had to formulate a response, but Sandpiper didn't demand one. He squeezed her hand and removed his own; the heat of his touch remained.

CHAPTER SIXTEEN

Juniper woke with a terrible, dull ache that stretched from the top of her head to the tips of her toes, but the worst pain centered on the line that curved from her collarbone to her abdomen. She lay for a while, wishing to return to sleep, but a pressure in the lower parts of her middle refused her rest.

Great. Would she have to crawl to the bathing room?

"Squire?"

No one answered. If he had been in the sitting room, he would have heard. She would have to do it herself. She moved her arms first. They obeyed but felt sluggish and distant, like her bones had been replaced with wet sand. Her legs felt worse. She pulled her legs inward; a searing pain stretched across her abdomen, yanking a breathless gasp from her throat.

"Shit," she gasped.

The pressure in her bladder increased.

She adjusted her arms to push herself into a sitting position, but the moment she put pressure on her arms, pain ripped through her chest. She collapsed onto her back.

"Squire?" she called louder. "I require assistance!"

No one answered.

She would not have him return to a soiled bed. She'd rather jump out the window. She tried to wiggle toward the side of the bed, but the pain in her chest pulled tears to her eyes.

Finally, the door to her chambers opened.

"Squire?" Juniper called, not hiding the desperation she felt.

Quick footsteps, lighter than Sandpiper's, ran across the sitting room and burst into the bedroom.

Clara appeared at the bedside. "My lady?"

"I need to use the bathing room," Juniper said at once.

Clara hooked Juniper underneath the arms and hoisted her upward, using strength that the blousy sleeves of her servant's dress kept hidden. Juniper leaned heavily on Clara as they walked the short distance, which felt forever long, to the toilet in the bathing room. Juniper held her gaze on the floor between her bare feet. She couldn't bring herself to look Clara in the face, not as she took care of her business. She might never be able to again.

At least it hadn't been Sandpiper. She would not have been able to survive the humiliation.

When Juniper finished, Clara assisted her back to the bed.

"Don't be ashamed, my lady," Clara said as she smoothed the blankets. "I've heard that a demon's poison does horrible things to the human body. You're lucky you can move at all."

"It's hard not to feel ashamed when a stranger helps me with things that have always been a private matter."

"You're the first to feel that way," Clara half laughed, pulling the blankets to her shoulders.

Juniper blinked. Clara wore a servant's passive expression—no disgust or teasing.

Clara glanced down at the bedspread, smoothing nonexistent wrinkles. "Of the ladies I've served, most feel that their servants are..." Clara stopped herself from saying anything further.

Juniper finished her sentence for her, "Less than human?"

Clara swallowed. A slight nod of her head came as her answer.

"You must not have served many kind women."

Clara toyed with her apron. "Getting this job was a blessing from Boxel. Kind servants to work with, a kind family to serve. An entire city to explore on my days off. I hope to work here until my fingers can no longer hold a teacup."

Juniper swallowed. What to say?

Thankfully, she was saved from answering by a knock at the door. Clara swiftly went to answer it. Clara returned a few moments later with a stern-looking older woman a step behind. Her silver-streaked charcoal hair was cut in a short boy's style, but her face retained a feminine charm.

"You are?" Juniper said, impersonating a lady who had been interrupted.

"The royal healer," snapped the woman in a harsh voice. "We've met before, but you were unconscious. I doubt you remember much of it."

"Oh, my apologies." Juniper gave the older woman a curt nod.

"Yes, well, let's see how you've healed up overnight." The royal healer yanked the blankets down to her knees. Another reason to be glad Clara had arrived instead of Sandpiper.

The royal healer proceeded to undress and inspect the snaking wound, her nimble-fingers poking, prodding, and healing a little as she went. She explained that, thanks to the demon's poison, her healing magic could only do so much. The poison had a special agent within it that made it immune to magic, and Juniper's body had to slowly process the poison out the natural way, which led to stiffness, pain, and other unpleasantries.

"You are healing well," announced the royal healer at last, her fingers on the edge of the long wound. "Is Squire Sandpiper not present?"

"He was needed this morning at the Knights' Hall," answered Clara.

The healer wiggled her fingers toward her bag. Bandages and soft cloth flew out of it. Orchestrated by the healer, those bandages fluttered and snaked around her middle. The soft cloth lay against the seam of the wound, cooling the skin where it touched—*magic*—and the bandages snaked tightly around her, fitting perfectly from her shoulder to her hip.

"Ah. Much faster. More secure than if I'd done it with my own two hands." The royal healer inspected the magically wrapped wound. "And I trust Ison brought the tonic like I asked?"

Juniper did not miss the slight change in Clara's attention at the mention of the court magician's apprentice. "Yes. He brought one yesterday. Knocked me right out," she answered.

The royal healer chuckled. "Good, good. That young man knows his tonics. Very well. I shall return tomorrow morning unless something goes wrong." She glared a warning at Juniper, who tried her best to look innocent. "Until then."

"Good day," Juniper said in parting.

The royal healer packed up her things and bowed herself out.

Clara pulled the blankets back up to Juniper's shoulders. "Is there anything else you need, my lady?"

Juniper exhaled. She had nothing to do but stare at the ceiling until she fell asleep again. "Stay in here, and keep me company," she said. "Unless you have pressing matters to attend to, which I understand. Keeping a castle running must be a tiring routine."

"Yes, it is, but I have been given the primary duty of attending to Lady Roslyn, and so I will do as you ask."

"Then please, come sit with me," Juniper said. "It won't be long until I fall asleep again."

Clara walked to the bedside and sat carefully. The bed barely moved.

Juniper asked, "What are your thoughts on the healer?"

"She is very skilled and professional," Clara said, her eyes on the bedspread. "Her apprentice healers are always kind, and they never ask too many questions."

"What about Ison? The court magician's apprentice?"

Clara's cheeks turned a light shade of pink. "Ison is... He is nice." Clara kept her gaze on the bedspread, tracing the intricate pattern with her forefinger. "He is knowledgeable about herbs, alchemy, and potions. He never acts like he's too busy to talk. The alchemist before him was a mean old man, sneering and ordering people out of his way."

"Ison isn't hard on the eyes either."

Clara's eyes jumped to Juniper, wide and fiery, almost fierce. She swallowed. Her words came out a bit clipped: "I suppose. Why do you ask?"

Juniper smiled wickedly. "Because you're blushing like mad."

Clara's eyes went wide, and she smacked her hands against her reddening cheeks. "I—I don't know what you're talking about."

Juniper laughed, although it came out as more of a hum. Too much motion jarred her middle. She said, "I've heard that Marca mages are exceptionally skilled in *particular* areas."

Clara's face burned hotter still. Her voice quavered. "I—I've heard those rumors."

Everyone had. The rumors told that mages in the Marca were not only fluid in their sexuality, but also remarkably skilled when it came to the act, for besides magic, they had little else to occupy their time.

"Do you think that Ison fits those rumors?" Juniper asked, her voice velvet soft.

Clara's face went as red as the burning fire. "I—I can't say. I haven't had the pleasure of finding out for myself."

"Have you talked to him?"

She bit her lip and shook her head. "Nothing more than a greeting here and there."

"Why not?"

Clara twisted her fingers together. "He is..." Her expression turned sheepish. Juniper motioned for her to continue. "He is the court magician's apprentice. A mage. And I am just a servant in the castle. I have no money to my name, no family here in the city. I'm no one when compared to the fine ladies of the court or of the city."

"That is nonsense," Juniper scolded.

Clara blinked.

"You're talking yourself down, but you haven't even spoken to him." Juniper lifted her sluggish hand and patted Clara on the arm. "Before you tell yourself that he's not interested, find out for sure. I don't know why in the world he wouldn't be. You're pretty *and* sweet."

"Thank you, my lady."

"I only speak the truth as I see it," Juniper said, and a plan formed. "Ison will no doubt bring me another tonic this afternoon. You are more than welcome to stay here and keep me company."

"Are you certain?"

"Yes. If you leave, I will be left with no one to talk to. Only the ceiling to stare at." Juniper glanced up the top of the canopy. "Until Ison brings his tonic to sweep me into sweet oblivion for the night."

Clara hesitated, then asked, "Does Squire Sandpiper not provide adequate company?"

"Oh, he is fine." Juniper waved away the idea, but then Clara's expression turned curious. "I think he worries that people will get the wrong impression if he stays in here too much. He is dear friends with Adrian. He doesn't want those types of rumors spreading."

"I understand." Clara nodded. By her tone, those rumors had already spread to some extent.

"Although, I do feel safer when Squire Sandpiper is here. After that"—she hesitated to say *demon*, in case it summoned another from some hidden shadow in her room—"thing attacked, it is nice to know that there is someone trained to protect me should the need arise."

"I apologize for not being trained with the sword," Clara said. "There are two guards stationed outside the door, however. I am talented with the duster, but it is unladylike to brag."

"I've seen your handiwork. The room is spotless!"

Clara laughed, and a shade of pink came over her cheeks.

Clara stayed, talking as she cleaned. She shared stories of her native city of Caindale, of the white sand beaches where the wealthy had sprawling beach homes, of the spats between Caindale's fleet and the pirates who scattered the southern coasts and islands. It made the morning pass delightfully fast.

Lunch arrived, along with Sandpiper, who looked none too thrilled about his morning. He said not a word about it as Clara sat by Juniper's bedside while she ate her broth and drank her herbal tea.

"Are you not eating, Squire?" Juniper asked.

"I ate before I arrived," he said sharply.

In a bad mood by midday. It did not bode well for the rest of the day.

He took in each word exchanged between her and Clara, analyzing it; no doubt, he would wait until later to discuss all of the things she had said wrong.

After lunch, a knock signaled Ison's arrival. Clara fluttered to the main door. Juniper held her breath to listen. Sandpiper started to speak, but she held up her finger to shush him.

"Afternoon," came Ison's clear, calm tone from the sitting room.

"Yes, this way," came Clara's sweet reply.

Clara led Ison into the bedroom. Her cheeks were a slight pink, although she had done a marvelous job of keeping her face neutral.

"Afternoon, my lady." Ison walked his silver tray to her bedside. Clara made her way to the other side. Sandpiper took up his post at the foot.

Surrounded on all sides.

"Afternoon, Ison," said Juniper. "I'm glad I can say hello this time. I see you've met my friend, Clara. She's been keeping me company this morning."

"Yes." Ison nodded, handing Juniper the tonic. It smelled of blueberries, mint, and lemongrass. It did not taste as good as it smelled. "We've had the pleasure of meeting a few times."

"It is a pleasure to meet you formally." Clara gave Ison a polite curtsy.

"And you, as well." Ison bowed his head toward her.

Juniper sipped her tonic, glancing between the two. Their eyes met for a prolonged moment. And her job appeared to be finished. Sandpiper, however, did not look as pleased. He glared at her, his eyebrows scrunched together, his mouth tilted downward.

What did you do? She imagined him asking. She only smiled. Now she could add *matchmaker* to her list of talents. She drank the tonic slowly, giving the new lovebirds plenty of time to silently size one another up, and she regretfully handed Ison the empty glass.

"Until tomorrow, Lady Roslyn. Miss Clara. Squire Sandpiper." Ison bowed to each of them as he left.

Juniper waited for her chamber door to close, then glanced at Clara. She whispered, "Miss."

Clara's cheeks burst into a bright pink.

"I can take things from here, Clara." Sandpiper stalked to the hearth and added another log. "You're dismissed."

"He doesn't mean to sound so rude," Juniper added on the heels of his words.

Clara winked at Juniper, curtsied low, and said, "Until then, my lady."

Juniper reached out to her. "Before you go, Clara, best take another visit to the bathing room. I'd rather not wake up in the middle of the night."

Sandpiper found something very interesting to stare at out the window while Clara helped Juniper, almost naked, shuffle across the room. It didn't feel nearly as embarrassing as it had the first time, and by the time Juniper returned to her bed, she felt the tonic working its herbal magic.

CHAPTER SEVENTEEN

The herbal magic wore off late that afternoon, and a fierce restlessness gripped Juniper's mind. She was too sore to move but not tired enough to sleep.

"Squire?"

"Yes?" he answered from his position in the sitting room.

"Tell me a story. Anything."

He huffed. A nonanswer.

"Please?" She would beg if she had to. "I'm so bored, I'm about to die! It doesn't have to be a good story, or even a happy ending, although I'd prefer one. Please?"

Sandpiper let out a sigh and stalked into the bedroom. Without his armor, he made hardly any sound. A warrior's grace. His armor was being cleaned, he said. He sat on the bedside.

"When I was ten years old, Adrian, myself, and a friend of ours snuck out of the castle and into the grounds." He found something on the bedspread to stare at. He absently traced the golden seams. "We were going to hunt dragons, or so we told each other."

"Are there dragons in the Royal Grounds?" She looked to the window, then back to him. His eyes met hers.

No, there were not.

"We skipped our afternoon lessons and wandered into the forest, looking for a legendary dragon that would only live in the thickest, deepest part of the forest. We wandered for the better part of the day. At last, we came to a glen." He paused and glanced at her. "Do you know what we found?"

"A dragon skeleton?" She could almost see it in her imagination, but the part of her that loved stories knew the real answer would not be as fanciful or pleasant.

"Bandits." He shifted to see her better. His honey eyes held a grimness that pulled her heart into her stomach. "Four of them, armed to the teeth. They'd made camp on the west side of the Royal Grounds, unaware of where they were. Imagine our terror when they unsheathed their swords. Real blades that had slaughtered."

90

She whispered, "What did you do?"

"We tried to run. We weren't stupid enough to take on four bandits."

A pregnant pause filled the space between them. Only the crackling of the hearth remained.

Juniper gripped the sheets. "What happened?"

He sighed. "I'd like to tell you how three ten-year-old boys kicked their asses, but we didn't. They surrounded us. Thank the gods one of the royal guards had followed us and intervened before the worst could happen. We all made it back. Mostly."

She raised her brows. "Mostly?"

"Hailen, the third boy, received a wound on his arm from a bandit who swung at him. It wasn't a terrible wound, but infection soon set in. The blade was filthy. He lost the arm, nearly to his shoulder." Sandpiper drew a line across his bicep.

"Couldn't it be healed with magic?"

"His father abhorred magic and mages. He refused his son magical treatment."

"He cost his son his arm, then, not the bandits." Juniper frowned. Stupid, ignorant fool.

Sandpiper didn't argue. "Hailen couldn't become a guard without both of his arms. His father sent him out of the castle to find work."

"He sounds like a marvelous parent," she said with a huff. Typical magic-hater. "What happened to him?"

"He works at the Marca. In the clinic. He asked for it, so don't give me that face. He said he wanted to be an example of what could happen to people who refuse magical healing. He says it boosts the confidence of those who fear magic."

She released her grip on the sheets. "I suppose that's not a horrible ending."

"That wasn't even the point of the story." He half laughed. "The guard who followed us defeated those bandits single-handedly. I'd never seen anyone fight like that without getting even a scratch. I knew then that I'd made the right choice. I wanted to be able to defend people like him. I never wanted to be defenseless in the face of danger."

"Who was he?"

"Kalder Darvel. He's since joined the Order and become a knight." He paused, and a gloom came over his face. "That day was also the first time I'd seen anyone killed."

"A bit nasty, isn't it?" She bit her lip. He'd given her a personal story. It only felt somewhat fair to return the favor. "I remember the first time someone died in my presence. I also remember the first time someone died by my hands. Neither left a pleasant feeling behind."

"Who?"

She swallowed. "The first was a thief who'd been struck in a fight. He meandered back to the Undercity and died. The second... I'd prefer not to name names."

He narrowed his eyes at her.

"I was thirteen. I'd gone...somewhere to retrieve something, and he caught me. I didn't want to kill him, but I didn't want to die either. I killed him to save myself. I couldn't sleep for nearly a week afterward. I kept seeing his face, alive, then not. I still do sometimes."

Sandpiper looked at his hands. "I thought I knew how it felt to kill someone, but it was awful that first time. The blood, the smell, the feeling that goes through the blade when it connects with bone and slices through the rest." The muscles in his jaw flinched. "I hated it. I still do."

She glanced at his hands. Did he see blood on them? She felt it on hers from time to time, slick, warm, and gooey. After her first murder, she had taken countless baths and washed her hands until they'd turned raw. Maddox had finally intervened, holding her raw, red hands between them, telling her that the blood she wanted to wash away could never be washed away and that she either had to learn to live with it or lose her hands.

"Thank you, Squire."

"Reid," he said.

She blinked.

"My name. Reid."

She nodded. "Thank you, Reid."

Although it hadn't been the most uplifting story, something between them had shifted for the better.

CHAPTER EIGHTEEN

Rain beat against the castle windows, wind howled, and thunder crashed and rolled. Juniper napped off and on. Clara came by to help her with bodily duties. Dinner came in the form of broth and juice for her and a plate of roasted pork and other butter-smelling dishes for Sandpiper.

After dinner, Ison came by with a tonic.

"Another?" Reid asked.

"The court magician suggested a nightcap tonic," Ison said carefully, his words charged with dislike. He handed the tonic to Juniper.

His fingers, soft compared to Reid's, brushed hers. He hesitated to make sure she had a hold of it before he let go. By his fingers, he'd never held a blade in his life. Of course, the mages in the Marca learned only what the Order deemed necessary. She doubted swordplay to be one of those things.

She sniffed the greenish tonic. It smelled like mint.

"Drink all of it," Ison instructed. "The herbs it contains are...potent but can only be used with certain other herbs, and...it's complicated to explain."

"A simple nightcap tonic?" Reid asked, accusation on his tongue.

"Brewed specially to combat a demon's poison," Ison said, a bit peeved. He straightened his shoulders. "If it was a demon, then the nightcap will help her sleep deeply. She won't move around or agitate her wounds."

"*If* it was a demon?" Reid repeated. Ison blushed slightly; he had said too much. "Does the court magician believe it not to have been a demon?"

Juniper did not miss the emphasis on *court magician*.

She glanced down at the nightcap. As disgusting as it was, she wouldn't mind being unconscious until she had healed.

Ison's gaze narrowed into carefully masked distaste. "The ash he retrieved from the scene is still being analyzed." He gestured to the tonic. "He would rather be safe than sorry, as would the royal healer. If there is no demon poison, then the tonic will do no harm."

Juniper swallowed the tonic a little bit at a time. It had the texture of thin pudding and the taste of an herb garden. It did not go down the easiest.

Reid asked lowly, "What is your unofficial word on the matter?"

Ison held his gaze. Each held a ferocity, and Juniper thought that if those two gazes could physically meet, they would result in a thunderous collision.

Ison said, "From the blood samples, both from Lady Derean and the creature, I would say that it was not of this world. From the reports, it sounds like a Hound, but I've only seen pictures." Ison glanced at Juniper, then at Reid. His gaze softened. A tint of fear leaked into his steel eyes. Ison looked like he wanted to say something else but withheld it.

Reid noticed. His gaze on the mage narrowed.

As if sensing it, Ison swallowed. He whispered, "I know what you think, Squire. I am not responsible. This position means too much to me to fool around with black magic. I am smarter than that. If I wanted to kill, myself, I know much better poisons than a demon's."

Reid didn't say anything.

Juniper sipped the tonic loudly, breaking the tense silence. She tipped the glass back, letting it slide into her mouth. It clung to the inside of the glass and slid down the sides like slime. Oh, why did she have to compare it to slime? She fought back her urge to cough it back into the glass.

While she drank the tonic, she felt both pairs of male eyes on her, fully aware that she wore only a thin layer of bandages. Surely a bare shoulder wouldn't trigger some feral male response.

When she had finished it, Ison set the empty glass on the tray. He walked to the door with enough grace that the glass didn't rattle. Reid followed Ison out, then returned to the bedroom, scowling.

Of course, as a squire, he would blame the demon on the first mage he saw. Typical.

Juniper settled into the pillows. She felt the nightcap's effects worming through her skin, her blood, her bones; it nullified the pain and her senses. In a sleepy voice that didn't feel like her own, she said, "You don't like Ison?"

Reid tightened his hand around his pommel. "Of course I don't. He's a mage. They're far too sneaky for their own good. Gods only know what he put in that tonic."

"Well, we'll know what happened if I don't wake up tomorrow."

He growled.

"Do you think Ison knows anything?" she asked. "Do you think the court magician told him everything?"

"I'm not sure." He sat in the chair beside the bed and stretched his legs out. "I don't speak much to the court magician, and he's been busy with this demon affair. Mason keeps to himself, as does Ison. He will answer questions when I ask but never volunteers information."

That tone—she lifted an eyebrow at him.

"I don't trust him. The man has far too many secrets," he explained.

"The man or the mage?"

He blinked, then focused on the hearth. "He's a powerful mage. He might be the most powerful in the kingdom. In the city, definitely. You'd be a fool not to be cautious of him."

"Oh, trust me, Squire, I am cautious of him." She relaxed further into the pillows. She felt the tonic taking hold. "Why do you hate mages so much?"

Reid didn't answer. His cool eyes met hers. "That is a story for another time."

"I'd love a story to put me to sleep. Tell me a happy one, though. I'd prefer one where no one dies or gets maimed or doesn't get to spend forever with their true love."

"Then it is a story for another time," he said darkly.

"Why do you have so many horrible stories?"

He turned toward the door, walked a few paces, and turned back to her. "Enough talk. You need your rest, and so do I."

She watched him walk through the bedroom door with eyes she could barely keep open. She never saw it close.

CHAPTER NINETEEN

Juniper rolled out of her narrow bed beneath the window, inhaling the honeysuckle and lavender that blossomed outside. She slipped through the side door and into the garden. The sun-warmed dirt softened her bare footsteps; the basil, thyme, rosemary, and mint sweetened the breeze.

She wandered through the grapevines, picking a handful of red, green, and black. She plucked the second to the last grape from her palm, poised to toss it into her mouth, when a strange scent blew in on the breeze. It smelled awful, worse than the fertilizer that came from the farm next door, worse than the outhouse on a sweltering summer day, worse than anything she had ever smelled before.

Found you.

Juniper ran from the monster. The grapes above her darkened into an inky, unhealthy black. They shriveled as the monster came closer. Her feet grew tired. Her breath grew ragged. Her side ached. The grapevines grew taller, wild.

She stumbled, and the shadows lunged.

Juniper lurched awake, a scream on her breath.

The bedroom door burst open. Reid dashed inside, sword drawn, hair disheveled; his wide, sleepy eyes scanned the room for trouble. Seeing none, he scrunched his brows, relaxed his shoulders, and sheathed his sword. The top button of his brown tunic was undone. His throat bobbed as he swallowed.

"What is it?" Reid demanded.

Juniper willed her breath to slow. A cold sweat chilled the surface of her skin and traveled to her bones. Pale gray sunlight filtered in through the seams in the curtains. Dawn. A rainy dawn, by the glow. Frost lined the edges of the windows, evaporating with every moment. The air had thickened. Humidity clung to her skin.

"Juniper?"

She met his gaze. Her panic must have shone on her face, for it mirrored on his; his brow furrowed deeper at her silence. Could he hear the thudding of her heart?

"Are you all right?" he asked, a tone softer.

A dream. She'd not had that dream in months.

Stupid demon.

"Juniper?" A footstep closer. His knee touched the bedspread. He grabbed her hand before she could move; her heart lurched into her throat. "You're cold. And you're shaking."

She took her hand out of his and huddled the blankets around her. She swallowed and hoped her voice wouldn't sound as weak as she felt. "Yes. It was only a dream."

"Dreams don't normally make a person scream."

Had she screamed? She placed a hand over her throat. "That would explain why my throat is sore."

His grim line of a mouth loosened. "I'll call for tea."

She took each breath as it came, in and out, in and out. A dream, she reminded herself. Just a dream.

Reid returned shortly. Not long after, Clara delivered a tea tray on which sat a simple teapot, two matching cups, and a jar of honey. She placed the tray on the table, and although she wore a wide smile of greeting, she bowed without a word and left.

Juniper pushed aside the blankets to make herself a cup, but Reid held up his hand. "Let me," he said.

Reid poured the steaming amber into a cup, added a healthy dose of honey, and held it within her easy reach.

She gaped at him before she took the cup. "Thank you."

The warm china oozed heat into her fingers, her hands, up her arms.

Reid raised a brow. "Not used to people doing things for you?"

She shook her head, mindful of the tea. She brought it to her lips. A little strong and a little too sweet. "People don't do things for other people in the Undercity," she said. "Not unless they want something."

"They trade in favors," Reid added darkly.

She nodded. Everyone wanted favors. Favors were worth more than gold in the Undercity. Most of the time.

He made himself a cup, adding just as much honey. He asked casually, "What did you dream about to make you wake up in such a state?"

Her fingers on the cup tensed. A ripple quaked the surface of the tea. Despite her nerves, she twisted her lips into a mischievous smile and teased, "Such a personal question from a man who wouldn't help me to the toilet."

A blush warmed his cheeks. "I am bound by certain rules of chivalry set forth by the Order. It would be unfitting for me to put a lady in an indecent situation."

She lifted a brow. "But those rules don't forbid visits to brothels?"

Juniper knew Amery had at least two clients among the Order, though she had never named names. Juniper had friends in brothels; they had always been a quick place to hide from the Watch. She had peeked at the books once, and even she had been surprised at some of the clients.

He sipped his tea loudly, holding the cup like a gentleman. "You woke up looking like a ghost. I thought for a moment that...something had happened elsewhere."

That Adrian had been attacked, and she had received the wounds.

Reid walked to the window closest to the bed, where the sunlight had grown imperceptibly brighter. Holding the teacup with one hand, he pulled the curtains aside with the other. Blue-gray daylight flooded inside. His tunic and trousers were wrinkled.

"Did you sleep in here?" she asked.

He walked toward the next window. "On the couch in the sitting room." *Swish*. Blue-gray light filtered in, leaving a lattice pattern of shadow on the floor. "More comfortable than the chair."

She glanced at the bed. It was far large enough for him to have slept on either side of her without being a nuisance, but the very idea of sharing a bed brought a warmth to her cheeks. She held the teacup to her lips to hide it.

"The king has ordered a guard to be stationed outside your door at all hours, but as of last night, the guard had not arrived." He opened the curtains of the last window just as a low growl of thunder sounded. "I felt my presence necessary. A precaution."

"While I thank you, the demons are attacking Adrian, not me. You would be better suited to follow him around."

His softened expression hardened into an unreadable mask. "The king assigned me to look after you, not him."

She heard the disgruntled kernel in his tone.

"It must be difficult for you to have been demoted to nursemaid," she said bitterly.

Reid didn't respond. He lingered, his unreadable gaze on her, then he stalked back into the sitting room.

She'd hit a nerve, it seemed.

She drank the rest of her tea—it did help with her throat.

Clara arrived with breakfast, and the royal healer arrived shortly after. Clara stayed while the healer worked; Reid stepped out.

Reid did not return for lunch.

Juniper lay awake in bed, alone in her room, staring at the ceiling. The dark wood of the canopy had a certain beauty to it, not just from the dark red of the finish, but from the wood itself. All the streaks of color and eddies and little knots. The more she stared, the more it felt less like the top of a bed and more like something else, like looking down into something, a world of its own. What did the gods see when they looked down at the humans scattered frantically below them?

How long had it been since she'd been attacked?

A few days? A week? A month? Time felt nonexistent, measured only in the flickering of the hearth fire.

The door to the bedroom opened, and Reid walked inside. He held two books in one arm and wore the simple clothes of a noble.

"You look like you're about to keel over." He sat down in the chair beside the bed. His grin faltered. "Do you need anything?"

"I'm bored." And tired beyond reason, but her body refused to sleep anymore.

He sighed and crossed an ankle over his knee. He opened one of the books to a marked page.

"Are you going to read to me?" A desperate hope found its way into her voice.

"No." He set his bookmark aside. His brown eyes started to read silently.

"They why come in here with books?"

"I need to study."

She glanced at the book in his lap. The dark leather cover revealed nothing about its interior. "What are you studying?"

"I can't tell you."

She frowned. "Why not?"

Frustration drew a line between his eyes. "Knights keep most of their training secret. It is to prevent untrained or unskilled people from trying to learn anything that might get them or others killed." He picked up the other book. Its lighter cover had faded lettering on the front, but she couldn't make it out. "This is a history of the knighthood."

"What secrets do the knights keep in their training?"

"I can't tell you that."

She'd heard rumors, none she could confirm, about what sort of training the knights received. Some were darker than others. Some said they subjected themselves to magic torture in order to teach their bodies to resist it. Others said they ingested magical powders and potions to achieve the same effect. One shady merchant told her that knights had runes carved into their flesh to ward off unwanted magical influences. A one-armed man had sworn up and down the Order slaughtered apostates like cattle and fed the meat to the knights. Another, slightly more reliable source suggested the knights learned a bit of black magic themselves. He'd called it unnatural magic because the knights manipulated the magic already in the air through unnatural means, whereas a mage used the natural magic within themselves.

"I've heard that knights learn how to disable magic," Juniper said. "Is that one of those secrets you're reading about?"

His eyes darkened. "Who told you that?"

"No one in particular. The Undercity. The rumor mill. The street vendor where I prefer to buy my apples."

Reid didn't say anything, but he kept his stare on her.

She smirked. "Does that look mean I'm right?"

He returned his gaze to the book with a huff.

"I suppose it would make sense for them to be able to defend themselves against angry mages," she said, more to herself than to him, if only to fill the silence. "It would make them better qualified to go after them." Even if it made them hypocrites for using the same magic they accused apostates of and killed them for using.

Reid didn't say anything.

After a moment, she said, "What about your history book? Is it off-limits to non-squires like myself?"

"No."

"Can I read it?"

"You'd find it dreadfully boring."

"I'm already dreadfully bored."

He half laughed and handed her the tan hide book. It was heavier than she'd imagined—or maybe she had lost strength in her arms. The faded lettering across the front read *A History of the Order of the Knighthood*. She worked herself into a careful sitting position and propped the book up on her bent knees.

Reid was right; the history was dreadfully boring, but it gave her something other than the universe contained in the wood above her bed to think about.

The knights, according to the history book, had been formed nearly a thousand years ago, during the Great War. They had existed before that as pockets of anti-magic warriors. The man who brought them together was a monk by the name of Roderick Vanten, a warrior of legend and the first Knight Commander.

Vanten rallied the anti-magic warriors against the Iluvin mage, Nexon, who had used his magic to conquer what would become Collatia, Duvane, and Galamond. After discovering how a regular human could withstand magic—which the history book did not further explain—Vanten and his banded-together soldiers started the movement against Nexon. Their numbers grew, and Vanten and Nexon had one final battle in what became known as the Blackwood Wylds, a dead land in the center of Collatia where magic had tainted the earth.

When Juniper asked Reid about how a regular human withstood magic, he only shrugged and said, "That's one of those secrets I can't tell you."

Although, she detected a bit of pride in him that she'd gotten through the first chapter of the book. After the first chapter, however, the book took a turn toward boring. It detailed Roderick Vanten's campaign to unite his anti-magic soldiers.

It took him nearly thirty years to do so after the first king of Duvane passed and his son took up the throne. Vanten's wife, a mage whom the book left nameless, founded the Marca for the protection and education of mages.

Juniper sluggishly turned the page but did not make it far before the pulls of sleep wormed their way in. She did not remember Reid taking the book away or him straightening her legs or pulling the blanket up to her chin.

She remembered Vanten and Nexon, and the two ancient men fought a battle in her dreams in a forest of gnarled, blackened trees.

CHAPTER TWENTY

Prince Adrian Bradburn tried his best to look attentive, but his father's meetings bored him to no end. His father's chief advisors, Rourke Hendle and Destin Ulgan, argued politics; discussed reports from the provinces, borders, and neighboring kingdoms; and theorized possible supply routes, threats, diseases that might plague the livestock—and whatever else. Adrian's attention had drifted after the possible resurgence of blue-tongue fever in the southwestern ranches.

"And speaking of the south, another caravan has complained of bandits along south Wayland Road. That makes three this week," barked Hendle, a short middle-aged man with tied-back blond hair and a matching beard, both streaked with gray. He held himself like a soldier, a lingering effect of his years in the Royal Army. "More patrols are needed to guard our supply chains to the south of Duvane. The city is losing stock, as are most of the central and northern parts of the kingdom. The merchants are growing wary of their chances of surviving a trip to port."

"Let the caravans hire their own guard," suggested Ulgan, a man in his fifties with a strong jaw and thinning brown hair. "We can't send a group of foot soldiers to guard every inch of the road. Bandits, while deplorable, are a risk of travel these days. Have been for centuries. We need to keep our forces where they are most needed, not where they are wanted."

Hendle eyed Ulgan with distaste. "You'd risk Rusdasin's supply of goods and trade?"

Ulgan retorted coolly, "You'd risk soldiers and guards on cheap merchants who want free guarding when there are demons lurking in our halls?"

Adrian shifted in his chair. The air had gone uncomfortably warm. He felt his father's eyes on him, but Adrian refused to acknowledge any lingering worry of the attack. Yes, he had been scared nearly to death by it, but he needn't show it. Not in front of the advisors.

Ulgan let his words sink in and then said calmly, "We need to deal with the obvious threat *here* before worrying about possible threats elsewhere." He turned his pointed face toward the king. "Especially since I have received word from my people in Chata."

His *spies.*

The king's attention showed little sign of interest. A perfect stoic mask of indifference. "What have they to report?"

Chata was an age-old city in the northeastern province of Onumit, nearly touching their neighboring kingdom of Collatia. Ulgan had a number of spies stationed there to keep eyes on the ruined northern part of Collatia, just like he had eyes on every border, city, tavern, whorehouse, and theater of note.

"They heard whispers of the northern rebels gathering strength," Ulgan said darkly. "As Collatia has been known to spit out powerful mages, we should keep an eye on them...in case they come looking for revenge."

The king narrowed his gaze at Ulgan.

Ulgan elaborated, "It takes a powerful mage to summon a demon."

Eyeing Ulgan warily, Hendle said, "You think the mage responsible is a Collation rebel?"

"Duvane sided with the south," Ulgan said plainly. "The northerners would see it as revenge for all they had lost. My spies reported negativity toward Duvane, and toward you, Your Majesty." His clever light blue eyes snapped to King Bradburn.

"Then why not kill me outright?" The king gestured to himself, the single golden ring he wore on his left hand catching the light of the torches: a modest, elegant wedding band, the unadorned twin of the queen's.

Ulgan folded his short fingers together. "Maybe they yet plan to. I suggest we keep the Royal Guard on alert. Increase patrols on the walls. Leave no window or door unwatched. And do a search of the castle, each room, closet, cabinet, and shoe cupboard."

Hendle nodded. "I agree. If a normal thief could get in unnoticed, a mage could easily magic themselves past our defenses. We should take no chances. However..." Hendle paused so as to not let Ulgan make all the ideas. "I also think, if it is indeed a mage we are hunting, we should increase the presence of the Order in the castle. I would sleep better knowing there are knights patrolling the halls."

Ulgan's lips twitched downward. Instantly, he smoothed his expression into one of schooled indifference.

The king spoke first. "Adrian, what are your thoughts on adding more knights to the guard?"

Adrian had been looking at the wooden table, marked with gashes where blades had pinned down maps for centuries. The entire surface was marred with pocks. Centuries of kingly meetings. Currently, four smooth black stones held down the map of the continent, each kingdom, province, waterway, major city, and road outlined and named. He met his father's gaze and hoped his own matched the cool authority.

"If not for Squire Sandpiper, I would not be sitting here. Surely, that demon would have slain Roslyn and I both." Adrian looked down at the table, pretending to be horrified at the notion, which didn't take much acting. Juniper's terrified face as the wound had transferred had scarred the back of his eyelids. "If increasing the number of knights will increase the safety of the castle, then I agree."

King Bradburn nodded in approval. "Then, so be it. Hendle, send word to Knight Commander Fowler at the meeting's end."

"Of course, Your Majesty." Hendle bowed his head.

Ulgan pursed his lips.

"Ulgan," said the king. "What of your eyes on the southern half of Collatia?"

"Nothing of note," Ulgan said. He paused; then his thin lips twisted into a smile. "However, there are rumors that King Crespin Balendin will step down and willingly give his crown to his sister."

Hendle's brows rose. "I have heard similar rumors but nothing solid. I suspect the king will not give in so willingly. Not if he has any of his father's treasonous blood in him."

"Crespin is aware of the lingering feelings toward his father," Ulgan added, "which is why he is willing to hand his sister the crown. The people adore Myrisha."

Myrisha and Crespin were the only children of Sabian Balendin, who had stirred the coup that had killed his brother, the king, and sent the kingdom into civil war. The conflict took the lives of the king's children, leaving Crespin and Myrisha as the only living heirs to the Balendin throne.

"She is only eighteen," Ulgan added. "But she has the trust of the people."

"If Crespin steps down as king to crown his sister, we will honor that choice." King Bradburn held his stare on Ulgan while maintaining his graceful posture.

"I suppose that will eliminate the possibility of a marriage between Adrian and Myrisha," Hendle said lightheartedly. He smiled at Adrian.

Adrian chuckled. "I will forever wonder what could have been."

"Still," Hendle said, his smile vanishing. "The Balendin's have magic in their family. Old magic. Powerful magic. They claim it reaches back to the

Iluvin. King Balendin has so far been resistant to establishing a school of magic. We should not push aside the possibility that he sent an assassin."

"Crespin also saw what that magic did to his kingdom," Ulgan said, his eyes cold as he beheld Hendle. "It if weren't for wild magic, his family would still be alive, his kingdom wouldn't be in broken halves, and his royal city wouldn't be crumbling under his feet."

Hendle continued, "My eyes in the south of Collatia report that Crespin's spies haven't been returning from the north."

Ulgan's attention snapped to Hendle, his brow furrowed.

Hendle looked pleased with himself. "Have your eyes not told you the same?"

The crease between Ulgan's eyes deepened.

"Either they are getting lost in the Blackwood Wylds," said Hendle, "or the northern rebels are picking them off. It suggests the rebels are readying themselves to make a move. It is possible the rebels sent a scout to infiltrate the castle, but the question is *why*."

"They could have been paid handsomely," Ulgan said grimly. "The mages there are known for their power. The Iluvin bloodlines run thick in the north."

"Most of the Iluvin people were killed a thousand years ago," Hendle countered. "The old magic died with them. Unless you are suggesting it is an archmage?" Hendle chuckled.

Ulgan glared. "Archmages are a myth," he spat. "I do not claim to know how Iluvin magic works. These are things I have heard. It is possible, not definite."

"Archmage?" Adrian asked.

"According to Iluvin legend, there was an archmage for every element of magic, a mage more powerful than the others," Hendle explained.

Ulgan twisted his lips into a frown. "But if archmages even existed, they fought and died in the Great War."

As the talk drifted to what-ifs regarding the northern Collatian rebels, bandits, and possible Iluvin mages, Adrian's attention wandered. It wandered out of the meeting room and to where his thoughts had been drifting for the past week.

The demon.

He could still feel the ghost of that demon's poisoned talon slice through his flesh. He absently lifted a hand to his chest. He shuddered. He hadn't been able to scrub the image of it from his mind: its patchy skin and matted fur, its dog-like brown eyes, its muscles and bones shifting underneath its leathery skin.

That thief had done her duty to protect him. He could still hear her cry when the wound—his wound—sliced into her, the panic on her face, the ghostly white of her cheeks, the blood seeping into the cream of her dress. It made his stomach twist. It made him wish that he'd been the one sick all this time.

At least he wouldn't have to sit through these dreadful meetings.

Juniper Thimble. Adrian had heard her name in countless meetings, on the lips of guards, victims, and admirers. Thief. Murderer. Scoundrel. The girl he met hadn't seemed like any of those foul things. The criminal he had seen in the dungeon had—dirty, shifty, prowling—and he had anticipated dealing with that for however long, but when she had walked through the door to the lounge, dressed like a lady with the posture to match, he'd been at a loss for words.

"...Lady Derean?"

Adrian's attention snapped back to the meeting.

Ulgan was speaking. "The attack happened so soon after she arrived. In the middle of the night, I will remind you. I hate to be the one to suggest this, Your Majesty, but what are the chances that her arrival and the demon's attack are connected?"

"Galamond is not as tight with the few mages they have," Hendle said, nodding toward the vast northern country on the map. "It is possible that one slipped in with her or knew the guards would be attentive to her and slipped in elsewhere unnoticed. A thief got in and out; I doubt a mage would have trouble."

"I doubt Lady Roslyn brought a mage with her," King Bradburn stated flatly. "Needless to say, I have eyes on her. After this attack, I have doubled those eyes."

Eyes that knew her real name and eyes that did not.

Adrian cleared his throat. "Roslyn arrived in the middle of the night because she refused to camp so close. She is a stubborn girl, and I have already reprimanded her for it, although I doubt it will do much good."

Ulgan and Hendle both cast masked glances in Adrian's direction. He did not falter underneath them as he had done as a child. He knew what they thought—what many people thought—of his relationship with Roslyn. He heard enough of it from his mother. They thought her a savage, wild woman, unfit for the role of queen.

"Perhaps it was a smuggled Janti mage who snuck into the castle,"

Ulgan suggested, if only to taunt Hendle. He gestured to the kingdom to their west.

"Don't laugh," Hendle warned. "That's a possibility. There are plenty of holes in the patrols along the western forests."

"We will keep eyes on our borders, all of them, especially on those known to harbor mages." King Bradburn stood—end of discussion, end of the meeting. "We will not take these threats lightly, but we will not show our enemy fear."

"Agreed," Ulgan and Hendle said in unison.

The advisors gathered their reports, letters, and notes and left the meeting room. Adrian pushed away from the table and made a lap of the room to stretch his legs. His thighs had gone numb where he'd crossed his knees. Such long, tedious meetings. He wished the meeting room had windows. Give him something else to stare at beyond the drab stone.

Too easy for spies, was his father's reasoning for the windowless space.

On his second lap of the room, the door opened. Captain Sandpiper and three of his most trusted men—three who had been there the night Juniper Thimble signed her life in blood to him—came inside.

Casually, to deter any listening ears, Captain Sandpiper said, "I've just been to see the new recruits. They're a promising bunch. They may be young and inexperienced, but they are eager to please."

Captain Sandpiper walked along the table and stopped halfway, close enough to King Bradburn to whisper. His men stationed themselves on either side of the door—listening.

His men listened, then nodded.

No one stood in the corridor to overhear.

"Ulgan seems eager to blame the northern Collatian rebels for the demon," said the king to the captain. "I think he means for me to set the wheels of war into motion."

"We have nothing to gain from a war with Collatia," argued the captain.

King Bradburn nodded. "I agree. Hendle seems eager to pretend that it didn't happen, that the knights will sort it out."

"He wants knights here, does he?"

King Bradburn put a hand to his chin. "I agreed. It is undoubtedly an apostate roaming the halls, whether an assassin from Janti or rebel from Collatia. A mage is a mage, and the knights are better suited to track them down. Have you any leads on the missing servants?"

Adrian's chest squeezed. People had been vanishing under their noses.

For months now. Servants, just gone. Had a demon been lurking for them too?

"None." Captain Sandpiper's face turned grim. "There is no evidence of foul play. The people just vanish. Leave their things behind. Leave washing in the water. Leave the bread in the oven. However, there is one connection that I have managed to find."

The king's brows rose.

"The people who have vanished have supposedly been alone when it happened."

"Someone is targeting them?" Adrian asked.

"It is possible," the captain answered. "I've suggested the servants and staff not go anywhere alone until the matter is put to rest. And, in regard to this recent attack,"—his eyes shifted to Adrian—"I suggest that you and Roslyn stay within the castle. Under supervision."

Adrian put a hand over his heart in mock hurt. "You dishonor me with your assumptions, Captain."

Captain Sandpiper smirked. "Not at all, but I highly recommend you spend time with your lady where the guards can easily dispatch any and all threats. Let your guard enter a room first. Stay clear of dark broom closets."

Adrian laughed, and the feeling warmed his entire being.

"I agree, Captain," said the king. He turned his stern stare to Adrian, which dispelled any good feeling he'd found. "You will both have guards at all times. I will ask a knight be assigned to you as I've assigned Squire Sandpiper to the...Lady Roslyn."

The thief was what his father almost said.

King Bradburn's fingers squeezed the arms of his chair, the same chair his father had occupied and his father before him. The same chair Adrian would one day inherit, with its sturdy wooden arms that had seen the stress of a thousand years of Bradburn kings.

"I will have the knights scour the castle from top to bottom," said King Bradburn. "We will find whoever is responsible for this attack. We will find the apostate hiding in my walls."

Adrian held his breath at the word his father hadn't used, not in front of the captain. *Traitor.* It was not the captain, not in a thousand years, but Adrian knew his father hated the word too much to even speak it.

CHAPTER TWENTY-ONE

Ison Rolin yawned, pausing his work with the mortar and pestle. He shook his head to rid the drowsiness and gazed out the only window in the workroom—cloudy mid-morning sunlight drifted in through the leaded glass. It made the stone-walled workroom only slightly more inviting.

Ison returned his attention to the jasmine and bear bones he was supposed to be grinding into powder.

What time was it? His muscles ached. He couldn't focus. A crick in his neck told him how horribly he'd slept the night before.

Ison set the pestle down and examined the powder. No bits of bone or petal remained, so he carefully funneled the powder into its slender jar, corked it, and replaced it among the hundreds of others that lined the wall of the court magician's spacious yet cluttered workroom.

He took a break from his work and strolled to the window. He stretched his hands out to the sunlight and flexed his fingers—they ached more than anything else. His fingers had been so stiff that morning, Ison hadn't been able to button his trousers. He finally gave up and used magic to do it. He blamed it on all the work he'd done the day before, crushing minerals and dried herbs to refill the stock.

Ison washed the mortar and pestle and replaced them in the cabinet with the others. He would finish the remaining herbs later. Instead, he did his daily inventory of stock, noting what herbs needed to be ordered, what raw ingredients were running low, and how much of everything there was currently.

Another tedious job to keep him busy.

Mason Hobbs had stepped out, leaving Ison to himself. He tidied up the workroom as best he could without disturbing his master's things and proceeded to clean up the main study and the library: he shelved the books left on the table or stacked on the banister; he used his wind magic to sweep the dust off every surface without disturbing even the most delicate of instruments.

Mason refused to let the castle servants touch his space, and so Ison became responsible for its general upkeep—a small bit that had been left out of the initial job description. But Ison understood. Mason had magical artifacts scattered about his chambers and study, and Ison knew how to handle things of unknown magical properties. The castle servants didn't.

Finished and utterly exhausted, Ison sank into one of the plush armchairs in Mason's study. Why was he so tired? He leaned his head back into the soft fabric and let his gaze wander to the purple and silver banner behind Mason's large desk—the Marca's banner. A silver owl had been embroidered onto the purple, its wings open.

Sometimes he missed the Marca. He missed the other mages the most. He didn't miss the glowering knights or early morning classes or the hook-nosed overseer. Ison had thought becoming the court magician's apprentice would involve more magic, but he felt like a glorified errand boy. He hadn't spent his entire life in the Marca learning how to control and utilize his magic to order stock and clean. It was, however, better than life in the Marca. Ison reminded himself of that each time the job felt useless.

He would rather be cleaning the court magician's study than selling his potions at the Marca's small shop, under the suspicious stare of the knights.

The ornate grandfather clock chimed. Two o'clock. He yawned again.

A book lay open on the desk as if the old man had paused mid-reading. Ison glanced at it, but he couldn't read it. The characters were angled and curved, a harsh and magical combination.

The Iluvin language. The Iluvin were ancient mages, most of whom died a thousand years ago in the Great War. The knights forbade any study on the Iluvin; only the advanced mages could get permission, like Mason Hobbs. Not that it mattered. Ison had never been good at foreign languages. He had been chosen for this apprenticeship for his brilliance in potion making, not his magical talents.

Ison yawned once more. He leaned forward, elbows on his knees.

He rarely got the chance to sit in the study without Mason there. Ison stared at the carvings on the rosewood desk, countless little scrolling diagrams, runes, and symbols. Complicated charms, more complicated than anything Ison had ever done or even attempted. According to the castle lore, each court magician left his or her mark on the desk for their successor.

The desk and matching chair had been made for a grand mage, a master spellcaster. When Mason died or retired, they would find another master spellcaster to replace him. Ison would forever be the errand boy.

He shut his eyes and fought to open them again. He'd done his duties;

Mason couldn't scold him for taking a nap. Gods, he felt like he could sleep through to the next morning.

A small knock landed on the door.

Ison straightened his robes and headed for the door. On the other side stood the pretty girl from Lady Roslyn's chambers. Clara. In her arms, she carried a freshly laundered set of robes. His robes.

"Special delivery," she chimed. She held up the robes, wearing a bright smile that stretched into her pink-tinted cheeks.

"Thank you, Clara." Ison accepted the robes and gave her his best smile, trying not to look too tired. She held his gaze a long moment, then turned to leave. His heart began to fall. "How is your day going?"

Her face brightened. "Oh, it's never-ending, but it's work. We wash one robe, and another appears. I shouldn't complain. It's better than anything I could get outside." She tucked her hands into her apron. "And you? Make any grand magical breakthroughs?"

He chuckled. "Not in the slightest."

She glanced down the corridor, then whispered, "Have they figured out what attacked the prince? They aren't telling the servants anything."

His hands trembled underneath the fresh robes. He shook his head. He quickly lied, "No, they haven't told me anything. But aren't you supposed to go places in pairs?"

She nodded. "Marcy's got another load of laundry. She's a corridor that way. I told her I wanted to bring these to you."

"Thank you. It's always a pleasant day when I see you."

She blushed. She started to say something else when Marcy's voice drifted down the corridor. Clara pressed her lips together, then quickly said, "Another time, Ison. When we're not in mortal danger."

"I look forward to it." He gave her a bow of his head.

Clara walked away, and Ison slowly shut the door. It took a moment for his heart to stop fluttering.

Ison stored his robes in his small dressing room and returned to the workroom to make sure he'd put everything away. As he walked through the study, his eyes grazed over the glass-front cabinet behind the desk. He paused. He had spent enough time in the study and had cleaned it often enough that he knew exactly how many, how high, and where; through the frosted glass of the cabinet, he counted five scrolls instead of the normal four.

A new spell had joined the others. A powerful spell to need a scroll. A dangerous spell to be locked in the cabinet. Mason locked the cabinet by magic. Ison didn't know the unlocking charm—they were as unique as any key—and even if he did, even touching the scroll might alter whatever spell had been cast.

"Ah, yes, you're far too observant," mused Mason from the doorway, a heavy book in each arm.

Ison straightened his spine. He hadn't even heard the door open.

Mason walked into the study and set the books on his desk. "Unfortunately, I have been sworn to secrecy and cannot enlighten you to the contents of the scroll."

"I understand," Ison said, and he meant it. He assumed it had something to do with the demon that appeared right under the court magician's nose. "I've laid the inventory on your desk," Ison reported. "The last of the ingredients have been stocked."

"Ah, thank you, Ison." Mason sat down at his desk, absently picking up the inventory list. "Hmm. Unicorn hair is going fast this year. I'll be glad when that round of winter sickness is gone."

"Should I put in another order for it?"

Mason considered, eyes intent on the list. "It wouldn't hurt."

"It will be done."

Mason set the list aside and pulled one of the books into his view. He set it directly atop the Iluvin book. From where Ison stood, the book was in the same language.

Ison started toward the workroom to fill out an order for unicorn hair when Mason spoke. "The order can wait until tomorrow." He didn't take his eyes off the book. "Go take that nap first. You look exhausted."

"Thank you." Ison walked instead into his bedroom. He had long since stopped wondering how Mason knew such things. One didn't become the court magician for nothing.

Ison pulled off his boots and collapsed onto his bed. Even with the dulled sunlight streaming in over his face, sleep claimed him quickly.

CHAPTER TWENTY-TWO

For the next few days, Juniper read while Reid studied. Clara, appalled at her reading material, brought her a few books from the Royal Library. Ison arrived in the afternoons with tonics, some green and some blue. His small smiles never quite reached his eyes. He brought no more nightcap tonics. She hadn't forgotten the daydream-like memory of Reid holding the tonic to her lips.

Every day, she could move a little easier.

"Reid?"

"Hmm?"

"I've heard some gossip," she said, unsure of how to phrase her next words. Reid huffed in response without taking his eyes off the book. "About servants going missing."

His lips twitched downward. "How do you know that servants have gone missing?"

Clara, mostly, but she didn't tell him that. "People talk. Guards. Servants. The healer." She waved the question aside. "Secrets don't last long when the remaining servants are terrified they'll be next on some deranged man-eating ghost hound's list." Clara brought stories of what could be happening, all strange and fascinating.

"It is being looked into," Reid said flatly. He turned the page in his book.

"What's happening to them?"

"It's none of your concern."

"So you don't know?"

He released a slow, calming sigh.

What would be taking the servants? Could something be lurking within the lowest levels of the castle? Ancient as the oldest stones? The demons most likely had a hand in it. How could they not?

Reid didn't offer any more conversation. She huffed and settled back into her pillow. She had the itch to move, yet she couldn't. "I hate this. I hate not being able to do anything."

"You're healing."

"Not just about that." She inhaled, feeling the skin around her wounded abdomen stretch, but not as painfully as before. "If a demon broke into the keep or the Undercity, I'd hunt the damn thing down myself. And this...laying around is grating on my nerves."

"You'd rather be out with the knights tracking the demon?"

"Yes." She glanced at him. "Are they finding anything?"

His frown told her they hadn't.

"It's settled. When I'm able to walk, I'm going demon hunting." She didn't glance at Reid to see his disapproval. She heard it in his humored huff.

Reid leaned forward on his knees, brows raised, a slight smile on his lips. "And how are you going to do what the Order and Royal Guard have yet to accomplish?"

"Easy." She gave him a wicked smile. "They're not me."

He frowned, although he had a glint in his eye.

It wasn't hard for Juniper to imagine strangling the apostate responsible when she couldn't move. A few days, and she could hobble on her own to the bathing room. When Clara wasn't there, Reid followed a step behind. Just in case. He lingered outside the door too, for the same reason.

She'd never had someone be so mindful of her. She couldn't decide if she hated it or not.

A few more days, and her hobble became a limp. She healed enough that she didn't need to wear as many bandages, and Clara assisted her with a much-needed bath. Clean, Juniper wrapped a pink dressing robe around herself and returned to freshly changed linens.

She read a while longer, and when the words danced around on the page, she looked up at Reid and blinked the strain away.

Reid was reading with a crease between his brows, and he kept making the same small flourish with his fingers: he would pull his fingers toward his palm, not as tight as a fist, then slowly spread them out.

He sighed in quiet frustration. Looking up, he met her gaze. He tightened his hand into a fist.

Before she could ask, a knock sounded at the door. With all his strong grace, Reid jumped to his feet. He left the book on his chair, but it didn't matter. By the time she could get it, he'd be back in the room. Several sets of footsteps entered, at least one of them armored. Guards.

Juniper's entire body seized, and then—

"Where is the lovely lady?" Adrian's chime floated in from the sitting room.

Something tight in her chest loosened. She closed her book just as Adrian appeared in the doorway to the bedroom.

"Ah, there she is," Adrian said warmly. He strolled to the bedside and placed a sweet kiss on her forehead.

"Luckily, I bathed earlier," she mused, "or you would not have come this close."

"You could be covered in mud, blood, and gods know what else, and I'd still hold you."

She grinned, though she did not believe him. She wouldn't hold him if he were covered in any of those things, let alone all three.

A tall, broad-shouldered man in silver armor walked into the bedroom. The owner of the armored footsteps. A knight. The sunlight shone off the crest that adorned his breastplate, an owl with its claws clutching a chain. At his side hung a sword in a dark blue scabbard. Mage's Bane.

Her heart fluttered.

The knight looked to be in his mid-thirties. His light brown hair was cut short, not unlike Reid's. Maybe they had a personal groomer who kept all the knights and squires looking identical.

Adrian cleared his throat. "Ah, Roslyn, this is my new...escort. Sir Destry."

Destry bowed. "Greetings, Lady Derean."

She gave a subtle nod of her head. "Sir Destry."

Adrian had come by for dinner, she learned shortly; servants brought enough food for them and his guard. Clara arrived with the servants and helped Juniper into the dressing room—while the men found other things to look at—and helped her into the simplest gown in the assortment, one that wouldn't irritate her injuries.

She sat at the small table in her bedroom with Adrian, Reid, and Destry.

During their talk, Adrian referred to her only by Roslyn, and Reid had taken on a formal tongue. She gathered that Destry did not know about the arrangement. He assumed her to be Roslyn, and she played the part accordingly. She held Adrian's hand on the table, ran her fingers along his, and blushed when his knee grazed hers under the table.

Lovers. She'd never had one. Lovers were not something found in the

Undercity. She could buy one, of course, but she'd rather not spend her hard-earned money on *that*.

After the meal, Reid and Destry left the two of them alone and stood on the other side of the room. They wore frighteningly similar expressions of deadly seriousness. Monitoring for demons, no doubt.

She caught Adrian's eye and motioned toward the two of them. She whispered, "Are all knights so serious?"

Adrian half laughed, considering the pair. "Those whom I've met seem to be. I think it's a qualification."

"I suppose I wouldn't want to put my life into the hands of a funny one."

"I'd rather not."

She smiled. Her chest and her middle did not enjoy the feeling of laughter. Soon, she would be healthy, and she would hunt down the apostate and make sure he couldn't move for a long while.

"Have you had any trouble, Reid?" Destry asked, his voice low enough that Adrian and Juniper—*Roslyn*—wouldn't hear him.

"No," Reid answered, keeping an eye on the couple on the other side of the room. "It's been quiet."

"Good." Destry stood like he'd been carved from marble. "The others haven't found a single trace of the damned beast or a summoning site."

Reid held in his surprise. "Nothing?"

"There are traces of the Underworld's essence where the beast died, but there is no trail leading to where it appeared." Destry's eyes darkened. "There have been whispers that it might not have been a simple demon, but no one is sure."

Reid didn't say anything. Demons left trails from their portals. Those portals, however big or small, left a trace for a considerable time after being opened. If the knights couldn't find a trail or a portal...

Reid dared to ask, "Something worse?"

Destry did not answer. Instead, he asked, "How is your training coming? I hope this situation hasn't put you behind."

"Never, sir. I train nearly every day." Reid shifted his eyes back to the table, where Juniper traced her slender fingers along Adrian's. "This past week, while unfortunate, has given me the chance to catch up on what I've missed."

"I notice you're reading about magical defense." Destry glanced toward the book Reid had set on the small table beside his chair. "I trust you haven't told her about it?"

"No," Reid answered. "When she asked, I answered honestly: that I couldn't tell her."

Destry gave a small nod. The only approval he'd get. "Magical theory and defense are guarded secrets. We can't afford mages getting ahold of that kind of information."

Reid nodded. "I haven't let the book out of my sight."

If there was indeed an apostate roaming the castle, the last thing they needed was a book detailing the knights' defense of magic laying open on a table. It had taken centuries for the Order to understand how magic worked and how a non-mage might be able to harness magic to defend against a mage's magic. If an apostate were to discover that information, they could use it against the Order. It was also how the knights detected magic, and if apostates understood the system, they might find ways to avoid it.

Reid hadn't refreshed himself on detection in a while, yet he could feel a ghost of magic lingering in Juniper's room. An effect of the healer, likely.

Destry glanced at Roslyn. He dropped his voice and said, "She's quite a sight."

Reid followed his gaze. "I am inclined to agree."

"Be careful."

Reid blinked.

The knight clarified, "Women have brought down more men than armies, though they hold no blade. Dangerous creatures. Especially those on the arms of friends."

He glanced at Lady Roslyn and brought his gaze back to meet Destry's. If only he knew the truth. "There is no risk of that happening," Reid said.

"You are with her more than her lover is."

Reid nodded but did not relent. Be she Roslyn, his friend's lover, or the thief Juniper Thimble, either woman stood beyond his reach for good reasons. "I keep my heart and my head separate."

"Be sure that you do, Squire."

Why it sounded so grave, Reid didn't know. Destry need not worry. Once the demon business came to an end, Roslyn would return home to Galamond and would no longer be his problem. The thief, however... He would worry about that when it came time. He had told her he wouldn't let

Maddox claim her, but how? What would he do with her? He might be able to find her honest work somewhere, maybe in the castle, maybe in the Marca, somewhere that wasn't Maddox's keep or the Undercity.

He had a while to think on that, however. Reid returned to the problem at hand. What did the Order think could be worse than a demon?

CHAPTER TWENTY-THREE

A few more days of rest, and Juniper woke to a clap of thunder. Scuttling came from the sitting room, of dishes and soft-soled feet—along with a delicious aroma of real food, not broth. Juniper shrugged on her dressing robe and let herself into the sitting room. The two servants arranging the table for breakfast jumped at the sight of her.

Reid stood by the hearth, supervising.

Both women bowed their heads and quickly finished setting the table. They skirted out the door with something shy of terror on their faces.

"Are they all right?"

Reid set the book he was holding on the table by the hearth. "For all the servants know, you could be their future queen. They do not want to be on your bad side."

"It's strange to be doted on like this," she admitted. The sight of the servants bowing to her, like she meant something, bothered her. "If they knew who I really was, they'd more quickly spit on me than bow."

"Ah." Reid's brows rose. "Is that guilt?"

Ignoring him, she sat and reached for the basket of fresh, steaming biscuits. "Maybe it is."

"I didn't think thieves could feel guilt."

She didn't lower herself to take the bait. Instead, she sipped her tea. Lying to the servants wasn't the same as taking something from a rich bastard. The servants were perfectly good people who didn't deserve to be lied to, and if she were being honest, she didn't deserve to be doted on. And next to Reid, the honorable squire, she was just a lowly street rat thief.

Worthy only of the gallows.

They ate for a while in silence; all the while, the storm picked up. Rain and wind pushed against the walls. Wind howled.

She let her gaze wander to the book resting on the small table by the hearth. Marks on the edges showed where a good number of hands had held the book open. The title had long since faded.

"What were you reading?" She motioned to the book.

He blinked, eyes settling on the book as though he had just spotted it. "Aldric's *Magical History of Duvane*." He heaved a sigh. "One of the required reads for a squire. Nine hundred and seventy-three pages of names, dates, and stuffy history. Dreadfully boring. However, whenever I can't sleep, I find its long-winded passages and flat narration to be quite relaxing."

"Were you reading it last night?"

"I was. It's not as exciting as the romance novel you were reading." He smirked.

Her face warmed. She should not have left that book on the bed.

After the raw edge of her hunger had been calmed, she asked, "What is on my agenda for today, my dear squire?"

"Until the healer deems otherwise, you are on bed rest."

Juniper sighed through her nose. "She will deem me fit."

"You sound certain of that."

Juniper ate a spoonful of porridge, swallowed, and tossed her spoon upward and caught it by the handle—she held it like a dagger about to strike, or in this case, a spoon about to scoop out an eyeball. "I will threaten to kill her otherwise."

Reid laughed. "I doubt mere threats from you will scare that old bat. She's seen through enough cranky invalid guards and royals."

She lowered her spoon into her porridge. "I suppose it would be rude to actually kill her, then."

"Yes." He took a bite. Swallowed. "We'd not find another healer like her on short notice."

Juniper heaved a dramatic sigh. "But I'm so bored locked in this room!"

"What would you do otherwise?"

She sipped her tea, holding the cup in front of her lips as Reid had instructed her so that people did not see her lips while drinking. "Normal things for any woman: read; train to keep myself sharp, strong, and flexible; go to shows in town; wander along the shopping district on market day; scout potential targets; test my pickpocketing; maybe go to a tavern or club."

He eyed her suspiciously. "And how is your pickpocketing?"

She winked, then motioned to him and asked, "What do *you* do all day?"

"Before being assigned to you, I spent most of my days studying and practicing."

"What does a squire study and practice?"

"Swordplay, archery, magic theory, knight protocol, and ceremony, just to give you a few subjects."

"That sounds awful." She'd never been one for schooling. Maddox had to threaten to beat her to get her to sit still long enough.

Reid shrugged. "Better than sitting on my ass."

She scoffed. "I have not been sitting on my ass. I've been *resting*."

"Resting on your ass," Reid corrected dryly. He took another bite. He hadn't yet donned his armor, and without it, the muscles of his arms and shoulders stretched the well-made tunic. "You need to stay out of sight. In your chambers."

"I'm wasting away in here," she whined. She leaned onto the table. "Can't we go for a walk? I need to move." Her legs ached with all the sitting and laying she had been doing.

"Is that a ploy to see the rest of the castle?" Reid asked, eyes on his tea, not her.

She released a short sigh. "I would like to keep myself strong." She leaned further onto the table. If whining didn't work... "You've been sulking around here like a housecat. I'm surprised you haven't wasted away. Your arms are smaller, I think."

He frowned at her.

"You're wasting away," she said dramatically.

He heaved a sigh of annoyance.

"Since you refuse to let me out of your sight," she started, desperation to get out of her chambers loosening her tongue, "and neither of us want to be trapped inside this room, why not go for a walk? Find an empty room so I can hand your ass to you. I've been needing someone to beat up since I got here, and you have repeatedly given me reasons to hit you."

He half laughed, and his lips twitched upward. "I'm not sure you could keep up with me, *my lady*."

"Oh, I know you couldn't keep up with me, *Squire*."

He met her gaze. "Are you challenging me to a duel?"

She shrugged. "Unless you're afraid to lose to a girl."

She smiled at him, and his smirk widened in response.

A knock sounded at the door, jarring her from her stare. She hadn't realized she'd been looking so intently into those honey eyes of his, and by the startled look on his face, he shared the surprise.

"The healer," he murmured. He stumbled as he stood to answer the door.

✦

Passed with good remarks by the royal healer, Juniper set off with Reid down the corridor and into a wide empty room.

A rack of wooden staves stood by the wall, and scuff marks dotted the floor. Thick curtains held off the stormy daylight. Rain smacked against the windows and stone walls, thunder roared and growled, and lightning flashed.

Reid walked to each of the six torches and lit them, giving them plenty of light to see by.

"A spare practice room," Reid explained as he grabbed one of the well-used staves and tossed it to her. She caught it easily. The wood had been smoothed by countless hands. "For when the Royal Guard needs a space not too far from the royals they protect or when Adrian needs a place to break things. He was an unruly teenager."

She snickered.

Reid harrumphed and chose a staff for himself. He turned it over in his hands, and then he came at her. He closed the distance between them with a frightening speed, even for a guard, and smacked his staff into hers with a force that shook up her arms and into her shoulders.

He paused after his initial attack to let her adjust. She retaliated, and the fight began.

The two staves smacked together as they danced about the floor. Juniper had the feeling Reid went easy on her. For a trained guard and squire, he didn't land a single blow on her. Her wounds protested, but she ignored them.

She managed, just once, to slip past his defense and whack him on the leg, at which she shouted, "Aha!"

She laughed as they moved. Her chest loosened with the movement, with the freedom. Fun. That's what it was. When had she last had such fun?

They danced about the floor, and soon, too soon, they both grew breathless. Reid started to try harder. He moved faster and hit harder, and it took all of her concentration to block his offenses. He feinted and smacked the staff on her rear.

"Ouch!" She yelped and put a hand to where he'd hit her. "I'll bruise! You'll have people thinking you beat me."

He laughed and set the end of his staff on the floor. "I won't leave welts in obvious places. You still have appearances to uphold."

She twirled the staff. It didn't have the same balance as a dagger. "If you would have handed me a wooden dagger, I would have beaten you by now. You've got the advantage."

He grinned. "That sounds like an excuse."

She flipped the staff to a defensive position. "Again!"

"You want a matching welt on the other side?"

She twisted her hands around the staff as countless guards had done before her. "I want to leave a welt on your ass too and see how you like it."

He tossed his staff up and caught it in an effortless motion. "If you can even touch me."

"I hit you!"

"Because I allowed it."

Though her body cried for rest, though her wounds had not fully healed, she came at him. He blocked her, turned onto the offense, and smacked her on the thigh with his staff.

She laughed, and she thought she heard Reid chuckle.

Round after round, they fought. He won most of them, and those that he didn't, she suspected he let her win. Reid had a marvelous control of battle. When he fought, an intense, focused calm erased all emotion from his face. A battlefield calm. He moved with learned grace but with a natural ability to calculate and judge an opponent. Juniper felt herself in awe by it, although she would never tell him so.

Reid ended the battle in a graceful twist of his body into hers—he disarmed her.

"How did you—?" Juniper gaped at her empty hands and then at her staff in his hands. She hadn't the time to finish her thought—from behind her, Reid used both staves like twin swords, one at her throat, one at her gut.

"Years of practice," Reid said, his words a breath in her ear. He stepped away and returned the staves to the rack.

Juniper put a hand to her throat. She'd had plenty of blades against her neck before, but they had been sneak attacks, not an open battle maneuver. "What in Rappa's name are they teaching you in squire school?" she asked.

He chuckled. "It's not squire school. When one first joins the Order, they become a pledge. Once they prove their worth and mettle, of both blade and mind, they become a squire. The entire process of becoming a knight is referred to as squirehood."

"Squire school sounds more appropriate." Juniper stretched out her arms and legs and sat underneath the window, where a cool spring draft seeped inside, ushered by the stormy wind whistling through the turrets and towers and battlements like a thousand warbirds.

"For all the studying, I am inclined to agree." Reid strolled over to where she sat, each step calculated, careful. "I will admit, I didn't expect a thief to know how to fight. You did better than I thought you would."

"I suppose that's a compliment." She stretched her legs out in front of her. She would be sore. She already felt the strain in her legs and back. "Do you think I spend all my time lounging about? I spent years learning how to fight with blades and daggers. It takes effort to keep this body strong." She motioned to herself and fought the urge to smirk when his eyes traveled the length of her. "I am better with daggers and shadows than I am with open combat and staves."

"The Royal Guard and the Order train with every weapon, but most favor the sword. It's easier to manage."

"If we were fighting with daggers and stealth, I'd have you pinned to the floor with a dagger to your throat before you could blink."

The corner of his mouth twitched upward. "Remind me never to leave daggers in your room."

"Were you planning on bringing them into my room?"

"That first day I was sent to watch you, I was armed to the teeth," he said. "I didn't know what to expect from one of the most notorious thieves in Rusdasin, so I arrived armed and ready."

Which had been the reason why he had clanked so much.

"Is that why you haven't worn your armor lately?" Juniper cast her eyes up to Reid, to his muscular arms, shoulders, and chest. She brought her focus then to his eyes; they'd gone unreadable. "You don't feel the necessity of carrying so much weight in weapons into my room every day?"

He waited a moment before answering. "I suppose."

"I am glad to say that I, too, have stopped plotting your death."

Reid sat on the floor beside her. Lightning flashed; it glared through the seam in the curtain, and a white streak sliced down the floor between them. Not a moment after, a crash of thunder shook the window. A crest of wind brought a thick torrent of rain against the glass.

Reid shifted, then asked, "Juniper, why do you stay with Maddox? Why not leave and find honest work?"

The question caught her off guard—she had no answer ready. She felt a tingle in the center of her back. "It's complicated," she said at last.

"You don't think I'd understand?" His tone was soft.

She felt him looking at her, but she kept her gaze on her knees. She didn't want to see the pity in his eyes. "You were raised in the castle. So, no, I don't think you'd understand."

His legs twitched like he meant to stand, but he remained sitting. "I've heard plenty of stories from the Undercity and what goes on down there. Give me yours." A request, not a command.

Thunder crashed, rattling the window.

"It's not that exciting." She smoothed a wrinkle in her pants.

"Tell me anyway."

She heaved a sigh, and as it left her chest, she felt the sinking feeling pull her heart into her stomach. "Maddox put a roof over my head. He made sure I had clothes and food. He taught me to fight. I get most of my jobs through him. After all he's done, I owe him."

Reid grunted his disapproval. "Why not just leave?" he asked softly.

"I can't." She felt the burning pressure between her shoulder blades, like a white-hot iron against her skin. "If I left, he would see it as desertion and hunt me down himself or send someone to kill me. It's the Undercity; plenty of people owe him down there. Like you said, it runs more on favors than gold." Favors and blood. "With Maddox...I have a place."

Reid's brow furrowed. He motioned to the training room. "What about all of this? What will Maddox do about you being here? He won't be able to send anyone to find you or kill you within these walls."

She wanted to argue that someone had infiltrated the walls and had nearly killed the prince, but she didn't. Reid knew. Like the unknown apostate, Maddox had his ways.

"I don't know. He might think me dead and leave it at that. It's a rule that if you get caught, you're on your own." She chuckled, but it didn't alleviate the sinking in her chest. "I'm looking forward to seeing his face when all this is over. I get so few chances to surprise him."

Silence returned with nothing but the raging storm between them. After a long moment, Reid stood. He offered his hand to her.

"Squire and a gentleman. It's a wonder you're unmarried. I suppose the Order has rules against that?" Even as she spoke the words, it brought a blush to her cheeks. She slid her hand into his, the rough calluses from holding a blade sliding against her own. He pulled her to her feet—oh gods, her legs would be sore in the morning.

"They do not," Reid said as he released her hand. "Many knights marry, but it would be a strenuous relationship. Knights are ordered all over the kingdom and sometimes beyond to do tasks others see as impossible or deadly."

"Like slaying dragons?"

Reid nodded, a faint smile tugging on his lips. "Like slaying dragons."

✦✦

They started back toward her chambers at a leisurely pace. Juniper did not want to return so soon, and after some bullying, Reid agreed to a walk.

They walked through the Royal Chambers, with him pointing out such and such king, queen, duke, or knight in their respective portraits. He had been well versed in Duvane's history and rattled off names and dates and battles with ease.

From the Royal Chambers, they drifted through the castle's countless halls, corridors, and breezeways. To better keep her from being seen, they stayed to the quiet parts of the castle and used empty servants' passages to move through the corridors. They stopped at several of the rooftop courtyards, most of which were closed off due to the rain. Through the windows, Juniper saw the bushes, flowers, and trees—all well-tended and manicured—swaying in the wind. Many of the flower beds had turned into muddy slops.

Juniper paused in an empty breezeway. Tall leaded glass windows lined the breezeway, filling the space with stormy daylight. Through the windows, Juniper had a lovely view of the Royal Grounds. With the storm, the view was a shade more terrifying. Thrilling.

Through the blue-gray downpour, she spotted the stables. In the distance, barely visible on the other side of the Royal Grounds, were the pale green dome-like structures of the Royal Greenhouses.

"You keep staring at the greenhouses." Reid tried to see what she saw, but he brought his confused gaze back to her.

"It reminds me," she said hesitantly. It was a piece of her that few knew.

His brows rose in soft curiosity.

"I remember greenhouses from when I was little, before..." She didn't want to finish that thought, and he didn't push her to. "I remember there being greenhouses. We grew grapes and apples and peaches and all manner of herbs. There were honeysuckle and lavender outside my bedroom window. I'd leave the shutters open at night just to wake up and smell them."

She inhaled like she might catch a whiff. She didn't.

"Do you remember anything of your home?" Reid's tone softened, but he didn't offer her pity. "If you can, we might be able to find it."

She shook her head. "Just little things, like the smell of the herbs. The feel of the freshly tilled dirt under my feet, and..." She hesitated again. Reid wore no judgment, no pity, only indifferent warmth. It was that warmth that loosened her tongue. "I remember my mother, kneeling at a tree. Crying. I don't remember why or when, but I don't remember it being strange, like she did it all the time."

The memory became clear as if she stood in the garden. Her mother, her dark hair tied loosely behind her head, knelt before a scraggly tree.

And then she was fighting for her life in the Undercity while Reid played in the castle, having his ass saved by guards.

The breezeway returned with a crack of thunder. Juniper pulled her arms around herself.

"What's wrong?" Reid stepped into her direct view.

In a small voice, she answered, "I've never told anyone that before."

He put a hand over his heart, the tanned skin flecked with tiny white scars. "I will take it to my grave."

She smiled, but it felt forced. "It's not a secret; it's just...not something I dwell on." She looked down at her fingers, the pale scars blending in with her skin. "I accepted that the girl who lived in that garden died the night she was sold in the Undercity, and I was born. There's no going back, so there's no sense crying about it."

"Do you remember their names?"

She blinked.

"Your parents."

She bit her lip and again found the little scar on her thumb shaped like a half-moon. "No."

Reid let out a slow exhale. "I'm sorry. Things like that shouldn't happen. Families should not be torn apart. Children should not be sold."

Bile rose in the back of her throat. "But you would take mage children away from their families and send them to the Marca."

His lips became a thin line. "That is different."

Though she wanted to, she didn't argue. She didn't feel like it anymore. A coldness had settled over her bones. Reid offered her his arm, and she took it. Without looking back at the greenhouses, they continued their leisurely walk through the castle. She thought about anything other than those greenhouses and, in her desperation to think about anything else, found her thoughts drifting to the squire beside her and to his seemingly never-ending well of Castle Bradburn history.

CHAPTER TWENTY-FOUR

"Any breakthroughs on the demon and the apostate?" Juniper asked as she and Reid walked into an empty courtyard. The morning rain had become a dreary spring drizzle; however, the veranda of the courtyard kept them dry. The blooming green looked impossibly vibrant after yesterday's storm.

"Unfortunately, no."

She puffed up her chest and shoulders. "I suppose it's up to me, then."

Reid laughed. "Oh? And where would the lady like to begin her investigation?"

"At the scene," she said. She pulled her braided hair over her shoulder. She wished she'd had Clara tie it up. The humidity felt awful between her hair and her neck. "I want to see it with my own eyes, without guards peering down at me like some porcelain doll teetering on the edge of a high shelf."

He didn't object like she thought he would, and instead, he walked her to Adrian's chambers. Reid nodded to the guards on either side, neither of whom fussed about them going inside.

Adrian had stepped out, leaving his chambers open for her to investigate. His chambers resembled hers, only his were larger and grander and had an air of being lived in. It smelled like him, like that butterscotch oil or tonic or whatever it was. His shelves were packed with books—a few of the authors she recognized. She hadn't noticed the reddish wolf pelt rug on which the well-used plush seating was arranged. A dire wolf by the sheer size of it. Its yellow glass eyes forever looked into the hearth with residual hunger.

The staff had cleaned up any trace of the demon. Books had been replaced. Blood had been cleaned. The only trace that Juniper could find was a set of scratches on the topmost bookcase the thing had leaped from.

Juniper shivered and continued into the bedroom, where that demon had met its demise at the edge of Reid's blade. They had cleaned his bedroom too. No ash remained, not even in the grout of the stone or the tight threads of the rug. Magic, she assumed. Reid leaned against the doorframe to the bedroom, watching her. She ignored his curious gaze as she meandered into the bathing room, a marvel of white marble, gray stone, and gold. No windows.

The bedroom had four windows. None would open, not even a fraction. Sealed, Reid informed her. To prevent assassins from using the obvious choice of entry. She walked into the sitting room, where the demon had appeared. Again, she glanced up at the bookcase.

"Is there always a guard standing outside?"

"Yes." Reid glanced toward the door, then back at her. "Why? What are you thinking?"

"If the windows in the bedroom are sealed, and there is always a guard standing outside, then how did a demon get inside without anyone noticing?"

"You've discovered the knights' conundrum."

"Where does that go?" She pointed to a simple, elegant wooden door on the far side of the sitting room. Her chambers did not have such a door.

"The study."

Not waiting to ask permission, she strolled to the door and let herself in. The four walls of the room held wooden shelves full of books, ornate figurines, small paintings, and glass globes of varying colors and sizes. In the mid-morning sunlight, each dazzled like a star.

The two windows of the study overlooked a courtyard. Underneath each window was a plush seat, one of which had been stacked with books halfway up the window. The other, however, looked to have been used frequently for sitting.

It was to that window she walked. "Demons can't phase through walls or doors, can they?"

"Not that I am aware."

"And they can't just appear wherever their sender pleases?" She opened the window a few inches. Cool, humid air rushed in. "Then, this window is the only way anything is getting in or out."

Reid's gaze settled on the window. "Do you assume the knights fool enough not to have realized that?"

She stuck her tongue out at him and opened the window further. The drizzle kissed her cheeks. She ignored it as she examined the courtyard. The veranda made it hard to see much of it beyond the bushy trees. She brushed her hand along the stone underneath the window. Uneven. Enough for something to climb up. From the courtyard, it would have been easy to reach Adrian's study. She had no doubt that a demon could scale the side of the castle. *She'd* done it.

She crossed her arms. "Any good assassin or thief will use a window. It's the best way; that's why it's the obvious way. In, out, no one knows you're there."

He raised a brow. "Is that coming from experience?"

She shrugged, a non-answer. "I want to see the courtyard below." She said it as a command, as any lady would, and turned to see Reid furrowing his brow at her. "What?"

Reid stalked to the window and shut it, firmly locking it. "I've heard that a demon can squeeze through an opening like a cat. If its head fits, it fits."

"I can't deny or confirm that." Juniper imagined that horrible, mangy beast squeezing in through the seams in the window, snout, eyes, shoulders... She shivered.

They left Adrian's chambers, walking in near silence. They passed a few servants, each too preoccupied to give more than a passing glance in their direction.

Reid and Juniper arrived in the courtyard. Apple trees had been artfully planted to welcome walkers into the grassy knoll in the center. The drizzle sounded against each budding leaf, a hum of pitter-patter. Four corridors branched off the courtyard, one on each side. Four corridors for the demon to have slithered down.

"Are we still in the Royal Chambers?"

"Yes."

Juniper doubted the demon would come from the Royal Chambers. Too many guards. Too many knights.

Still, demons weren't exactly inconspicuous. How could a demon walk around the castle at all with the knights sniffing for any sign of magic and guards standing at every corner? She voiced her thoughts to Reid. He agreed darkly, in such a way that told her the knights had already ventured down that path of thinking.

"They don't understand how a demon could be getting anywhere without leaving a hint of itself behind," Reid said. He glanced about the courtyard, then said in a near whisper, "There are traces of the demon in this courtyard, but then it vanishes."

"So, you knew about the window?"

He nodded. "I couldn't explain it all to you. I'd be in trouble with the Order if I did."

She made a lap around the veranda, thinking. She knew little of demons; she'd avoided the subject when she could. She wasn't looking at anything in particular, only walking as she thought. On the second lap around the veranda, she spotted something that made her stop dead in her tracks.

"What is it?" Reid appeared at her side instantly, hand on his pommel.

"What is that?" She pointed to the ground where a grate was set into the stone. It blended in so well with the gray stone, she'd nearly missed it.

Reid frowned. "A drain. Leads into the sewers or the dungeons. Or both."

The dungeons or the sewers. Of course.

Juniper knelt down beside the grate, carefully sweeping the edges of her dress from her feet. A small trickle of rainwater dribbled down into the depths, echoing upward, blending in harmoniously with the drizzle. The edges of the stone were worn where the grate had long rested. The grate itself had been shifted.

"See that? Someone's moved this. Recently."

Reid bent down beside her. His eyes narrowed. "Gods."

"Could the knights have looked here and moved it?"

"It's impossible to say."

Juniper glanced down into the darkness on the other side of the grate. Water hit a surface not too far away. She grabbed hold of the grate, the cold iron biting into her fingers, and pulled. It shifted but did not come out. Reid's hands mirrored hers on the other side, and between the two of them, they lifted the grate.

The darkness lightened only slightly.

She whispered, "If I were summoning demons, I would go where no one would look, a place people wouldn't visit very often."

"Like the sewers," Reid finished her thought. He scowled and shook his head. "The knights searched the dungeons, but I can't say if they searched the sewers."

She clicked her tongue. "What kind of knight doesn't think to look in the most obvious place?"

"The sewers are near impossible to get into from inside the castle unless one could travel through pipes a few inches wide."

"Unless you're a demon who can squeeze through a grate, scale a wall, and open an unlocked window in the prince's study," Juniper said, motioning to the likely route the demon took.

"I will reprimand Adrian for not locking his windows."

Juniper shifted her feet and scooted closer to the opening. It was dark and wet, but she'd been in worse places.

Reid started. "What are you doing? You're not going down there. You do realize what is in a sewer?"

She smiled at him, a retort on her tongue, when a strange, rolling gurgle echoed up from the sewer. It evolved into a low rumbling roar. Every hair on her body stood on end, and a feverish shiver ran from her neck to her toes.

Reid shifted his feet and jumped down into the sewer. His feet met wet, solid ground.

"Are you dead?" she called.

Reid scoffed. She could see him move against the darkness. He unsheathed his sword.

Juniper put her feet into the hole first, braced herself, and jumped. She landed on wet stone not that far down. Less than seven feet. The floor sloped downward, herding the water further into the depths. Trickling water echoed from every direction.

"We should've brought a torch," she whispered. Just because she had excellent night vision didn't mean Reid did.

Reid crept down the tunnel in front of her. He had one hand on his sword, the other against the wall beside him. Juniper mirrored him, tracing her fingers along the stone. Her eyes adjusted; the light from the grate glinted off the trickling water. The farther down they went, the darker it became.

Gods, the smell. She could do without the smell: like dank stone, stagnant water, and all the human waste from a castle full of guards and servants.

They did not walk far when another growl, closer than the first, sounded through the darkness. A warning growl.

Reid froze.

Footsteps, big footsteps of clawed feet, sounded from the gloom. They sloshed through water several inches deep.

Juniper's breath hitched. She had nothing to defend herself with.

Could demons see in the dark? Her gut told her they could.

The demon, however, made no hurry to get to them. The footsteps came closer, closer, then stopped.

The tunnel ahead of them continued to slope down, but she saw no movement ahead. Only stone. Only trickling water. The demon made no move to attack. Instead, lazy footsteps meandered in the other direction. The echo made it hard to tell how far away it was, or even where it was. It might be below them or beside or above. She didn't know the layout of the sewers. Another thing she tried to avoid.

Juniper tiptoed to Reid and set a hand on his back; he briefly tensed. She whispered, "How many grates are there in the castle?"

"Too many."

Reid's muscles tightened under her hand.

"It's looking for Adrian," she warned. "We need to find him first. We find him, that thing will show itself."

Reid considered her words, then nodded. "You're right."

Juniper and Reid backed up to the sewer grate. The drizzle had thickened into rain. Luckily, the courtyard remained empty. She'd rather not have to explain why Lady Roslyn and Squire Sandpiper were seen climbing out of the sewer.

"His guard will be with him. And Sir Destry," Reid said as they started back into the castle. "But if that thing is planning on attacking, we should at least give him some warning."

"It will wait for Adrian back in his room."

"Why's that?"

"That's where the other went. It waited for him." The words tumbled as she thought them, "Like whoever sent it knew he wasn't in his room and when he would be back."

Reid's brow furrowed. "Then, let's head that way and wait for it."

They did not have to go very far. As they rounded a corner toward Adrian's chambers, Adrian and his guard rounded the other corner. Destry stood beside Adrian, wearing the same expression as Reid. His serious eyes settled at once on Reid and Juniper, as if he could sense their urgency.

Juniper wouldn't put it past the knights to have some system of silent communication.

Adrian was smiling, but as he came closer, that smile faded. He, too, sensed something amiss. Adrian stopped. His guard stopped.

"Well, neither of you look very enthused to see me." Adrian put his hands on his hips and glanced between her and Reid. He stepped closer to Juniper. Concern flickered in his gaze. "Dearest, you look a bit ill. Are you all right?"

"Yes, love." She glanced down the corridor behind them. No sign of any demon. "This weather takes it out of me."

"I can understand that." Adrian glanced at Reid. "You don't look well either. How about tea in my room?" He gave Juniper's arm a squeeze and set a hand on Reid's shoulder.

Reid looked like he would object, but Juniper reached for Adrian's arm. "I agree. Tea sounds delightful, love."

Her gut twisted on the way to his chambers. With two knights and a small squad of Royal Guard, no demon stood a chance. Juniper had witnessed what Reid alone could do, but it did not stop her stomach from tightening.

They arrived at Adrian's chambers without complication. Destry went inside first and deemed each room demon-free. Six of twelve royal guards took up positions outside the room. The other six and Reid followed Juniper and Adrian inside. Two guards stood by the main door, mirroring those outside. Two stood by the threshold of the bedroom. Two stood beside the study door.

Juniper tried not to look off-put by it. They'd have no privacy in here with all the guards. Adrian must have thought the same, for he walked straight into his study. He called for tea then shut the three of them in his study. Adrian half laughed, glancing between Reid and Juniper, then rubbed his face.

Reid started to speak, but Juniper never heard his words. Her attention snagged on the window. The window they had closed and locked that now stood open nearly an inch.

She didn't get the chance to point it out.

Movement near the ceiling—she glanced upward to the small unlit chandelier. She barely had time to let out a cry as the demon lunged.

CHAPTER TWENTY-FIVE

Reid's sword met the demon's gaping maw with an ear-splitting *clank*.

Adrian gasped and stumbled backward, his face several shades too pale. Juniper threw herself in front of Adrian. She would rather take the initial blow than have it transfer. Less pain for her and less explaining for Reid and Adrian.

The study door burst open, and Destry charged through, sword drawn. The dark blade glittered a bluish black, spotted with feathery red. Mage's Bane.

Juniper tensed; every bone in her body went rigid.

Reid's blade slashed into the demon's face, and the beast clattered back into the bookcases on the opposite wall, the knobs of its hind legs knocking several tomes to the floor.

The demon's brown-black eyes looked at Reid, then Destry. Its nostrils flared. Its muscles flexed underneath its leathery brown skin. The patches of red-brown hair bristled. Blood dripped from its face. Then, with a strange twist of its thick neck, those eyes settled on Juniper.

Her heart fluttered as those eyes narrowed. It was *thinking*. Its nostrils flared once in her direction. A low growl, almost curious, escaped its bleeding jaw.

What was it smelling?

Adrian shifted closer to her.

The demon ground its teeth. Destry and Reid took a unison step closer to the demon, pinning it against the wall. The demon sensed the trap. Those brown-black eyes jerked from Juniper to the window—the open window.

It had been enough for the beast to get inside—

Before Juniper could alert their attention, the demon dashed to the window. Its snout went first, and like a wraith, the rest of it squeezed out after without slowing down.

Destry made it first to the window and yanked it open all the way. "It's gone!"

Juniper caught Reid's eye. He knew. The demon had not vanished. It had gone straight for the sewer.

Juniper pushed out of Adrian's grasp, but the guards were not enthused about letting her out. She placed a hand on her head and let out a dramatic sigh. "I need to lie down."

Reid appeared beside her and placed a hand on her back. "I've got her."

It appeased the guards. Reid and Juniper walked into the corridor and headed not for her room, but for the courtyard. Once out of the view of the guards, they burst into a run. Luckily, they didn't meet anyone on the way to the courtyard, and if anyone from Adrian's room looked down, they would not see them underneath the veranda.

The grate to the sewer had been left askew.

Reid bent down and yanked it off. Juniper bent down, meaning to jump, but Reid held up a hand. "You should stay here."

She blinked. "What?"

"It's dangerous business to be hunting a demon."

"I will not cower in my room like some pitiful ninny!" Juniper Thimble did not cower.

Reid glanced between her and the darkness below, considering. "Then, make yourself useful, and grab a torch."

She dashed into the corridor closest to them and yanked one right off the bracket. When she returned, Reid had already jumped down into the gloom. His brown eyes glinted back at her in the torch's flickering light. She knelt and jumped.

With the torchlight, the stone glittered with wetness. Reid led the way, sword out and ready. The torchlight gleamed off the wet floor, the streams running along the worn groove in the stone, the mildew growing in the creases. The flickering light shadowed every uneven crack and crag in the walls. The rank air worsened the farther down they went, step after step, following the trickling rainwater. They hadn't yet made it to the bottom when the demon's guttural murmurs echoed off the stone.

The tunnel finally reached an end and opened up into a larger tunnel. Sewage gushed down a channel in the center, unknown inches deep and at least six feet wide. Darkness stretched out on either side of them, blackening the ends of the main sluice. Juniper could see indentations in the tunnel's stone walls where other grates guided rainwater and gods knew what else into the sluice.

The demon's murmurs sounded, but with the gushing sluice, she couldn't determine which direction the beast had gone. Either path looked the same, only...the main sluice angled. The water flowed along a slope. She started to walk with the water, farther into the tomb-like sewers. Reid silently followed.

The path led steadily downward. The sluice deepened. The demon never appeared, not in front of or behind them. Its guttural moans echoed off the water, bouncing off each stone, sounding everywhere and nowhere.

The main sluice ended at a deep pool of what looked like water but smelled worse than any chamber pot or rotting bathhouse. Juniper coughed, but the rushing water hid the sound. The pool emptied into a flood channel; an iron grate on the far side caught the larger debris and let the water drain out on the other side. By the sound, the water crashed onto rocks far below. The sewers branched off from the pool in several directions, all wide sluices that angled upward, except for one. No water flowed from it. Its path didn't angle upward. It angled out.

That one.

Reid didn't object when she made her way along the stone walkway over the pool to the empty tunnel. It looked older than the sewer. Ancient. The walls were carved, not blocks. Solid stone. Even in the torchlight, the darkness seemed thicker. The very air seemed to be energized. Dread curled around her spine.

Reid stiffened and spat a curse. "Magic," he seethed.

Dark, vile, twisted magic, Juniper thought. It prickled against her skin and compressed her insides to the extent that she thought she might not be able to draw another breath. She inhaled deeply to make sure.

"That's not all." Juniper pointed to a spot on the ground that glistened in the flickering light.

Reid smeared it with the toe of his boot. "Blood," he confirmed.

Splotches of blood led down the cavern passage. A trail. "At least we're on the right track," she said.

She took a step, but Reid blocked her path.

"What?"

"It might get dangerous," he said. He unhooked a dagger from his belt and handed it to her. "Take this. Just in case."

She looked at the dagger, then him. "You mean it? You're handing me a weapon?"

He fixed his grim eyes on hers. "If that demon is waiting for us at the end of this tunnel, you need to be armed. I only wish I had something more than a dagger to give you."

She grinned. "You've obviously never seen me with a dagger."

The glint returned to his eye. "I better not find it in my back."

"Dear Squire, you think so little of me." She closed her hand around the dagger's worn leather hilt. She tested the weight. Royal Guard quality. Made for usefulness, not decoration, and of the best material the king could afford. It wasn't the typical junk they sold in the Undercity. No, this blade could break an Undercity blade in half.

Reid took the torch while she looped the leather strap of the sheath around her belt. She hadn't realized how much she'd missed the feeling of weapons on her person.

She walked with the torch angled so she could reach the dagger easily. Reid walked in front of her, with his back exposed, *after giving her a dagger*. He honestly trusted her enough to do that? She pushed the thought from her mind. She had a demon to find and revenge to extract on an apostate.

They followed glob after glob of demon blood. The tunnel broke off into branches, some narrow, some wide, all with the same carved look to the walls, streaks and gashes where a chisel once chipped away at the stone. In the distance, water dripped.

"How old do you think this is?" Juniper whispered.

"I don't know," Reid answered. "There are ruins below the castle, part of the castle that stood here before, but I've never heard of caverns beneath the castle. There have been people here for thousands of years. It's possible that some culture devised these tunnels for whatever purpose."

They followed the glops of blood into an old tunnel of stone blocks. It looked as though the cavernous tunnel had been blocked, but at some point in history had been reopened.

"Sewers," Reid breathed.

They'd taken a shortcut to a different part of the sewers. The stone blocks of the walls looked ancient. Some were crumbling at the edges. No sewage ran through the middle; the channel was dry.

In the middle of that dry channel was a bright, shining glob of blood. Fresh.

They did not walk far into the dry sewer. They came to a short offshoot where a hole had been knocked into the stone wall. The stones had been pushed out by the looks of it and scattered the floor. Whatever had made the hole had come from within the wall.

Across the threshold of that hole was a splotch of fresh demon blood.

Juniper unsheathed her dagger and held it at a killing angle. Reid nodded; sword at the ready, he stepped through. Juniper followed on his heels, eager to put this demon business to rest.

Perhaps if she defeated the apostate for them, the king would take pity on her and not throw her out so soon.

It looked like a natural cavern, with rocks jutting from ceiling and floor like teeth, but it felt unnatural. The air had changed. The torch's light did not reach very far. The shadows themselves seemed to grow, absorbing the light, drinking it, stealing it. Everything about the space felt wrong. Stifling. It compressed worse than the air before it had.

"Get out," Juniper whispered.

Reid either didn't hear her or didn't listen. He stepped further into the cavern and held his sword higher.

Juniper's breath hitched. Her body felt frozen. Icy fingers ran down her neck and back. Movement, and then—

The demon jumped from the shadows, yellow teeth and black talons glittering in the torchlight. Juniper didn't have enough of a voice to even scream. Reid acted fast, countering the demon's lunge with his own.

Juniper's grip on the dagger tightened. Reid threw the demon off. It skidded and turned, ready to attack again, but Juniper didn't give it the chance. She dropped the torch; the light flickered. She jumped onto the demon's back and thrust the dagger through its thick neck. She ducked as those talons came at her, slicing the air by her ear. She yanked the dagger free with a sickening twist and slid from the demon's back. Her feet had just touched the cavern floor when Reid thrust his sword through the demon's chest, where its heart should have been, and yanked the blade upward; he cleaved the demon nearly in two.

The demon collapsed to the floor, twitching and slipping in its blood. The body stilled and dissolved into black ash. The smell of it washed through the air like death, like vomit, like decay. Juniper's breakfast threatened to reappear.

Reid heaved a breath. "Damn."

"See?" Juniper crouched to pick up the torch—crouched to keep her stomach from sending anything upward. "I told you I could handle a dagger."

Reid was about to speak when a footstep sounded somewhere farther in the cavern—neither of them had moved. They were not alone. Juniper held up the bloodied dagger, and Reid positioned his sword to strike. But nothing moved. Not even the shadows.

"Who is there?" asked a hoarse, hissing voice.

Juniper tightened her grip on the dagger. The apostate? No. It sounded...inhuman. It came from within the passage, but deeper. Juniper took a careful step farther into the cavern and held the torch out. There—where the demon had appeared was a small opening in the rock.

That's where they were coming from. She glanced at Reid; he nodded. She took a step closer to it, dagger at the ready. The opening led down a narrow and steep tunnel. She picked up a small rock and tossed it into the tunnel. It rolled down the passage and out of sight. She wouldn't be able to stand up inside it. She would have to crawl. Her gut twisted at the thought.

If she went down there, she might not get back up. Her gut told her to back away, but she didn't see any other way in or out of the cavern. The demon had come from it. They all had. Going down there seemed a horrible, stupid, awful idea, yet if the apostate lurked at the bottom...

I can smell you.

Juniper froze at the intimacy of the voice, softly spoken into her ear. She felt no presence beside her, yet it was there.

I know what you are.

The voice spoke playfully but with a viciousness that felt like talons clawing along her bare skin.

You've come to me.

"Juniper?" Reid stepped closer.

The shadows moved—converged, twisted, unaffected by the torch's light.

"We need to leave," Reid commanded. "Right now."

She forced her right foot to step, but something solid and cold pressed against her back. A ragged breath sounded in her ear. A sharp, cool edge of steel pushed into her neck. The thing behind her, whose chest pressed against her back, lived; breaths expanded its chest. A heartbeat thudded from within.

But it was not human.

Don't move.

CHAPTER TWENTY-SIX

Long bony fingers grasped her arm. Cold seeped through her dress, chilling her skin, her bones.

"Juniper?" Reid's eyes met hers and shifted over her shoulder—and widened. Fear twisted in those eyes. He shifted his sword to attack.

The thing holding her let out a low rumbling laugh.

"No, no, that won't do," said the thing in her ear. It seemed to whisper, yet the voice sounded as loud as a scream. It felt as cold as the walls of the sewer around them and dry as death. "Put your sword away, Squire."

Reid hesitated, hatred twisting with his fear. The cold blade at her neck pushed, slicing easily into her skin. She gasped; Reid lowered his sword.

"You too." It nudged her throat with the blade.

Her dagger clattered to the floor at her feet. The blade at her throat didn't retreat.

"I told you to put it away, Squire." It hissed. It squeezed her arm; pain scorched from its touch, into her fingertips and up into her shoulder. The torch fell from her grasp but did not go out. The light shifted. It glinted off Reid's blade as he sheathed it, eyes on the beast behind her.

Reid held up his empty hands. "Let her go."

"Why would I do that?" it drawled. Its cold breath snaked against her ear. It inhaled, its face close to her hair. Smelling her.

You could stop me, you know.

Juniper shook. If she hadn't already dropped the torch and the dagger, she would have dropped them then.

"What do you want, demon?" Reid demanded, fists tight, eyes burning black in the torchlight.

"A taste," it hissed.

Of you. It's been so long.

She trembled. She held herself as still as possible in fear of slicing her own throat on the demon's blade. Reid held his ground, assessing, calculating.

If she fought the demon long enough to give him some time... The demon pressed its face into her hair and inhaled deeply.

"Release her," said Reid.

"Do you know what this girl is?" the demon hissed, its voice lithe with excitement.

Reid didn't move. His eyes snapped to Juniper, her throat, at the knife poised there, then back to the demon.

I can smell you.

"Raw. Primal. Unrefined." The demon's breath grazed the shell of her ear, ice slithering into her mind. "It's been so long since I've smelled something so lovely. So delicious."

Her entire body shuddered. She felt it, a leeching—her very soul easing out of her body and into...somewhere else. Somewhere dark. Somewhere she did not want to be.

The demon closed in around her, its darkness folding over her.

"Release her, beast." Reid's eyes burned like fire. "You are trespassing on royal grounds. You have no place here. This ground is protected by the Knights of the Order."

The demon chuckled lazily. "Your words mean nothing to me, Squire." The blade at her throat wiggled. A hot droplet of blood slid down her throat, over her collarbone, and soaked into the neck of her dress. Another followed it, using the same bloody path. "What would you give me in exchange? Hmm?" It laughed. "What could *you* offer *me* in exchange for this lovely creature?"

She looked to Reid; she pleaded. *Don't let it take me.*

He was a squire, a future knight, a knight-in-training—Reid could take on a demon. He could win. He would win if the demon weren't using her as a shield. Because it knew. It knew Reid would win.

"Nothing." Reid's hand flexed. "I will not make deals with demons."

"Is that so?" The knife pressed into her skin.

She winced.

"Harm her further, and I will end you. Leave her be. Leave now," Reid demanded, his voice firm.

The demon laughed, a sickly sound. "You humans are so territorial."

It leaned in closer to her. Its face, cold as ice, rough as sand, nuzzled her neck. She wanted nothing more than to wrench her head away, but the blade held her still. Chapped, cracked lips met her bare skin. Uneven teeth grazed her skin as the demon nipped at her and left a kiss where those teeth had been.

I know what I would do with you.

Shivers ran over her skin like she'd been plunged into icy waters. The hand on her arm slid to her shoulder and down her side, those long fingers grazing over her breast, down her stomach, where it rested on her hip.

Reid stood still as death on the other side of the cavern.

The demon's fingers grabbed a fist full of her dress and pulled it up, inching the hem closer to her hip. Its hissing laughter tickled her ear with *yearning*. Those teeth pricked her neck.

No, no, no, she begged any god who listened. Any who still cared about her.

A distant gong came from within the cavern. The demon pulled his mouth from her throat. The hand inching up her skirt slackened. The blade against her throat loosened.

"I am called," it hissed.

It dropped her skirt. The blade shifted. The demon moved. Juniper saw Reid move, and she dropped to the floor. Reid swung his blade at the demon.

Had he been faster, he would have sliced the monster in two. Instead, his blade met the demon's side. The demon howled but did not fight back. With its cry, the entire cavern submerged into unnatural darkness. The demon hissed, and she felt its presence slink away.

In the dark, she didn't mind the heat building behind her eyes or the burning tears as they started to leak or the sobs as they quaked in her chest. That monster had wanted to...

A hand, a human hand, found her shoulder. Its twin found her cheek, where the tears streaked down her cold skin. Strong, gentle calloused fingers wiped them away. Reid knelt on the ground in front of her—she felt him there, his presence, a ward against the darkness that abounded.

She reached for him, found his chest, felt his heart thudding beneath his tunic, steady underneath her trembling hands.

He pulled her to him, and she wrapped her arms around his middle. She buried her face in his shoulder, letting his warmth seep into her frigid bones as she cried. His hands rested on her shoulders, on her back. Steady. Solid. Secure. The calmness of his spirit sank into her.

When the tears stopped, his hand once again found her face in the dark.

"Are you all right? Are you hurt?" Reid's warm breath met her cheek.

"No," she whispered, voice scratchy and wet. Then she remembered her throat, the blade held there. She felt for it. "I'm not bleeding out, so I suppose I'm all right."

They sat there, knee to knee, as the darkness slowly ebbed. The torch began to glow, first a flicker, then a flame. She sat there with Reid, his arm around her shoulders, until she stopped shaking. He never once asked her if she could stand, if she could walk. He waited until she stood. Then he stood with her.

In the light of the torch, Reid reached for her chin. He held it between his thumb and forefinger and tilted her head upward. His eyes searched her throat.

"It's not deep." Reid released her chin.

She swallowed. She felt the torn skin move, but it didn't hurt that bad. She'd live. "I'm gathering a zoo of scars."

He tried to smile, but it didn't meet his eyes. It didn't last long on his lips either. Reid cast a wary glance back to the narrow passage in the back of the cavern, where that demon had vanished, where it had been called back to.

By its master. The apostate.

"Should we go after it?" she asked.

"No." Reid nudged her toward the opening in the wall. "The Order needs to know about this."

She bent down for the torch and the dagger she'd discarded.

She stepped back into the ancient sewer first; she felt the change instantly. The air lightened, her chest loosened, and she could breathe easier. Magic. Reid stepped into the sewer and took a deep breath. He'd felt it too. She started back the way they'd come. She never wanted to go back to that place. Let the knights deal with it.

They made it back to the tunnel that would connect them to the sluice pool when Juniper finally broke the silence. "I'm sorry," she whispered, "for losing it back there."

Embarrassment warmed her cheeks.

"You have nothing to be sorry for. That demon would have frightened anyone. I was terrified, and it wasn't me the beast was touching."

She knew. She'd seen his face.

Reid pulled her gently to a halt. His seriousness softened into something she couldn't identify clearly in the torchlight. The sight sent a warm pulse down her spine and into her stomach.

"We will stop this." A promise. He reached for her hand and held it between them. "We will stop whoever is pulling the strings of those demons. We will end this reign of terror. I won't let that demon or any of its brothers touch you again."

She didn't know what to say; no one had ever promised such a thing.

She folded her fingers around his. She nodded. "I will hold you to that, Squire Sandpiper."

They stood for a moment, looking at one another. She watched the flames flickering in his eyes. She wondered, did he watch the flames flicker in hers?

"We should go back before we are missed," Reid whispered. With a gentle squeeze, he released her hand.

CHAPTER TWENTY-SEVEN

The next day, Reid left Juniper to escort two knights to where they'd found the demon.

Reid hadn't breathed a word of her breakdown or the demon. She still felt a twinge of guilt and embarrassment at the thought of it. She could still feel those spindly fingers sliding down her body, especially as she fell asleep.

Juniper was reading in the sitting room when Reid returned. By his grim face, it hadn't gone so well.

"It's gone."

"What's gone?"

"The hole in the wall." Reid started to pace in front of the hearth. The firelight glinted off his armor. "I led them back to where it was, but the wall had been fixed. It looked like it had never been there."

He huffed and ran his hands through his short hair.

She knew what he wanted to say. Magic. No other explanation.

"You're not going crazy." Juniper set the book aside. "I was there. I saw the hole and the demon and...that other one."

He halted his pacing. "I suspect that demon, the other one, was no ordinary demon. Not like the others." He glanced toward the fire. It burned his brown eyes molten. "The other demons walked like wolves, acted like rabid animals, but that one spoke. It stood on two legs. It wielded a weapon. It tried to bargain."

She felt the ghost of its lips on her neck. She instinctively raised her hand to where it had touched her, flattening her warm palm over it. "What does it mean?"

Grave seriousness shone in his eyes. "I believe someone summoned that demon, a Greater Demon, and it has been summoning the lesser demons. That way, the real summoner, the apostate, could be in the castle while the demons were summoned. It would give the apostate a watertight alibi."

She sighed. "So, someone is still summoning demons."

"Yes." Reid sat down in the chair beside her. "That demon...its master called it back. To be able to hold a demon's leash would require power. It would require a trained mage. Someone who knew what they were doing when they called that monster."

"The court magician?"

"He is the only logical suspect. He would be the only one in the castle capable of producing such magic." Reid glanced toward the doors as if he might appear. "Ison isn't strong enough. Sir Darvel told me why they didn't suspect him. He's not a strong spellcaster. He doesn't have the magical strength to summon such a monster."

Juniper thought back to the way the court magician had looked at her when he had magically pricked her finger—like a test subject. Less than human. "But that means the knights will be watching the court magician from now on, right? If he tries anything, they'll know."

He nodded. "He allowed them into his study to prove that he isn't guilty." Reid chuckled. "They stood in his study all yesterday. The court magician didn't so much as flinch at their presence, but they made Ison a nervous wreck."

Poor Ison.

"It could also be someone framing the court magician," he said. He leaned forward on his knees and let out a sigh.

"Like who?" she asked. She frowned. "Ison? You said he didn't have the magical strength."

"Black magic works differently," he said darkly. "I won't rule him out entirely until proven otherwise."

Juniper huffed but didn't argue. She leaned back in her chair. She didn't know Ison that well, but he did not seem like a killer.

Reid shifted. His armor moved with him. She liked him in his silver armor—it looked stunning when clean, even when he slouched—but she preferred him in a tunic and pants. It made him look human. It made him look less like a brainwashed knight. The armor also hid his powerful body, which, Juniper would never admit out loud, was nice to look at.

Reid broke the silence in a voice no louder than a whisper. "Do you... Do you remember how the air felt down there?"

She nodded. She remembered the stifling, suffocating air.

"Someone is keeping that demon down there." Reid frowned. "I told Darvel about it, and he confirmed what I suspected. We walked through a magical barrier, a ward."

"What does that mean?"

"It was a barrier to keep magical things inside it and to suppress magic unwanted by the caster. It too is powerful magic." Reid ran his hand

147

through his hair, leaving the longer strands leaning in the wrong direction. "That demon couldn't have left that cavern."

It wouldn't be hunting them down. With those words, a weight lifted from her chest. "Still, the tunnel the demon returned to was too small for humans and too steep. If the apostate were down there, he would've had to go in a different way."

Reid's brows came together. "Which means there is another way down there from the castle."

"If the caster is indeed in the castle."

He glanced at her with suspicion.

She continued, "Those were old caverns. For all we know, the summoner lives down there. There might not be an opening to those caverns for miles."

Reid's gaze drifted into the fire, thinking. "To leash a demon is dangerous and foolish. It will sooner devour its master than anyone else."

She nodded, although she had little experience. From that night in the cavern, she believed him. She would be content with never seeing, hearing, smelling, or being in any contact whatsoever with a demon again.

Reid's gaze flickered to the thin white line across her throat. The scar would be minimal, if at all there against her pale skin. Just like the others. His eyes lingered on it, and she felt the skin there prickle.

"I'm starting to think that being a royal protector is more trouble than it's worth." She tried to smile. "The king isn't paying me enough for all of this. Being a thief didn't include nearly as much heroism."

He returned her smile, but it looked as hollow as hers felt. "You never chased a demon into the sewers?"

"Oh, no, it was usually me who got chased into the sewers by the City Watch."

He laughed. "That's another reason why you can't leave the castle. Some of the Watch might recognize you."

"I'm surprised no one has." She leaned back into the cushy chair and fingered her black hair. "I've been told that I am a rare and distinguishable beauty."

"Who told you that?" His tone was dry, but he smiled.

She huffed in pretend offense. "More than one person, just so you know."

He laughed again, harder this time, more genuine.

✦

That afternoon, Reid left to attend the knight's meeting. He offered to station a guard inside Juniper's chambers, but she refused. She didn't want a stranger in her room, guard or no. Reid didn't argue with her, but she heard him order an extra guard outside her door.

When had he become so fussy?

Juniper began a routine of simple stretches and exercises, the same she had done nearly every day at Maddox's keep. Her arms, her legs, her back—all of her had weakened. She couldn't do the same number of repetitions as before, and she felt the strain much faster.

Had that poison taken so much out of her?

She was hauling her chin to the bathing room door when she heard the door to the sitting room open. Five more. Her arms burned. Four more. Sweat dripped down her spine. Three more. The door to the bedroom opened, but she didn't look to see Reid walk in. Two more. Her arms felt like dough. One more. She couldn't do any more—just one more.

She dropped to the floor.

"Look at you!"

She turned; it was not Reid standing in her bedroom. It was Adrian.

His eyes were sparkling. He wore a fine gold and white tunic with a red sash embroidered with the royal seal. He must have come from a meeting, or at least somewhere he had to look official.

Juniper shrugged, loosening her shoulders. "I can't let my body go to waste, now can I? All this southern food is making my dresses tight. Father won't be happy if none of my clothes fit when I return."

Guards stood in the sitting room, no doubt, extra guards if Destry had joined the knight's meeting.

Adrian's lips stretched into a wicked smile that sent gooseflesh along her sweaty scalp. He pushed off the bedpost. His hazel eyes scanned her body. "That would be a travesty."

"Did you come alone?" she purred.

"I asked my guard to wait outside. I didn't think you would appreciate so many intruding in your space." He took a few leisurely steps toward her. "How are you doing? Well, I assume, but I'd rather hear it from you."

"Better," she said, stretching out her wobbly arms. She then flexed them up to show off the muscle she had been carving.

Adrian's gaze wandered over her bare arms, and the corners of his sensual mouth turned upward. He let out a small chuckle. "I know Roslyn would love you. She once complained that the southern girls were too skinny, no meat on the bone."

"She's right," Juniper agreed in a sigh.

She leaned against the wall behind her, and Adrian joined her. He let out a carefree, calming sigh. Juniper met his eye, and she saw something there she hadn't before; she couldn't immediately identify it. Longing? As she watched him, the sunlight faded as clouds slipped in front of the sun, dousing her room in shadow.

"Is everything all right with you?" she asked.

He blinked; even his eyelashes moved with regal grace. "I miss her," he said softly.

Roslyn.

"You really love her?"

"I do," he said, no hesitation. "I knew it from the moment I saw her. I know how childish it sounds, but I saw her, and the world vanished. It was just the two of us in that ballroom." Something liquefied in his eyes. "I love Roslyn, but..."

"But what?"

He let out a slow sigh. Juniper caught the sweet, sweet scent of wine on his breath. "She's there, and I'm here," he whispered. "Her father hates me. My mother hates her. While I hate to admit it, a part of me knows we will never be able to be together. The politics of our parents will inevitably keep us apart. She would never be happy down here, and I know I'd hate the north. Besides, my place is here. I will succeed my father."

Maybe she had been reading too many romantic adventures, but the whole thing seemed utterly obvious to her. "So, that's it?" she asked him.

His eyebrows rose at her tone.

"You're going to let her go because you don't think it would work out? You haven't even tried."

He studied her a moment and then said, "I know. I know. You're right." He ran a hand through his blond hair and let it fall back into place, a bit disarrayed. "You're right."

"Has Roslyn ever been here before?"

"No."

"Then how do you know she'd hate it?" Juniper met his gaze and raised her brows in question. "She might enjoy Rusdasin, especially if you're here. She might be just what the kingdom needs."

He blinked at her. "You might be right about that too." He laughed genuinely. "Look at me, taking romantic and political advice from you."

"What's the city come to?" She returned his smile.

"All this romantic advice wouldn't have anything to do with those smutty books you read, now would it?" Adrian's smile grew.

Heat flooded her cheeks. She stuttered and stumbled over her words, "I don't know what you're talking about." She cleared her throat and glanced behind her into the bathing room. Adrian chuckled, and her face became warmer still. "Reid told you?"

"He did," Adrian said, his tone casual. "Remarkable how often he speaks of you. And sometimes even fondly."

Her face heated like fire. Why did it matter to her that Reid told Adrian about her? He would have to report to the king about her too. It shouldn't matter, but it did.

Adrian started to speak, and the window creaked. The shade in her room changed. Darkened. Her heart fell into her stomach. Juniper twisted her body toward the window, and she saw it before the image registered: the window slightly open; the long, boney fingers pulling it upward; and the shadow on the other side of the glass blocking out the sunlight. A snout poked through the open window.

Every hair on her body rose. Her blood froze. "Adrian!"

CHAPTER TWENTY-EIGHT

Reid hated meetings, and this one had been especially taxing.

He stood in front of the Council of the Order and retold his story of chasing the demon into the sewers. The dark stone walls of the circular chamber made him feel small and too large at the same time, and his voice echoed.

He had carefully plotted Roslyn's part in the tale, of how she pointed out the sewer grate to him while they had taken a walk, and how he had put the pieces together, not her.

Knight Commander Fowler sat in the center of the council. When Reid's story finished, he spoke in his calm, knowing voice, strong despite his old age.

"You followed a trail of blood to the passage?"

"Yes."

"From the wound that you inflicted on the demon?"

"Yes, sir."

Fowler stared at him, his eyes thinking, debating. Reid had always suspected the old man disliked him for his lack of reputable lineage, but Fowler treated all the squires the same, like they were unworthy of his presence.

Fowler said, "The knights did not find your passage when they returned to the location you mentioned. You led them there, correct?"

"Yes, sir."

"Our apostate is getting crafty," Fowler said to the Council. "He knows we are looking for him. He will no doubt know that Reid stumbled into his territory."

Reid held in his anger at the tone. *Stumbled*. Like he hadn't meant to, like he hadn't been intelligent enough to have done it on his own. Sir Darvel, standing near the back wall, seemed to gather the same from the Knight Commander's remark and winked at Reid.

Don't let the old man get to you, Darvel had said many times over the years. *He's been cranky since they made him retire.*

Reid was not the only squire. Two others, Henry Julian and Penet Berwick, attended the meeting. Neither of them spoke nor dared move while the Council discussed the demons, the culprit, and what Reid's discovery meant.

"We'll have to keep an eye on the prince while we investigate the caverns," said Sir Hogarth, a beefy man in his late fifties with a thick black beard and a thicker neck.

He glanced toward Destry, who nodded. "The sooner this meeting is over, the sooner he will be under watch. I don't trust the Royal Guard to be able to handle a demon. They've already proven themselves useless. First the thief in the Royal Chambers, and now demons. They're slipping."

Reid dared not breathe a word about the thief. That other thief had escaped, to the guard's disliking, and to the king's luck. It had been easier to keep Juniper a secret when everyone thought the thief had escaped. It made Reid wonder if they had let the second thief escape on purpose.

"They're not trained for demons," argued Sir Ashwin, a former Royal Guard. "They are made for swordplay, not fighting demons. That is why the Order exists."

The meeting seemed to go one for hours. Back and forth, the knights argued of what to do, where to search, what precautions to take, what wards to place around the Royal Chambers, and whether the king would allow a charm to be cast on Adrian. The knight commander firmly ended that discussion.

Finally, the meeting ended. By the time Reid, Henry, and Penet were walking into the barracks, they all needed to let out the steam from standing silent for far too long.

"Don't you have a lady to get back to?" Henry asked, his lips curling at Reid.

"She'll be fine without me for a while longer." Reid cracked his neck as he approached the sparring ring. He had positioned extra guards at her door, one of whom knew who she was. Besides, he needed something to do with his hands.

Reid grabbed one of the dulled practice swords from the rack and flourished it at Henry.

Henry laughed. "I've been practicing while you've been playing nursemaid."

"Then prove it." Reid took a stance in the ring.

Henry grabbed a sword, tested its weight, and stepped into the ring. Penet stood beside the ring, eager to watch either get their ass handed to them and to fight in the next round.

Reid rolled his neck along his shoulders. Henry had joined the Order a month after Reid, and they had spent many hours practicing their swordplay against one another.

They surged toward each other, dulled blades clanking. They danced about the ring; Reid countered; Henry feinted; they parried. Neither landed a blow. Henry moved with an expert's dexterity and grace, but Reid kept up with him. Then, at last, Reid saw his chance. He feinted; he knocked his sword against Henry's side.

"Ha!" Darvel laughed as he walked up into the practice rings. He beamed at Reid. "Well done, Reid. Don't fret, Henry. It will take a few years before you can defeat Reid on the battlefield. He's got his uncle's blood in him."

Reid nodded, trying not to let the compliment burn through his cheeks. "Thank you, sir."

"Give me a year, or a few months," Henry said with a shrug of his broad shoulders, cocky grin wide. He pushed his sandy hair out of his eyes. "I'll catch up to you. Then maybe the king will make me the royal nursemaid."

Reid frowned.

Darvel laughed and clapped Reid on the shoulder. "I doubt His Majesty would allow you to be anyone's nursemaid, Henry. And remember who you're fighting. Reid here was partially trained by Captain Sandpiper, by far the best swordsman I've known."

Reid felt a surge of pride at the statement. His uncle had refused to accept anything less than perfection from blood, and Reid had refused anything less of himself. A knight did not settle for subpar, and neither would he.

"Still," Darvel said, hand on Reid's shoulder. "I'm not surprised that you've kept up your stamina." He winked.

Henry and Penet howled with laughter.

Reid pushed off his hand and allowed himself a chuckle. Did they all assume he had already bedded Roslyn? Did they think that little of him? Or her?

"What did you do to be appointed nursemaid to the prince's sweetheart?" Henry set the practice sword back into its place on the rack.

"Is that jealousy I detect, Squire Julian?" Reid smirked. He wouldn't trust Henry to stand in Juniper's room. He would be the sort to insist he guard her while she bathed. Juniper, however, would be the sort to insist that he fall onto her blade.

"I could do without the frilly bitches." Henry shrugged. "I just thought all that standing around and following her like a lapdog would be hard on your battle sense. But, as Darvel pointed out, it hasn't bothered your stamina." His fierce eyes pinned Reid, smirking.

Reid didn't let it bother him. He chuckled. "It's not the frills, Henry. It's what's *underneath* the frills that counts."

Henry, Penet, and Darvel howled. Between their laughter, a commotion started on the other side of the practice hall. Someone yelled, a boy.

"What's that?" Darvel said, smile fading.

A fearful young guard, barely a man, stumbled into the practice hall. He gasped for breath.

"What is it, boy?" an older guard demanded, bending down. The lounging guards took notice, looking away from their half-drunk tankards, card games, and dice.

"An attack," gasped the boy, glancing at Darvel, then at Reid, then at the guard beside him. "A demon... Prince Adrian..."

The floor fell away from his feet. Reid didn't wait to hear anything else. He bolted around Darvel, through the gathering crowd, and into the corridor, running as fast as he possibly could.

He should have gone straight back there after the meeting.

If anything happened, it would be his fault.

CHAPTER TWENTY-NINE

Juniper shoved Adrian away. He stumbled into the wall; she felt the bruise starting underneath her shoulder blade where he'd smacked into something.

The demon slithered into the room through the window, body unfurling like a shadow. It let out a low growl and bared its teeth at her as if it knew she was the only thing standing in its way. It stepped toward her, sizing her up, narrowing its eyes, snapping its yellow teeth.

The demon lunged. She dropped into a forward roll as it came at her, and shoved her feet upward, into the soft underbelly of the beast. It yelped and careened to the side. She didn't wait to see where it landed; she reached for the iron fire poker from beside the hearth.

Not a sword or a dagger, but the end looked sharp enough. It would have to do.

The demon flopped and rolled, banging against the bed. It came at her again, jaw stretching to tear into her, and she shouted as she slammed the iron poker into the beast's head, not nearly hard enough to kill it, but hard enough to push its head out of the killing trajectory it had been on.

Footsteps shuffled in the sitting room—the guard. The demon lunged at the door, kicked at the handle, breaking it off—preventing anyone else from getting inside.

Her panic rose hot and feverish. The demon was smart enough to break a doorknob. It meant to kill her. Adrian too. With her being the only obstacle between the demon and Adrian, she didn't feel very confident about her odds.

The guards slammed against the bedroom door. The wood near the hinges groaned. No time. The demon came at her, teeth bared. She lunged; she had one shot. She thrust the poker up, aiming it like an arrow. She thrust all her strength behind it.

The demon lunged; the poker hit home. The sharper end of the poker rammed through the demon's mouth and smashed upward into its skull, propelled by the demon's lunge. Cracking, crushing, and squishing.

Dark blood spat from the wound. With a gut-wrenching yelp, the demon yanked its head to the side, ripping the poker out of her hands; one of its longer fangs sliced through her arm. She felt the poison burn on her skin, worming through her bloodstream. Yet it didn't feel as powerful; the burning seemed to vanish as she thought about it.

The demon stumbled. It grabbed the poker and yanked but couldn't dislodge it. Juniper reeled back and kicked the demon's chest, sending it crashing onto the floor. It kicked and yelped and whimpered, but the iron poker lodged in its skull stayed firm. Juniper didn't feel remotely bad about not killing it outright. Let the monster suffer.

Juniper stumbled backward; her back hit the wall. Adrian remained where she'd pushed him. His face had gone deathly pale. He stared unblinking at the demon's flailing body.

The door gave one final whine and burst, falling inward with a ripping of wood. Reid charged through, sword drawn. With one heave of his sword, the demon's head parted from its body. The head clanked to the floor, iron poker preventing it from rolling. The body collapsed.

And it was over.

Juniper sank to the floor. The demon's body shook, stilled, then dissolved into black ash. The iron poker clattered onto the floor.

Juniper glanced down at her arm. The demon's tooth hadn't dug as deep as she thought. It had barely grazed her at all. Even as she looked, the scrape seemed to vanish... No, it had gone deeper than that.

Adrian's sharp inhale made her heart sink. He cradled his arm. Blood was seeping into his sleeve, in the same spot where the fang had scraped her. She crawled to him and shoved his sleeve up. Her heart turned over.

There, on his creamy skin, a wound had appeared. Was appearing. It seared slowly into his flesh, breaking apart the skin as if a blade was being dragged across. In the exact spot the demon's tooth had grazed her.

The guards examined the demon's remains. They were shouting orders for servants, for the healers, for the king to hear of it at once.

Juniper looked up at Adrian, and he met her worried, confused look with his own.

"I'm sorry I pushed you," she whispered.

He nodded. His lips parted, but no words came out.

Reid stalked over to them, sword bloody.

"What the hell happened?" Reid demanded. His burning bronze eyes went from Juniper to Adrian, to the cut on Adrian's arm. The cut that hadn't healed, hadn't transferred. "A healer. We need the healer now. The prince needs her attention."

Reid stood by Juniper and Adrian as the servants quickly cleaned up the room and as the healer made quick work of Adrian's arm.

When the worst had been dealt with, Reid pulled Juniper aside.

"It came in through the window," Juniper whispered breathlessly.

"Why did you leave it unlocked?" Reid snapped.

She met his gaze. "I didn't."

He did not look at all happy at her answer. She knew he double-checked her windows every evening before he left; he knew those windows would have been locked. The demon had unlocked the window from the outside.

No room in the castle was safe.

CHAPTER THIRTY

Reid stood guard by the window. The demon had *unlocked* a window. By magic. This changed things.

He shouldn't have left. He should not have shirked his duty like that. Adrian had been hurt because of it. Not just his prince, but his friend, had been hurt. Could have died. They both could have. He could feel the lingering chill left by the beast, just as its vile scent tainted the air.

They had moved into the sitting room while the servants cleaned up the mess in the bedroom. Juniper sat in the chair by the hearth, fingers knotted together. Adrian sat beside her, sleeve torn and arm bandaged. Adrian's wound hadn't transferred. By the way Juniper kept fingering the identical spot on her arm, he suspected the worst. It had been inflicted on her. Her wound had transferred to Adrian.

Juniper had fought the beast, had been able to keep it back, had driven that poker through its skull. Despite everything, Reid felt a bit of pride at her for it.

He would speak when the servants finished in the other room, when the three of them were alone. Of course, it would be hard with Destry standing by the door, solemn and stoic as a statue. He too must have felt the shame at having the demon attack while they had been away.

One of them had to stay with Adrian and Juniper at all times. No excuses.

But the timing... He couldn't be the only one to suspect it. The demon had attacked when all the knights had been occupied. The apostate knew about the meeting, knew that Adrian wouldn't be as well guarded, and knew that he had gone to Juniper's chambers instead of his own.

The apostate was in the castle or had eyes in the castle. No doubt about it now.

He'd like to see the court magician weasel his way out of this one.

The four of them sat in silence as the servants cleaned the bedroom. Finally, when the ash had been swept, the blood had been scrubbed, the sheets had been changed, and incense had been set to burn the unpleasantness from the air, Juniper walked into the bathing room without a word.

Reid followed her and stood in the bedroom doorway. The doorway that no longer had a door. The incense smelled strongly of citrus and pine.

Behind him, Destry shifted on his feet.

"I think it's time we talked," said Destry. He escorted a silent Adrian into the bedroom.

When Juniper exited the bathing room, she merely blinked at the three men waiting for her.

Destry grumbled, "What the hell is going on?"

Reid said, "We need to speak with the court magician and the king. At once."

✦

Less than an hour later, Juniper stood in front of the court magician's large desk. Reid stood between her and Adrian, and Destry glared at her from the other side of Adrian. Captain Sandpiper stood by the door, looking so much like his nephew with his furrowed brow and straight-line mouth. King Bradburn stood on the other side of the desk, beside Mason Hobbs.

"This is all of us," said the king. His hazel eyes focused on Juniper, eyes that so resembled his son's, only colder. "Explain what happened. Exactly what happened."

Juniper opened her mouth but glanced at Destry. Confusion and anger had whittled away at his stoic mask.

"Don't worry about him," the king said, his voice softer. "I trust that he will understand."

Destry glanced from Juniper to the king, brows knitted.

The king didn't engage. He motioned to Juniper. "Speak."

"Adrian came to see me." Juniper swallowed and left out the bits that no one needed to know. "I saw it unlock the window. The demon. I used what I had to fight it." She touched her arm where the tooth had torn through her skin. "When I impaled it, one of its teeth scratched me."

"The wound transferred?" Mason Hobbs asked. His bushy white brows rose high on his forehead. He shook his head. "No, no, that's not how the spell was designed. I know. I spent days sorting out the equation."

"Then, please explain why her injury is currently on my son's arm." The king's tone felt like ice in the room.

Destry remained silent, but his eyes darted between Juniper, Adrian, and the court magician.

Mason shook his head. "I designed the spell to transfer his wounds to her, not the other way around. It has worked up until now, correct?"

Juniper nodded.

"Then why has it suddenly stopped working tonight?" Mason asked.

"You tell me. It is your spell," said the king.

Mason Hobbs met the king's eye. He nodded. He turned to a glass-front cabinet behind his desk. Through the doors, Juniper spotted a stack of scrolls identical to her binding spell. Mason waved his hand in front of the cabinet, and a heavy lock clicked open. No keyhole was visible on the cabinet; he'd unlocked it by magic.

He'd unlocked the cabinet by magic, just as someone had unlocked her window.

Juniper glanced briefly at Reid. He met her eye; he thought the same.

Mason opened the doors and carefully retrieved the top scroll. With a wave of his hand, the books on his desk returned to the bookshelf, and the scroll magically unrolled and flattened on the desk. Mason let out an angry huff immediately. Juniper blinked at the archaic slashes and symbols. It looked the same as it had the night she had signed it.

"What is it?" King Bradburn demanded. He looked over the scroll as if he could find the answer.

"Someone has altered the spell." Mason seethed. He pointed to the scroll but did not touch it. "See here, the final part of the equation, originally Adrian's blood signed the giver's side, and Juniper's blood signed the taker's side."

"Yes, I remember." King Bradburn nodded.

"Someone has added Adrian's blood to the taker's side and Juniper's to the giver's side. It is not a clean alteration... Did the wound not transfer completely?" The court magician's eyes flashed to Juniper.

She lifted her sleeve to show him her arm. A scratch remained where the demon's tooth had sliced. "No."

"I see." Mason glared at the scratch on Juniper's arm and the bandage on Adrian's.

"Who could have altered the spell?" The king's cold gaze lingered on Juniper's arm. His brow furrowed, and he shifted that accusative glance to her face.

He blamed her? How? She couldn't have possibly altered that spell! And, more importantly, how had someone gotten samples of her blood?

Reid stepped ever so slightly closer to her.

The court magician shook his head. He focused on the scroll, eyes calculating. "The lock on the cabinet has not been broken or tampered with. The only evidence of the alteration lies in the scroll itself. The seal has been defiled."

"Someone altered the spell without opening the cabinet?" Captain Sandpiper looked skeptical.

Mason nodded. "To do so would require powerful magic. I have wards against people entering my study with intent to harm. It would seem that not only did someone alter the spell without opening the cabinet, but they did so without stepping foot inside my office."

Captain Sandpiper stepped forward. "The only person capable of such magic would be you, Court Magician."

The court magician frowned as he beheld the captain. "I suppose that is true."

"What of your apprentice?" Destry asked.

"Ison is a talented mage, but he lacks the power required to perform such magic. If you doubt me, Knight, check his records at the Marca. You will find his scores in magic casting to be low." Mason glared at the knight, a silent challenge.

"If it is not any of the mages we know are in the castle," Reid interrupted, his voice calm, albeit a bit worried, "then our original suspicions of an apostate hold true. This apostate might be working to frame Mason for his deeds."

"I agree." Destry nodded, to Juniper's surprise. He looked at the court magician. "We've had knights watching you both. If you or your apprentice had been summoning demons, it would have left a trail. The knights would have known."

"And yet you've found nothing." Mason didn't seem surprised that knights had been following him.

"However"—Destry regarded the court magician coolly—"the only person who can justify your claim that no one entered this office is you. How do we know you are not lying to protect yourself or your apprentice? Or the true apostate? I do not put it past you to help an apostate."

"What motive would I have for assisting a murderous apostate?" Mason straightened his shoulders. He matched Destry's glare. For a moment, the two men stared at each other, one clad in armor and armed with Mage's Bane, the other clad only in mage's robes, although Juniper doubted the court magician of Duvane needed weapons to inflict bodily damage. "I wish to keep my job and my life, Knight. I do not put up with

162

such nonsense as black magic. I can guarantee you that if I discovered my own apprentice partaking in such arts, I would sooner slit his throat myself."

"Enough," growled the king. The chamber silenced. "I trust Mason to tell me the truth, Sir Destry."

Destry nodded once. He said no more.

"And there is still the problem of the apostate trying to murder my son. Sir Destry, I gather you have put the pieces together by now."

He nodded. He glanced at Juniper with dislike. "You've taken in a criminal to protect your son and disguised her for secrecy. Any father would have done the same."

King Bradburn nodded. "Please, refrain from asking anyone outside this room anything. The fewer people who know about our situation, the better."

"Understood."

"Mason," said the king, "I must ask the knights to stand guard by you."

The court magician nodded. "I will rest easier when this fiend is caught as well. I will explain it to Ison when he returns."

"Where has he gone?" asked Captain Sandpiper.

"I sent him to the market for supplies," the court magician answered shortly. "There are some ingredients I don't trust to simple couriers. Some are rather volatile."

The king said to Destry, "I want you beside my son at all times." He turned his gaze to Adrian. "I do not care where you go. I want a knight and a dozen guards within arm's reach of you in case another beast attacks." He snapped his attention to Reid, not even glancing at Juniper. "Squire Sandpiper, do not let her out of your sight."

Reid nodded. "Yes, Your Majesty."

Her. Such distaste in a single word. As if she had done nothing to save his son and everything to throw him headfirst into the jaws of the demon. Juniper had pushed the thought of stealing the king's crown out of her mind, but she entertained the thought again. When she got out of this mess, she would take it with her.

If she got out.

CHAPTER THIRTY-ONE

Reid escorted Juniper out of the meeting and toward her chambers. His uncle walked beside him. They walked in silence until they reached the corridor where they would part. One hall led to the Royal Chambers; another led to the barracks.

"Your aunt misses you," said his uncle. "She's complaining about how little we see each other when we work within walking distance of you. She wants to have dinner."

"Of course," Reid said, nodding. "Name the night, Uncle, and I will be there."

"Your duty will not keep you?"

Juniper let out the smallest of sounds.

Reid didn't answer immediately. *Don't let her out of your sight.*

His uncle paused, waiting for his answer.

"No," Reid answered.

"Dinner, then," said his uncle. "I will inform your aunt. She'll be delighted."

The captain glanced at Juniper, who had kept her eyes to the floor for the better part of the walk. His uncle didn't bother to hide his distaste, just as Destry hadn't when he had realized who she was.

After a quick goodbye, Reid and Juniper started toward the Royal Chambers. Reid could have sworn Juniper released a sigh of relief.

The servants had filled her chambers with scented candles and oils to banish the lingering stench of demon ash. Juniper meandered into her bedroom, holding her scratched arm.

Don't let her out of your sight.

Reid hesitated in her bedroom doorway. Someone had taken the broken door, the door that he had assisted in breaking down. He barely remembered it; he'd heard the demon on the other side, heard Juniper shout. He didn't remember the door, although a large bruise on his shoulder suggested that he'd used himself as a battering ram.

"I can't say when another door will be installed," Reid said, picking at the stone where the door had been ripped from the hinges.

Juniper didn't respond. She glanced at the floor where the door had been, her face vacant. Her black hair had fallen from its braid. Sweat had dried on her skin, scrunching the loose hairs around her face.

"Are you all right?"

It took her a long moment to respond. "I've fought bandits and cutthroats and assassins, but nothing..." She met his eye. Her voice became a whisper. "I've never been so afraid before. I thought...I thought it would kill us both."

"It didn't," Reid said, taking a step closer. She had skewered it on an iron poker. "It is theorized that some demons can instill fear into their enemies."

"Do you think that's what happened?" She clutched her shirt. "You weren't afraid of it."

"You know that for certain?" He lifted his brows. He closed the space between them until he stood within arms' reach of her. "In truth, I was terrified. I was terrified that I would be too late, that when I got the door open, I would find corpses and a demon with a full stomach. It isn't that I wasn't afraid, but that I knew I needed to act in order to prevent that fear from happening."

"It hit the door so no one could come in. It knew what to do in order to trap us in here with it." Her fists tightened, whitening. "Someone altered the binding spell. Someone sent that demon here, to my room. It came at me first. It knew." Her brow scrunched. "Why?"

He didn't have an answer. He desperately wanted one to give her, to soothe that worry in her eyes, but he didn't have one.

Reid unbuckled one of the daggers at his waist. The same dagger he'd given her to defend herself before. He handed it to her. "It makes for a better weapon than a poker, although you did a decent job with one of those."

She gave him a small, hollow smile and took the dagger. She coiled her slender fingers around the sheath. She glanced toward the window, now latched, where the evening stained the sky purple and gold. The emptiness in her eyes hardened.

"I will make sure the bastard behind all this gets what he deserves," she said darkly.

"We will find him and end him," Reid assured her. She turned her gaze back to him, and he felt a shudder; hardened eyes and ill-intent gave her a madness, one that belonged on wanted posters and behind bars. He fought the urge to reach for his sword, if only for the comfort.

He had never seen eyes quite like hers. Dark blue like midnight. Flecked with tiny stars of silver.

Juniper meandered to the bed and hid the dagger underneath her pillow, then started toward the bathing room. Reid started to turn, to step out of the bedroom, when Juniper spoke: "Whoever has resorted to summoning demons for parlor tricks, they're either a monster or demented. Who would be so bitter against the prince?"

Reid's thoughts went first to the court magician, but he didn't have an answer as to why he would want Adrian dead. "I've heard Adrian has left more than a few broken hearts about the country," Reid said. He half laughed. "It is possible that he scorned the wrong woman in his adventuring. One of his former paramours might have taken it upon herself to right the wrong. Or *himself*. I wouldn't put it past Adrian to go exploring."

Juniper rolled her eyes as a calm laugh escaped her lips. "You think our demon-summoning apostate might be an ex-boyfriend? I could have sworn the prince preferred women."

"Oh, he does." Reid laughed. "But he's also the curious type."

She laughed, a genuine, friendly, heart-melting laugh that made him want to take her to the bed and show her his preferences. He lingered in the bedroom as she fetched fresh clothes from the dressing room and lit a few extra candles in the bathing room.

She reached for the door handle.

"Just for reference..." he said.

She paused, glancing over her shoulder at him.

He hesitated a beat before asking, savoring the pregnant air between them. "Men or women?"

She blushed pink, then winked and shut the door.

The following morning, Juniper bullied Reid into taking her for a walk about the castle. The sky was a clear, bittersweet blue, and she wanted to visit a courtyard, any courtyard, to get her fill of the spring air. Her lungs had been inhaling the stuffy air of the stone castle too long. She'd wanted to go back to the sewer grate, but Reid refused; if she sustained any injury, even a scratch or a bruise, it would transfer to Adrian.

Before they had even reached the courtyard, Juniper counted twenty knights.

166

"I didn't realize there were so many of you," she said to Reid as they passed a grumpy-looking knight with flaming red hair.

"I don't know exactly how many knights there are at a given time," Reid said. "They can't leave the Marca unguarded, so there are even more. They are scattered about the kingdom too."

Hunting mages, is what he didn't have to add. She knew. Every week, more apostates were cut down, and more young mages were brought to the Marca.

They left the Royal Chambers, and a short walk later, a pleasant, chilled breeze greeted her as they walked into the courtyard. She took a deep breath and closed her eyes to feel the sun on her face.

"At what point in a mage's life does the Marca consider them apostate?" she asked.

Reid blinked at her. "What do you mean?"

"Say a child grew up a mage but never went to the Marca, not because they were evading it, but because they knew no better? A five-year-old child is considered a mage, but if that same child is twenty, they are considered an apostate?"

Reid nodded. "I suppose that is something for the judgment of the knights who find the mage. Although, in this day and age, it is difficult for a mage not to have heard of the Marca. They should know, by twenty, that they are a mage and that the Marca exists. Those who reject the idea become apostate."

"Even if they've not done anything wrong?"

He nodded. "The Order defines an apostate as a mage who rejects the Marca."

"Even if it's not a rejecting but a declining?"

He glanced at her, brows raised.

"Can't a mage accept that the Marca exists without going to it?"

"That's rejecting it."

"It's declining the invitation."

"It's not an invitation," Reid said firmly. He curled his fingers into fists, then relaxed. "A mage needs to be taught how to use their magic."

"You don't see how that could be considered a form of imprisonment?"

A trio of servants walked past. They paused briefly to bow their heads to Lady Roslyn. She nodded back, though not as low.

Reid pulled her to a stop. "Are you defending the very people who have produced the person who has nearly killed you three times?"

"How many killers have come from non-magical people?" Juniper fought to not curl her hands into fists. "Yet we do not herd them into camps."

Reid huffed. Footsteps sounded in the corridor behind them, and he pulled her along the courtyard's walkway.

"I'm sorry if my confusion on the subject bothers you," she said.

He shook his head. "I've seen what apostates can do when unchecked. What kind of power they have... It is different from a sword."

Reid looked like he might say something else when a wad of smoke exploded from the corner ahead of them. No, not smoke—a girl in a layered dress of pale gray and white. At the sight of Juniper, her overly-painted face broke into a wide, court-trained smile.

"Oh, Lady Derean!" she chirped. "It is a pleasure to meet you."

"Lady Nadine Dudley," Reid said in quick greeting, more so to Juniper than Lady Dudley. He looked as thrilled to see her as he had Juniper that night in the dungeons.

Juniper gave a small bow of her head, adding, "Lady Dudley."

Despite her outward cheeriness, Lady Dudley's eyes looked at Juniper with all the friendliness of a pissed off snake. Juniper forced herself calm. If this were the Undercity, she would have killed Lady Dudley for such a stare or, at least, left her a bloody pulp on the ground.

"Taking a walk about the courtyard?" Lady Dudley asked.

"I am," Juniper answered, and she thought quick: what would a lady do in this situation? They loved to mingle and gossip. "Care to join me?"

Lady Dudley's eyes brightened, and she looped her arm with Juniper's. Her stout floral perfume wafted, but Juniper kept her face well-humored. They started a slow meander along the courtyard. Reid followed a safe distance behind, looking murderous.

"Not the talkative sort, is he?" Lady Dudley asked, tilting her head toward Reid.

"Oh, my dear lady," Juniper said, faking exhaustion. "You have no idea! You can't imagine what a bore he's been. So serious all the time."

Lady Dudley laughed. "All the knights are like that, I'm afraid. They refuse to stop and talk. Not at all friendly like the Royal Guard."

"Squire Sandpiper has refused my requests to go into the city," Juniper whined. "I haven't heard a single word of news or gossip since I arrived."

Reid let out a low huff. Lady Dudley noticed, and both girls giggled.

"Please, kind lady, tell me what's happening in this city!" Juniper wiggled Lady Dudley's pudgy arm.

Lady Dudley puffed herself up with importance; women like her loved to hear how important they were and how important what they said was. Juniper had learned that early. It didn't extend just to the rich either, but all women loved to be important, loved to be the conveyor of news.

"Well," said Lady Dudley, "the entire kingdom is raving about these..." she dropped her voice to a whisper, "demon attacks. It's been absolutely dreadful what's nearly happened to you! Everyone is on edge in the city. Everyone is petrified that we'll get the news of our prince's murder."

"I've heard mention that it is his evil twin."

Lady Dudley laughed. "I've heard that myself. No one knows, which is why everyone is talking about it. The knights can't even figure it out!" Lady Dudley glanced over her shoulder at Reid. "Obviously, it's something far stranger."

Juniper wouldn't deny that. "What is happening in the world? I feel like I've been locked up here, without any news at all."

Lady Dudley patted her arm sympathetically. "Well, there are rumors of rebels from northern Collatia causing trouble. Some say it's one of them causing trouble in the castle, for revenge on the king. He sided with the south in the war, you know. The City Watch have apprehended a few of them in the city too, but they've tried to keep it as hush-hush as possible."

"Collatian rebels in Rusdasin?" Juniper pretended to be shocked.

Lady Dudley nodded grimly. "And they've got all that dark magic too."

"Perhaps they want to plunge Duvane into a war for spite," Juniper suggested. "It is hard to believe that some people in this world are that dreadfully spiteful."

"Oh, I agree, Lady Derean."

"No need for the formalities," Juniper crooned. "Friends don't refer to each other by their titles."

Lady Dudley beamed. "Of course, Roslyn."

"Nadine."

They rounded the corner and Nadine glanced back at Reid. "He is the serious sort. Does he ever smile?"

"Rarely," Juniper said, glancing back at Reid's scowl. "I've told him he's prettier when he does, but he doesn't listen to me."

Nadine glanced at Reid, and both girls giggled as Reid blushed.

They passed the open doors of a corridor, and Juniper opened her mouth to ask a nosy question, but her words vanished—a pinprick of pain started on her thigh. It blossomed into a searing pain, something pushing its way into her body.

She gasped, released Nadine's arm, and fell into the cool stone pillar that held up the veranda.

"Roslyn?" Reid appeared in a blink.

She couldn't breathe. The object in her thigh felt like steel, a thin blade. It slowly made its way down her thigh, burning her skin around it.

"I have to go...all this southern food," Juniper gasped to Nadine and started for the corridor. Away. She had to get away. She placed a hand over her stomach for emphasis. *Get out of the way or be puked on.*

Nadine flattened herself against the far wall. Reid grabbed Juniper's arm, and she fell into him. She felt the warmth of blood beading on her leg. Reid ushered her into the nearest corridor faster than she could walk on her own.

Not again. She begged any god who would listen.

CHAPTER THIRTY-TWO

Reid hauled Juniper into the first empty room he came to, a storage closet. He kicked the door closed and let go of her long enough to shove a broom handle against it. He didn't want Lady Dudley *accidentally* stumbling upon them like she had in the courtyard.

Juniper collapsed to the floor. The color had drained from her face. She stretched out her legs, and her shaking fingers started to pull up the skirt of her dress to assess the wound.

Not fast enough. Reid knelt down, grabbed a fistful of the hem, and yanked the skirt up to her hip. He immediately saw the long, bleeding wound that ran along the outside of her thigh. He touched her knee and tilted her leg to better see the wound while trying his best to see only the wound, not the pale flesh around it.

"It doesn't look to have struck anything vital," he whispered. No arteries, at least, or she would be bleeding much faster.

She trembled, fists curling in her dress. "Reid."

"Is it the poison?" He tore his eyes away from her leg to her face. She shook her head.

"I don't feel it," she whispered, voice raw with pain. "It's not poisoned. It was a blade. I felt it...not a talon. Not a demon."

"A blade?" Reid felt his heart flutter. Demons didn't carry blades. Unless they'd suddenly started. He didn't like that idea at all.

"Adrian?" she gasped.

"He has his guard and Sir Destry." Reid realized he still held her knee in his hand. He released her. "It doesn't look to be getting worse. Do you feel anything else?"

She shook her head. They waited a moment, a long moment of her bleeding, but no other wounds appeared on her person.

"It would appear the guards did their job." Reid looked again at the wound on her thigh. "We'll wrap this as best we can until we can send word to the healer."

She nodded. He cut strips out of her underdress and gently wrapped her thigh. If she felt invaded by his hands, she made no mention of it.

It was his duty, he told himself every time his brain reminded him of where his hands were and how close to other things they were.

He tied off the quick bandage. "It's staunched the bleeding, at least."

"Thank you."

He stood and carefully helped her to her feet. She tested weight on her leg and deemed it all right. Luckily, no blood had seeped through her dress. Reid opened the door first. Lady Dudley had not stuck around to snoop, and he walked into the corridor without notice. Juniper followed and took his arm in hers to better hide the limp.

They crossed into the Royal Chambers; the guards on either side of the doors gave them little notice other than a slight bow of their heads. The corridor beyond was quiet.

Juniper whispered, "Doesn't it seem quiet in here for having thwarted an assassination attempt?"

Reid glanced at the knights stationed at an intersection of two corridors. Neither had moved. They both looked remarkably bored. "Yes, but you need a healer."

"After I know Adrian is all right."

The sharpness of her tone irked him, but he knew there would be no arguing. On the way to Adrian's room, they passed three servants carrying empty tea trays. Reid stopped them and informed them to call for the healer to meet them in Lady Roslyn's chambers. The servants scurried off without a glance toward Juniper.

They came to Adrian's doors, guarded on either side by stiff-backed, pale-faced guards. Neither so much as moved as they approached. Reid opened his mouth, but a certain stench entered his nose. Juniper inhaled; she smelled it too. Bitter. Sickly. Sticky.

Blood.

Juniper limped to the first guard and put her hand against his chest. He didn't move.

"Dead." Juniper pointed to the guard's throat where a short, slender dagger had been wedged. Barely visible. "That's an assassin's trick. Keeps them standing. Enchanted to keep them from bleeding."

The other guard had received the same trick, it seemed.

Reid felt the color drain from his face, but he schooled his features into a stoic mask. Juniper reached for the door, and he unsheathed his blade. He held it ready, and Juniper opened the door. She didn't charge inside, but she paled at what she saw on the other side.

Adrian's guard scattered the sitting room. All dead.

Gods.

Juniper followed a step behind him, her midnight eyes scanning the shadows, the hiding places, the corners, and behind-spaces—quicker than a guard could. She stepped with caution. A thief's steps. She held herself in a mid-stance, ready to pounce or run.

This was Juniper Thimble the assassin-thief.

Reid made his way to the study; fewer bodies lay in there. No Adrian.

That left the bedroom. Juniper had come to the same conclusion. She, unarmed, made no motion to go first. Reid made for the bedroom, sword first.

One step into the bedroom, Reid froze. Adrian sat on the floor, slumped against his bedpost. A cut ran along his thigh, cutting through his pants, but his skin was intact. Transferred. At the sight of them, Adrian looked nearly grateful, but he looked sick. His hazel eyes flickered to the corner of his room where thick shadows gathered.

A subtle scent of silver polish and flowers lingered in the air, a combination of unnatural and natural magic. Once Reid and Juniper had crossed the threshold, the bedroom door slammed shut of its own accord. They both jumped.

"It *is* you," said the figure from the shadows.

Juniper froze. Her face paled.

A man stepped out of the shadow—no, the shadows around him dissolved. Magic. He wore shadow-black from head to foot, with only a sliver of his dark brown face visible. Blue-gray eyes shimmered at Juniper with amusement. Even from a distance, Reid spotted a dozen weapons on his person, daggers, throwing knives, and gods knew what else.

An assassin. A mage. An apostate.

Juniper spat, "Xavier."

"Jun," the assassin crooned. "Is that any way to greet your brother?"

Brother? Reid glanced only once at Juniper. She didn't look remotely pleased by her brother's presence.

"What are you doing here?" she demanded.

The smile vanished from Xavier's eyes. The ruthlessness of a seasoned assassin replaced it. His voice softened into a cold purr. "Checking in on you, dear sister. Maddox is worried about his little princess."

Juniper seethed. Her fingers twitched. She blinked—a strange calm came over her features. She straightened her shoulders and shrugged. "And here I am. Safe and sound. Now get out before I kill you."

"With that? I came armed to the teeth, and all you've got is..." He looked her up and down. His eyes glittered with amusement as he took in her dress and dyed hair.

She breathed, "It's enough to twist your head off your shoulders."

Reid's skin prickled at the ice in her voice. He'd never heard her speak like that.

Xavier chuckled, a mirthless sound. "How I've missed your temper!"

"I'm only going to tell you once more."

"Or what?" Xavier spat, his humor gone. "You'll sic your guard dog on me?" Those blue-gray eyes slid to Reid. "I'll do to him what I did to the others who got in my way. You saw how that turned out for them. Not even the king's knights could stand in my way."

Reid's blood froze.

Xavier noticed. He motioned to something on the other side of the room, behind Reid. Juniper stepped closer to Reid, eyes pinned on Xavier.

So he could look.

He glanced back. Whatever blood had retained heat in his body went cold.

There, against the wall leading to the bathing room, was Sir Colin. His throat had been slit. The blood seeped over his silver breastplate. A dagger poked out of the older knight's shoulder, another from his hip, all the weak places in the armor.

He'd killed a knight.

Reid schooled his face into neutrality, then looked back at the assassin. Xavier's blue-gray eyes glittered with amusement. Reid took a step forward; he would gut the bastard himself.

Juniper's hand landed on his chest. *Don't do it.* The impact lessened; her fingers were not rigid. It was a warning, not an order. Reid lowered his sword.

"Smart man," Xavier crooned. His eyes swept between Reid and Juniper. Then he laughed, a belittling laugh. "And here we all thought you'd given up your place among us to bed a prince. A squire too?" Xavier clicked his tongue. His cool eyes examined Reid. "You're just the castle plaything, aren't you? I'm surprised at you, Jun."

Juniper clenched her fists, then released them. She steadied herself and took half a step in front of Reid. Her hand slid down his chest, to his side, to the dagger at his waist—the dagger Xavier couldn't see. Her hand tightened around the hilt.

"I didn't intend to kill the prince. Just hurt him a little. Mostly to piss you off." Xavier's blue-gray eyes narrowed. "What happened?"

174

"Hm?" Juniper tilted her head as though she couldn't hear him.

"I cut the prince. Then it vanished. You're limping." Xavier's eyes traveled to Juniper's thigh. "That is interesting."

"Did he send you here to assassinate the prince or just piss me off?" Juniper's hand gently lifted the dagger. Slowly, as to not draw Xavier's attention to it.

Xavier chuckled. His cold eyes glanced from Adrian's leg to Juniper's. "I came to see you, dear sister. I've missed you. But you were busy with that frilly bitch in the courtyard. Your loyal hound wasn't far behind." Those glittering eyes flickered to Reid. "I saw the foolish prince open his window. I took my chance."

"Assassinating a prince? Without a paycheck? That's a fool's chance."

Reid stiffened. Juniper was digging Xavier for information. Clever.

"Not to kill," Xavier said, fingering a dark handle of a blade tucked into the leather at his side. "Just to...remind him of who you belong to. To remind you. Maddox doesn't like to share."

Juniper laughed. "Maddox, the king of thieves, is mad because someone stole something from him? I'm touched he cares enough to send someone to look after me."

"I've rarely seen him so angry." Xavier's head tilted downward. His eyes darkened. "When Amery came home to tell him that she'd seen you with the prince... On your way to the Temple of Bala, no less. I'm surprised she didn't smite you at the gates."

Juniper shrugged, the comment sliding off her shoulders.

Reid adjusted his grip of his sword. Xavier noticed but didn't move.

Juniper took a step toward Xavier. She slid the dagger further from the sheath. "Just get out. I'll come crawling back to Maddox when I'm finished. I might even tell him you helped."

Xavier seethed. He took a step; Juniper took a step. She slid the dagger from the sheath at his waist. In a blink, the thief and the assassin collided, blade to blade. Despite her wounded leg, she danced about the bedroom floor with Xavier, neither landing a blow.

He *hadn't* seen her with a dagger. Gods. She knew what she was doing. So did Xavier.

Reid adjusted his sword, ready to join the fight and end it, when a thudding came to the main door. A heavy hand, knocking.

Destry's voice came from the other side. "What is this?"

The door burst open. A sword unsheathed. Armored footsteps clamored inside, a curse spat at the bodies on the floor. Destry kicked down the door to the bedroom, face ashen but full of rage. In that moment, Juniper cried out; Xavier had landed a blow to her upper arm. Red bubbled into her ripped sleeve. Her eyes drifted to Adrian—with the small distraction, Xavier dashed behind her. He pressed his blade, already bloodied, to her throat.

"You threaten us with the life of a thief?" Destry half laughed, but it lacked the mirth. "Go ahead, Assassin. Kill the girl."

"Really?" Xavier's dark brows rose. He pressed the blade into her throat.

Adrian gasped and clutched at his neck; both Reid and Destry froze. Already, red leaked into the sleeve of Adrian's shirt.

Xavier laughed. "Strange magic you've got working here." His humor vanished. "Now get out of the way. Unless you're hard set on seeing this one dead."

No one moved. Xavier, holding Juniper in front of him, took small steps toward the door. Neither knight nor squire breathed too hard as the assassin walked between them, through the sitting room, and into the study.

That damned window. Reid would make sure it was sealed before the day ended.

In a flourish of shadow, Xavier shoved Juniper forward and dashed through the open window. Juniper caught herself on the edge of the desk. She and Reid rushed to the window—Xavier had already vanished.

"Shit," Destry spat. He slammed his fist into the wall, rattling the picture beside him.

Without Xavier there, Juniper took the weight off her wounded leg and leaned into Reid; her heart thumped erratically against his arm.

"Anyone else need a stiff drink?" Adrian asked from the bedroom doorway. Blood smeared his throat and his upper arm. His hazel eyes went glossy as he regarded the bodies on his floor. "And a few servants to clean up this mess." He ruffled his hair. "Better make that order into a few bottles. I fear it will be hard to sleep tonight."

Chapter Thirty-Three

Juniper sat up in her bed while the healer cleaned her wounded thigh. To better heal the leg, the healer had requested she remove her dress and underdress, which left Juniper sitting in nothing more than her underthings. They'd fixed her bedroom door while she'd been gone, and Reid stood beside it with his back to her, gazing intently out of the window.

The healer mumbled to herself, her brows furrowed. Her green magic prickled against her skin; the wound stitched together but did not entirely heal.

"An enchanted blade," mumbled the healer. "It's no match for me. The enchantment wasn't done correctly or very well by the looks of it. It doesn't matter." She quickly wrapped her leg. "You'll be better in a few days."

"Thank you." Juniper carefully swung her legs over the bedside. She limped into the dressing room, chose a simple dress, and shut herself into the bathing room. She washed herself as best she could around the bandage, dressed, and returned to the softness of the bed. A folding table awaited her with dinner.

Juniper settled the tray over her legs and uncovered her dishes; the delicious smells pushed any thought of Xavier from her mind and made her mouth water.

Reid remained by the window.

"Are you not eating?" Juniper swallowed a spoonful of the buttery soup. Delicious!

Reid turned, worry mixed with his unreadable seriousness. "Your brother?"

She blinked—what? Oh, she knew who he meant.

"We're not related by blood." She took another spoonful, then another. "When they sell kids in the Undercity, they sell them in groups. It's tradition for those in your group to be considered your siblings. Xavier and I were in the same group. Our kidnappers gave us the name Thimble."

"Do you consider him your brother?"

"In a sense." Juniper hesitated, staring into the dark wine. "But that doesn't mean I won't kill him if I have to."

"Would you have?"

"Yes." She didn't have a doubt about that. "If he had tried to kill me or Adrian or you, I would have killed him. You saw how many people he killed just to get to Adrian, just to piss me off. He didn't care about them. They were just in his way."

Xavier's heartlessness was part of what made him a favorable assassin. One of the best.

Reid meandered to his dinner, waiting on the table. He stirred his soup absently, then took a spoonful. He washed it down with wine. "He said he came to look after you."

"Maddox knows I'm here." What that meant, she didn't know. "It's a taunt. A game. I can't even say for sure if Maddox sent Xavier here or if he came of his own accord."

"That's quite cutthroat."

"It's the Undercity."

Reid didn't argue. His eyes held nothing of prejudice, only warm curiosity. He held his stare on her; all the while, the steam from his soup gently rose and twisted.

She wiggled her spoon at him. "Eat your dinner before it gets cold."

While waiting for her leg to heal, Juniper kept herself busy reading books Clara brought from the Royal Library: romance, mystery, and adventure.

Reid kept to his studies while she read. One afternoon, Reid left to assist the knights and posted another young squire, Squire Berwick, in the sitting room.

Juniper paused her reading; her eyes needed a break. She found a spot on the far wall and blinked until they felt normal again. In the other room, Berwick shifted.

"Why are there no female knights?" Juniper asked, loud enough that Berwick knew she meant to speak to him.

"It's tradition, my lady," Berwick answered in a small voice.

Right, right, he spoke to Roslyn. She'd nearly forgotten. She had gotten used to being herself in her chambers. She straightened her shoulders. "Step in here so I don't have to shout."

Berwick did as she asked. He stood by the door, where he could see the sitting room door should someone enter. No hair graced his young face, and he kept his ash blond hair cut short. He lacked the easy confidence and seriousness that the knights wore, but his dark brown eyes spoke of intelligence.

"How old are you?" Juniper held her chin high.

"I'll be nineteen in a few weeks, my lady."

Older than he looked. "How long have you been a squire?" she asked.

"Four months."

"Why do you want to become a knight?"

His gaze flickered to the floor. "I want to protect people from apostates." When she didn't interrupt, he lowered his voice and added, "When I was young, I witnessed an apostate use his powers to burn fields and homes of those who opposed him. Knights came and took care of him, and I knew I wanted to help people. No one should suffer at the hands of an apostate."

No one should suffer at the hand of a tyrant, no matter the manner of control.

She asked, "Have you been to the Marca?"

"Yes, my lady."

"How do you find it?"

"It's a safe place for mages. There, they can learn how to use their powers for good. There, they can learn and practice safely."

Under knight supervision.

"What do you plan to do once you become a knight? Stay here in the city or travel?"

"I would love to travel." His gaze drifted to the window. He blinked, and his eyes returned to her. "But the tasks that traveling knights are given are often more deadly and dangerous."

"But by the time you are a fully trained knight, you will be ready for such tasks," she said matter-of-factly.

He blushed. "I wish I could be as sure as you, my lady."

She gave him a small smile. "I'm sure Reid wasn't as stony and arrogant when he became a squire."

Berwick's small grin faded. "The older knights say he's the best squire they've seen since Sir Fowler."

"Fowler?"

"He is the current knight commander."

Reid came back before she could ask anything else; his lips twisted into a deep frown when he beheld Berwick standing in the bedroom. Berwick looked almost guilty under Reid's stare. Reid didn't speak to her until Berwick had left.

"He's nice," Juniper said. "You should invite him over more often."

"What did you say to him?"

"Nothing horrible." She waved her hand dismissively. "Don't worry, Squire, I was the epitome of a lady. Nose high and proud."

Reid didn't look convinced.

✦

Though it had been an assassin, not a demon, the healer still recommended Juniper drink a tonic, in case the enchanted blade had been cursed or poisoned. Ison brought them by in the afternoons, as he had before. For the first three days, Reid had been there, glaring at Ison as though he had summoned the demons, but on the fourth afternoon, Reid had stepped out. Berwick stood in the corridor. She had no doubt Reid had stationed him there so she could not talk with him.

Ison brought her a bluish tonic on a silver tray.

She drained half the glass and paused for breath. "This one tastes good. Less like grass and more like blueberries."

Ison gave her a small smile. Without Reid glaring at his back, he didn't appear nearly as nervous. "I added a small amount of juice to make it less...thick. It shouldn't alter the tonic, and it helps with the less flavorful ingredients. Guarding against unknown enchantments is harder than a known poison. How are you healing?"

"Well, thank you." She downed the rest of the tonic and handed him the glass. She could move fine, but she'd rather stay in and read than go out and play Roslyn.

He smiled, and it reached his steel eyes. "I'm glad to hear it." He hesitated, then turned to leave.

"Wait," Juniper said.

Ison paused.

"Stay and talk to me. It's dreadfully boring in here."

The next chapter could wait. She hadn't gotten the chance to speak with Ison without Reid there to intimidate the poor mage. Ison didn't move at first. He stood by the bed, still as marble.

"Unless you're busy. Then, I understand. I tried to speak with Squire Berwick yesterday, and Reid moved him into the hall. I think he wants me to be bored."

Ison blinked. "Reid?"

"Oh, Squire Sandpiper."

Ison took careful steps to the chair that Reid occupied when he studied. He set the tray on the table, now free of study books and notes. "I have time. Nothing I do is vital. Mason handles those tasks himself."

"You're the potion master?"

"Mostly." Ison nodded. "Mason has started to trust me with the more complicated potions now that he has seen what I can do. I'm not very good at spells or charms, but I consider myself well in the art of potion making. It comes easier to me than other things."

"Is that something you learned at the Marca?"

He nodded. He folded his fingers gracefully in his lap. "What do you know of the Marca?"

"Not much. I know it is a place where mages are taught." Juniper saw the gentle flinch in his eye. When he didn't speak for a moment, she added softer, "You don't have to speak of it. I understand."

"It's fine, my lady." Ison twisted his fingers. "There are masters there who teach. We learn control and how to harness our magic, but we also learn the typical things a student studies, history, mathematics, music. As we get older, we can select certain things to study more. I was best at potions, so I studied it. I taught a few classes to the younger mages, but...I'm no teacher. I made potions for the local clinics, healing tonics mostly."

Ison smoothed a wrinkle from his sage robes.

She said, "I suppose the castle is a fair improvement over the Marca."

Ison's steel eyes held nothing of emotion. After a beat, he nodded. "The staff is friendlier. The food is better. I have my own room. No more sharing a dormitory with eleven other mages. The décor is about the same. It's still drafty."

She nodded. "The food here is good. I thought the kitchens were just trying to impress me with the cooking."

"No, the food is excellent all the time." Ison offered a short-lived smile. "Do you miss your home? I've never been farther north than the greenhouses."

She swallowed; the tonic's taste lingered in her mouth. She'd never been to Galamond either, but she couldn't tell Ison that. "A little. Although, there is so much to see and do in Rusdasin. I feel so cooped up here in the castle. If I'd have known it would be this way, I would have put off my visit until Adrian and I could go into the city." She thought of mentioning the visit to the Temple of Bala but then changed her mind. "All these...this demon nonsense. And now assassins. It's thrilling, to say the least, but it's also frightening."

Ison nodded, eyes on the tray. "I imagine so."

To prevent him from asking anything personal about her home in Galamond, she said, "I suspect that, as a mage, you've been questioned about it."

He nodded but didn't meet her eye. "Yes, I have. But I haven't done anything, my lady. I swear it." His voice shrunk with each word, and he looked utterly terrified.

She blinked. A mage in a castle full of wary knights. "I believe you, Ison."

His eyes widened. "You do?"

"I've been told that I'm excellent at reading faces," she lied. That voice she had heard in the cavern had not belonged to Ison. It hadn't come close to his calm tenor; it had been full of venom, hatred, and lust. "Why? Do you think I shouldn't?"

"No, no, it's not that, my lady." Ison bit his lip, then quickly stopped. "It's just...I'm a mage."

As if that alone made him guilty.

"So are the court magician and the healer." Juniper motioned toward the two of them, wherever they may be. "If anything, the court magician would be the one behind it all. I've heard the knights talking. It would take someone with immense magical power to summon a demon."

Ison nodded. "I've heard that. I can't say for certain. I've never tried."

"Good for you." Juniper adjusted herself, careful of her leg as though it were still injured. "It's only logical that the more powerful mage be the prime suspect. Of course, I don't mean to imply that you are a weak mage. I doubt they would have employed you if they thought that."

"It is quite all right, my lady. I see the power Mason has. He is far above my skill by decades."

Juniper nodded. She still held her suspicions against the court magician. She did not like the way he looked at her or the way he had secured himself in the king's pocket. He saw her as a bit of the spell, nothing more, not a person.

Silence fell, and then Ison glanced up at her. His steel eyes were slate after a storm. "May I ask a question of you?"

"You may."

A beat, then he asked, "Who are you?"

She blinked several times at him. Her heart sped up.

But before she could answer, Ison continued, "I know you are not Roslyn Derean. I do not know who you are, but I know you are not her." His gaze intensified. "You were brought here to protect the prince. You've taken his injuries for him. You carry yourself like a lady. You are treated like a lady. Yet they've given you a task which very well could kill you."

His stare did not relent.

She didn't know what to tell him. She swallowed, but her throat had gone a bit dry. "You're observant."

Ison glanced at the tonic glass. "The court magician doesn't bother to shut his study door sometimes." He looked ashamed. "I've overheard him speaking to Captain Sandpiper and King Bradburn about a binding spell and how important it is for a knight to be with Prince Adrian and you at all times. I put the rest of the story together myself, from your injuries, the prince's lack of injuries."

She inhaled deeply and released her sigh slowly. "Some of that might be true."

Ison stood and grabbed the tray. "You don't have to tell me. I understand." He turned to meet her gaze. "I thought they had brought another prisoner to the castle."

"Prisoner?"

His shoulders slumped. "The castle is no better than the Marca. Always, someone is looking over my shoulder, judging my work, scrutinizing my actions, waiting for me to commit some act of black magic so they can run me through and be done with it. I'm just another mage to be eliminated." He glanced to the bedroom door as if one of them might have appeared. It took a moment for her to realize he might be looking for Berwick. "I can feel them watching me. There's nothing I can do to prove my innocence to them. I'll always be a troublesome mage."

Juniper swallowed. Something had lodged itself firmly in her throat; she had never heard Ison talk so much, so freely. He turned his gaze back to her, and it was not rage in those eyes, but grief.

He heaved a breath. "I'm sorry," he mumbled.

"It's all right," she said, her voice a whisper. She released the fistfuls of the sheets she had unknowingly grabbed. "I am sorry, Ison. You are right about me. The guards watch me wherever I go. I can't leave this room without supervision." She sighed. Not that she minded Reid's supervision. "If you ever need someone to talk to, you can come to me. I won't think any less of you."

Ison considered her, then nodded. "Thank you, my lady... Do you have a name?"

"For safety, Roslyn will do." If anyone heard him calling her Juniper, there would be questions. No, best to keep him out of it.

Ison nodded, and a small smile came over his lips. "As you wish, Lady Roslyn."

CHAPTER THIRTY-FOUR

The morning after the healer deemed Juniper's wound healed, Reid found her hoisting herself up to the bathing room doorway. She twisted her bare feet up behind her; her toes curled with each repetition. Her eyes passed over Reid, but she said nothing. Sweat glistened along her brow and neck and soaked into her shirt. She went without anything underneath it.

Each repetition pulled a strained grunt from the back of her throat, each more strained than the last, until Reid didn't think she could manage another. Her arms shook, she gasped with the effort, but she managed to hoist her chin to the doorframe. Finished, she untwisted her legs and dropped to the floor. She walked to the table and poured herself a glass of water from the pitcher.

Maddox's brand stood out a shade darker through the sweat-soaked shirt. Had she been wearing white, the brand would have been clear. So would have other things. He shoved those thoughts away. Quickly.

She drained the entire glass before she spoke. "What? I can't let all this bed rest reduce me to a flabby mess."

"That would make your lifestyle a bit difficult."

She chuckled. "You try scaling a castle wall with twenty extra pounds. Although, all that armor weighs more, I suppose."

Those midnight eyes looked at him head to toe. He hadn't donned his armor that morning. "And in the summer, it becomes a personal oven," he said.

"I can imagine." She drank another glass of water and then closed herself in the bathing room. While she washed up, servants brought in breakfast. For two. She walked into the sitting room, sniffing the air.

"What will we do today, Squire?" Juniper asked as she scooped strawberry preserves onto a piece of toast.

Reid could think of a few things, but he wouldn't say them aloud. "Whatever you'd like. Within reason."

Juniper folded her toast in half and nibbled on the end while she thought. "I'd like to go for a walk. I want to see the Royal Library."

He considered that request. It would not be strange for Roslyn to want to see the library she had borrowed so many books from. Juniper stared at him, awaiting his consent.

He nodded. "All right."

She changed into a dark blue tunic and trousers, braided her hair loosely over her shoulder, and slipped a silk shawl over her shoulders. He thought about asking her to wear one of the dresses the seamstress had made but changed his mind. She looked lovely in a tunic too.

They started toward the library, and she looped her arm through his. They passed through a sunny corridor, and the light illuminated the blue tones of her black hair. She didn't bat an eye as servants and guards glanced in her direction.

Juniper was a lovely young woman, despite her flaws. She abounded in...something Reid couldn't identify. She glowed with it. Servants and guards noticed. Reid noticed. He reminded himself of her occupation—thief, criminal, assassin. Yet, as they walked, she didn't seem like any of those things.

They entered the library, and her face lit up. She took in the three stories of books that rose up the tower. A spiral stone staircase connected each floor, books carved into the stairs. At the top, a glass dome let in copious natural light. Small alcoves of comfy seating dotted each floor. Scholars in dark brown robes lingered about, researching, maintaining the collection, dusting, and shushing. Dozens of people scattered the first floor, sitting at the wooden desk and tables, reading in the alcoves. No one spoke above a gentle murmur.

"The library is open to the public," Reid whispered as they made their way to the second floor. "The king entrusts the library to the scholars. They deem who may enter and who may not."

"How do they determine that?" Her brows furrowed at an older scholar currently pouring over a thick ancient text. His bushy graying brows were knit in concentration. Long, bony fingers held the pages aside.

"I can't say. I've always been allowed in." Reid glanced at a scholar carrying an armload of books. The scholar paid them little mind. "But I have seen them call the guard to escort people out. Troublemakers mostly, people who talk too loudly and ignore the warnings, the occasional thief."

She smirked.

Reid steered her to the third floor, where the sunlight came in brightest. Birds tweeted and fluttered on the other side of the dome. Juniper meandered through the towering bookshelves with childlike wonder on her face, eyes bright and lips parted. She walked around one shelf and came back on the other side—she stood at the wooden railing and glanced down at the floors below.

On the third floor, the murmuring of the library rose in a quiet rumble, none of the words distinguishable from the others.

"I used to come here for the peace and quiet," Reid whispered to her. "It was easier to study here than in the barracks." He glanced at the familiar coves, many of which he'd been scolded for sleeping in. "There were weeks when I spent more time here than anywhere else."

When Nanette had run away with her florist, he'd spent weeks in here, studying, hiding from everyone's pitying expressions and empty words.

"How long until you become a knight?" Juniper whispered, turning her back to the railing. She slid her slender hand along the wood, her fingers easy with grace.

"I remain a squire until the king gives me a quest," he answered. She blinked at him. He forgot how little she knew about the Order. "I must fulfill a king-given quest, whatever it might be, and deem myself worthy of knighthood."

"What kind of quest?" Juniper asked as she walked toward a small alcove of closely arranged seating. She sat down on one end of a red couch.

Reid followed her into alcove, hesitated, then sat beside her. "It depends on the needs of the kingdom. History is spotted with grand adventures and quests of knights, of dragon slaying, apostate hunting, and bandit clearings. Sir Darvel, my mentor, was sent south to deal with a pirate captain who dealt in slavery."

"Apostate hunting?" Juniper's brows furrowed in disagreement. "What, he sends them out to kill as many apostates as possible?"

Again, defending mages.

He clarified, "No, just the worst ones. The apostates that have made themselves into threats by killing people or burning villages."

She nodded, but that furrow between her brows didn't recede. She glanced toward the skylight. "Which do you think you will receive?"

"I don't know, but I have thought about it." He stretched out his legs. He'd thought about it a great deal, laid awake at night thinking of when the king would call him into the throne room and officially grant him a quest for knighthood. "If I had to choose between those, I suppose hunting down an apostate wouldn't be bad. Better than hunting a dragon. Fewer teeth."

She tried to smile, but it looked forced.

"You'd rather pit me against a fire-breathing dragon with teeth as big as I am?" Reid twisted to look at her. "I am better suited to fight a mage."

She frowned. "No, I understand not wanting to fight a dragon."

He said lowly, "The apostates that knights are sent to kill aren't nice people. They are murderers. They are criminals. They aren't people you would want living next door to you." Lowering his voice even more, he asked, "Do you know an apostate?"

He had suspected it for a while, from her comments and mannerisms.

Her face told him nothing. "There are mages who live in the Undercity so they won't have to go to the Marca. Not all of them are horrible people. Most just want freedom," she said.

"They would rather live in the Undercity than in the Marca?" Reid blinked. What did people think the Marca was? Who would want to live in the Undercity, a place of criminals, black markets, thieves, and assassins? Of course, who knew what sort of market for magic the Undercity had.

"In the Undercity, a mage can wake up when he wants. Go where he wants. Speak to whomever he wants. He doesn't have to ask permission to piss, as they say. The Marca is no better than a prison. There is no going home at the end of the day. There is no getting away."

Reid nodded. He understood, but it didn't matter. The best place for a mage was in the Marca.

"It wouldn't be so bad if they just let them leave," Juniper said, looking at the skylight. "If they treated it more like a school and less like a prison. Let them go into the city, go to shows, go shopping, let them socialize and go to taverns. Don't lock them up because of something they didn't choose for themselves."

Reid smoothed a wrinkle on his pants. "I've never thought of that."

They were silent a moment.

"When you become a knight, where will you go?"

Reid blinked. He'd thought of that too but didn't have an answer. "Wherever the Order needs me to go. Knights travel all over the kingdom and beyond."

"If they asked you to leave Rusdasin, would you?" Her midnight eyes met his.

"Yes." He would. For the Order and all it stood for, he would.

"Even if it meant leaving all this behind? Your family? Your friends?"

He nodded. "It wouldn't be permanent. My uncle and aunt will do fine. Adrian, I hope, could take care of himself without me."

He hadn't forgotten his words to her. To keep her from being dragged back to the Undercity. He had the wild notion to ask her to go with him, but he kept his mouth shut.

"Have the knights gotten any closer to finding the apostate?" she asked, her voice small.

"No, unfortunately." Reid sighed. "They're running in circles trying to find someone who has carefully hidden himself. They've gone into the sewers to try and find a trail or a trace, but they've found nothing. They've even..."

Juniper raised her brows, nodding for him to continue. He swallowed. He didn't know if it was a secret or not.

Reid whispered, "Some have been looking into old texts for answers, black magic texts."

"Black magic texts?"

"There are some that exist in the Order's care."

Her brows furrowed, and her curiosity turned to spite. "Ah, I see. A knight can read a banned book, but a mage cannot."

"They are doing it to learn what their enemies might be doing, and the knights can't perform any of the magic in the books. A mage might be tempted." The magic in those texts required natural magic. "If it makes you feel better, the court magician has been helping. Some of the books are in the Iluvin language, and he is one of the few people that can read it."

"So, the court magician has been given books containing black magic?" Her whisper dripped with accusations.

"I agree," Reid said, nodding. "The knights are watching him day and night for any signs that he might know more about the apostate than he admits. Speaking of, you've been spending more time with Ison Rolin."

"I have."

"What do you two talk about?"

"Books. People. I ask him about the Marca. He asks me about the city."

"Does he know who you are?" Reid asked quietly, lower than a whisper.

She hesitated; her lips twisted downward. He did.

Reid felt his face pale. He spat, "What?"

She quickly held up her hand, whispering, "He doesn't know who I am, but he knows that I am not who I say I am."

Reid curled his hands into fists. First Clara, now Ison. He didn't like how many people were learning the secret.

"I didn't tell him," Juniper defended. "He figured it out himself. He's smarter than most of the staff." She reached forward to pluck something off his shirt. "Oh? What's this?" Her fingers came back empty. "*Jealousy*, Squire Sandpiper?"

She laughed and poked him in the chest. He growled and swatted her hand away.

Footsteps sounded on the stairs—purposeful footsteps. A scholar walked into the third floor with a deep frown on his face. He made a lap of the third floor, staring in Juniper and Reid's direction every chance he got. The scholar paused at a bookshelf not far from them.

Juniper leaned closer to Reid and whispered, close enough that her breath warmed his skin, "Do you think he's pretending to look for something, or is he mad that we're up here, and he wants to look for something without being watched?"

He smirked and whispered back, "They've chased out the occasional pair of lovers."

She glanced at him, scandalized. "People actually come here for a tryst? It's a public space."

Reid grinned wider. Had she not met Adrian?

The scholar made another pass, glancing shamelessly at the two of them before finding another shelf to search.

Juniper leaned in, a smile warming her face. "I think he thinks we're being inappropriate. That gives us two choices."

He glanced at her, brow raised.

"We leave in a huff for being intruded upon." She grinned wickedly. "Or we start being inappropriate to give him something to watch."

She pulled her lips into her mouth, inviting him to them. Whatever thought he had vanished. Her hand flattened against his chest—he hadn't seen her move—and his heart jumped underneath. Blood surged south at her touch.

No. No. Gods no. He shoved those thoughts away. Far away. Not in the library.

That wicked glint in her eye gleamed like fire. She slid her hand down the front of his tunic, but he snatched her away before she reached his belt buckle. She held in the most of her giggle, but some it slipped out.

The scholar, a bookshelf away, snorted a sigh and slammed whatever book he'd been pretending to read.

Reid yanked her to her feet. Best get out before the scholar figured out who he'd been watching. He did not want gossip of him and Roslyn to circulate any more than it already had. Without glancing back at the scholar, they started down the stairs and continued their morning walk.

CHAPTER THIRTY-FIVE

Ison made his way to Roslyn's room for lunch, only to be told by the guard standing outside her chambers that she had gone with Squire Sandpiper.

"Do you know when she might return?" Ison asked.

"No." The Royal Guard said no more. His tone implied that Ison shouldn't have inquired in the first place.

Ison did not retort at the guard's tone or frown, which deepened every moment Ison stood there. No, he understood. Whoever-she-was had obligations and appearances to keep. He was just the court magician's apprentice, a troublesome mage asking too many questions.

Ison walked away, the smart decision for any mage in Duvane.

He didn't let himself wallow in the lone hour that would now be his lunch. He took the long way back to his chambers and made a point to walk through his favorite of the rooftop courtyards. It was a wide oval of green with blazing star, queen's lace, and wild chicory. It reminded him of his home, where the roadsides and meadows had abounded with wildflowers.

Ison took a deep breath of the long-ago scents. Home. Home didn't exist anymore. Not for him. Not for a mage; the knights would make sure of that. When he thought of home...his mind blanked. He did not consider the Marca home. He did not consider his room at the castle home.

"Ison?"

He nearly jumped out of his skin—standing at the archway of the courtyard, dressed in her immaculate servant's clothes of brown and white, stood Clara. Two other servant girls stood behind her, watching with wide, careful eyes.

"Clara," Ison said in greeting.

"I didn't meet to startle you," she said sweetly. Her friends giggled.

He shook his head. "You didn't, I didn't hear anyone coming."

Clara turned around to her two friends and waved them on. "I'll catch up."

They hesitated but didn't argue. The two servant girls continued down the corridor and out of sight, arm in arm. Clara meandered into the courtyard, strands of hair floating around her face where it had loosened from her bun. She came to stand beside him and flickered her gold-yellow eyes at him. This close, he saw dark gold flecks in them. Embers.

"I know I'm not supposed to be out alone." Clara laced her slender fingers together. "Not with people going missing and all, but you'll walk me back, won't you?"

"Of course." He wouldn't want anything to happen to her.

Clara glanced out at the grounds.

Ison flinched; a sudden throb, like someone had pierced his brain with a dagger, sent his vision blackening. As quick as the feeling came, it vanished but left a lingering sensation behind. He rubbed the spot on his head where it had appeared.

Maybe he needed to see a healer. Those headaches had been happening more of late. He blamed the stress. Demons. Knights.

"Are you all right?" Clara's sweet voice chimed.

"Yes." He dropped his hand from his head. "I haven't eaten yet. I suppose my body is trying to tell me something about it."

Her lips stretched into a girlish smile. "I haven't eaten much today. Would you... I mean, I understand if you'd rather not have company, but—"

"Would you like to join me for lunch?" Ison pushed the words out with a smoothness he didn't know he possessed, but there, looking at Clara, those lovely golden yellow eyes looking at him, not at the mage or the apprentice, but *at him*, he felt a strength he had forgotten about.

Her grin flourished. Her cheeks turned a shade pink. The embers in her eyes danced. "I would love to. I've got friends in the kitchens. We can ask for anything we'd like."

He offered his arm to her, and she linked her elbow with his. Ison walked them out of the courtyard, but she led the way toward the kitchens on the other side of the castle. For once, the long corridors didn't feel so lonely.

CHAPTER THIRTY-SIX

Juniper slipped her arm through Reid's as a token of friendship and apology, but she couldn't for the life of her figure out if he accepted it or not. He wore his guard's face well, never telling, never suggesting.

She had meant to make him uncomfortable, but not like this. Had she crossed a line?

She still felt the squeeze of his fingers around her wrist. He had grabbed her with a warrior's quickness, and his eyes had held a ferocity she hadn't seen since those first few days in the castle.

Don't.

He had looked at her like a stranger, like an intruder. He'd flinched under her touch. A reaction to *her*. He didn't want her touch, not the touch of a murderer, a thief, common-born street scum. She shouldn't have done it. It had been a stupid, impulsive move.

She felt the rift between them grow, no better than it had been before. She did not belong in the castle, she reminded herself. She played a part. A possession. To be used and tossed aside like a dishrag. She silently scolded herself for thinking otherwise.

By the time they reached her chambers, Juniper felt a widening pit in her stomach, black and endless and gripping. It pulled her heart and lungs into her ankles.

She walked straight for the bathing room and shut herself inside. Why did she feel so horrible? Her chest felt like it might collapse at any moment.

Damn her for getting attached. She knew better. People came and went like flowers; soon she would be gone, and Reid, Adrian, Clara, and Ison would be nothing more than memories. She would return to Maddox, to the Undercity, and everything would return to its original state.

No. She wouldn't. She'd changed, somehow, even just a little.

She washed her hands and face and dappled a bit of perfume on her neck for the hell of it, even if no one would appreciate it.

Juniper walked out of the bathing room to find Clara humming as she set a tea tray on the table.

"Welcome back, my lady." Clara gave her a quick bow of her head. Her cheeks were flush like she'd been running, but she looked bright.

Happy. Juniper tried to soak in that happiness, even as Reid's presence felt like a weight in the opposite direction.

"Someone is in a good mood." Juniper had not seen the young woman in such elation. Clara's face reddened. She looked down at her simple brown shoes and then glanced at the open bedroom door, to the sitting room, where Reid no doubt stood, listening to every word they said.

She opened her mouth, but Reid's voice came from the other room. He announced that he was leaving; he had stationed Squire Berwick outside. Then, the door shut.

Clara closed her mouth, then opened it again. A furrow appeared between her brows. "Is the squire all right? He seemed colder."

Juniper didn't feel like explaining the incident in the library to her. She waved her hand toward the door, toward him. "I'm sure it's a boy thing. But what's got you in such a good mood? I've not seen your eyes so bright."

She smiled, truly smiled, and it was a lovely sight. No amount of makeup could have made her prettier.

Over tea, Clara told Juniper about her afternoon with Ison. Apparently, the rumors of Marca mages were true; Clara's cheeks reddened, and her voice vanished to a near whisper as she retold of their steamy interlude in a broom closet.

"He used magic," Clara admitted. "He told me so, but he didn't go into details. I've been with men before, but gods..." Her hands squeezed the teacup. Her knees twitched. "I see why mages make popular courtesans. Anyone with extra pocket money would pay for that."

Juniper tried her best not to frown at the idea of someone's tongue *there*. With magic *squirming*, as Clara had put it, over every sensitive part of her. A voice that came from her stomach, not her head, said it would be sinfully fun. However, she didn't think she could trust anyone like that. Especially when she doubted anyone wanted to touch her like that.

Clara sighed. "All that time, all that speculating, and it's true."

Juniper tried her best to smile. "And now every girl in the castle is going to be hunting down poor Ison for his skills."

Clara giggled. "No. I want him for myself. I'm not sharing."

"Not even with me?" She raised a brow, sipping her tea loudly.

Clara's cheeks reddened, and her lips stretched wider. "Only if you share the prince with me."

Juniper chuckled. "He does seem the type, doesn't he?"

Clara drank a cup of tea, gathered an armload of laundry, and left when a group of servants walked by, leaving Juniper alone. She drank another cup of tea and picked up her book where she left off. With no one to disturb her, she might finish it.

Five chapters in, a knock sounded on her door. She paid little mind to it until the second knock. Then she realized no one would open the door for her, and she rose to answer it.

"I'm coming," she called.

It was Ison, and he looked better rested than he had in weeks.

"Ison," she said in greeting and stepped aside for him to enter.

"I apologize for intruding, but I was in the corridor and thought I'd stop by. I came earlier, but your guard said you'd stepped out for lunch."

She didn't want to explain the library to him either. "Reid and I took a walk. Come, the tea might still be warm." She led him into the bedroom and sat down at the table. He sat across from her, in front of Clara's cup. "Don't worry, Clara drank out of it."

He blinked at her; she worked hard to school her face into neutrality. He poured more tea into it. It no longer streamed, but he didn't complain. He held the cup in both hands—slowly, steam began to rise from the tea.

"Oh?" Juniper blinked. She poured herself another cup. "Mine too, please."

He obliged.

"Clara tells me you're good with your mouth."

She leaned back in her chair, expecting the bluntness to throw him off, to stun him, to do anything except what it did—nothing. Ison merely blinked at her, his face calm, nonplussed.

"Ah, she told you about that." Not even a little concerned.

"She did." Juniper smiled and crossed her legs. She didn't want to give him the idea she wanted a firsthand account. "I didn't pin you for the type."

Not even the slightest bit of embarrassment came over his cheeks. "It's not the same here as it is in the Marca." He shrugged, the only emotion being his inability to explain himself. "We, as in the adult mages, have ways to entertain each other. We don't hide it. We're trapped in the Marca together. Might as well enjoy each other."

"And you got good at it, I've heard."

"Practice."

"Have you ever done it in a group?"

He laughed. "Are you trying to embarrass me?"

"Maybe, but now I'm curious."

"Then, yes, I have."

She raised a brow. She hadn't expected him to say yes. She had only read about those. "Do you have a preference?"

"Why so interested?" He laughed, a genuine humor.

"My love life is nonexistent in comparison. A few spare kisses with Adrian is all I've got to go on. You're a well of knowledge and experience on the subject." She uncrossed her legs and crossed them the other way. She laced her fingers together and set her hands upon her top knee. "You're a library, and I want to learn."

"In theory or in practice?"

She blinked. Not an ounce of shame on his pale face. Her face warmed considerably.

"I'm sorry. I forgot how blunt that might be to you." He waved his hands between them, eyes and brows reflecting guilt. "There's no shame about it in the Marca. A body's a body, and everyone has needs."

She laughed. A silence fell; Ison waited for another question, or as she feared, an invitation. She quickly said, "And now Clara's laid a claim to you."

"Yes, the solitary claim. Another thing the Marca and the rest of the world don't have in common." Ison twisted his fingers together. "We don't handle coupling very well. It works best if we...share."

"For all the horrors in the Marca, you're making it sound more like a pleasure hall." A pleasure hall guarded by knights.

As if reading her thoughts, he said, "We had places where we were not so closely watched."

"When do you see Clara again?"

"Tonight, for dinner," Ison said. He grinned. "I suppose I could try this solitary claim route for a while."

"I'm sure Clara would enjoy it thoroughly."

Ison smiled in a way that meant she already had. "She tells you've been reading smutty mage novels, my lady. These questions wouldn't be connected to those books, would they?"

"Of course not!" Yes, but she'd never say it out loud. She added, "I also read adventure. I'm fond of pirate tales, myself."

"Have you read anything of Gerynd Rugbear?"

She knew that name. She looked for it whenever she visited bookstores. She rarely bought anything, but when she had the money, it went toward books, sweets, or new weapons. Juniper clapped her hands together. "Oh, she writes of dragons and romance! You're a fan?"

Ison nodded. "I enjoy adventure." His face darkened. "To a mage trapped within stone walls, anything outside is an adventure."

Juniper slumped back into her chair. No sense in pretending with Ison. He already knew she was no lady. He poured himself another cup and warmed it magically in his hands. Juniper rolled another question around on her tongue. She'd been wanting to ask him, and sensing that the previous conversation had ended, she asked it.

"How old were you?"

"Hmm?"

"How old were you when they brought you to the Marca?" She wanted to say *taken*, but she didn't want to remind him of it.

He didn't answer at once. "I don't remember, but the knights recorded me as five years old."

"That's so young!" She gaped at him. They'd been brought younger.

He nodded solemnly. "I had a brother, or I still do, two years older. Idel. He told me he would write me every day. He did for a while; then it became once a week. Once a month. Once a year. On my birthday. I haven't received a letter in two years. I only hope it's because he's forgotten me and not because he's dead."

Footsteps sounded outside the door. A smooth, familiar male voice spoke; Berwick spoke back. Reid walked into the sitting room without so much as a knock. He stalked into the bedroom, and at the sight of Juniper and Ison sitting together, alone, his frown deepened.

Ison drained his tea, cleared his throat, and stood. "I must take my leave, my lady. Squire Sandpiper."

Reid nodded to Ison but offered no parting words.

Ison walked past Reid, every step under his watchful gaze, and left the room.

"You could at least have said hello. Or goodbye." She hadn't meant to sound so bitter. She drank from her teacup.

"I don't like him in here alone with you." Reid looked to where Ison had been sitting, as if expecting a curse to have been left.

"Ison is fine." She felt Reid's gaze but refused to meet it. She beheld her tea instead. When he did not relent, she met his cold stare with her own. "What? Am I not allowed to have friends?"

His voice turned to ice. "He is a mage."

"What?" she gasped, hand over her heart. "I never would have guessed. That scoundrel!"

He scowled. His voice dropped to a seething whisper. "Are you forgetting that there is a mage somewhere in this castle who has tried to kill you and nearly succeeded?"

"Please, don't insult me." Or Ison. "I've been much closer to death than that."

"I'm serious, Juniper," he hissed her name. He took several steps closer to her and grabbed the wrist of her hand that held her tea. It sloshed, nearly out of the cup. Fire lit his eyes. "Stay away from him. At least until we find the apostate responsible for all of this. For all we know, Ison's helping him."

Anger flared. At his words, his accusation, his implications. At his hand secured around her wrist. If the tea had been in her free hand, she would have thrown it in his face.

She spat, "Because all mages are horrible, vile creatures who do nothing but torment the innocent, is that it?"

His scowl deepened.

"Ison is harmless."

"They all seem harmless until they're shooting fire out of their fingertips and burning villages to the ground," Reid seethed, anger like she'd never seen on his face.

"I've met plenty of killers, Squire, and Ison doesn't fit the type."

"I've met plenty of *innocent* mages who then slaughter," he hissed. His knuckles tightened. His shoulders tensed. He looked ready to kill.

She gingerly took the tea from her restrained hand and set it on the table, then yanked her wrist from his grip. Standing, she said, "You're so damn adamant that because someone was born with magic in their blood that they're inherently evil. You're just like all the other knights that bully and push the mages around because they can. You're no better than them!"

"The knights are there for their protection."

"With permission to kill if they deem necessary? What kind of backwater, biased logic is that?"

"A knight must use his judgment!"

"To end someone's life?" Her voice cracked. "All because of something that a mage can't control. They didn't choose to be born with magic. They are no more dangerous than a man with a sword."

Rage, pure and raw, seethed around him. The muscles in his arms tightened. His fists shook.

She stood her ground. "Hit me. Prove to everyone what sort of man you are."

He took a single step to her, never breaking her gaze. She fought the tendril of fear that ran up her spine at his proximity. He could reach for her neck if he wished, strangle her until the breath no longer flowed through her throat. He stood close enough that she could smell the sweat on his skin, the leather, the musk of the barracks, lye soap and something...woodsy.

Footsteps came down the corridor, a horde by the sound. They stopped outside her door; the handle turned.

Reid stepped away from her as the door to the sitting room opened. Several sets of footsteps entered. Prince Adrian sauntered into the bedroom, followed by Sir Destry. Adrian smiled, then it faltered; his hazel eyes went between them, reading more than he showed.

"Reid, Roslyn." Adrian threw his hands out toward them. He cleared his throat. "I can't stay, but I thought I'd stop by myself since I was here. I wish for you to join me for dinner. In the Flowering Atrium."

"Of course, love," Juniper crooned.

Adrian crossed the room and placed a sweet kiss on her lips. He clapped Reid on the shoulder, and whispered so that only the two of them could hear, "Please try not to kill one another before then."

Adrian left; Juniper grabbed one of her books, then stormed into the bathing room. Not once did she look at Reid.

CHAPTER THIRTY-SEVEN

Juniper reclined in the scented bath, reading an adventure novel with plenty of romance, until the water turned too cold for her liking. She applied a sweet-smelling tonic to her skin and hair, one that left her feeling silken. She walked into the bedroom wearing only one of the fluffy white towels, mostly to annoy Reid, but also because she'd left her robe in the bedroom. Reid, however, did not stand his vigil in the bedroom. Instead, she found Clara humming in the closet.

"Fighting with the squire, my lady?" Clara raised her brow knowingly.

"He started it."

Clara didn't ask for details, and Juniper didn't feel like giving them. Instead, they spent a prolonged time going over Juniper's clothing options for dinner in the Flowering Atrium. Juniper finally settled on a lovely gold dress with blue threading. After fixing her hair, Clara walked with her into the sitting room, where Reid was brooding over a few books of his own, studying.

"Best not keep His Highness waiting," Juniper said. Each word clipped.

The three of them walked into the corridor. Clara vanished with two other servants, and Juniper took a step—then realized she didn't know the way to the Flowering Atrium. She motioned for Reid to lead the way, a lady's snap of the wrist.

The Flowering Atrium was aptly named. Every wall but one held nothing but windows, which gave a marvelous view of the coming sunset. As the sun set, the stunning view of the castle's towers, breezeways, and windows would be lit with the liquid gold of twilight.

The atrium itself was a magnificent space of flowering plants in hanging pots of varying heights and colors. Forget-me-nots, lavender, spots of heather and clover, baby's breath, nightshade, and other plants she recognized but could not name, all artfully arranged. Adrian sat at a low wooden table on a small patio in front of the windows. His guards and Destry lined the space.

Juniper put on her lady's smile and sauntered over to the table. Reid took up a place with the other guards. Adrian's hazel eyes slid from Juniper and fell over her shoulder. She knew who he looked at.

"Reid," Adrian called. "Come join us."

"It would be inappropriate of me." Reid's voice came out strained.

Adrian held out his hand as Juniper's approached the table. He placed a chaste kiss on her knuckles.

Adrian said to Reid, "Nonsense. Sit." He pointed to the seat beside him.

Ah, he wished to sit beside Reid. A small pang of jealousy hit her, but she brushed it aside. Juniper sat across from him. Reid came over to the table, one step at a time. All the eyes of the room fell on him, and he knew it; he looked uncomfortable.

"What do you think of the view, my love?" Adrian asked, leaning onto the low table. The wood had been polished and shone like honey.

"It is lovely." Not a lie. The sun turned the dull gray stone yellowish, almost like sandstone. The sun shone off the haze like fog, making it glow. "It looks enchanted."

Reid huffed at her tone.

Adrian's smile drifted from her to Reid and back again. His smile widened, and his intelligent eyes sparkled. "Fighting, are we?"

Reid huffed again. "No."

"I would never." Juniper placed a hand over her heart. "You insult me, Adrian, to think I would stoop so low and petty."

Reid made the smallest of sounds. Aggravation.

Adrian laughed and nudged Reid's shoulder. "It will do you no good to argue with a lady, Reid. They are always right. Even when they are wrong."

"That is sound advice." Juniper dared a glance toward Reid, whose stony face barely contained the anger beneath it. "You should listen to Adrian more often."

His eyes narrowed in silent warning. A silent threat. She silently threatened him right back. Juniper Thimble did not balk at the threats of men.

A servant poured three cut-crystal glasses of wine. Juniper gladly sipped hers. It tasted like spring, like sunshine, like a field of yellow and blue wildflowers. She shifted and spotted Reid's clenched fist resting on his thigh.

Had she riled him that much?

A part of her felt sorry for it, but not enough to apologize. Not yet.

Maybe in a day or two or at breakfast that next morning after she had slept on it.

Dinner went surprisingly smooth, snide glares and subtle, sharp comments aside, none of which slid underneath Adrian's notice. He seemed to enjoy the tension between Juniper and Reid like a show, one he could participate in, which irritated Reid further, which then brought delight to Juniper, which caused Reid to be nastier still. An endless cycle.

The food vanished; the wine diminished; the sunset tottered only a moment on the edge of the world before sliding onto the other side, pulling its gilded light with it. The night took over. Dark, inky clouds blew in from the north; a storm bubbled on the horizon. Lightning flashed in the far distance, its thunder not yet reaching Bradburn Castle.

"Ah, I'm glad I didn't pick an open courtyard," Adrian mused, hazel eyes glittering at the storm. "I almost did, but I thought the atrium had the better view of the sunset."

"I'm glad you chose this spot," Juniper added before Reid could speak, something she noticed irritated him most.

Reid wore an expression of exasperation; if they had been outside, the evening would have been over.

Juniper smirked. She loved storms. There was something energizing about them, something pure and raw, something sensual and powerful. A low, steady roll of thunder drummed over the castle. She felt it in her chest, in her bones. She glanced out the window at the bruised clouds briefly illuminated by flashes of bright white.

And then she saw it.

Outside, on the other side of the courtyard, perched on the angled roof of a breezeway. A figure. In the flashes, she saw it. Perched, crouched. Assassin.

Any wonder she felt at the storm vanished. Darkness returned to the rooftops, and she hoped that she had imagined it all, that it had been a trick of the light, of the storm, but as another bolt of lightning flared across the sky, spiderwebbing in countless directions, she saw the assassin again.

Moving toward them.

Juniper jumped to her feet, ready to go after him, but quickly remembered her place. Roslyn wouldn't run after an assassin. Not with guards surrounding her.

"What is it?" Reid demanded, standing in his warrior's grace. His hand flew to his sword and pulled it several inches out of the sheath.

"There!" Juniper pointed, her finger pressed against the glass.

Lightning flashed; the figure was gone.

"I don't see anything," Reid snapped, shoving his sword back into the sheath.

Juniper focused her eyes on the dark roof, as did every other pair of eyes in the room. The hair on the back of her neck prickled. The air thickened, energized.

Her breath caught in her throat at the smell.

Through the soft pit-pat of the first raindrops against the windows, she heard something else, a sound she sometimes heard in her dreams: a claw sliding along glass. She saw nothing outside. No lightning illuminated the would-be attacker. She dashed around, eyes turned from the windows to her.

"Roslyn?" Adrian said carefully, standing. A warning and a question.

She glanced sideways, at the darkest window pane. She barely saw the shadow slip between the panes; the lock slid open. She opened her mouth and shouted—the windowpane slammed upward, cracking the glass just as lightning illuminated the beast.

A dozen swords unsheathed at once.

The demon slid in among them, brown hair matted and leathery skin taut over lithe muscles. It brought with it the stench of wet dog. Its elongated snout was wide as a bear's, long as a wolf's, enough to snap a man in half and swallow the first half in one bite. Golden yellow eyes took in the room, the challenge.

Juniper glanced to where the assassin had been—no, not an assassin. The apostate. The real problem.

The guards began to close ranks around the demon, with Destry and Reid leading them.

"Roslyn, get back," Reid commanded, his voice unwavering.

The apostate had been there. Right there!

The window still stood open behind the beast. She could end the problem tonight.

Lightning flashed. Just beyond the breezeway, through the drizzling rain, the figure watched, hiding in shadow. Watching its creation.

Juniper jumped for the window as the demon lunged past her for Adrian.

CHAPTER THIRTY-EIGHT

Reid didn't have time to shout at Juniper. He swung his blade, but the beast jumped to the side as though a great wind pushed it out of the way of the slice that would have—*should have*—taken its head clean off.

The beast landed on the grassy atrium floor. It ripped through the dark soil with ease, grass and flower roots sticking between his black talons. The demon bristled, letting out a low growl that rumbled the windows worse than the thunder. The guards closed in. Destry readied himself. Reid stood his ground.

Adrian backed away, toward the wall, out of the way.

The demon turned toward Reid; its nostrils flared. It picked its feet up and set them back down, testing the ground on which it walked. The muscles beneath its leathery skin shifted and rippled.

It shifted its golden yellow eyes to Reid. The beast almost seemed to be hesitating. No. It was a trick. Demons did not hesitate, for they did not feel. Did not think. Reid stared it down—the whites of its eyes were yellow tinged with red.

Destry swung first. The demon moved swiftly out of the way. The guards followed, blocking the demon's path with swords, but the demon nimbly avoided each slice. It swatted at the incoming blades with its thick arms, receiving nothing more than a few nicks. A guard darted forward and landed a blow to the beast's back, but the blade barely made a dent in the thick leather skin. With a kick of its hind legs, the demon sent two guards into the opposite wall; they hit, slid down, and stayed.

Destry charged the beast, landing a blow on its shoulder—the Mage's Bane blade sunk enough into the flesh to infect it, but it would take too long for the bane to work.

The beast knocked Destry to the side like he weighed nothing. His armor clanked viciously against the stone. The demon, hissing and growling, turned its attention to Reid, the only thing standing between it and Adrian.

Thunder cracked overhead. The demon let out a vicious, ear-splitting call in response. Reid felt the call resound in his head, a pulsing headache, lights in his eyes.

It was enough for the beast. It lunged at Reid, claws out, poised to strike. In that short moment, he knew what he had to do.

Reid lunged forward at the demon, through its outstretched arms. He drove his sword straight through the beast's chest, where its heart should have been. Blackish blood oozed down the blade, over the hilt, and onto his hands. The beast gurgled; the blood oozed from its bleeding heart, but underneath the pain, it seemed to laugh. It shifted its head to look at its killer. Its golden yellow eyes slowly lost the light of life.

Reid yanked the sword from the demon's chest, using his foot to push it away. The demon fell free with a sickening rip of flesh and wet smack of blood. The talons on its front feet, which Reid had jumped between to avoid, were glittering red.

His heart sank. Reid spun; the beast had hugged him, exposing its chest, but had dug its talons into Adrian. Every single talon had pierced his body, leaving five stab wounds on either side of his torso, each bleeding fresh, bright blood.

The sight stole any breath remaining in his throat.

Adrian slumped down the wall, his hazel eyes wide. He coughed, each breath struggling. Blood in his lungs. Reid collapsed on his knees before Adrian, his friend, his prince. He never heard the demon behind him burst into ash or the calls of the guard for the healer or the sounds of chaos as it exploded through the castle.

Reid watched in horror and relief as the wounds lining Adrian's middle magically began to shrink, the torn muscles stitching back together, blood vessels knitting, the skin repairing. Transferring. To a thief who had run out into the night.

Reid found Adrian's eyes; he held them on the window where Juniper had vanished, and Reid found his own unspoken fear in that gaze.

Juniper scaled the castle roof with ease. She kept her eyes on the dark figure running ahead of her, clad in smoky black. The broader shoulders and narrow waist were of a man. She'd kill him for all he'd done. He had summoned the demon. He was the reason she'd spent all that time in pain while the poison pumped through her body.

Thunder crashed as they ran along the rooftop of the castle, the rain thickening with every step. The dress did not help. One slip, and she'd be done for. Splat, on the ground. If she'd worn pants, she would have caught the apostate by now. Sooner. Tripped him and sent him falling to his death.

No—she wanted to feel her hands around his neck. If only she had a dagger. She could have thrown it straight into his spine, his heart, his neck, wherever she wished.

She chased him steadily north, toward the Royal Grounds.

They reached the back of the castle; the apostate scaled down the wall with ease, despite the rain-slick stone. Juniper launched herself downward onto the stone, like she had done many times, but found her chilled, wet hands slipping and her dress cumbersome.

How she made it to the ground without falling, she would never know. By the time she jumped to the sodden ground, the apostate had a good head start on her. Too much of one. She dashed toward him, willing all her strength into her legs. She had halved the distance when a sudden, ripping pain seared through her middle. She screamed, her vision blackened, and she collapsed. The cool mud cushioned her fall with a wet splat.

The demon. She could feel the poison burning. Five punctures, maybe more. She couldn't tell. The pain blurred together, searing through her middle, slowly stabbing deeper, ripping through muscles, blood vessels, scraping bone.

The pain paralyzed her. The poison burned her into stiffness. Blood flowed freely from her body. More blood than she could afford to lose, but she had no way of staunching it. It flooded internally. She felt it.

She could do nothing.

They would be busy with the demon. They wouldn't follow her. They wouldn't find her in time. Time that she was quickly losing. At least Adrian would live. From this, she likely would not.

Breathing became hard. Labored. Each breath choking between the blood filling her lungs.

To die here, of all places. The Royal Grounds, at night, during a storm, alone and unwanted, and certainly without anyone looking.

Anyone else in her position would have been praying, but Juniper had never been one to pray. Not that the gods listened when she did.

Through the rain, footsteps approached. Calm, steady, muddy footsteps. He came within her view and knelt beside her with feline ease. He wore smoky black, head to toe, except for his eyes. His cold expression settled on her, and she knew a scowl stretched across his hidden lips. She'd seen it enough to know.

Not an apostate. Assassin.

She shouldn't be surprised that he would come looking for her himself. He watched her, calculating, debating whether to leave her or put her out of her misery. Did he know what would happen if he did? Did he know how close he crouched to assassinating the Crown Prince of Duvane?

"I thought you above the role of courtesan." His cold eyes ran along her muddy, blood-soaked body. "Those wounds don't look good. I'm not sure they can be fixed." His eyes flickered back to hers, pity and remorse. He brought a gloved hand to her cheek. "Shame, though, to lose such a promising thing like you. Wasted on a frivolous task." He pushed wet hair out of her face. He fingered a lock of it and clicked his tongue. "I liked you better as a redhead."

The rain came down harder still, beating against her face, her neck, the raw flesh of her middle.

He pulled a smooth, simple dagger from his arm and held the edge to her throat. She couldn't move. She couldn't fight. Either by him or by the wounds, she'd die tonight.

Somehow, this end didn't surprise her.

Then, his attention shifted upward. The blade slackened. Thunder rolled, roaring through the clouds as lightning lit up the swaying, wind-bent forest behind him and his wide, watchful eyes. He withdrew the blade. He stood. She blinked, and he vanished.

A small mercy. She couldn't feel anything. From the cold, from the poison, from the blood loss, she didn't know; but she had gone entirely numb. The rain beat her, slipping into her eyes, her mouth, her nose, soaking her to the bone. Maybe she would drown before bleeding out. Her thick, unresponsive lungs agreed.

The trees swayed in a blast of lightning. Dark shapes grew on the edges of her vision, pulling closer, closer, closer.

She closed her eyes. It felt a lifetime before she found the strength to open them again. Which blink would be the last? At what point did the body stop seeing? Stop thinking? And...cease?

Through the stormy darkness above her, a different shadow appeared. More solid than the others. Quicker. It came closer.

Look at me.

The voice hammered at her ears, but it felt as though she'd gone underwater. Had she drowned without realizing?

Look at me.

Her head moved on its own—no, he moved it. Calloused fingers touched her chin, her jaw, her cheek. His face hovered above hers, blocking the rain. She blinked, and his hand flattened against her cheek. So warm. She closed her eyes and leaned against his hand.

The ground underneath her moved. She felt something solid against her shoulder, her back, and then she felt nothing at all.

CHAPTER THIRTY-NINE

Juniper blinked several times before she realized she was awake. She felt wonderful, like sunlight, like a cloud. A low fire burned in the hearth, spreading its warmth over the bedroom. The flickering light played along the red and cream curtains of her bed.

Underneath the comfort, she felt the exhaustion, the stiffness. It felt like she had been cut into tiny pieces and stitched back together. By the worst cobbler in the entire kingdom.

No light streamed in from the window. Night? Or had the curtains been drawn tight enough to block out the light?

Reid occupied the chair beside the bed. He slumped, fast asleep. He slept with his sword over his thighs, one hand loosely around the hilt, the other on the scabbard. He looked so peaceful while he slept, with the scowl wiped from his face, with his indifference replaced by a somber calm.

She inhaled, and the feeling of comfort utterly dissolved.

Searing hot pain ripped through her sides, fresh blades jabbing into her flesh. She cried out at the pain. Tears pooled in her eyes; a few ran out.

Reid jumped from the chair and pulled his sword free. His warrior-ready eyes scanned the room. Finding no enemies, they fell on her. He returned his blade to the sheath.

She stopped moving. Moving was bad. She forced her limbs still as a corpse and focused on each breath as it came. In, out. In, out.

Reid took a heavy sigh and sat back down, slumping and beholding her with tired eyes.

"What happened?" Her voice came out as a hoarse whisper. Her throat squeezed; every inch of it felt raw.

"I should be asking you that." His brows knitted. "You saw something outside and ran for it like a crazed cat after a mouse. The demon attacked. You're lucky it didn't go for you first. I had half a thought that you'd taken the chance to run for your life."

The figure. The rooftop. She remembered. "I went after someone. I saw him... I thought..."

Reid's face scrunched. "The apostate?"

"That's what I thought." Each word grated on her throat. "But, no."

His grave eyes burned. "Who? Did you see his face?"

"No." Not a lie. He had kept most of his face hidden.

"Whoever it was vanished into the Royal Grounds," Reid said. The fire reflected in his eyes. "Do you think he had something to do with the demon's attack?"

"I don't know." She tried to swallow; her mouth felt like she had eaten sand.

Without shifting his eyes from the fire, Reid said, "You could have died. From the look of those wounds, and from how long the healer took, you *should* have died." A beat. "You should not have gone after him, regardless of what you thought. If it had been the apostate, then he would have known the way to kill the prince would be to kill you."

She wanted to argue that Juniper Thimble was not easy to kill, but her throat refused to cooperate. She glanced at the table by the window, where the water pitcher sat. Reid made no move to follow her glance.

"Water?" she croaked.

Reid didn't move at first. He shifted his eyes to her as if she had interrupted him. She repeated her request, quieter than before. Reid fetched a glass of water from the table and held it against her lips. She reached for it, her fingers numbly touching the cut crystal and his strong fingers around it.

She drank the entire glass. Her throat felt infinitely better. By the herbal taste that lingered in her mouth, they'd added something to the water.

"I knew..." She felt sleep pulling at her—whatever they'd put in the water. "I knew I would die there. I felt it." Then his eyes appeared. "But you...you were there."

"I had no idea where you'd gone." Reid curled his hands into fists. He spoke it like a threat. "You ran, and the demon sank its talons into Adrian." He gestured to her torso, numbed by pain and stiff with poison. "You're lucky one of the servants from the kitchen saw you dash onto the grounds, or else you very well might have died out there." His voice softened, just a bit. "You're lucky to be alive this night."

He'd saved her. He'd found her in time.

"Thank you," she said, "for saving my life."

His gaze turned cold. "I saved my prince's life."

The cold, frank way he said those words stung, the way he implied that if the prince's life had not been connected to hers, Reid would have left her out there to drown in her own blood in the rain.

Juniper closed her eyes. "I'm sorry."

Reid didn't say anything.

"I'm sorry for running." She opened her eyes. Reid stood by the bed, still as marble, eyes watching her every word. "I'm sorry."

Reid smoothed the sleep wrinkles in his shirt and reattached his sword belt to his waist. He started toward the bedroom door. In a softer tone, he said, "I'll inform the kitchens you're awake. You need to eat something."

He left, his footsteps sounding across the sitting room. His voice rumbled, too low to hear. Reid returned a moment later, but he did not come to the bedside. He walked to the hearth and stoked the fire, then resumed a post by her bedroom door, hand on his pommel.

Juniper woke with Reid's hand gently touching her bare shoulder. He helped her sit up by stocking pillows behind her back and shoulders.

A familiar servant girl, no more than sixteen, stood beside the bed with a folding tray in her arms. She wore an expression of utter fear. Bags clung underneath her eyes, and her dusty brown hair was swept back into a messy bun.

It took a moment, but Juniper placed her. "Marcy?"

Where was Clara?

Marcy's shoulders rose nearly to her ears. The silver on the tray rattled. She held her eyes downcast, obedient; she must believe her to be Roslyn. "Yes, my lady?" she asked, her soft voice strained.

"Are you all right?"

Marcy blinked at the question. "Yes, my lady. I have brought you something to eat. It isn't much, but the healer ordered the meal for you." She set the tray down over her legs. Seasoned broth. Herbal tea.

Juniper's numb limbs refused to listen to her, and Marcy fed her. The broth warmed her mouth, down her throat, and flooded into her chest like a blooming fire-flower. Herbs, no doubt. She'd have to thank Ison for those.

Several spoonfuls later, Juniper glanced up at Marcy's vacant expression.

"Marcy," Juniper whispered, "are you sure you're all right?"

"Yes, my lady."

Lies. Juniper narrowed her eyes at the servant, daring her to lie again.

Marcy bit her lip and looked down at the broth. "I—I did not sleep well last night, my lady." Marcy twisted her free fist in her apron. "I don't know if you have heard, but Clara has been missing these last few days."

Juniper blinked. Surely, she'd misheard. "These past few days? Nonsense. Clara was with me just yesterday."

Marcy blanched. Her hand holding the spoon shook.

Reid didn't look much better, which startled Juniper. Despite the soup warming her insides, she felt cold. "Reid?" she pleaded.

Reid held her gaze, his stare steadfast. "That was five days ago, my lady."

Five days? Juniper felt her breath shortening. She'd been asleep for five days. Clara had been missing for five days.

"We have guards looking for her as we speak." Reid's words were short, clipped.

Juniper stared into her broth. Clara. She'd dared to think of her as a friend, and now— No. Clara would be found, just as the others would.

She ate what she could stomach of the broth, and then Marcy helped her to the bathing room. The healer had again bandaged Juniper and left her without a shirt. The bandages hugged her from below her breasts to nearly her hips. Five wounds on each side. Five talons. Someone had undressed her: rather than her evening gown, she wore a simple, short chemise and underthings.

At least the herbs and the pain numbed her sense of embarrassment.

After helping Juniper back into bed, Marcy left. Reid paced from the hearth to the window, back and forth. Patrolling, she realized.

Juniper had never wished for the herbal sleep to take her, but she wished it would now. She wanted to sleep until she felt better, until her mind stopped spinning.

"What happened to Clara?" she asked.

"I don't know." Reid stopped his pacing, but he kept his gaze on the window. "The Guard is looking for her."

"She helped me get ready that night."

"She never made it back to the servant's quarters."

The pit in her stomach opened wide, swallowing her whole.

Reid continued to pace. It felt strange to be nearly bare in the presence of a man, but the pain and the herbs numbed her sense of modesty too. Reid had already seen most of her. Still, it felt strange to be in so little, and in so vulnerable a state in the presence of a man who wielded a sword with such skill. It felt oddly safe too.

He caught her stare. His neutral face dipped into a frown.

"You don't have to stay in here." Although, she'd rather he did.

"You're defenseless like that." He returned his gaze to the window. "The king put you in my charge. Should something happen to you, it would be my fault."

"You mean, if something happened to me that caused something to happen to Adrian." She said it with more bite than she'd intended. At his frown, the anger she'd felt toward him returned. "Then it would be your fault."

Reid gazed at her, the fire burning in his eyes. "Yes."

A thing. A possession. A shield for the prince. That's all she was.

She didn't know why she expected it to be any different.

✦

Reid slept fitfully in the chair, woke before dawn, washed up, and stood guard as Marcy came to help Juniper to the bathing room. The healer arrived shortly after to heal, which Marcy assisted with while Reid paced in the sitting room.

He tried to focus on his studies, on the things he should be learning, but...those golden yellow eyes kept resurfacing. The way they had looked at him as the beast had died, as if in gratitude.

He knew those eyes.

Clara's eyes.

The more he saw them in his mind, the more sure he was. But what did it mean? The demons, the missing servants...thinking about it made him sick.

The healer finished, rewrapped Juniper's middle, and left. Marcy returned, along with a few others so she wouldn't have to walk alone, with lunch for both Juniper and Reid.

Marcy never stayed long. He'd heard the rumors. Strange things were happening around Lady Roslyn Derean. The demons went after her. Her servant went missing. It was enough for any servant to be wary. This last attack had only made those rumors worse. The guards had seen Adrian's wounds—wounds that mysteriously vanished, and now Roslyn was sick once again. Strange things, they whispered.

The strange, silent tension in the castle was thickening by the day.

Reid ate in the bedroom. His meals were more substantial than hers, but she never complained of her herbal broth and spiked tea.

Before she had finished her lunch, a knock sounded at the door. Reid stomped through the bedroom and through the sitting room. He opened the door and found Ison standing on the other side, a tonic resting on a silver tray. He looked exhausted; his skin had paled since the last time Reid saw him. His gray eyes had dulled. Bags hung underneath. His cheeks had sunk, sharpening his cheekbones.

Ison's steel eyes met Reid's; the young mage seemed to shrink inward. Reid bristled. Did he detect guilt? What did a mage have to be guilty for? Gods only knew what he did when the knights weren't looking.

Ison didn't speak. After a moment of their standoff, Ison glanced down at the tonic. "Good evening, Squire Sandpiper." Ison's voice sounded as tired as he looked. Raw. Had he been crying?

Oh. He and Clara.

Reid stepped aside and held the door. "Evening, Ison."

Ison walked into the bedroom with a grace that Reid disliked. The tonic barely rattled, barely moved in its glass. Reid followed a step behind.

"I brought you a tonic, Lady Roslyn."

His eyes went from the tray to Juniper, who sat up in bed, with the blankets at her hips. She wore fresh bandages across her middle and a clean swath across her breasts. Ison blinked once. Nothing of embarrassment or shock came over his face at the nearly naked woman.

"Thank you, Ison," Juniper said sweetly, the soup and tea working its magic on her already.

Reid watched the mage's every step. His lack of modesty grated on him, although he'd heard about mages from the Marca and their fluid sensualities. Yet Ison regarded Juniper without a hint of desire in his eyes. Reid would make sure it stayed that way too. For the sake of Roslyn's reputation, he told himself. She didn't need rumors flying about her and the court magician's apprentice too.

Juniper drank the tonic slowly, pale hands grasping the glass that Reid held for her. Ison watched the tonic; only once did his gaze slip from the glass and to her, to her bare shoulders, to the strip of flexible fabric around her breasts. He blinked, and his eyes snapped back to the glass.

Once the tonic was gone, Ison left, holding the tray and glass with his strange grace.

Reid saw him out. He returned to the bedroom to find Juniper's eyes closed. He stalked to the fire, rubbing the soreness from his neck. Gods, he hated that chair.

"If you keep glaring at him, Ison won't be inclined to like you." Juniper's voice drifted to him, sleepy and causal.

Reid glanced over his shoulder. Her eyes were barely open, just enough for him to see the midnight blue dancing with the reflection of the flames. He crossed his arms. "Who said I cared?"

A tiny smile curved the edges of her mouth. "Who doesn't like having friends?" That smile vanished. "Oh, wait. You're *you*, and he's a mage. It would never work out."

Damn it, was she still on about that? Reid took a deep breath. As he did, she closed her eyes. It would do no good to stay mad at each other. "Are you finished eating?"

A grumbled confirmation came from her lips.

He removed the tray and set it in the sitting room. She'd eaten most of the broth. How much herbal additions the healer put in it, he didn't know, but when he returned to the bedroom, Juniper had fallen asleep.

He pulled the blankets to her chin. She didn't so much as bat an eye.

CHAPTER FORTY

"How long was I out?" Juniper asked Reid.

He glanced up from his book; her midnight eyes met his. "Just the afternoon," he said.

"How long has it been?"

"About eight days."

She blinked twice and turned her face to the ceiling above her. She wore no emotion that might reveal what thoughts moved through her mind. Reid returned to his study. Wards were not easy to learn. Reid had been able to summon a simple ward yesterday, but Darvel had broken it with a thrust of his pommel. A proper ward needed to be able to withstand both physical and magical attacks. A strong ward could even ricochet magic back at the mage. Harnessing the unnatural magic of the world sounded easy in theory but, in practice, proved difficult. How easy would it be for a mage to summon a ward using the magic within them, rather than gathering from outside?

"Keep studying," Darvel had told him. "It takes time to summon a strong ward. You've already surpassed most. Don't always expect the extraordinary from yourself, Reid."

Juniper's soft voice interrupted his thoughts. "You slept here?"

"Yes," he said. He shifted in the chair he'd slept in. It had not been made for comfort. He couldn't fathom a more uncomfortable night; his lack of solid sleep might be his problem with understanding wards. But even if he returned to his bed at night, he wouldn't be able to sleep for the worry that something would happen without him.

Juniper started to say something else, but he interrupted her.

"Like I said, you are my charge," Reid told her. "If assassins are coming after you in addition to demons, I would be a fool to let you out of my sight again."

He fought a yawn and failed.

"Will you be staying here again tonight?"

"Yes." Gods, could his back take it?

"Are you planning on sleeping in that chair?"

"You'd rather me sleep on the floor?"

Her expression did not change. She regarded him plainly, her drowsy calmness unreadable. It bothered him to no end when she looked at him like that, and it bothered him when she looked away too.

"My offer of the other side of the bed still stands."

He bristled. "It wouldn't be fit."

She blinked. "Is it not soft enough?" She blinked again. Her smile stretched. "Hard enough?"

Blushing, he cleared his throat. "It would be inappropriate for me to share a bed with a lady."

She smirked, albeit groggily. A soft chuckle fluttered out from between her pale lips. "Luckily, I am no lady."

That look, her laugh, her tone...did she mean that as in the other kind of sharing a bed? No. Ridiculous. Reid shoved those thoughts down.

She chuckled again, a warm sound that heated his face. "I'm not asking you to bed me, Squire Sandpiper. Although, I doubt I'd be much fun in this condition." She chuckled again. "I am simply offering you a more comfortable spot to sleep while you keep the demons and assassins from killing me in my diminished state. There is plenty of room for two. Maybe three."

Indeed, the bed could fit several people comfortably. And this chair...

Reid stood, closed his book, and set it on the table. He stepped up to the bedside. They kept Juniper closer to the fire, which gave one side of the bed more room than the other. The fire flickered, casting half her calm face in shadow and glinting off her angled eye like an ember. The firelight shone off Juniper's bare shoulders, gilding her exposed skin.

Horrible, terrible, awful idea.

Yet, as sleep pulled at his eyes and exhaustion pushed him down, he found himself unbuckling his sword belt and setting it against the bedside table, within easy reach. He sat on the bed, careful not to jostle her, and removed his boots. His belt. His tunic. He kept his undershirt and pants and socks, just in case, and slid into bed with the most notorious thief in Rusdasin.

Juniper didn't move as he slid his body underneath the same covers.

"How high are my chances of being killed in my sleep?" Reid glanced at her. He settled his head on the pillow, and his body sank into the bed. Much more comfortable than the chair.

"Considering my state? Low."

He nodded. She couldn't move with those wounds and the medications, and if she tried, she'd make enough noise to wake him.

Satisfied, Juniper closed her eyes. She quickly fell asleep. Her chest rose and fell with each breath. Every breath, however even, hitched. Pain. Her face showed none of it, but he knew she felt it. Felt it with every breath, every movement.

The hearth fire crackled behind the screen, shadows of the flames darting across the ceiling and canopy.

Twice now, Juniper should have died from poison. Twice she'd barely lived. It baffled even the royal healer.

Juniper let out a gentle breath. Her lips parted slightly, and he found himself fixated on them. He thought about how smooth they looked, the pale rosy tone that had returned with a few meals and deep rests, and how those lips would feel against his own.

Damning thoughts. They would lead him nowhere. He shoved those thoughts as far away as he could. He closed his eyes. He would need his rest to be able to focus on his wards in the morning.

Her breathing halted. Her next inhale came sharper. Her exhale followed, jagged and sudden. He wrenched his eyes open. Her eyes remained closed. Her brows scrunched together. Her hands fisted the sheets. She winced; a sudden, high-pitched whine echoed out of her throat.

He reached for her, setting his hand on the soft, pale skin of her shoulder. "Juniper?"

The demon, growling and hissing, chased her from the warmth of the castle and into the endless, shaded woods. The demon behind her became two red-eyed beasts. Razor-sharp teeth and talons snapped at her, tearing her clothes, her skin, ripping through her like water.

I know what you are.

She ran harder, pushing her limbs to the limit.

I can smell it on you.

The demons ran behind her, ever gaining ground, ever growing into massive beasts, their hot breath licking the back of her neck.

I know what you are.

A demon appeared in front of her, birthed from the shadows of the forest. He stood on his hind legs like a man, but he was no man. He hissed her name on his too-human tongue. His hands clamped on her arms. His breath heated her cheek. His teeth grazed her neck.

I found you.

"Juniper?"

Two strong, warm hands replaced the demon's.

The demons, the forest, the shadows—the nightmare dissolved. The demon vanished, and a brown-eyed man appeared. Reid's hands clutched her bare shoulders. He knelt beside her, nearly over her, with the fire flickering across the worry on his face.

She waited for her ragged breathing to ease, for the numbed pain to relax, all the while, looking into his calm eyes, letting his steadiness ooze from his arms, through his hands, into her shoulders. She blinked, once, twice.

"A nightmare?" Reid didn't move. His calloused hands remained at her shoulders, the warm, dry skin against hers.

The demon's voice hissed in her ear, a memory from her dream, from within her mind, not outside it. She couldn't speak without the residual fear inside her twisting her words into sobs. She bit her lip to keep it from trembling. It was all she could do to nod.

Reid held his stare on her. Any demon would have to go through him. She had seen him in action; no demon would stand a chance. His thumb twitched, drawing a line over the outer edge of her collarbone. Over the top of her scar. In that moment, she didn't care about his reasons for being there. She didn't care that he only protected her because his king had commanded it, because it meant saving his friend. She just wanted him there.

Reid settled back into the bed, closer to her than he had been before. His arm grazed hers, reminding her how close he was if she needed him. He wouldn't go anywhere.

Juniper wanted to curl into him, to hide underneath his muscular arms, to pretend that she wasn't pretending to be some frilly lady in a demon-infested castle. But she couldn't move. Her wounds held her still.

That, she would tell herself in the morning, had probably been for the best.

CHAPTER FORTY-ONE

Ison struggled to wake up. His body cried for more sleep, yearned for a few more minutes in the dark, endless abyss of sleep, where he didn't have to skirt knights or squires, where he didn't have to face his blank memory, where he didn't have to think about Clara.

He gave in. He rolled onto his other side, to the cool blankets, and tumbled back into the abyss. Again. And again.

Ison woke several times, each time he gave into that voice, that yearning for sleep—until he knew that something had to be wrong. He never slept this long.

Wrong. He felt it.

He forced himself awake. He forced his uncooperative limbs from the confines of the blankets. His legs didn't listen; he fell from the bed and onto the rug, his shoulder taking the brunt. Using the bed for support, he crawled onto his knees. He stood, wobbly, against the bedpost.

What happened? His head throbbed. Ison stumbled to his bedroom door and half fell into the large study beyond.

"Easy, son." Mason's chair scooted. His brown boots appeared in Ison's view; then purple robes fluttered as the old man knelt. A steady hand lifted Ison's chin. Mason regarded him with the same indifferent, clinical stare with which he viewed experiments. "You've had a rough night."

Ison felt his breath tremble in his throat. "What happened to me?"

"You're ill," Mason said. "You should rest."

No. No. No. The voice in his head screamed. *Don't let him. Don't listen.*

Ison tried to move, but with a wave of Mason's hand and a murmur off his tongue, Ison felt his body go slack. Magic crawled over his skin, binding him.

No. No. No!

"You've been ill." Mason's voice drifted as he moved about the study. He went into the workroom and returned with a fat flask. From it, he poured a greenish liquid into a crystal glass. To it, he added an assortment of herbs—herbs that Ison had crushed and pressed. "You're not yourself."

"You..." Ison gasped.

"I have done my best to keep you here," Mason said, adding a powdered herb that turned the drink pale blue. Mad Weed. An herb notoriously given to the mad to subdue them. "I can't have you wandering about."

Ison shook his head. Mason knelt beside him, Mad Weed potion in hand. He handed Ison the glass, but Ison turned away as best he could.

"Drink it, or I will put it in your stomach myself." A command.

Ison was not powerful enough to break the magic holding him. Not in one hundred years would he be that powerful. Mason pressed the glass to Ison's lips, and he drank it.

He means to harm you, said the voice. *He isn't to be trusted. Look at what he does to you.*

"I should have seen the signs months ago." Mason watched the drink vanish into Ison's mouth, watched his throat swallow. "The dreams...I feared I realized too late then. You might already be too far gone for me to reach."

Ison drank the entire glass of Mad Weed. Ison thought over all the ways to make a body sick, to make it empty the contents of the stomach, but already, he felt the Mad Weed taking hold, pulling him into the blackness of an inflicted sleep.

No!

"I will not allow these things to happen in my care," Mason said, though his voice sounded distant.

The Mad Weed pulled Ison into its embrace, but sleep did not come at once. He felt it move, the voice, the thing he hadn't noticed; he had noticed it before, and only when he noticed it again did he realize he had forgotten it.

Mason lifted Ison's limp chin, peering into his eyes. His bushy white brows knitted. "What are you?"

He did not mean Ison.

He does not know.

Ison blinked. The foggy memories. Restless nights. Mornings where he felt as though he hadn't slept at all. The utterly impossible-to-describe feeling of being watched. The thing, the voice... Was he the apostate? No, no. Impossible. He hadn't the magic for it.

"He's made quite the blockade." Mason's grip on Ison's chin tightened. The old man's magic came over him, pushed past his own, and touched something else—the thing, the voice.

Pain ripped through his body like a serrated knife, pulling a cry from his throat.

Mason fell backward, clutching his hand. "Gods..." His eyes searched Ison, but Ison hadn't the thought left to think. Darkness claimed him.

CHAPTER FORTY-TWO

Reid stationed Squire Berwick in front of Juniper's door first thing the next morning. He set off at once toward Knight Commander Fowler's office.

Knight Commander Fowler kept his main office in the castle, a moderate space of Marca purple and the Order's silver, in the wing of the castle that housed the knights and squires. It resembled the rest of the wing: drab gray stone, iron torch brackets, and drafts.

Reid approached the simple wooden door to the office and knocked.

"Enter," came Fowler's dry tone.

Reid walked inside to find the knight commander at his desk. The corners of the old man's wrinkled mouth turned downward naturally, and at the sight of Reid, his frown deepened. Reid had rarely seen the knight commander laugh or smile.

"Knight Commander," Reid said in greeting and gave the old man a respectful bow of his head.

"Yes, Squire?" he drawled.

"May I have a word with you, sir?"

"Regarding?"

"The demon attacks and the missing servants."

Fowler didn't say anything for a moment. He pinned his placid stare on Reid, debating, thinking. He spoke in an arrogant tone, "I suppose you think the two incidents related?"

"I do, sir."

Fowler harrumphed. "As do a great number of knights. But tell me, Squire, what can you offer the investigation that has not already been discussed? Another mysterious passage for my knights to waste their time hunting down?"

Reid kept his expression cool. "No, sir. The last demon, the one that appeared in the Flowering Atrium, it wore the eyes of the servant girl, Clara, the one who had been doting on Lady Roslyn."

Fowler pursed his lips but did not interrupt. He looked almost worried.

Reid continued, "All of the beasts have had strangely human eyes. I didn't think more about it until I saw Clara's eyes in that beast. She went missing the afternoon before that dinner. She helped Roslyn get ready, and she never made it back to the servants' quarters."

Fowler tapped his gray-skinned fingers on the wooden desk. "You think this beast somehow stole that servant's eyes?"

Reid fought his disbelief. He knew the knight commander to be a smart man. He'd read about his accomplishments, even the books that he wrote on the Order. Was he being deliberately stupid?

"No, sir," Reid said. "I believe that the demon *was* the servant girl."

Fowler didn't say anything for a long moment. He stared at Reid, barely blinking, gauging every breath; it reminded Reid of his first days as a Pledge. He had felt so small and inadequate next to Fowler, next to any of the knights. That feeling of insignificance returned and grew with every moment Fowler didn't speak. Reid schooled himself still. Any movement could cause the commander to call out a weakness that didn't exist.

Reid continued, "It would explain how no trace of a portal has been detected and why there have been no demon trails found. Because there aren't any of either."

"What research have you done regarding such things?" Fowler's words were sharp, clipped.

"None, sir."

"Have you mentioned this idea to anyone else?"

"No, sir. You are the first to hear about it."

"Good." Fowler rose. Without his armor, he looked like a shriveled old man, skinny and gray. Once a thick-muscled man, now his entire body seemed to be shrinking in on itself. "These are serious accusations, Squire Sandpiper. Do not breathe a word about this to anyone else, especially the servants or the royalty. I will bring this to the attention of the council, and we will decide what to do from here on. Thank you for bringing it to my attention. I knew you were a good seed. Your uncle was right about you. You've promise in the Order."

Fowler pulled a heavy jacket over himself and proceeded through a side door in his office, a breezeway that connected to the Council Hall.

Reid stood for a moment, alone in the commander's office.

A good seed.

You've promise in the Order.

Knight Commander Fowler had never breathed a word of goodwill toward Reid, toward anyone. Had he truly been impressed? To be

225

complimented by the commander himself... Reid hadn't the words, the gratitude. And yet he could tell no one about it. Not yet, anyway.

Reid started back toward Juniper's chambers. He couldn't tell her either. Not until he knew for sure that Clara was gone. If he was right, however, it meant that none of the servants would be coming back.

But, as he made his way through the barracks, he pushed thoughts of Clara and Juniper aside. The commander's words resounded through his mind, over and over.

You've promise in the Order.

CHAPTER FORTY-THREE

"Shouldn't you be awake?" Reid asked louder than he ought to. If Juniper hadn't already been awake, it would have woken her.

Juniper rolled onto her back and pushed the blankets away from her face. She had pulled them closer to block out the sunlight. Reid had conveniently opened all the curtains before he'd left that morning.

"I ran into Adrian on the way back," Reid said. "He wanted me to remind you about Bala's Ball."

All thoughts of sleep vanished.

"Bala's Ball?" Juniper squealed. She squirmed to sit up, sure that in her sleepy state she had misheard Reid's announcement. He stood at the foot of her bed with his arms crossed. Late morning sunlight streamed from each window, shading everything a hue of blue. Another stormy day.

Reid did not correct her.

"Bala's Ball!" She, Juniper Thimble, would be welcome at the grandest event of the year. Bala's Ball attracted dignitaries and nobles from all over the country. Every year, she and the other thieves would flitter around the drunken nobles as they departed, picking pockets like flowers in spring.

Reid smirked. "Unless you don't feel up to attending. I'm sure Adrian would understand."

Juniper pouted; she had weaseled out of training with Reid the day before, pretending to feel worse than she did, because she wanted to finish a book. Juniper knew he knew she'd lied, but she didn't try to hide it. The ending of the book had been worth it.

"I am feeling remarkably better this morning."

"Are you sure?" Reid's brows shot up. "You're looking a bit pale. You don't have to go."

"Of course, I want to go!" She swung her legs over the edge of the bed. She stood too fast, and a dizzy spell had her grasping onto the bedpost to steady herself.

Reid grimaced. "Are you sure?"

"It's the event of the year." Juniper started toward the bathing room. "No woman in her right mind would give up a chance to go!"

Juniper turned the tap for warm water and rolled up her pajama sleeves. She returned to the bedroom to find Reid staring out of the window. He'd been absently staring more in the past several days.

Reid had slept on the other side of her bed the entire time she had been bedridden and unable to move. He didn't seem to be as angry at her, and she liked to think that her hazy apology had helped. For the past two days, however, Reid had slept in the sitting room. They had woken up three mornings ago in such close proximity that they had shared breath; Reid had hurriedly gotten out of bed, leaving his boots and tunic in the bedroom, and found something to do in the sitting room.

She hadn't told him how cold it seemed with only her body to keep her warm.

She would leave him behind, anyway. No need to get attached. To anyone.

She pulled her dressing gown over her pajamas and reminded herself of the look on his face when she had touched him. Repulsed.

"You would be attending with Adrian, should you desire to go." Reid shifted his foot, then bent down to adjust a knife tucked inside his left boot. She'd not noticed it before. The leather hilt blended in well with the dark boots. He noticed her eye and frowned.

"Oh, I desire to go." She planted her hands on her hips. "When is the ball?"

"At the end of this week."

She blinked.

"Five days," he clarified.

She gaped at him. "*Five* days?"

Bala's Ball was mid-spring. Had she honestly been in the castle that long?

"You've been out of it for most of the decorating and planning," Reid said dryly. "Lucky you. But, since you want to go, I will inform the seamstress and Adrian of your decision."

She wanted to giggle with delight, but she held it in. Most of it. A girlish squeal escaped her lips at the very thought. Bala's Ball! "I will get a dress especially for the ball?"

He raised his brows at her. "Of course. You'll be on the arm of the prince. You will need to dress accordingly."

Juniper squealed and grabbed fistfuls of her dressing gown, imagining the most beautiful dress: brocaded silk, shining lace, beaded bodice, embossed threading, polished buttons.

"Glad to know you're excited." Reid's voice softened. "You will be a guest of honor. All eyes will be on you, the mysterious Lady Roslyn Derean who stole the prince's heart right out of his hand with a single meeting."

It sounded so romantic when he said it like that. She turned to him, smiling, and before she could stop herself, she said, "*All* eyes? Even yours, Squire Sandpiper?"

The corners of his mouth tugged upward. "I'm already looking at you."

She blushed. *Repulsed.* She turned her gaze into the hearth so that he might not see the red on her cheeks.

Then he added, "It is my duty to do so."

She swallowed. Professional. Curt. She could be those things. She changed the subject, "Have you heard anything about the missing servants?"

Reid didn't answer.

Did his silence mean bad news or a lack of? He was staring into the fire with that unreadable expression of his, one that she had come to learn meant thoughts roiled around in his mind, blanking him of easily read emotions.

"Reid?"

"No." He blinked his gaze to her. "We haven't heard anything."

"Have you found anything about Clara?" Her voice shook.

Reid shook his head. "She and Ison went to dinner. They were in one of the courtyards. Advisor Ulgan saw Ison depart with Clara at one of the servants' passages. After that, nothing. She didn't return to her quarters."

"Something is nabbing them from the servants' passages?" Her voice had gone to little more than a whisper. "Do you think..." She swallowed. "Do you think it's because of me?"

Reid's eyes darkened. "I don't know. I can't say. But none of the others had a connection to you. This had already been going on for months before you arrived."

She nodded, although that little voice in her mind said it was entirely her fault. She looked to Reid for any lie of reassurance, but he did not give one. His eyes had returned to the fire; his thinking face had returned.

Miss Jenson came after breakfast with a book of swaths. Juniper settled on a brilliant spring pink, almost white. The seamstress nodded, spoke over key design elements, took a few measurements, and promised the most stunning gown at the ball.

Bala's Ball. A real ball, not the grungy parties in the Undercity where she had to fight off pickpockets and groping hands, avoid piles of vomit and puddles of piss, and try not to get into any brawls that broke out. And she would be dressed by the Royal Seamstress. Perhaps the gods didn't hate her after all.

Juniper dressed in a tunic and trousers. She didn't quite feel like walking about the castle, but she knew Reid would frown if she wore her pajamas into the afternoon. And she still had another book to read. She was thinking of ways to weasel Reid into letting her stay in bed and read while he studied, but when she walked out of the dressing room, she found Reid leaning against a bedpost. He held two wooden swords. One rested over his shoulder, and the other rested point-first on the toe of his boot.

She blinked. "Where did you get those?"

"I went down to the barracks while you two were talking fashion." Reid shifted the swords easily. "I asked a knight to stand watch at the door; don't worry."

"Did he act offended when a squire stationed him?" She grinned.

Reid shrugged. "If he did, he held it in well. I asked nicely." He flipped the sword up from his boot and caught it by the wooden blade. He held the hilt out to her. "I can't afford to get rusty. Show me if that sword arm of yours has dulled with all your lazing about."

Ah. A challenge. She scoffed and repeated, "Lazing about."

She sauntered over to him and wrapped her hand around the wooden hilt of the sword. Worn and smooth, like the staves. They positioned themselves in the open space of the bedroom. Reid started off slow, and then they danced about the bedroom, back and forth, clanking wooden sword against wooden sword. Reid was an excellent swordsman. She had to focus to keep up with him, to avoid his swings, to defend and counter, and as he quickened his pace, she found herself barely dodging attacks that would otherwise cleave into her arm, her thigh, her ribs.

Her breath turned ragged. Sweat glistened along her brow and along his. Her middle ached. She saw her chance; she feinted, but he caught her. His sword came swiftly to her exposed side.

It would not have been a lethal hit, but as the sword's swat surprised her, his foot came around to her opposite ankle. She tumbled backward; he moved too fast for her to counter. Her back collided with the stone floor. Reid knelt over her, sword's edge to her throat.

"Cheap shot." Juniper nudged her own sword upward, swatting him harmlessly on the calf.

Reid chuckled. "Yet you are the one with a sword at your throat. If this were real combat, you'd be dead."

He offered her his hand. She grasped it, and he easily hoisted her to her feet—and she stood much closer to him than she anticipated. The smell of him hit her: leather, sweat, and that woodsy scent. That scent clung to the pillow he'd slept on.

She found his eyes. Solid as the rest of him. Build like a warrior, inside and out.

"Round two?" he asked.

Her lips twitched upward. "Thought you'd never ask."

They sprang apart. The swords clanked, feverish and quick, around and around, until again, Reid's skill outmatched hers. He used the same feint-and-trip maneuver; however, this time, he used her lack of balance to spin her. Her back collided with his chest. The edge of the wooden blade met her throat.

She felt the muscles of his chest heave against her back with each breath he took, his powerful lungs pumping underneath, his heart thudding.

His hot breath met her ear. "That's twice I've cut your throat."

Neither moved. She wasn't sure she wanted to.

The sword at her throat moved, and his hand replaced it. His calloused fingers brushed against her pulse. Did he note how it quickened? His hand flattened against her throat without the slightest pressure.

Anyone else's hand at her throat would have sent her panicking, flailing to defend herself, but not Reid's. He wouldn't harm her, not with his prince's life bound to hers.

A part of her was glad she faced away from him. Otherwise, he would have seen how red her face was.

Reid's mouth came close enough to her ear that his lips dusted the shell. Her breath hitched; her heart skipped. His hot breath tickled her skin, and every muscle in her body seemed to go numb. The wooden sword slipped from her grasp, but she tightened her fingers around it before it fell.

His breath collided with her jaw, her neck. Her gut twisted as his breath traveled, as his lips grazed the skin where her shoulder met her neck.

Mistake.

Every fiber of his being screamed at him—*mistake, mistake, mistake.*

Almost every part of him. The other part of him wanted to feel the skin of her throat against his mouth, to see if she felt as soft as she looked, to see if she tasted like she smelled, to hear the sounds she would make. That part of him, the part of him he'd done his best to ignore these past several weeks, wanted to toss the swords aside and pin her to the bed.

It was to that part of him that he yielded. He let his eyes wander from her smooth neck to the collar of her tunic, to the soft skin exposed at his angle, to the forbidden flesh that lay underneath it, to the curves of her breasts.

She tilted her head slightly, exposing more of her neck. Did she do that on purpose? Gods.

Juniper Thimble, that logical voice reminded him shrewdly. Thief. Assassin. Criminal. But the other part of him spoke louder, pulling his eyes toward her skin with ravenous hunger. Her throat pulsed wildly underneath his fingers. He waited for her to push him away, to do something to stop him, to tell him no. She didn't. She seemed, if it were possible, to have gotten closer.

He could barely breathe. He dropped his sword. Instantaneously, she dropped hers. They clattered to the floor, one after the other. Reid brought his now free hand gingerly to her hip and pulled her even closer.

Mistake.

✦

Juniper inhaled, unsure if she could still breathe. His hand slid along her stomach, along her ribs, with strength but without pressure. Gods...she wanted to feel that hand *everywhere*. His other clung loosely at her throat. His hand paused high on her ribs, a finger away from her breast.

And then he yanked both hands away from her like he'd been burned.

She turned, but he had already stepped away from her. He looked flustered and angry. What had she done?

"Reid?"

He stalked toward the door, leaving the swords where they lay. He left without a word.

Juniper stood where he'd left her. She stood there until she could no longer hear his footsteps, until the door to her room closed, until she heard the guard from outside step inside to resume Reid's position.

He hadn't even waited for a knight or to call for a squire.

Repulsed. A horrible pit opened up in her stomach—suffocating, lightless, and never-ending—wide enough to swallow the whole world into the black depths.

With numb hands, she picked up the wooden swords and set them against the wall. She thought about a bath but decided against it. She didn't feel like a bath. She felt like curling up into a ball and vanishing until this loathsome feeling subsided. Until she figured out what she had done wrong. Until she could push Reid and the feeling of his hands out of her mind.

She stretched out her limbs, then washed the sweat from her face. She wandered back into her bedroom, to one of the sealed windows, and pondered the thought of escape that had drifted in and out of her mind since she'd been locked in this damn room. She could do it easily. She could slip out of a window or through a courtyard, move along the rooftops, over the wall, and into the city beyond. They'd never find her.

Of course, all they had to do was slit Adrian's throat. The wound would transfer to her, killing her. An easy way for them to get rid of her. They couldn't have her wandering about the city when any wound she received would transfer to Adrian. She could ransom any amount of gold for his safety. That itself was a damn good reason to lock her inside.

She pushed those thoughts away and climbed into bed. Without Reid there, she didn't need to make up excuses to spend the day in bed reading. Surely, he'd rather spend it elsewhere, with other people. His reaction to her had been evidence enough he did not think about her like *that*.

Not that she thought about him like *that* either.

She started reading; Ison had promised this book held plenty of sword fights, adventure, witty heroines, and smutty forest scenes. She immersed herself so thoroughly that she didn't hear the door open, the guard talking, or the person talking back. She became aware of someone else when her bedroom door closed louder than it should, jerking her attention upward.

Reid stood in her bedroom, brown eyes on her. He wore a look she'd never seen on him before, and it sent a warm spark down her spine. Slowly, he started toward the bed. She closed the book, not bothering to mark the page, and swung her feet to the floor. She set the book on the table beside her dagger.

"I'm sorry," she said at once.

He blinked at her; his warm expression dissolved into one of confusion. He shook his head. "No, I am the one who should be sorry. I shouldn't have... I didn't mean..." He sighed. Confusion knitted his brows together. "I didn't mean to offend you in any way."

What? Her brows rose. Is that what he thought?

She laughed. "*Offend* me? Dear Squire, you are going to have to try much harder to insult me than threaten to nuzzle my neck."

Red warmed his cheeks, but he did not look away. Damn that look of his. It melted her bones and stirred something warm where that pit had been. Juniper closed the distance between them, lifted onto her tiptoes, and placed a swift kiss on his blushing cheek.

Her heels had not yet met the floor again when he pressed his lips against hers.

CHAPTER FORTY-FOUR

Juniper's gasp vanished against Reid's kiss. His lips moved against hers with precise, controlled grace. His arms pulled her closer still. She touched his jaw, his neck. Taut with muscle.

They broke apart, but neither moved. His gilded brown eyes met hers, unreadable expression gone. Desire danced in its place. She felt each of those things swirling around in her stomach, her gut, tugging lower. For him.

"And here I thought you hated me," she whispered.

He laughed, a soft sound that pushed against her lips. He kissed her again, pulling her as close as possible.

His lips found a tender spot on her neck, and he coaxed sounds from her throat that she didn't know she could make. The rest of the world faded. They collapsed onto her bed, but his hands never went underneath her clothes, never tugged on the strings of her tunic, never pushed her for anything more.

Reid could barely breathe. Not with her lips against his, not with his hand in her hair. He couldn't keep his hands off her—he never wanted to let her go. He ran his hands along her back, pulling her close, and then he felt it. The too-smooth skin, the ridges. The brand.

He broke their kiss. "When did he do this?"

Juniper blinked. He traced his fingers along the jagged spiral. "I was twelve," she whispered.

He hissed. That man had burned a brand into the back of a twelve-year-old girl, claiming her. The bastard. Reid would find the time to make him pay, but for now, he hugged Juniper closer.

"That's when he knew he'd keep me," she said softly. "The Undercity guild masters trade orphans until they find what they're good at or until they die trying."

Reid huffed.

"It's better than dying on the streets." She flattened her hand over his heart. "Maddox, for all his faults, did put a roof over my head and food in my stomach. He pushed me to see what I could do, to see where I'd fit in, testing me, drawing my limits."

Reid followed the jagged spiral with his fingertips.

"Maddox kept me," she whispered. She shut her eyes and laid her forehead against his shoulder. "I wasn't pretty enough to be a courtesan, not an expensive one at least, and I didn't have the right personality for it. He said I'd only piss my clients off."

"You're more than pretty enough." Reid brushed a strand of hair off her shoulder. He touched her cheek. "Far more than pretty enough. He knew how valuable you were."

Her midnight eyes widened. Her lips parted. Silver lined her eyelids. He had opened something vulnerable, something underneath the bravado and arrogance, and he loved it. He leaned down and kissed her tenderly.

"Reid," she breathed against his lips.

"When your job here is finished," he said, a promise, "I will not let you go back to him, to the Undercity. I want you here. With me. Even if I have to hide you in my room."

She smiled against his lips, but it faltered. "You'd do that?"

"Yes." No hesitation.

"Why?"

"I want you here with me."

Her gaze softened. The silver in her eyes intensified. She blinked, smearing tears across her eyelashes. "Why me?"

He had an answer but not one he could put into words.

"I'm not good at anything." Her voice had gone to a near whisper. "I don't have anything. I'm just a worthless thief."

"Don't say that." He angled himself over her. She had nowhere to look but at him. "Don't ever say that."

"But it's true."

"Who told you that?"

"Would you like a list? The king, your uncle, and Maddox are just a few names on it."

He kissed her forehead, the tip of her nose, and then her lips. "They don't know you like I do. I've spent enough time with you to know you're worth far more than they realize." He kissed her. He would never tire of those lips.

"Enough to hide me in your closet when the king finally kicks me out?"

He smiled and kissed her again. "If that is what I have to do to keep you. It's a big closet. Not as big as yours. You'd have to keep your clothes to a minimum."

"Well, that's a deal breaker." Juniper laughed, a lovely sound, and a lovelier sight. "How am I supposed to downsize my dresses to just a few?"

"I'll see what I can do."

Smiling, she leaned into his shoulder. "Just remember to let me out at least once a day. And feed me at least twice, or I'll get cranky."

"As you command, my lady." He wrapped his arms around her, unsure if he had the will to let her go. He would worry about his uncle and Fowler and the Order later. Right now, all that mattered to him was the girl in his arms.

CHAPTER FORTY-FIVE

We are running out of time, said the hissing voice in Ison's ear.

When he had first heard it, he didn't know. He'd stopped thinking about it. He'd heard it many times before, but he had almost always forgotten it until it spoke once more. It never said much to him, but the words sliced through him like ice, through his mind—an intrusion.

I will help you. He won't hold you here.

He knew who the voice meant.

I will open a door for you. Go through. Go left, toward the end of the corridor. I will open another door there for you.

The instructions sounded familiar. He'd done this before. Doors where no door should be.

Tonight, you will go to the library. To the archives below. There will be a knight alone there. Use him.

No, he wanted to argue, but words failed him. He couldn't disobey the voice.

Use him, the voice hissed darkly, a warning not to question. *The next will need more power than the others. Use the knight. He will not see you. I will make sure of it.*

He didn't want to do this, but even as he wanted to say no, he felt his body responding to the order, committing the commands to memory. He stood, his eyes hardly seeing, and he started to walk through an archway beside the hearth that hadn't been there before. The light from the hearth did not go farther than the threshold, as if the stone had been painted black.

He walked through and into the darkness. The stone behind him swallowed the light. His feet knew the way. The voice knew the way.

He knew it didn't matter to object. He would follow the hissed orders. His body no longer belonged to him.

Soon, hissed the voice. *I will reward you for your service. Soon. But the prince must be out of the way. The king must be out of the way. The impostor must be out of the way.*

He knew all of the names of those the voice mentioned. He knew all of their faces. He knew he did, but he could not summon them to his mind. As he made his way through the corridors, through the stone arches that

238

disappeared as quickly as they appeared, his mind left those things behind. Hid them away.

His mind was lost until the master released it once more.

CHAPTER FORTY-SIX

Juniper and Reid were eating breakfast the next morning when a quick knock sounded at her door. Reid stood to answer, pecking her cheek as he passed.

It was Squire Berwick, and he looked shaken. His skin had paled, and he panted. Reid glanced once at Juniper, worry on his face, and then stepped into the corridor with Berwick.

Something, she knew for certain, was wrong. With every beat, with every moment that Reid didn't return, her heart inched further up her throat. She could hear them just outside the door, whispering. She gripped the table, her nails digging into the wood.

At last, Reid came back inside. The color had drained from his face.

"Is Berwick all right? Reid? Are you all right?"

He swallowed. His darkened gaze met hers. "Another has been taken."

Her chest tightened. The stone shifted underneath her. She shook her head, as if it would do anything to reverse the news. She'd stopped asking, nearly stopped hoping, but a sliver of it remained that Clara would burst into the room one morning with a wild story of abduction and a harrowing escape.

Maybe she'd been reading too much.

"Who?" Her voice shook. "Not Marcy?"

Reid shook his head, that darkness thick in his eyes. "Sir Geol."

Her face blanched. The food turned sour in her stomach. Her voice came out a croak. "A knight?"

Reid returned to the table and sat. "He was in the archives,"—he pushed his unused knife into perfect alignment with the plate—"looking up records of missing people in the castle. There is one door into the archives, through the library. According to the scholars, he went in, but he never came out. They had eyes on the door the entire time. They're owls, those scholars."

She nodded. She remembered.

"They went in to kick him out for the night, but he was gone. His Mage's Bane blade was on the floor, books and scrolls still on the table."

"They left his Mage's Bane?" What did that mean?

Reid nodded grimly. "I've heard rumors that the knights suspect the apostate is responsible for the missing people."

Her hands shook. She clenched her fists and hid them beneath the table. "Gods...but why? Midnight snacks for his beasts?" Her throat threatened to close. "I thought the knights were supposed to protect us from the apostate? What's going to stand in his way now?"

Reid shook his head. "I don't know, but it's shaken the Order. They've called an emergency meeting, but I declined to attend. I am needed here."

She felt much better with Reid within reach. "What does this mean?" she asked.

"We remain on guard. In pairs. Two guards and a knight will be posted outside your room."

"I want you." As the words left her throat, a mad blush warmed her entire face. She clarified, "I feel safest with you."

"And you'll have me." Reid stood and made his way around the table. He cupped her cheek and placed a tender kiss on her lips, one that lit a fire underneath her skin. "He won't take you," he whispered. "Nor will a demon lay a talon on you. Not while I breathe."

"I'd like to see it try," she whispered back. She kept the dagger he'd given her on her bedside table.

Reid smiled and stood. "I do have some other news." He cleared his throat, and his professionalism returned. Her breath hitched. "I must visit my uncle and aunt's for dinner. I've been planning to come by more."

She nodded. He didn't have to add the rest. *With all the demon attacks and missing people, who would be next?*

He added, "I can't leave you here unattended."

"I can look after myself for a while. No need to drag me along." His brows scrunched together, and she added, "I'm sure your uncle would rather me not be at your dinner."

Reid knelt down on one knee. His unrelenting gaze stared into hers. "A knight was taken. A *knight*, Juniper." He set a hand on her knee. "A trained knight who should have been able to detect and dispel any magic, who should have been able to take on an angry mage. He failed. I don't know what this means for the Order or for our apostate problem. But I refuse to let you out of my sight."

"You wish to keep an eye on me yourself?" She laced her fingers with his. "So attentive."

He brought her hand to his lips.

You're more than pretty enough. She wrapped her arms around him, pulling him close. She buried her face in the taut muscles of his chest. If anyone else had spoken those words to her, she would have laughed and called them a liar. But Reid... He had looked at her with only sincerity in his eyes. Honesty.

Those words had nearly made her heart stop. They still did when she repeated them to herself. What power did this man have over her to make her feel so?

✦

Captain Sandpiper knew her real name, but Juniper still took the time to get ready. She chose an elegant blue gown from the first selection the seamstress had brought up.

She did her own hair, not caring enough to call for a servant. She didn't want anyone else touching her hair but Clara. Every time Marcy or another servant stepped into her room, they acted as though they might be the next victim.

She chose a simple necklace from the rack, a yellow gem on a silver chain.

"That one," Reid whispered over her shoulder. He pointed to a string of sapphires, each roughly the size of her little fingernail. Before she could question his fashion sense, he whispered, "It matches your eyes."

She blushed. She carefully picked up the necklace and laid them against her neck. Reid nodded, and she glanced at herself in the mirror. Indeed, the sapphires reflected the dark blue of her eyes.

"You look lovely," Reid said from behind her, his brown eyes glancing over her reflection.

She met his eyes. Should she say something? What did people say after receiving such compliments?

He lifted a brow. "Do you not believe me?"

She blinked several times. "No, no, I'm just not used to compliments." Especially from men. Especially from people who didn't want something.

He gave her a warm smile. His hands came around her waist, pressing her into him. "You better get used to them." He kissed her cheek.

Oh, she could stay in his embrace forever. But they had dinner to attend. They disentangled themselves and stepped into the corridor as Squire Sandpiper and Lady Roslyn.

Reid led her through the castle, passing guards, servants, and a few nobles, none of whom walked alone. Reid walked with one step between them, ever the professional.

They arrived at the barracks, ripe with clanking swords and the grunts of guards fighting against one another in the practice rings and full of tired men after a long day, chatting and laughing.

Reid steered them into the Captain's Corridor. While windowless and a bit drab, it held paintings of famous captains, a few scenery paintings picked by someone with horrible taste, and enough torches to leave lengthy shadows between each stone pillar. For anyone having to visit the Captain of the Guard, the corridor certainly set an air of horror. Juniper scanned each shadow for anything that could be lurking, be it demon or assassin or whatever else.

They arrived at the only door in the corridor, a set of oak doors with dark brass handles, and Reid knocked thrice.

Soft footsteps padded across the floor, and the door swung open, revealing a smiling woman in her early forties. She stood a head shorter than Reid but held herself like the tallest woman in the room. Her flaxen hair had been pulled back into a bun, not unlike what the servant girls wore, and she'd donned a simple dress of white and brown that flattered her matronly figure.

"Reid," she said, stepping across the threshold to embrace him. "It's been too long." Her light brown eyes shifted to Juniper. Her smile faltered. "And you've brought company."

"Yes." Reid cleared his throat and motioned between the two. "Aunt Glenda, this is Lady Roslyn Derean. Roslyn, this is my Aunt Glenda. She oversees the servants."

"It is a pleasure to finally meet you," Juniper chimed, her voice sweet as a song.

Glenda's smile turned sweet as frostbite, full of cold, lethal venom. The captain had told her, then. She knew exactly who Roslyn was. "It's a pleasure, my lady."

Yes, she knew.

Juniper held in her reaction as best she could.

"Please, do come in." Glenda held the door open.

Reid motioned for Juniper to go first. Captain Sandpiper and his wife occupied a space as large as a nice townhouse. The first floor, all open, contained a sitting room, a dining room, and a kitchen. A stone staircase led to a second floor. They decorated modestly. Juniper wandered into the sitting room, where a painting of Captain Sandpiper hung over the mantle.

"A gift from the king," Reid said to her. "Uncle had to find a place to hang it."

"I thought I heard guests," Captain Sandpiper said as he descended the stone stairs and walked into the sitting room. He wore a simple tunic and pants, along with a thick leather sword belt. He approached Reid, hand outstretched. "Reid."

"Uncle." Reid took his uncle's hand, but his uncle pulled him into an embrace.

"It's been too long." Captain Sandpiper's eyes shifted to Juniper. He, unlike his wife, had a better skill for keeping his expressions masked. "Lady Derean."

"Captain." Juniper dipped into a curtsy.

Captain Sandpiper huffed a laugh. He said to Reid, "You've trained her well."

Juniper shot a sharp glance at the captain, to which he laughed.

Captain Sandpiper led them into the dining room, to the oak table capable of seating six, and took the seat at the head of the table. He bade Reid sit to his right. Juniper sat on Reid's other side.

"You've been well?" Captain Sandpiper asked.

Reid nodded. "Yes. As well as one can be with all that's been happening."

His uncle's eyes shot to Juniper. A warning.

"She knows most, if not all," Reid quickly clarified.

The captain nodded. "How wise is that?"

Juniper tensed; she did not like to be spoken about as if she wasn't present. Reid gently nudged her knee with his. "Fairly, I'm sure. I wouldn't have found the sewer grate had it not been for her eye."

His uncle's eyes searched his with a masked indifference, as one might use when examining a painting for flaws. Peculiar how much they looked alike. They shared the same chestnut hair, strong jaw and nose, and broad shoulders. His uncle had greenish eyes, not the honey-brown of Reid's.

Glenda emerged in the archway. "Dinner is almost ready. Juniper, help me bring it in."

Juniper did not jump at the sound of her name. She stood politely and followed Glenda out of the room and into the spacious and well-used kitchen. The pots and pans had the dents and dings and scorch marks of one who loved to cook. By Glenda's healthy figure, the woman knew her way around a kitchen. Glenda had several pots over the stove, some bubbling, others steaming.

"It smells amazing." Juniper closed her eyes and inhaled the herbs, the butter, the spices.

Glenda nodded toward an array of serving dishes on the shelves. "Grab me the large flat dish for the pork," she said flatly.

Juniper did as instructed and selected the dish that she felt fit the description of large and flat. She carried it to Glenda, who didn't scold her for making the wrong choice. Neither woman spoke while Juniper held the dish and Glenda transferred the tenderloin from pan to dish. It looked as delicious as it smelled. Glenda then set the pork on a two-tiered wheeled wooden cart, similar to those the servants used to bring Juniper her meals.

The process continued with each dish Glenda had prepared. Glenda described the dish she wanted, Juniper found and brought her said dish, and Glenda filled it with food. Juniper tried to ignore the woman's coldness, her indifference, but couldn't.

"I am sorry for intruding on your family time." Juniper held the servicing dish steady as Glenda skillfully transferred the cooked beans and the herb-rich juice into it. "I suggested Reid leave me in my chambers, but he refused."

Glenda set the empty pot in the sink. She took the beans from Juniper and carefully added it to the cart. She gave no indication that she'd even heard.

Juniper inhaled, holding in what she could have said to the woman. She could handle the silent treatment. At least she had the food to look forward to. She would not be mean to Reid's aunt. The aunt who had raised him. Practically his *mother*.

Who knew who she was, what she was, and what she'd done.

"I've known Reid most of his life," Glenda said at last, her tone sharp. A warning. She turned to Juniper with a glare that matched her tone. "He is an honorable soul, just like his father." Glenda's gaze narrowed. "I see how he looks at you."

Juniper blinked. How had he looked at her?

Glenda's chin jutted. Her voice turned into a deadly whisper. "You don't see it, do you? Well, I do. I've dealt enough with the young servants to know when a man's in love."

Juniper froze at that word.

Glenda took a step closer to Juniper. Her eyes burned. "You have noticed."

She swallowed; underneath Glenda's hard stare, she felt small. The older woman looked like she might strike her.

Glenda hissed, "You'd best not break his heart."

"I do not plan on it."

They put the rest of the meal into serving dishes, grabbed butter for the warmed rolls, and Juniper volunteered to push the cart into the dining room, which Glenda allowed. Reid and Captain Sandpiper were sitting in near silence, but Juniper had the sinking suspicion that a conversation had just ended and that she had been called out of the room for more reasons than to assist with the food.

CHAPTER FORTY-SEVEN

With Bala's Ball two days away, the entire city was preparing for it. Reid took Juniper to one of the highest courtyards to see all the vendors along Royal Avenue and the side streets, selling everything imaginable: jewelry, clothing, woodwork, candles, perfumes, food, and drinks. The Undercity didn't celebrate Bala's Day like the rest of the city. Thieves and pickpockets prowled the crowded streets for easy prey.

When the seamstress arrived with a garment bag behind her—two servants carried it between them—Juniper tripped over herself trying to stand. Miss Jenson instructed the two servants into the bedroom, and Juniper followed eagerly behind. She gripped fistfuls of her dressing gown while Miss Jenson carefully unwrapped the dress.

Juniper's mouth fell open. She had never seen a more beautiful gown—not in the shops along Royal Avenue, not in the paintings that littered the castle corridors, not on the hundreds of nobles that flocked to the royal balls each year.

"So, you like it?" Miss Jenson grinned, glowing with pride.

Juniper didn't have the words for the glorious gown displayed in front of her. She let out a girlish squeal. Reid, standing by the door with his arms crossed, jumped at the sudden sound.

The dress was a soft pink-white with yards of flowing, shiny silk. Pearl beading and silver-white thread embroidered the bodice. The scooping neckline left much of her chest and shoulders bare. The pink-white silk of the sleeves fluttered from the shoulder to the white-cuffed wrists, and split down the length of the arm, leaving much of her arm exposed. Silver thread detailed down the sleeves.

Juniper felt a pressure welling in her eyes as such a lovely dress. For her.

"You will look like a goddess," said Miss Jenson. "Or I will chop it up and eat it. Now, are you ready to try it on?"

The seamstress glared at Reid, who found something to do in the sitting room.

Miss Jenson and the two servants helped Juniper into the gown, and it took all three of them. It felt like wearing a cloud of silk, albeit a slightly squeezing cloud once the corset was tied.

Juniper gasped at her reflection. Gone was the skinny rat from the Undercity. Her reflection showed a healthy young woman in a gown worthy of Bala herself. The pink-white flowed like dawn light.

"Absolutely stunning," said Miss Jenson. "You will have every pair of eyes on you."

A part of her, the part that delighted when Maddox bragged about her to the other thieves and guild masters, loved the idea of all the other women being green with envy at her and her gown on the arm of Prince Adrian Bradburn.

But she would rather be on Reid's arm.

He would attend the ball as Squire Sandpiper, her guard, not as a guest with whom she could dance. It might be better that way. If Lady Roslyn danced with Squire Sandpiper, her lover's best friend, it would raise suspicions. They didn't need any more suspicions than they already had.

"I will take your speechlessness as approval." Miss Jenson stepped around her and reached for the ties on the dress. She hesitated, giving Juniper one last chance to disagree.

"I love it," was all she could say.

Satisfied, Miss Jenson and the servants helped Juniper out of the dress and carefully hung it. Miss Jenson set her matching shoes underneath it and laid out her jewelry on the vanity. Juniper dressed in a simple gown, drab in comparison to the ballgown, and stood in the doorway to the closet as Miss Jenson left.

"It's a lovely gown," Reid said from the doorway of the bedroom. His sure footsteps started across the room. "You will look marvelous in it."

"Bala will be jealous."

Reid chuckled and came to stand beside her. "Do you really want to poke Bala before her own ball? Some might consider it asking for disaster."

She grinned and looped her arm through his. "Haven't you met me? I often ask disaster to dinner. We get along just fine."

Reid laughed and pulled her into the open space of the bedroom. He reached for the wooden swords against the wall and tossed one to her. She caught it by the hilt.

"Before that—"

She sighed dramatically. "You need your ass handed to you, I understand."

He chuckled. They took up their stances. The swords clanked together, and the two of them danced about the floor. Reid won all but one round, which ended with a kiss on her lips.

Juniper hoisted her chin to the top of the bathing room door frame until her arms shook and shoulders felt raw. She dropped to the ground. Two breaths, three breaths, five breaths. She rolled onto her back and hauled her shoulders to her knees. Again. Again. Again. Until she couldn't bear to do another.

She would gather her strength as best she could, despite the half-read book on the bed. She wagered with herself: she could read only after she'd tired herself out from working her body.

Juniper rested on her back, letting the burning in her abdomen settle, when a hasty knock came to the main door of her chambers.

It took a moment for her to remember that Reid had gone, something about a meeting for the ball's security. Squire Berwick and two guards stood outside her door. She rolled onto her hands and knees and wobbled to her feet. Her visitor knocked a second time as she walked through the sitting room.

"Coming," she chimed.

Hopefully, her visitor didn't mind her sweaty appearance. A lady needed to keep strong, she'd say. The real Roslyn Derean would surely agree.

She opened the door; Ison stood on the other side, looking worried. He looked smaller, narrower without his mage's robes. The red of his tunic made his eyes appear cold.

"Lady Roslyn," Ison said, nodding in greeting.

"Ison?" She stepped back to let him through. Berwick didn't look at all pleased by it, neither did the guards on the other side of the door. She ignored their stares and shut the door. "Ison, it's been ages. I've been told you were ill. Are you all right?"

"Ill?" Ison blinked at her. Confusion passed over his face. His steel eyes darted to the door, to every corner of the room, and to the doors and windows with an urgency and panic that she did not like. "I'm fine. Now."

"Were you not?"

Those panicked eyes turned to her. He gave a mirthless laugh. He glanced to the door, then he motioned toward the bedroom.

Whatever it was, he did not want the guards listening in. Or the squire.

She followed him into the bedroom. He stood stone still in front of the hearth. She shut the bedroom door and asked, "Ison? Please, what is it? Are you all right?"

He swung his arms out to the sides. "Considering everything? No, I'm not all right." He started to pace. "Something is happening inside this castle. Something horrible. Something evil."

Her heart dropped into her stomach. Her voice quavered, "The demons?"

"I—I don't know." The heart that had always been behind Ison's voice crumbled. His shoulders shook with each breath he took. "I overheard Mason talking, him and the king. He doesn't think the demons are demons. I—I don't remember the entire conversation, only that he thinks it's something horrible. Something worse."

"Worse?" She took a step toward him. "What do you mean?"

Ison turned his cold eyes on her. His frown became a grimace. In a calm, cold voice, he said, "I think you know."

Juniper felt as though she had been dunked into a lake of icy water. She swallowed, forcing the feeling away, thinking of the hearth fire burning behind Ison, of the heat of the flames, of the warmth of Reid's body against hers as he slept.

She met Ison's uncanny stare. She mustered all the venom she could and said, "I can assure you I do not, but since you are already here, skip the dance and tell me what you're accusing me of."

Ison didn't flinch. "It started after you arrived. The demons. The suspicions. The nightmares. The voices."

She fought to keep her expression calm. "Nightmares and voices? Neither of those is good. Especially for a mage." Or her fault.

His left eye fluttered slightly, the only reaction he gave. "I've seen things, splotched memories of things I don't remember doing, but...I've done them. I know I have. My hands know it."

"You..." What had he done? Did he know more about the demons? No. She didn't want to believe it, but under that stare, doubt crept in. There was something menacing underneath his calm panic.

"I couldn't remember it well at first. I thought they were dreams. But they've come back to me, a little more each time." His voice was small yet powerful, spiteful, and strong. "It started with you. That first time I met you. I brought you a tonic." His hands came together over his chest. "I touched your hand. Do you remember?"

She nodded. "Yes."

"I felt it." His eyes burned like the fire behind him. "The magic."

She tensed; every bone felt like iron; every hair felt like a needle. She dreaded the words even before they left his mouth—

"You're a mage."

Juniper didn't move. His cold stare met hers, daring her to deny it, to try and lie her way out of it. But before she could speak, the door to the sitting room opened, and Reid's feet met the floor.

Thank the gods.

Juniper spun and dashed toward the bedroom door but paused. Her hand trembled against the wood. What would Reid think when he found Ison standing in her bedroom with such an accusation on his lips?

No, no, Reid couldn't know. Not yet. Not ever.

A soft whoosh came from behind her. She spun, her back hitting the door, only to find her bedroom empty. Ison was gone.

The stone beside her bathing room door seemed to shift. She blinked; it was gone. A trick of the light and her panic.

Reid walked through the sitting room, already unbuckling his sword belt from his waist. He walked into the bedroom, sighed heavily, and set his sword in the chair he'd once slept in. "If you ever feel like sitting through a boring meeting, try the security council. With all the demons, they're pulling every available man for Bala's Ball. Royal Guard, City Watch, and the Order. Every window, doorway, and sewer grate will be under watch. They've put me with the guards in the ballroom, to better watch Adrian and Lady Roslyn."

Reid stretched and walked toward the fire. He hadn't heard Ison. A deep relief lifted from her bones.

"I will be glad when this ball is over." Reid let out a sigh. "Are you all right? You look pale."

She opened her eyes; she didn't remember closing them. Reid was looking at her, brows furrowed, searching.

She nodded. "Yes, I'm fine."

Reid closed the distance between them and brushed a warm hand against her cheek.

What would Reid think if he heard Ison's accusation? She lied, "I was working myself too hard. I guess I didn't eat enough for lunch. I fainted."

Whether he believed her or not, he didn't let on. He kissed her forehead. "It's nearly time for dinner, and I'm famished. Is there anything special you'd like to eat?"

"Anything sounds good. I trust your judgment when it comes to food."

He grinned and started for the door, to give the order.

✦

That night during dinner, they didn't speak of Ison or the attacks. Reid told her about the meeting, about a squirrelly city guardsman who had been kicked out, rejoined under a false name, and kicked out again; he'd become a joke among the guard. Juniper laughed. With each heave of her chest, the panic of Ison's accusation settled down, down, down, into that place where she could forget all about it.

That night, eating dinner with Reid, she knew what she wanted. She wanted dinner with him every night. She wanted to fall asleep beside him and wake up to him. Not just until the apostate was found, but forever. His eyes, his voice—Reid held something that no one ever had before. He had become her stone.

Someone to come back to. A home.

CHAPTER FORTY-EIGHT

The day before the ball, Juniper woke in Reid's arms. He slept soundly, his breath warm on her neck. With the comfort of the bed, the laziness of the sunlight, and the sturdy presence beside her, she could think of nowhere else she'd rather be.

Reid's arm tightened around her. He'd woken. He hugged her close and pressed a kiss to her neck, then another.

They spent the day shut in her chambers while the castle beyond buzzed with last-minute decorations for the ball. Their meals came and went with the servants, all looking hassled and tired. Only when the sun began to sink did the reality of the following day settle.

That night, before settling into bed beside Reid, Juniper walked into the closet several times to make sure the dress of her dreams still hung there. It never moved, although she wanted to reach out and caress the soft silk each time she saw it.

"I'm not sure I'll be able to sleep," she confessed. She leaned against the doorframe. "None of it feels real."

Reid's arm came around her waist. "The ball?"

"Everything," she whispered. "The ball. You."

"What about me doesn't seem real?" A smile played on his words.

"I still find it hard to believe that someone like you—" she hesitated to find the words to describe him "—could find anything remotely attractive about someone like me." She could think of plenty of words to describe herself. His breath hitched, but she continued before he could speak. "And I wonder if everything else that's happened: getting caught, this binding spell, the demons... I wonder if it was all a ruse by the gods to bring me to you."

She turned in his arms. His stoic mask was gone, and he looked at her with something that set loose a mad flock of butterflies from the tips of her toes to the top of her head.

"I'm not sure what I've done to deserve you," he said, breath against her lips, "but I'm not going to question it." She started to argue, but he shushed her with a kiss. "I don't care what you've done, Juniper. You're mine, and I'm yours, if you'll have me."

"I will. Sour attitude and all."

He laughed, and she laughed in response. Reid's lips moved along her cheek, to her ear, where he whispered, "If you don't think you can sleep, I'll wear you out."

She bit her lip. Every time he touched her, every time they kissed, she thought about giving herself to him entirely. Reid pulled away just enough to see her. She wanted to. Gods, she wanted to.

"It's your choice," Reid said. "I'll wait forever if that's what you desire."

He started to pull away, but she grabbed his arms. "I desire you."

"Are you sure?"

"Yes," she breathed. "Everything I have is yours."

His arms slid around her and lifted her. She wrapped her arms around his neck, inhaling his scent as he carried her to the bed.

Juniper woke to Reid humming into her neck and hugging her bare body against his. She didn't want to move, but they both knew the servants would be along shortly to help Roslyn ready for the ball, and neither of them wanted to answer the question of their nakedness. Not long after, a horde of servants arrived with breakfast.

"How are you feeling?" Reid asked over breakfast.

She knew what he meant. "A bit hassled, but otherwise fine." Juniper said no more, not with servants listening in. She caught his eye.

Reid raised a brow.

She added, "The hassle is well worth it."

She had known her first time with a man wouldn't be the most pleasant, but she hadn't anticipated it bringing her to tears. He had asked if she wanted him to stop, but she had said no each time. Despite the pain, he had made sure she met her release. She could feel the ghost of his hand tangled in her hair, of his breath on her neck.

Reid stayed in the sitting room while the servants washed her, dried her, smothered her in lotions and oils, cleaned and filed her nails, and combed and dried her hair. By the time the pampering had ended, lunch had arrived.

They couldn't talk over lunch, not with the servants listening in, and their conversation remained professional and friendly.

After lunch, the servants helped her into her dress. They fixed her raven hair into a braided crown and fixed it with pearl-tipped pins. They touched her face with powder, lined her eyes with kohl, and painted her lips a darling shade of red.

Juniper didn't know what to think of the regal young woman who blinked back at her from the mirror. Before, she looked like a princess, but tonight, she looked like a queen. A goddess.

Certainly qualified to be on the arm of the Crown Prince of Duvane.

The servants led her back into the sitting room, where Reid stood by the door. He'd left to change; he wore a simple black doublet with blue and silver embroidery—the dress uniform of the Order. He wore his sword at his waist and a dagger beside it. He carried himself like a knight, shoulders square, back straight.

"You look lovely, Lady Roslyn." Reid bowed his head. He held his hand out for hers. She held her shoulders and chin high and gracefully set her hand into his. She forced her face impassive when he placed a kiss to the back of her hand.

"As do you, Squire Sandpiper."

A proper greeting between a lady and a squire.

Reid led her into the corridor. A guard had assembled, each black and gold uniform pressed and clean, each button and pommel shined. Each guard wore not only his sword, but a dagger on the side and a short sword on the preferred shoulder. None were ceremonial.

They came to Adrian's chambers, where a guard twice as large as hers waited outside, all seasoned and capable guards, armed to the teeth. By the sounds, several more waited inside.

"Tell Prince Adrian that Lady Roslyn has arrived," Reid said to one of the guards by the door.

"And that *she* was ready on time," Juniper added with a smirk.

The guard nodded and vanished into the room. A few moments later, the doors opened. Adrian and the rest of his guard, including the fully-armed and armored Sir Destry, emerged.

Adrian wore a fine red doublet with golden embroidery along the gleaming brass buttons. His cream-colored pants showed off his narrow figure, and his brown boots had been shined to a gleam. A sash of silk ran from his shoulder to his waist, signaling him as Crown Prince. His head remained crown-free, although, with all the dancing, she understood why. His dark blond hair gleamed like worn gold, a crown in its own way.

Adrian looked her up and down, a smile across his handsome face. Reid made a grand show of handing her arm to Adrian, who made a show of taking it.

Normally, she would have objected to such a handing-off of a woman, but at these events, ceremony stood above personal honor. Tonight, she was not Juniper, but Lady Roslyn. Tonight was all about the show. And for once, she was participating.

They started toward the ballroom, rightly named the Royal Ballroom for its wide marble floors and pillars, stained glass windows, and adjoining courtyards. They came to the closed doors that would lead into the ballroom; the clink of glasses, the harmonious chime of strings and wind instruments, and the chatter of hundreds of voices drifted through.

Adrian led Juniper to a set of clouded glass doors in the corridor.

"We'll make a dramatic entrance," Adrian whispered. A guard opened the clouded glass doors. Adrian tugged Juniper into the room. The guardsmen halted outside, but a few followed them inside. Shadows.

The room was a moderate lounge. King Bentley Bradburn stood at the hearth fire. He wore a suit worthy of a king. It was a glorified version of the same suit Adrian wore; however, the king wore his crown.

King Bradburn watched them enter. His gaze settled on Juniper; it narrowed when he noticed her gaze on that which set on his head.

"Humph," was all he said.

Adrian whispered loud enough that his father could hear, "That means you look nice, but he doesn't want to tell you so."

Juniper had a retort on her tongue but thought better of it. The king had paid for her dress, after all. She could play nice for an evening.

"He's never been good at compliments," Adrian continued, well aware that his father heard every word. "My mother goes on and on about it."

The king huffed.

Adrian smiled, noting his father's displeasure. "She's the reason we're waiting. Mother must be the last to arrive. It makes her feel important to keep others waiting. That's why she is always late."

King Bradburn didn't argue, but his gaze slid to where Adrian whispered to Juniper, to their linked arms.

While they waited, she listened to the distant party, to the high-pitch ding of ladies' laughter, to the rumble of gentlemen talking. She could picture it, a scene pieced together from memories of watching from a hawk's view: dresses and suits swirling about the dance floor, skirts spinning, the jewelry glittering underneath the candlelight.

Juniper didn't know how long she stood, arm folded over Adrian's, imagining the party beyond those doors, but her thoughts were interrupted by the sound of a pair of heels, accompanied by a dozen booted guards.

The doors to the lounge swung open, and Queen Catherine sauntered inside. Her crown perched on her curled and pinned hair. The queen's gaze settled on Juniper. Dislike squeezed her eyes together, and the queen held her chin too high to be natural. A reminder of the hierarchy.

"Oh, Roslyn, dear, you look simply amazing!" Queen Catherine chimed in a false tone of pleasantry. Petty dislike oozed with every word.

Juniper nodded. "Thank you, Your Majesty, but I pale in comparison to you."

She gave Juniper a small grin. Juniper glanced at Adrian. He winked. Juniper did look amazing, and Queen Catherine hated her for it.

No words were exchanged between the royal family as they arranged themselves in the hall. They stood in parade fashion behind the doors to the ballroom. Two middle-aged men, who looked like they had a dozen other places to be, joined them. The royal advisors, Adrian explained, Rourke Hendle and Destin Ulgan.

Both men kept glancing at Juniper, particularly the short one, Ulgan. His heavy brow and ice-blue eyes gave him a heavy impression. She ignored him as best she could. Hopefully, he did not recognize her from a wanted poster somewhere in the city. Maybe the makeup would hide any trace of Juniper Thimble.

Then, suddenly, the band on the other side of the doors stopped playing. The crowd, the tickling of glasses, the shuffle of feet—all silenced. Juniper knew this part. She had witnessed it. But it did little to quell the monster quivering in her gut. The dramatic entrance.

She could do this.

Guards on either side of the door moved in unison; the doors opened. They led onto a small balcony from which a set of wide stone stairs led to the ballroom below.

Dramatic indeed.

She clutched Adrian's arm a little tighter, and he gave her hand an affectionate squeeze.

A horn sounded. The parade started. The herald, a man of booming voice and impossible volume, stood at the base of the stairs. He spoke each name and title with a graceful articulation. The announced party stood at the top of the stairs, paused, and continued down the stairs to join the ball.

Stairs. Just stairs.

She could handle stairs.

Juniper and Adrian would be second to last in the parade, before only the king and queen. The line moved frighteningly fast, and then she and

Adrian stood atop the stairs. Every pair of eyes in the Royal Ballroom looked to them. Hundreds of them. Gowns and suits of every color. Banners of woven flowers, purples, pinks, golds, and blues, adorned the stone between stained glass windows, hanging onto the torch brackets, and woven into the hair of servants. It smelled like a field of wildflowers.

Another world. A world of the gods. And *she* had been invited.

The herald, a short, balding man in a fine black suit, held her gaze for only a moment. Adrian held himself a little taller.

"His Royal Highness, Crown Prince Adrian Bradburn and Lady Roslyn Derean of Galamond."

Adrian took the first step. Juniper followed. She felt each stare as she and Adrian descended the stairs. She fought the urge to look at her feet; she'd never felt so wobbly in a pair of shoes. She forced her chin high to acknowledge her superiority to the women around her—Roslyn's superiority—and took each step in unison with Adrian.

They reached the ballroom floor at last. The crowd didn't look as intimidating. She took a calm breath.

Adrian led Juniper through the parted crowd, toward the dais were the royalty sat, his eyes full of awe and curiosity. She grinned back at him.

Look how well the thief plays a lady.

"His Majesty, King Bentley Bradburn and Her Majesty, Queen Catherine Bradburn," said the herald.

Adrian continued toward the dais, and Juniper felt eyes shift to her as she moved. Wouldn't the queen be furious? Adrian and Juniper reached a pair of smaller thrones and stood as the king and queen made their way toward the dais. As they moved through the room, heads bowed and skirts curtsied.

The queen's mask did not hide the icy glare she gave Juniper, the impostor standing where only royalty should tread.

Juniper turned her lips upward into a sweet smile and leaned toward Adrian, who met her halfway and gave her his ear. "Does your mother know?"

Adrian glanced toward his parents. "I can't say for certain. My father wanted to keep it the highest of secrets, but Mother is smart enough to put the story together for herself."

Like Ison.

The king and queen stepped onto the dais and, after a dramatic pause, sat. Adrian and Juniper sat a heartbeat after.

The king waved his hand toward the band, tucked into a safe corner of the room, and at once, the fluttering of woodwinds and strings filled the air. The crowd shifted back into itself, closing the path to the dais.

Adrian stood, holding his hand to Juniper. "Dance with me."

Juniper uncrossed her ankles and set her hand into his. Adrian led her through the ballroom to the dancefloor, amid a flurry of watching eyes. They fell easily into a simple dance. Her body moved with the delicate music, following Adrian's lead. Her hand rested on his shoulder, his hand on her waist, and their other two hands locked together. He spun her, and she cast her gaze over the crowd again. She found Reid; he stood in a guard's position by the wall.

You're mine, and I'm yours.

With those words, something settled in her chest.

Adrian saw how the other women looked at Juniper, like an intruder upon their sacred court. He spun her again. Her pink-white skirts shimmered in the light. What would they say if they knew who he really danced with?

Juniper returned to him, and he caught a whiff of jasmine and eucalyptus. Her oils and perfumes. Juniper's midnight eyes drifted over his shoulder and back again to his. A smile slid effortlessly over her red lips. Genuine.

Pretend, that's all it was.

Underneath her glossy court smile slept a hellcat. Adrian had been in the room when Captain Sandpiper revealed the extent of her criminal record. Murders. Thefts. Some of which had left him gawking; the skill required would have left anyone gawking.

Yet she looked at him with innocent eyes.

Adrian found it hard to believe that the girl he danced with was the same girl attached to such crimes of murder and impossible theft. Yet he saw it from time to time when her lady's mask slipped, and something darker glanced out—someone assessing each room she walked into and each body within it.

Juniper's gaze shifted from his once more, over his other shoulder. Her eyes remained there a beat too long. As he turned her, he followed that gaze to see what could be drawing her attention so often. Did someone wear a prettier dress? Wear a theft-worthy necklace?

He spotted no prettier dress and plenty of theft-worthy necklaces; however, it did not take him long to find what she had been looking at.

His gaze met Reid's. The squire looked away quickly. Oh? Adrian spun Juniper and brought her back again. Her eyes came to him, then over his shoulder. At Reid.

It would seem the thief and the squire had let something replace their animosity. He felt happy for them, yet jealousy burned in his chest. They had each other while Roslyn remained a kingdom away.

Juniper's midnight eyes found his. She gave him a small, reassuring smile. Had he been frowning? He gave her one in return and found that his lips had to move more—yes, he'd been frowning.

Juniper's smile widened. Her lips parted; the beginning of a word drifted upward from her throat but never made it to completion. Her nostrils flared. Her brows came together. The pretend-innocence of her eyes vanished, and something bloodthirsty and predatory took its place.

Before Adrian could question it, she whipped her head around.

Then, he heard the screams. Panicked screams of *run*, *get away*, and unintelligible fear. Then Adrian heard the deep, guttural grumble. A thunderous crash of a table overturning. The clatter of heavy claws on stone. Shoulders knocked into his—Juniper came closer, flattening her hands on his chest.

Then he saw it—the massive demon stood in the doorway to the courtyard. Its wide eyes settled on Adrian with a ravenous hunger.

Adrian froze; his very bones had been turned to ice.

CHAPTER FORTY-NINE

The demon fixed its eyes on Adrian.

Juniper felt every bone turn to ice, radiating her body with a numbing cold. The beast flexed it thick ivory claws. This demon walked on two legs, but it was not the Greater Demon from the passage. The patchy hair on its broad chest and shoulders looked reddish blonde, the leathery skin underneath a gray.

Howls echoed from the courtyard.

The demon hadn't come alone.

From the courtyard doors, five demons slinked inside on all fours.

The larger demon started into the room, its step thunderous. It moved toward them, toward Adrian.

Chaos spread like a contagion. Screams echoed off the stone and marble. The music screeched to a halt. Pushing, shoving, pulling—guests fled from the demons through any door or window, abandoning drink, food, and dancing partners. Glasses shattered, wine splashed across the stones, and fabric ripped underfoot.

The crowd surged around Juniper and Adrian. The guards shouted, but their voices were lost in the chaos. They tried to push through the crowd but not quick enough.

Away. They had to get away! Juniper shoved Adrian, who had frozen in place, eyes fixed on the demon. She pushed him harder, knocking him back a step. She beat a fist against his chest, and his hazel eyes snapped to hers.

"Adrian!" she screamed, voice breaking.

Juniper grabbed him by the arm, and they ran. The demon bounded after them. The guests ran in every direction from the demons, intercepting the larger demon's pursuit. Juniper heard the demon swat them out of its way like flies, tearing skin and fabric. And the screams.

At least they slowed it down, she told herself.

Juniper elbowed her way through the crowd, not caring for those she pushed; she cared more about herself and Adrian. She aimed for the stairs they had come down. They hit the bottom step, and guards swarmed—Juniper paused long enough to find Reid among them, his sword at the ready.

On the other side of the ballroom, the sound of screams had lessened, and the sound of fighting had started.

"Come on!" Adrian's voice shook. He pulled her up the stairs and into the safety of the corridor. She stumbled more than once with her heels, but Adrian never slowed.

"Move, move!" came Reid's voice.

Something in her chest loosened at the sound of his voice so close.

"Close these doors!" Reid shouted.

Juniper turned to see him, just to make sure, and wished she hadn't. From the top of the stairs, she had an unobstructed view of the ballroom. The horde of demons slithered like spiders, slashing, biting, clawing. Blood splattered the stone. Bodies scattered the floor, unmoving.

"Move!" Reid shouted, and the doors swung closed. "Get away, to the passage."

Reid and five guards shepherded them down the corridor, moving faster than she would have liked in her shoes, but with a horde of demons behind them, she would run until her feet bled.

The sounds of the slaughter died out behind them, the screaming, clawing, scratching, tearing... Juniper stifled a cry of her own. It would help no one.

She barely paid attention to where they ran. Finally, the guards led them into an unremarkable room of a few paintings and unlit torches. Three of the guards took torches and lit them. Another walked to a painting of a fat man in a red coat. No plaque identified the fat man. The guard pushed against the far left side of the painting, on a book half-hidden in shadow, and the painting clicked—it swung open like a door. Behind it, stone stairs led down into darkness.

"Inside," Reid commanded, ushering them forward with his bloodied sword.

A guard with a torch took the lead. Adrian, holding onto her hand, went next. Juniper lifted the hem of her dress with her shaking hand and stepped inside. The torchlight illuminated several steps ahead, but the rest sank into darkness. Holding onto Adrian, she started down the passage. The others filed in, and the painting closed with an echoing click.

The stone soaked in the sounds of their steps, their breaths, and in return, emitted a hollow silence. No one spoke.

How many people died tonight? How many would die from their injuries?

Adrian looked sick, his skin ashen. His eyes held enough worry for a dozen men—a king's worry.

She focused on her feet. She didn't trust her beautiful, cursed shoes not to betray her and sprain an ankle or send her tumbling down the unforgivable stone steps.

Down, down, down they walked, until, at last, they came to an unassuming, if not a bit drab and unwelcoming hall. The torches flickered off the ancient stone. Water ran somewhere nearby, dropping into a larger pool; the sound echoed through the halls. They walked and walked, each step bringing them closer to the source of water.

At last, the hall opened into a cavernous dome. Water gushed from a dozen sluice channels on the far side of the cavern. It flowed down a stone slope and underneath a walkway and then out of sight. The guards started across the walkway, just wide enough for two people to walk abreast.

The other end of the walkway was bathed in darkness.

"Where are we?" Juniper whispered to Adrian.

"Underneath the castle," he answered softly. "We will wait out the chaos in a safe room."

In a castle full of trained guards and knights, they still had safe rooms? Of course, she shouldn't bash the idea. Not with ravenous demons hunting them down.

The torches illuminated a stone arch at the end of the walkway. Beyond, darkness.

"Almost there," Adrian whispered as they walked through the archway. "Hopefully, the demons will be looking for us and not kill anyone else. With the best of luck, the guards and knights have already taken care of them, and we won't be down here long."

She swallowed. Her throat had gone frighteningly dry.

The stones on the other side of the walkway were ancient. Older than those of the castle. Much older. Did this passage connect to the one she and Reid had found? Juniper shivered at the thought.

They walked down a narrow hallway, then another. The guards, at last, came to a halt by a plain iron door set into the stone. Old iron. Strange iron.

She didn't like it.

With the dank air, the iron should have rusted. Yet the door hadn't the tiniest spot on it. In the firelight, she spotted the engraved emblems, whorls, and strange wording, vine-like archaic symbols.

Warded. Old magic.

One of the guards turned the heavy handle on the door and pushed it open. The light of the torch swarmed into the old room. It was no more than a glorified prison cell with a few furnishings. A table and chairs. Barrels. Extra torches. Shelves of sealed boxes and glass containers and candles. A room meant for survival, not luxury.

A guard with a torch walked inside first. Juniper gazed behind her at Reid. In the firelight, the blood on his sword looked black. He met her gaze. The shadows turned his honey eyes into pools of darkness.

The death in the castle would bother him worse than it did her. As former Royal Guard, he would see the demons' attack as an invasion.

A second guard entered the safe room, and Adrian started toward the threshold, Juniper beside him, but as he made to step into the door, the iron door screeched. It moved.

Juniper grabbed Adrian, and they barely stepped out of the way as the door slammed back into the frame, hard enough to rattle.

"Hey!" shouted one of the guards inside the safe room. The handle rattled. "The door's not budging."

The guards tried to open the door, but it refused to move. Adrian let go of her to assist, and she backed up until her bare shoulders met the cool stone of the wall.

Wrong. Everything about this place felt wrong.

She met Reid's eyes. His brows furrowed as if he sensed the wrongness too.

Juniper opened her mouth to voice her concerns to Reid, but she *felt* it before she heard it. A low, hissing voice that sent a feverish chill down her spine.

"You can't evade me. There is nowhere else to run."

CHAPTER FIFTY

The wrongness magnified. Malice oozed, thick as fog. Juniper felt it against her skin like humidity in summer's peak, pressing in from all directions—stifling and suffocating. It was the same wrongness, she realized with no amount of comfort, as the passage she and Reid had found.

The one that had vanished.

The Greater Demon appeared from the other end of the hall, slinking from the dark, its black eyes glittering like diamonds.

It looked nothing short of a nightmare. Its body, although humanoid, had been twisted and warped. Its arms and legs had been stretched to gangly claw-tipped hands and feet. Dark leathery skin clung close to its bones, shifting with every breath the beast took. It had the facial shape of a human, but an elongated nose, broad forehead, and tilted eyes gave it a wolfish appearance.

"You've nowhere to go," hissed the demon in the voice that Juniper still heard in her dreams. "Trapped. And I've grown tired of chasing."

Reid jumped in front of Juniper and Adrian, sword at the ready. He wore the calm, deadly mask of a predator.

"All this time, confined underneath the castle like vermin," the demon hissed as it inched closer, "but now the master has undone the lock, set me free."

Something moved in the other end of the passage. Juniper dared take her eyes off the Greater Demon—her heart sank at the sight. The larger demon from above, its snout and teeth bloodied, blocked their only exit. Pieces of cloth and flesh stuck between its claws. Blood clotted in its reddish hair. Several sword-shaped gashes tore at the beast's skin, but none had been lethal.

A demon behind, the Greater Demon before.

They were trapped.

She met Adrian's eyes across the corridor. He knew the odds of them both escaping were slim, that the odds of any of them escaping were slim.

The remaining three guards arranged themselves around Adrian and Juniper. The reddish demon struck first. It moved fast, slicing the head of a guard clean from his shoulders. Body and head thudded on the stone floor.

Juniper screamed, or she might have—she felt her throat squeeze, but she never heard the sound.

The demons came at them from both ends. Reid engaged the Greater Demon. The remaining two guards surrounded the others. Swords, claws, and teeth—one guard fell, and the second used that moment to thrust his sword into the demon's chest, burying it to the hilt. The demon bellowed in pain and grabbed the guard by the neck, snapping it.

The torch the guard had been holding fell to the floor, the flames licking the pooling blood. The reddish demon tried to yank the sword from its chest but couldn't dislodge it.

Juniper felt her shoulders quiver as something icy crawled up her spine. The sword had missed anything vital.

Two demons. Only Juniper and Reid stood in their way of Adrian. With those odds, none of them would make it out alive.

Reid was faring much better against the Greater Demon. He moved with frightening efficiently and smooth control; he moved quicker than he ever had while fighting with her. Of course, he hadn't been fighting to his best abilities. He hadn't been fighting to survive.

But with two demons... Tears welled in her eyes. She couldn't watch Reid die. She just couldn't. But she couldn't take her eyes off him, not as he blocked, swung, and nicked the beast's arms and chest.

Adrian's hands tightened around her arms. She blinked, smearing tears on her painted eyelashes. The reddish demon slunk closer, unopposed, lazy in its approach. It knew they had no way out.

If only she had a dagger, a sword, a club—anything!

Reid cried out, pain in his voice—her heart seized and stopped. Reid stumbled backward, hand on his chest. The Greater Demon laughed; it wiggled its talons, slick with Reid's blood. Reid took a knee, head bowed, shoulders slumped.

No, no, no!

"Nowhere to run," hissed the Greater Demon.

"Nowhere," echoed the second, its voice scratchy and raw. Animalistic. Pained. Nowhere near as refined as Greater Demon.

Reid wobbled to his feet, his face paling as the poison coursed through him. Juniper knew—the sluggishness, the pain, the stiffness. Reid wouldn't stand a chance.

The reddish demon came closer still.

Reid readied his blade with the eyes of a man who knew he was about to die. He would go willingly too, for his prince, for his friend, for his kingdom. He would give his life for it, as the Royal Guard chose to do, as the Order chose to do.

Tears pushed against her eyes. Her heart threatened to burst. If Reid gave himself to protect them, it would. It would die along with him.

"No!" Juniper screamed, to stop Reid from doing it, to shield him with her own worthless life, but Adrian grabbed her shoulders and held her back.

"Are you mad?" Adrian gasped in her ear.

She was. Mad at Adrian for holding her back while Reid stood ready for his death, at Reid for being such a noble ass, at the demon for baring his bloodied claws at him, at the stranger who'd brought the demon into their world in the first place.

She would tear this castle apart, stone by stone, and find the bastard responsible. She would kill him, slowly, painfully, and relish every moment, every scream.

For Reid, she would do anything.

"Get out of the way," the demon hissed at Reid. "I will let you live; it is not you I am called to take."

"No," Reid said firmly. He held his sword at the ready. The rest of him shook; his skin had gone a frightening shade of gray.

His grip never faltered.

Tears began to roll down Juniper's cheeks. She didn't hold in her sobs.

"Then you will die like the others," hissed the demon. He pointed a bloody claw at Juniper. "And then your prince will die. Then she will."

Reid roared at the demon and charged. The demon slashed its claws. Reid deflected the blow with his blade, but the demon's other hand slashed upward, across Reid's chest, crossing the previous wound. Reid fell backward onto the ground, blood shining on his chest, over his torn clothes.

Juniper felt her throat vibrate and crack, but she didn't hear the sound she made over the blood gushing in her ears. Every bone in her body had gone cold, her blood like liquid ice.

Reid collapsed onto one knee, blood dripping onto the floor below him, but refused to release his blade.

The Greater Demon laughed. The other came closer.

Not Reid.

Not Reid.

Not Reid!

She could save him. She had to save him. No matter what he thought about her afterward.

Adrian gasped and let go of her, but she didn't stop to assess him. She saw only Reid, his blood, his life. The demon threatening him. She made her way toward Reid, toward the Greater Demon.

Reid spat a curse at her, a command, but she didn't acknowledge it. Everything had gone cold. Her breath fogged as it tumbled from her lips, her nose—her skin frosted. She felt it tingle against her skin, but it didn't hurt.

The Greater Demon hesitated, eyes on her. It knew. The reddish demon didn't know. Laughing, it threw itself at her, talons out.

Juniper knew what she wanted to do. She felt it. She saw it.

The demon never touched her.

The ice grew from nowhere, faster than she could blink, running its slivering tendrils over the stone walls, over the ceiling, and onto the demon—freezing it solid. The reddish demon froze with its longest talon an inch from her chest. The crystalline ice thickened, frosting the air as it crawled up the demon's body until the entire beast had been covered. It held its gaze on her as it froze—to death.

The demon's life snuffed out, and as it did, the redness of its eyes faded, and its brown eyes became terrifyingly human.

The Greater Demon laughed.

Juniper spun and flung her ice at it, but it did not obey her command. She flung bits of ice at the demon, which it knocked aside. She tried again, but she couldn't. The ice wasn't listening. Panic flared in its place. Underneath it, pain squeezed in a place deeper than her bones, in the place she had shoved her magic all this time.

"Out already?" the Great Demon taunted. "Tsk, tsk, tsk." It sauntered a step toward her. "I have changed my mind. I will kill you first."

It lunged. Juniper silently willed her magic with everything she had. A spike of ice shot from her palm and lodged itself in the demon's shoulder; it let out a howl. Its arm went slack, and it yanked out the ice spike with the other. It threw it aside, shattering it on impact.

Juniper tried to shoot another, but only conjured a bit of frost on her palms.

"Why don't you freeze me like you did the other?" The demon chuckled. "A mage who can't cast. Shameful."

The demon took another step. She willed the magic, but nothing happened. She felt for the magic in the place it had been hiding; she felt nothing. Panic flared alongside fear.

"Not a very good mage, are you? Not very good at anything from what I've been told." The Greater Demon sauntered closer. Its eyes glittered with humor. "What will you do now? Hmm? He will not want you now. No one will. A worthless mage. A worthless bitch. He can do better."

She tried again to throw ice at it, but as she willed the ice into existence, pain seared along her insides, a spasm centered in her empty well.

"My master finds you curious," hissed the demon. "But not enough to let you live. You've gotten in the way, little mage."

The demon came at her again. Juniper didn't have time to think. She threw herself to the side, barely dodging the demon's outstretched talons. She rolled back to her feet. As the demon came at her, she bolted down a side passage. A glance over her shoulder confirmed that the demon slinked after her.

She reached into the empty well. *Come on*, she begged, *just a little!* She found nothing.

"Why not freeze me? Hmm?" The Greater Demon chuckled.

"The irony is not lost on me," Juniper spat. All those years of shoving her magic down, hiding it, praying it would go away, begging the gods to take it away, and now that she desperately needed it, it refused her.

"My master could help you," said the demon. "He knows far more about magic than most alive today."

"Why help me if he wants me dead?" Juniper asked. She turned, facing the demon, but continued to step away. She didn't like having it at her back.

"It isn't you he wants dead," said the demon. "You are just in the way. It is the prince he wants dead, the prince and the king. You are merely an obstacle to those ends."

"Why the prince? Why the king? What could he gain from getting rid of them?" She stumbled on the hem of her dress and caught herself on the rough stone walls.

Chuckling, the demon slinked a step closer, faster. Her heart thudded. If it got too close... "Why would anyone want a king out of the way? Power."

The demon swatted at her, but she jumped back. Her back slammed into a wall as the demon's talons sliced through her bodice. She threw herself into a side passage and flattened her hand on her bodice; the talons had barely cut through the corset. Her skin hadn't been broken. With the demon right behind, she raced down a side passage. Her eyes adjusted to the darkness, but the dark didn't seem to hinder the demon's pace.

"Why the chase?" whined the demon, its tone slow and taunting. "I know I will catch you in the end. You know I will catch you. Why not stop running and save us both the trouble?"

Because Juniper Thimble did not and would not lay down and die. She never had before, and she never would.

She reached into her well, into her fledgling magic, and gathered what little had replenished. The result was a thin needle of ice that struck the demon's chest—its heart. The demon yelped and growled and threw a talon at her. She twirled out of its range, and the tips of its talons grazed the strings of her bodice.

Maddox's words echoed, *It doesn't matter how big your opponent's sword is. A well-timed dagger and wits can outmatch any blade.*

She dashed around a corner and down another dark passage. The demon slunk behind, its humored huffs tinged with rage. She careened around another corner, wishing her magic to replenish, hoping for a miracle from the gods, when she tripped. A yelp escaped her throat, and she tumbled onto the stone ground. Had she been wearing anything else, she would have rolled back onto her feet. But she wore her beautiful, cursed ball gown whose corset did not allow for quick breaths and quick movements.

As she pushed herself onto her feet, talons sliced through her upper back. She screamed for the pain and because she knew those talons would be soon felt by Adrian. As the wounds began to close, as her pain began to shrink, she heard the distant cry of sudden pain elsewhere. Adrian and Reid were not far.

"Stop this chase, and I will tell you what happened to your friend," hissed the demon.

"What friend?" she gasped, heels clacking as she ran.

"*What friend?*" The demon repeated, shocked. It gasped dramatically. "The one who blamed you in her final moments. Such a pretty thing too."

The ground fell from beneath her feet. She stumbled, hugging the wall for support as she wheeled to face the demon. Juniper gasped, "Clara?"

The demon halted just out of range. "I do not know names."

"What did you do to her?" Her voice cracked.

"Not what I did, child. What *we* did." The demon put a blooded talon against its chest. Blood seeped from the wound she had inflicted but not enough. "My master required blood. And we fetched him blood. Fresh blood. All the blood that he needed. The other did the fetching, I instructed."

"You..." Juniper couldn't form the words. Clara. All the servants. "You took them? You killed them?"

The demon shrugged, a non-answer. It sauntered a step toward her; she took a step back. For every step it took, she took two. She felt the passage open, felt the darkness open on either side of her as they entered a crossroads. The demons had taken the servants. Clara. The demons had killed her. They had killed her, whoever *they* were.

Rage bubbled from her empty well, a blinding, burning rage. Juniper screamed at the demon, throwing everything she could—two thin slivers of ice.

The demon snarled and came at her, talons extended. One sliver of ice entered its left eye, angled inward. The other cut into its chest, just underneath where the other had.

You're aiming too high, Maddox's voice echoed. *The heart is lower.*

The demon howled and stumbled backward. Blood gushed from its face, from its heart, and its breaths gurgled.

She took a step—ice crunched under her foot. They had entered the first passage. The demon staggered to its feet but collapsed, breaths ragged and wet. Juniper picked up one of the guards' discarded swords. She felt Adrian's and Reid's stares, heard their breaths. They were alive.

The demon soon would not be. She angled the tip of the sword and set it against the demon's chest. It growled, and she put her weight against the blade.

"Tell your master than I am much harder to get rid of," Juniper seethed and shoved the blade through the demon until it hit the stone on the other side.

CHAPTER FIFTY-ONE

The demon stilled. For a moment, only her breath sounded in the passage. Her ice had snaked up the walls, along the ceiling and floor—skipping only where Adrian stood and where Reid knelt on the ground. Each of their breaths puffed out before them. Behind them, the reddish demon stood frozen.

The ice began to crack—sickening, bone-shattering cracks. The reddish demon shattered into frozen demon ash; the greater demon dissolved, the ash feathering into nonexistence. In the torchlight, the pieces glittered like glass.

Juniper's breath puffed out of her mouth in white bursts. The torches began to melt her ice. It dripped from the ceiling and walls. As the air warmed, a pain settled in her arms and legs. A stiffness. She dropped the sword, clanking on the stones.

She'd done it.

She'd killed the demons and saved Reid and Adrian.

They would make it out.

"By the gods," Reid gasped, his voice strained with pain. He sat back on his heels, sword arm limp. He needed a healer at once.

Adrian had gone as pale as the ice that melted around him.

"Mage," Reid sputtered.

He struggled to stand. His knees gave out, and he collapsed to the floor. His blade skittered across the wet stones. Juniper started to go to him, but he looked up at her—his brown eyes were not warm, not loving. He stared at her with a coldness that stilled her to the bones. Hatred. Repulsion.

Juniper balled her fists in her gown. "Reid?"

"You're a mage!" Reid shouted with such vile anger that she took a step back.

Her heel sank into the wet ash. It grabbed onto the bottom of her dress, soaking into the fine pink-white, staining the edges black and gray.

"Mage!" Reid spat the word like a death sentence, along with blood from his mouth.

Footsteps, dozens of them, thundered from the direction they'd come. Guards. Knights. Reinforcements.

"Mage!" Reid breathed, his consciousness fading.

The guards thundered closer. Across the walkway. Armor clanked. Adrian glanced toward the walkway, relief on his face.

Reid never looked away from her, his gazing burning through her. Betrayal. Hatred. Blame.

She'd exposed herself. He knew what she was. He had seen what she'd done. The guards would see the ice melting. They would all know. They would kill her for it. The demon had been right. Reid didn't want her now.

Apostate. They were looking for an apostate hiding in the castle, one whom many suspected had arrived shortly after Roslyn.

They would blame her for it.

The footsteps thundered closer, calling, "Adrian, Adrian, Adrian."

Before they could see it, see her, she ran. She ran the opposite way, where the Greater Demon had appeared from, and into the darkness it held. Away from the knights, the guards, and Reid's hateful stare.

"Juniper!" Reid shouted after her.

Her name became a curse on his tongue, the name he'd whispered with love only that morning. Something deep in her chest broke, shattered like the ice. It squeezed the breath from her throat. Tears fell as she ran through the lightless passages, narrow halls, and low-ceilinged rooms. Up and down steps, alongside forgotten sewer channels.

Juniper ran until she couldn't, until her sides ached and her lungs burned. She collapsed in an unremarkable stone passage, and with no one to see or hear, she sobbed. She cried until her body had no more tears to give.

The Greater Demon was dead. She had killed it. She had protected Reid and Adrian. She had done right, she told herself. They were safe. They would make it back to the castle. The royal healer would tend to them. The castle would go back to normal.

Reid was safe.

For Reid, she would do it all over again.

Time. Never enough time.

The Wechun had been slain by that girl. He'd felt it. A severing. A shutting of an eye. The power that connected him to the beast had rebounded with a hard slap to the chest. Hard enough that he had doubled over, coughing.

"What is it?" the other man asked, annoyance underlining his outward concern.

He waved his hand toward the other man. Brushed the hand off his shoulder.

"Nothing. Just a cough. Must have swallowed wrong."

The other man didn't believe him. He could see it in his eyes.

It didn't matter. The Wechun had served its purpose. It had played its part, and its early departure caused only a minor wrinkle in the grand scheme of things.

✦

Adrian stood by Reid's side as the royal healer worked. Her graying hair was frayed, and the lines on her face seemed deeper. One of her apprentices had healed Adrian. The royal healer had wanted to tend to him herself, but he had refused. Reid needed more attention than he did. The guards had appeared in that passageway none too early, and Reid had gone in and out of consciousness as they carried him back to the portrait room. They dared not jostle him further.

Reid woke as the healer magically wrapped his wounded chest.

A nightmare. No other word fit what had happened.

Nothing seemed real. Not as he walked with a limping, silent, barely-aware Reid to Juniper's chambers, because it was closer than Reid's. He needed rest. Adrian slumped into one of the armchairs by the hearth fire as Reid took the bed in the other room, the bed Juniper had slept in.

Adrian hung his head in his shaking hands, barely aware of the guards who came and went. Gods, his back ached. He had received only a small dose of poison, but he felt it in every fiber of his being. News passed, but Adrian wanted nothing more than a stiff drink. Or eight. Enough to knock him out, enough to erase this feeling of uselessness.

Utterly useless. That's what he had been.

"What happened?"

It took a moment and a hand on his shoulder for Adrian to realize the question had been directed at him. He glanced up; Destry stood by the chair, his silver armor and Mage's Bane sword bloodied.

Destry repeated, softer, "What happened?"

Adrian blinked. With the guards present, he couldn't tell Destry what had really happened. "A demon was waiting for us. Another demon came in behind us, trapping us in the passageway. Reid and the guards fought them off, but...none of the guards made it out. Reid nearly didn't."

Destry glanced at the bedroom door with pride, sorrow, and admiration. "Reid will be a fine knight someday."

Adrian nodded.

He had never seen Reid so enraged, so torn. She had been a mage all along. Reid hadn't known. He'd had feelings for Juniper, but whatever those feelings had become, they'd shattered the moment Reid had witnessed her magic.

"What of my parents?" Adrian looked into the fire, terrified to see the answer written on the knight's face before he spoke it.

"Alive, both of them." Destry shifted. A dent in his armor glinted in the light. "Escorted to a safe room."

Not attacked by demons. If Adrian had gone with them, would the demons have followed? That demon had been called, it said, to fetch *him*. Adrian shivered at the thought, at the memory of its hissing voice.

"Lady Roslyn isn't with you?" Destry narrowed his gaze at Adrian.

Adrian shook his head. "She distracted the demon to give Reid a chance to kill it. It worked."

"And Lady Roslyn?"

The unspoken question hung between them.

Adrian didn't know what to say. "She... I don't know what happened to her," he whispered. "She ran to buy us time, and when the guards arrived, she was gone."

"Did she not realize that she could have gotten herself killed?" Destry's tone turned cold.

"If she hadn't, all three of us would be dead." Adrian met Destry's glare.

The knight nodded. "I will send word to His Majesty about her vanishing. She is a tough girl. She might turn up in another of the passages."

Adrian nodded, although he doubted Juniper would come back. Adrian glanced toward the open bedroom door, toward Reid. Juniper had saved their lives. The thief that she was, she had saved them. And he didn't know what to make of it.

"Extra healers have been called in from the Marca," Destry told him. "To help with the extent of injuries."

Adrian nodded. "Reid's wounds aren't deep, but the poison..."

"He isn't the only one." Destry shifted again. Had he been wounded? "Many received injuries. The death toll was not as high as originally feared. It seemed the demons only wanted to cause chaos." They succeeded. "Tonight will be long for the castle, I'm afraid."

Adrian slumped further into the chair. He wouldn't be able to sleep that night, and he took a small comfort in knowing he wouldn't be the only one.

✦

Juniper shivered. The cold of the stone seeped through the back of her dress. Her lungs ached with cold, with the dryness from crying until she could cry no more.

She was laying on the stone floor. Had she fallen asleep?

Dark, so dark. Where was she?

Then she remembered. Using her dark sight, she saw the stone passageway.

The demon had been slain. She'd killed it. Using magic. She'd protected Reid and Adrian from it and exposed herself.

She'd exposed herself to a squire trained and sworn to hunt down apostates like her. They had been looking for an apostate, and she had revealed herself to be one. Someone with magic had altered the spell binding her to Adrian, someone looking to harm him.

They would blame her for it all. She knew they would.

Reid. The darkness in her chest squeezed at his name. It forced the air out of her lungs and made it hard to draw in another. He had looked at her with such hatred, fear, and disbelief. If he had been able to stand, would he have killed her?

No, the binding spell would have transferred her wounds to Adrian.

What now? Were the knights scouring the castle for her that very moment? If she crawled out of the tunnels, would she be thrown to the gallows? Or would the knights have a mage's death waiting for her?

They would need to break the binding spell first. They wouldn't harm her while her life was bound to Adrian's. Again, the binding spell was the only thing keeping her alive.

Juniper shivered. The dank air chilled her to the bone. She forced her arms to move, then her legs. She used the uneven stone of the wall to guide her along the passage. Her feet ached where the shoes bit into her heels and toes, so she pulled them off and tossed them behind her. Where they landed, she didn't bother to see.

She had tried so very hard to keep her magic under control and out of sight. One of her earliest memories was of the tutor her parents had hired, an apostate, to teach her how to control her magic. How to hide it. How to pretend that it wasn't there.

Despite her sight, she tripped over a loose stone, stubbing her toe and ripping her dress several times. Her beautiful gown, ruined.

She walked and walked. Her feet went numb from cold.

She came to a narrow staircase like the one they had climbed down, and up she walked. It ended at a narrow landing. The wooden back of a painting greeted her, just like the one the guards had led them through. Another secret door.

She struggled to find a way to open the door, and when it swung open, a part of her expected there to be guards standing on the other side, waiting. A knight with his dark Mage's Bane blade ready.

The room was empty. The torches sat in their brackets, dark.

She stepped onto the carpeted stone and pulled the portrait of a red-haired woman closed. The handle was the collar of a cat perched on the windowsill beside the woman.

How many secret doors into the bowels were there?

Juniper crossed to the wooden door that would take her back into the castle, fastened her hand around the handle, blinked her sight away, and pulled the door open. The brightness of the torchlit corridor blinded her. She cast her eyes down, away. And gasped.

Her dress. Absolutely ruined. The ashy water had seeped up to her knees. Rips and tears marred the skirt. It hung in tatters. If she'd had tears left, she would have cried for the dress.

She walked a few steps through the corridor. It didn't take long to recognize it. She'd walked through it a few times with Reid. They would be watching her room, no doubt, and with the guards scrambling in the aftermath, no one would look for her here.

And, if she were to die tonight, she would rather it be at his hands.

CHAPTER FIFTY-TWO

Reid had refused to lay still the moment he'd come to his senses. He might have been content to sleep while his wounds healed, had he not realized whose bed he slept in.

Juniper's.

He'd spent enough nights with her to know the canopy, the layout of the room, the feel of the bed. The bed that they'd shared. Her scent lingered on the pillow, lavender and honeysuckle.

Despite his aching wounds, stiff from the poison, he forced himself to his feet. His shirt had been removed, and thick bandages wrapped his middle. Reid gritted his teeth as he made his way out of the room.

He blinked and saw the ballroom again. Blood and death.

Reid slowly made his way down the corridor, and he understood why each attack had left Juniper in such a state. His entire body felt stiff, and everything ached.

"What are you doing?"

Reid blinked several times. A mage stood in the middle of the corridor. He wore Marca purples with a green sash. A healer. He looked none too happy to see Reid.

"Get him inside before he passes out," snapped the healer.

Guards appeared on either side of him and hauled Reid into a room that had been transformed into a sick room. A dozen Marca mages in purple and green tended to as many wounded as the room could hold. Guards and nobles alike.

Reid didn't see a single knight overseeing them, but as the guards set him down on an unoccupied cot, and he realized just how horrible he felt, he didn't push the issue.

The mage knelt over him and magically removed the bandages on his chest. A soft yellow-green glow hummed between the mage's tanned hands and Reid's wounds, stitching the flesh back together, pulling tiny amounts of the poison out. Reid could feel the poison slithering through his blood like a barbed string, pulling and tugging and snagging. Tearing him apart from the inside.

"There," said the mage, scowling. Fresh bandages wrapped right around Reid's chest. "If you want to move around, you won't make it worse."

The mage stood and moved on to someone else.

Reid stood. He felt better than he had. Not good, but better. He started again toward his own room. He would be useless to the guard and the knights in his condition. As much as he wanted to help, a wounded soldier helped no one.

With each footstep, his thoughts returned to one word. Mage. Juniper Thimble was a mage. Had been a mage the entire time. Not just a mage. A damned apostate. He'd followed her around the castle for weeks, stood by her bedside, talked with her, bedded her, and yet he'd never glimpsed her true nature. How could she have hidden it from him? From the knights?

Reid paused on the other side of his door. She'd defended them. Damn it, he should have seen the signs! All those times he had attributed lingering magic in her chambers to the royal healer, to Ison. It had been her. He should have seen past those eyes of hers and the way she walked and how she moved and how her lips said his name. Damn it all.

He stumbled into his sitting room, nowhere near as extravagant as Juniper's, but moderate for a squire of his standing. Much better than the barracks the guards slept in. He kicked the door closed.

He stalked toward his bed, intent on a long rest. He was halfway to the bed when he spotted her. He didn't even jump.

Juniper slumped against the far wall, shadowed behind his bed. She sat with her legs drawn to her chest, head buried in her arms. Her dress was ruined, filthy with demon ash, torn and tattered. Her hair had fallen from its braided crown, strands of raven falling about her head. Dirty toes stuck out from the jagged, stained hem of her gown.

His anger at her deflated but not enough.

Reid stalked to the hearth and stoked the fire. All the while, she didn't speak. She didn't even move. Not a rustle came from her. He walked into his bathing room, washed his hands and face in cold water, and walked into his closet—he cast a glance in her direction. It felt like a metal brace clamped around his chest. He tore his eyes off her and grabbed a fresh undershirt but then reconsidered. With his injuries, the shirt would only get in the way. He left it crumpled on top of the others.

Juniper still hadn't moved.

He couldn't avoid it forever.

Reid crossed the room and stood in front of her. A twitch of her left hand—the only sign she gave.

"Why here?" His voice came out harsh.

"I didn't think anyone would look for me here." Juniper's once strong voice sounded small, weak, and afraid. The sound tore at his chest, but he held firm. He clenched his fists. *Mage*, he reminded himself.

When he didn't speak again, she glanced up at him. The hearth fire shadowed his face but illuminated hers. She'd been crying. The makeup around her eyes had run, dried, and started to flake. The color had faded from her lips and cheeks, and the absence left her ghostly pale.

Under his gaze, she seemed to shrink further into herself.

He fought the urge to go to her. *Mage*.

His anger seethed. "Why didn't you tell me?"

She bit her lip. "Because I was afraid of how you'd react."

And he'd reacted badly.

"You're an apostate!" The words felt like a curse.

Her midnight eyes softened. Water lined her bottom lids, silver in the light. She laid her head down on her arms. "I didn't do it on purpose."

He scoffed. "You killed those demons on accident?"

She looked up at him, lips parted, but she squeezed her mouth closed. He saw the flicker; she'd wanted to say something but didn't. She said, "I didn't choose to be what I am."

"Like you didn't choose to become a thief or a murderer?"

"I wasn't born a thief," she spat. "You'd rather me be enslaved at the Marca?"

"You're a danger," he hissed. She wouldn't have been able to hurt anyone else besides herself in the Marca. She would have learned the right way to use magic.

The flints of her eyes glinted. Her voice dropped. "No more than a man with a sword."

He clenched his fists. They glared at one another, but after a moment, her eyes dropped to the bandages on his chest. If she hadn't acted, all three of them would likely be dead. Reid sighed and sat on the edge of his bed.

"Will you kill me for it?" Her eyes lingered on his chest.

"I should." Reid set his clenched fists on his knees. "I should turn you over to the knights and let them deal with you. You should be sent to the Marca, but there is a chance the knights will blame you for this mess. The demons appeared after your arrival."

Her brows rose.

"Adrian and I haven't told a soul about it. The guards think you ran to save yourself in the tunnels. They're looking for you as we speak." Her eyes softened, and he hated the urge he had to crumble on the floor with her, to pull her into his bed. "You should let them know you've come back on your own."

"Why?" she squeaked, her voice raw. "I thought you hated mages?"

"I do, but I...it's you." He stopped himself before the words tumbled from his lips: *but I love you.* He didn't. He couldn't. Not anymore. "I'd rather not escort you to the gallows or to the execution chamber at the Marca. They would either make me do it or make me watch."

He hadn't said it, but by the downcast look in her eye, she understood. The Mage's Bane. No, he did not want to watch her die of Mage's Bane.

"I'm sorry," she whispered. "A long time ago, I wandered too far from my parents' house. There were three of them, and they kept saying how they had found me. I assumed them knights, and I ran from them. I stumbled into bandits who then later sold me in the Undercity. I told myself that a life of crime was better than a life in the Marca."

She had chosen to be a thief over a Marca mage. Reid balled his fists but didn't say anything. He didn't have anything to say. Juniper didn't understand.

He looked down at his boots, flecked with demon's ash and blood. He said, "Apostates killed my family. My father, my mother, and my older brother."

She jerked her eyes up with the swiftness of an arrow.

He explained, "They came by the farm one night, starving and desperate. My parents, the good-hearted people they were, gave them shelter and food. They asked for nothing in return." His eyes fogged at the memory. "Do you know what happened? Knights came looking for them. The apostates accused my parents of selling them out. I hid underneath my parents' bed like a coward as they killed my father, my mother, and my brother. I cowered underneath that bed for a day, unable to move until the knights found me. They knew my father's name, knew my uncle, and brought me here."

He could still feel the pain in his chest as everything was ripped out of his life. By magic. He could remember hiding, his father's body in his view, his eyes staring forward, lifeless, the smell of three bodies in the summer heat. He still felt the hatred toward those ungrateful mages. It came as a small prize that they had been found later and killed with Mage's Bane. He regretted that he hadn't been able to kill them himself, but he'd watched. His uncle had permitted him to. Just a small scratch on the upper arm of a Mage's Bane blade, and those mages had twisted against the restraints, eyes rolling, gasping, praying, squirming. They'd cried and begged and pleaded until they couldn't form words at all. It had been a slow death.

He did not want to see Juniper die that way.

Her small voice said, "I—I didn't know."

"I know you didn't." He stood, refusing to meet her gaze. If she stayed any longer, he would lose his anger at her. He would pull her into his bed. He stalked to the fire and stared into the brightness, willing his resolve to hold fast. "But now you know. That is why I chose to become a knight. I will avenge my family." He inhaled, held it. "We can't be together. I can't be with an apostate. Now, get out."

She shuddered.

He didn't turn around.

He listened to the sound of her dress swishing, of Juniper fumbling to stand. Her bare feet padded along the floor, away from him, her tattered dress moving with each step. He glanced toward her. Her shoulders slouched, and her posture sank inward like her dress was pulling her to the ground.

He wrenched his gaze away.

✦

"Now, get out."

Reid's cold voice drove spikes into her chest. Juniper wanted to go to him, to fold her arms around his strong middle and hang on for the rest of her life, but Reid couldn't even look at her without hate in his eyes. He kept his back to her, his eyes on the hearth fire.

She took several steps to the door, but he didn't move. She took several more, waiting, hoping for him to change his mind, to open his arms, to beckon to her, but he stood firm.

He didn't even glance at her when she opened the door and slipped out. A numbing cold settled over her bones—she didn't feel anything. Nothing seemed real, like she had drunk too much and drifted beyond herself, away from it all.

"Lady Roslyn?" Footsteps ran toward her. A guard. He stopped a step away. He wore a joyous smile on his clean-shaven face. "Thank Bala! We've been looking everywhere for you! Are you hurt? Do you need to see a healer?"

She shook her head.

"Please, Lady, let me take you back to your chamber."

She slid her arm into the guard's. On the way to her chambers, he told her that the castle had worried the worst for her. Adrian had told them she'd fled from the demon. The guard promised to send word of her safe arrival to the prince.

A part of her wished the demon had finished her off.

The guard took her to her chambers and asked if she needed anything. Juniper didn't answer. She went straight into to bedroom and started to rip the ruined dress from her skin.

She didn't remember falling into bed or dreaming, but she woke to sunlight streaming through the windows. The sleepy blue sunlight of dawn.

For a moment, everything was fine.

Then she reached for Reid and found the other side of the bed empty.

And she remembered.

Worthless mage. Worthless bitch.

She grabbed Reid's pillow and hugged it to her chest. That woodsy scent clung to the threads, and she buried her face in it.

No servants brought breakfast. Reid did not appear. The blue sunlight brightened and strengthened into gold and yellow.

Juniper forced herself out of bed and soaked in too-hot water until her skin pruned. She dressed in the pajamas she had lazily thrown into the chair in the dressing room when everything had been fine.

What now?

Reid's promise of her future had been burned. When they found the apostate, they would throw her into the dungeons or kill her.

Why had she thought it would be different?

A gaping hole in her chest opened wide, pulling her down, down, down.

A knock sounded at the sitting room door. Not minding her pajamas or loose hair, she went to answer it—the door opened as she stepped into the sitting room.

Reid limped inside, his gaze cold. "You're expected upstairs. His Majesty's orders."

"But I'm not dressed—"

"It doesn't matter." Reid motioned to the door.

She grabbed her robe and tightened it around her pajamas, then followed Reid into the corridor. He walked a step ahead, and not once did he look back.

He led her into the lounge where she had shared that first meal with Adrian. Through the wall of windows, Rusdasin looked the same as it had been before.

King Bradburn, however, looked worse for wear. He stood at the windows beside the court magician and a sandy-haired knight she had never seen before. Reid shut the door to the lounge, and a deafening silence pressed in.

The king looked her over, then pointed to one of the armchairs. "Sit."

Juniper pulled her robe closer and sat. *Here it comes.* The king would cast her out wearing nothing more than a dressing gown, or he was about to skip over the problem of *her* and send her straight to her execution. Perhaps that is why the knight accompanied them.

The king straightened his shoulders. "I hear the Greater Demon has been slain."

"Yes," she said.

"By Squire Sandpiper."

Reid shifted behind her. She felt the breath leave her throat—did they not know? She nodded. "Yes."

The king eyed her. The wrinkles on either side of his mouth had become more pronounced in the last few days. "And you did nothing?"

"If I would have gotten hurt, Adrian would have gotten hurt."

The king regarded her for a long moment. "You ran."

She nodded. "Like a coward."

The king continued, "Squire Sandpiper tells me that you distracted the beast to give him a clear killing blow."

All eyes were on her. Then, she understood. It was a cover story. "It happened too fast. I don't remember it clearly," she said.

"Whatever you did, it worked. Both demons are dead, and my son is alive," said the king. He let out a small sigh. "For that, I thank you."

She met the king's eye. To be thanked by the king—she didn't deserve it.

"I think it is worth mentioning," said the court magician, "that it was no demon you encountered. None of the beasts were."

Juniper's head snapped up.

Reid asked, "Then what were they?" Each word dripped with distrust.

"After examining the ash of the Greater Demon, as you called it"—the court magician motioned to Reid—"I have concluded that it was not a demon, but a Wechun."

Juniper blinked. "I've not heard of those before."

The court magician nodded. "Not many of this age have. They are ancient beasts and very rare. It is possible that the Wechun was nabbing servants from the castle, infecting them with its tainted magic, and turning them into the feral anomalies that we falsely identified as demons."

Juniper swallowed, but she couldn't force her throat to form words. She glanced between the three men, but none added onto the court magician's words.

"What does this mean?" Reid asked from behind her, his voice dry.

"It could mean many things," answered the court magician. "Most likely, it means that our demon crisis is over, for the Wechun can no longer snatch or infect."

Juniper nodded. The crisis was over. It meant either her death or her eviction. She slumped onto her knees. She had a sinking feeling about which the king would choose, regardless of his bargain with her.

"However, it is not the proof I require," said the king. "Thimble." Juniper lifted her gaze to meet the king's. "I ask that you remain here until I have solid evidence that my son is safe."

Her voice came out weak: "Yes, Your Majesty."

The king smirked. "You've gained manners since our first meeting. I suppose my thanks should be to you, Squire?"

Reid shifted behind her. The king chuckled.

Should she ask for another keeper? No, it would look foolish. She cast her gaze on the unknown knight. His pale gaze blinked to her. His face changed slightly, but not to one of disgust—it took a moment to place the expression. Intrigue.

"This is Sir Isaac Pinul," said the king.

Reid said, "We've not had the pleasure of meeting, Sir."

"I've been away most of my knighthood." Sir Pinul spoke in a soft, melodic voice. "We have met, but you were but a boy. I am glad to see you in the Order. I've heard good things from Fowler about you."

"Sir Pinul has been informed of the situation." King Bradburn laced his fingers together. "I have asked him to return to assist." He cleared his throat. His gaze landed on Juniper. "For the time being, you will continue under the disguise of Roslyn Derean. When the aftermath of Bala's Ball clears, she will return home, but you will remain here under the protection of Squire Sandpiper."

A prisoner.

"Until I can safely undo the binding spell," added the court magician.

The king nodded. "Until then, you will remain my son's royal protector. We cannot allow you to leave while your life remains bound to his."

She nodded. "I understand."

"Good." The king started toward the door. "Now that we've settled that, I've got a meeting with the advisors. Gods, they've both been in a tizzy since that damn ball."

Just like that, King Bradburn, the court magician, and Sir Pinul left. She sat alone in the lounge with Reid.

"Get up," he barked. "The servants will be by with lunch before long."

She stood on legs that did not feel like her own. She didn't feel enough of anything to argue. Reid led her back to her chambers and took up a post outside the doors.

She meandered back into her bedroom—her prison—to find something more suitable for a lady to wear for lunch.

Tomorrow, she told herself, she would start planning her escape. And that damned crown was coming with her.

AVAILABLE NOW

Mage in the Undercity

STARS AND BONES BOOK II

BOOKS2READ.COM/MAGEINTHEUNDERCITY

ACKNOWLEDGMENTS

There are a lot of people who helped this book come to life, and they all deserve more gratitude than words can give. But, as my friends can testify, I'm not good with words in person.

I want to thank Ryan and Laurel. You two have been amazing friends. You were the first to see *Stars and Bones: Thief in the Castle* and the first to give me the green light. Without you two, half of the characters and places wouldn't have names.

There's also my parents, who never implied, insinuated, or even mildly suggested that all those nights sitting alone in my room were wasted (at least not to my face or where I could hear them). You never complained about the keyboard noise either.

And the Authors 4 Authors team who gave me this chance, I'll forever be thankful for all the advice and guidance you've given me.

And of course, you, the reader. I've nothing but endless thanks for you.

ABOUT THE AUTHOR

Beatrice B. Morgan lives in southern Illinois. When she isn't reading or writing, she is most likely playing a video game. She is a night owl, caffeine addict, yoga enthusiast, dog person, hopeless romantic, optimistic, and a shameless Ravenclaw.

Follow her online:

www.bbmorgan.com
Twitter: @BBMorgan_W
Facebook: @BBMorganBooks

Authors 4 Authors Publishing

A publishing company for authors, run by authors, blending the best of traditional and independent publishing

We specialize in escapist fiction: science fiction, fantasy, paranormal, romance, and historical fiction. Get lost in another time or another world!

Check out our collection at https://books2read.com/rl/a4a or visit Authors4AuthorsPublishing.com/books

For updates, scan the QR code or visit our website to join our semi-monthly newsletter!

Want more female-led fantasy? We recommend:

Exile
by Melion Traverse

After killing a paladin in revenge for her family, Squire Bryn is cast out by order of the god Avgorath himself. Now she seeks atonement with the father of the dead paladin. But machinations far greater than a disgraced squire are at play. Unicorn riders—believed to be only legend—ride through the land. A young sorcerer needs help in finding his father, and a mystery brews that could hold the fate of two worlds.

books2read.com/exile